FLYING BLIND

Dave Jackson

Evanst

Published in Evanston, Illinois. Castle Rock Creative.

Scripture quotations are taken from the following:

> The Holy Bible, New International Version®. NIV®. Copyright © 1973, 1978, 1984, 2011 by International Bible Society. Used by permission of Zondervan Publishing House. All rights reserved.
>
> The New King James Version®. Copyright © 1982 by Thomas Nelson, Inc. Used by permission. All rights reserved.

ISBN: 978-0-9982107-3-5
eISBN: 978-0-9982107-4-2

Cover photos: mariyaermolaeva | Shutterstock
Fly_Fast | iStock

Cover Design: Dave Jackson, Julian Jackson

Printed in the United States of America

For a complete list of
books by Dave and Neta Jackson visit
www.daveneta.com
www.riskinggrace.com
www.trailblazerbooks.com

To Dean Berto,
my college roommate
and missionary pilot

Prologue

"*Hey, hombres!* Don't bunch it up. You know I can't afford to lose the whole unit." Actually, Lieutenant Fabián Ramírez couldn't afford to lose even one more of his men, especially not his thirteen-year-old son, Jesús, who walked twenty paces ahead and to his right as the ragged contingent of the Revolutionary Armed Forces of Colombia made its way down the muddy jungle road toward the small village of San Lucas.

Though this was only the third patrol Jesús had been on, Ramírez exhaled pride: The boy was quick to learn, didn't complain, a good soldier. But most of all, Jesús was his son, the only remaining member of his immediate family after the paramilitaries had attacked his village six months before. He could've sent Jesús to live with his aunt in Bogotá, but there was always the chance the government would discover he was the son of a FARC commander and use Jesús as leverage against the Revolution. No, officially his son might be too young, but it was better to keep him close at hand where Ramírez could watch over him. After all, there were other young soldiers serving the cause. Take Álvarez, walking just ahead of Jesús, only fifteen and . . . right now, not paying attention, strolling along as if he was dreaming of his *novia*. He'd get himself killed one of these days. Ramírez should keep Jesús away from him.

Like a creeping fog, the soldiers rounded a bend in the road. The jungle on the left had been hacked back some eighty meters: the first small farm on the outskirts of San Lucas. They stopped until Ramírez's radio clicked twice. His point man had checked out the cocaine farmer's shanty . . . safe.

"*¡Vámonos!*"

But when Ramírez passed the one-room shack, the stone-faced campesino stepped back into the gloom and closed his door . . . a little too quickly.

"*¡Alto!*" The hushed command passed up and down the column, stopping it while Ramírez and two of his men went to investigate. Nervous as a new bride, the gaunt farmer offered his receipt for the taxes he'd paid FARC on his latest harvest. These hardscrabble peasants had a tough life, and Ramírez no longer had any illusions *la Revolución* was improving their lot—not after nearly fifty years of fighting with nothing more to show for it than the worn-out soil of his pathetic cocaine field. Ramírez studied the receipt closely. Everything seemed in order, and yet . . .

Outside, he scanned the wall of jungle around the edge of the farm and then turned toward the men crouching along the road. "Álvarez! Jesús! Doctor Petro!" He beckoned them with a jerk of his chin. They rose and came. "Somethin's not right," he muttered in a tone too soft for the shanty family to hear. "Don't let these people outta here. And watch that road. No one follows us into town. *¿Comprendes?*"

He got his men underway again and then wrestled with himself. Was he giving his son special treatment by keeping him out of a town that might hold an ambush? Or was he just being prudent to keep his least experienced soldiers—and of course his doctor—out of harm's way? Well, so what if it was personal? Marxist ideology went only so far . . . then family, love, and loyalty took over. The specter of the mangled bodies of his loving wife, Peonita, and their three beautiful daughters chilled him like a high mountain downpour. He would never let that happen again. Never! Love, loyalty, family—that's what mattered. And on top of that, Jesús made him proud! He would look out for him, no matter what anyone said.

Tall and well kempt even in the field, Lieutenant Ramírez commanded the respect of his men. But he knew bullets gave no quarter to appearances. He touched his pencil-thin mustache absently and let his finger slide across his right cheek along the little scar that ended at his missing earlobe. He'd been lucky. Could he share that luck with his son?

The soldiers had advanced another five hundred meters when he keyed his radio. "You pass that little farm on the left, yet?"

"Sí!" replied the sergeant bringing up the rear.

Ramírez could trust Rodriquez with anything. "You see the three men I left there?"

"Yeah. They're sitting on—"

Boom! The explosion came first through the radio, then shook the jungle so hard Ramírez's teeth hurt.

"¡Ay, Dios mío!"

"¿Qué sucedió?" demanded Ramírez.

"Mortar. The shack—" *Boom!* "Ambush!" *Ratta-tat-tat-tat.* "Seven o-clock, across the field in the jungle. Get some help back here, quick. Where's the Doc?" *Boom! Ratta-tat-tat-tat.*

With no need for orders, Ramírez's men went running back.

"The doc's at the shack!" he barked into the radio as he followed his men up the road. There was no further response on the radio, but above the constant automatic fire, he heard Rodriquez shouting orders, deploying the men as soon as they arrived on the scene.

Once Ramírez got to the clearing, he glimpsed a shattered shanty, its front wall gone. He could see a bed and an upended table. Coals from the small overturned stove had ignited the splintered wallboards. A little child, naked from the waist down, stood screaming in the middle of the chaos, his hands held high, pleading for someone to pick him up.

But where was Jesús?

Bullets flew as Ramírez sprinted toward the ruins, and then he saw a green uniform on the ground by a rusty oil drum—the doctor, dark red spreading rapidly from a saw-blade neck wound. And there beyond him, face down was . . . was it Jesús? *No, no!* He'd left his son here to be safe. Ramírez's stomach convulsed as though it were full of snakes. No! This couldn't be happening!

He dove to the ground beside the boy's body. At least he was breathing, moaning softly—bravely, like a man. What a dumb thing to think about at a time like this. *But my son is brave!* Ramírez pulled out his field bandage and pressed it hard against the pulsing wound on Jesús' back. "*¡Ay Dios!* Not his kidney! Please, not his kidney!"

The intensity of the automatic fire moved away and got more sporadic as Rodriquez and the men chased the attackers into the jungle. But a new sound captured the lieutenant's attention—the drone of a small plane. Ramírez squinted upward. A white and red, single-engine aircraft flying low . . . *4-9-T*, its last three license numbers. He'd remember that: *4-9-T*. Grabbing the radio from his belt as he held the bandage on his son's back with his other hand, he barked, "Rodriquez! Take out that spotter plane before those paramilitaries are all over us again." He swore through gritted teeth. "*. . . 4-9-T!*" With all that big business money behind them, the paramilitaries had every advantage.

Suddenly, the fight for which he thought he'd lost his passion became very personal. *They hit my son! Gotta get a plane! Level the playing field!*

Several long bursts of automatic fire ripped the air as pink tracer trails arced above the trees. A moment later, the small aircraft peeled off to the west and disappeared over the jungle.

A charged silence followed, broken only by the labored breathing of his son. Would the paramilitaries counter attack? Ramírez waited and listened until his own breathing slowed and he heard his men tromping through the tangled jungle, their adrenaline-pumped voices cursing and nervously recounting the firefight. Enough noise to announce their location to the whole world. Careless fools!

"You're gonna be okay, Jesús. We'll get you out of here. Doc'll fix you up in no time." He looked back at Manuel Petro's still body. Yeah, he needed a doc, but it wouldn't be this one. He'd have to find another . . . and soon!

The lieutenant looked around, his responsibilities greater than family. Where was Álvarez? Oh yes. There, leaning up against the fence, slowly shaking his head as though he'd just awakened from a bad dream.

Bad dream all right! "Álvarez, get over here and help me with this man."

Álvarez made a move to obey, then cried out in pain as he grabbed his leg.

Ha! He'd be no help.

The smell of cordite still hung in the humid air along with acrid smoke from the smoldering ruins of the family's hovel. The child still wailed. Where was that cocaine farmer . . . or his wife? Why didn't someone pick up the poor kid? "*¡Madre de Dios!* What's happening?" The destruction looked like his own village after Peonita and his daughters had been killed. Ramírez let out his breath. It was getting away from him again! This time, he'd been unable to protect Jesús from . . . from *La Violencia!*

Would it never end?

Chapter 1

Nick Archer yanked the wheel of his Cessna 185 sharply left, then right, testing his ailerons. He'd felt a bump. Then saw the pink streak of a tracer. Someone was shooting at him! Leaning down to look along the bottom of his right wing, he saw three bullet holes just outboard of his fuel tank—too close. He shuddered involuntarily. If a burning tracer had pierced his half-empty tank, he'd be a ball of flame. Much too close! As he looked again, he saw a fourth hole through the aileron, probably the one he'd felt. He scanned his gauges—oil pressure, RPM. All looked normal, and the engine still purred smoothly, thank God! But he'd better face it: This was a war zone—like the insurgency in the Philippines, where his wife, Megan, had died.

Grabbing his global positioning system, Nick clicked through the screens. What were his exact coordinates when he'd taken fire? Should he call the government? Get the army out here?

Once he had the numbers, he dropped the small, hand-held GPS unit on the seat beside him and pulled the mic down from where it hung. "Florencia tower, this is Cessna five-three-four-niner-tango, over." No answer. He tried again: "Florencia tower, this is Cessna four-niner-tango. Please respond, over." Still no response! You could never depend on those jerks in Florencia. Unless they were expecting a commercial flight, they might be out for coffee. He flung the mic aside where it bounced from its curled cord like a bungee jumper. He'd have to wait until he crossed over the mountains and could pick up Neiva radio.

By the time he cleared the pass through the Cordillera Oriental, the eastern finger of the Andes, Nick had calmed down. What good would it do to radio in a report? Most likely the army wouldn't do a thing, and if it did, it would only send out a plane to bomb the site. Whether it had been the FARC or paramilitaries who'd shot at him, they'd have moved on by now. If it had been some poor peasant who thought Nick was going to spray his cocaine field and had tried to scare him off, what good would bombing him and his family accomplish? His neighbor would just take over, and the cocaine production would continue unabated.

Nick's insides twisted over the Catch-22 that was Colombia. He hadn't become a missionary pilot to bomb peasants, fight the government, serve the oil tycoons, or even stop the cocaine trade. He had come to . . . well, the right answer had always been, "to serve the Lord," but he knew his reasons were more complicated, and they did have something to do with the war zone this part of the country had become. Still, they didn't include calling in air strikes. He'd wait and make a report later so the government could have the incident on record, but he wouldn't trigger any immediate retaliation.

Again, he looked out his side window at his right wing. There'd been a lot of fire coming his way. The pink streak must have been a tracer, and those holes in his wing were so evenly spaced, they were probably from an automatic weapon. Many campesinos had AK-47s, but why would they pay extra for tracers? Only military units would have tracers. FARC—it had to be FARC . . . or the right-wing paramilitaries, or maybe even the ELN, the National Liberation Army. There were so many factions fighting in the country, who could know?

Nick took a deep breath and ran his hand over his tousled sandy hair. Then he adjusted the mixture and trim, and began his descent. For the first time in weeks, it seemed, he wasn't flying under a weeping cloud cover. The gray ceiling had broken up and blossomed into puffy cumulous clouds spangled across a stunning azure sky. Below, columns of sunshine returned color to his home beside the Magdalena River.

Home for Nick Archer was Finca Fe—Faith Academy—the First Peoples Mission station seventy-five kilometers southwest of the Colombian city of Neiva. Nick and his plane were assigned there by his own mission: Missionary Aviation Support Team or MAST for short. Finca Fe included a boarding school for some sixty children—nationals as well as the children of local missionaries and foreign business people—an infirmary, and an airstrip. Nick provided transportation for the students as well as logistic support for the academy and the dozen or so missionaries still working in southern Colombia.

As he cut his throttle, lowered his flaps, and flew the downwind of his approach, he could see kids playing soccer in the field beyond the manor house that had once been the estate of the coffee baron, Ricardo Vasquez. Nick had come just two years ago, feeling at first as if he'd been exiled to a paradise he was not sure he liked. But then Terri Kaplan, a dark-haired nurse, had arrived to run the mission's infirmary. Nick had no intention of testing the mission's policy against romantic relationships on the field, but that woman had eyes so large and dark he sometimes thought he might fall in and get lost forever if he didn't look away quickly.

But if he ever *did* get involved with another woman . . .

He glanced down toward the infirmary to see if she might be outside as he turned onto the final leg of his approach and cleared his engine with a brief surge of the throttle. Time to pay attention to his drift and line up with the narrow grassy strip. He slipped the plane to the left and then set it down without a bounce.

Terri Kaplan studied the tall, square-jawed pilot standing on the stepladder with his arm stuffed deep into the inspection hole under his wing. "Hey mister flyboy, don't get your arm stuck in there. You know we don't do amputations around here." She moved her head to the side to see what he was doing. Nick had removed the inspection plate and was trying to peer in with the help of a small flashlight. "So, whatcha doing? Getting an early start on your annual?"

"Nah." But he glanced at her quizzically. "Whadda you know about annual inspections?"

"More than you might think. So, what *are* you doing?"

He squinted back into the hole in the wing. "Well, seems I just got shot up a little. Need to make sure it didn't hit something vital, like the—"

"Nick!" she interrupted, looking along the bottom of the rest of the wing. "You did get hit!" She felt her gut clinch.

"Yep, that's what I said. Got hit." His smile was as bland as if he'd merely told her it was a nice day.

"Are you okay?" She could see he was, but— "Where were you, anyway?"

"Uh—" He shielded his eyes from the bright sun with one hand as he looked into the dark interior of the wing. "—'cross the mountains." He pulled back and glanced at her, his nose, still wrinkled from squinting, making him look like a mischievous kid.

"But that's El Despeje, the 'cleared zone' ceded to FARC. You know you're not supposed to fly over it."

"Well, technically El Despeje doesn't exist anymore. Ceasefire's off. But I was just taking mail and medicines to the Gustafsons. Actually, I fly over there all the time. Never had any problem . . . 'til today." He gazed at her closely, one eyebrow raised, but she wasn't buying his excuse. He shrugged. "Hey, it takes forever to fly all the way around that area just to get to their village." He peered back into the wing.

"Yeah, but . . . *Nick*, look at me!" What was with this guy? Didn't he have any sense at all? "I bet MAST wouldn't approve of you flying over El Despeje—for this very reason." She pointed at his perforated wing, stabbing her finger four times, once toward each of the ragged holes.

"You're not going to tell on me now, are you?"

His accompanying grin brought back those clothes-tumbling-in-a-dryer feelings. How was she supposed to deal with this? "Look," she said, "it's not about telling on you, Nick . . . or not telling." She struggled to control the quaver in her voice. "It's about . . . about you. Maybe you've got plenty of time to patch up your plane, but I've got too much to do to patch up *you*!" She felt heat rise up her neck and into her cheeks. Had she said too much? She didn't want to sound personal.

She turned away muttering. "Oh, Lord, *My people are fools . . . They are senseless children; they have no understanding.* Help him, Lord. Help him!"

"What're you doin'? Praying Scripture at me again?" Nick called after her.

"Somebody's gotta pray for you, or you'll never get back alive!" She shook her head and continued across the grass toward her infirmary. She shouldn't get involved.

To Nick, she seemed to toss her head as he watched her trim figure retreating in the afternoon sun—*so easy on the eyes.* And was that little scolding she'd given him because she cared about him . . . or did she just need to 'be right'? Nick raised his eyebrows and sighed. He had to admit, she *was* right. Shots like that could bring him down. For all his casualness when speaking to Terri, he wasn't inclined to take unnecessary risks—at least none beyond what it took to be a good bush pilot. He could control most of those risks with good maintenance, avoiding serious weather, and careful planning. But getting caught in a civil war? That was something else!

Terri was right. The conflict was heating up, spreading, and he should be more careful to avoid the danger zones. Civil war was a deadly wildcard he didn't want to face again. Been there, done that . . . with horrific personal consequences. Perhaps he should put in for a transfer. But to where? The whole world seemed to be going crazy with insurgents and terrorists. He remembered the stories he'd read as a kid about pioneer missionaries. They'd sailed halfway around the world to face exotic empires and savage tribes all too ready to kill outsiders. But now things seemed just as dangerous.

Terri wouldn't have paid any attention to the *chug-chug-chug* of Roger Montgomery's green lawn tractor as it came to a stop outside her infirmary had it not been for the anxious yells from a dozen students: "Nurse Terri, Nurse Terri, come quick! David's been hurt!" They all seemed to yell the same thing—though not in unison—before Terri got the door open to see David Tarkington sprawled across Roger's little tractor trailer like an NFL player being carted out of the Super Bowl. David was the son of Martha and David Tarkington, Sr., the CFO of SurPetro, the largest U.S. oil company in Colombia. Across the face of the boy in the trailer was painted both agony and ecstasy as he ate up the attention of his teammates while they tried to explain what had happened.

"David kicked a goal and put us ahead. Then he crashed into Lucy Mendoza. They both went down, but Lucy landed on top. And you know if Lucy Mendoza lands on top of you, you're gonna be in a world of hurt!"

"All right, all right!" Terri held up her hand to stop the chatter. "David, what seems to be hurt?"

"My leg! Right there above my ankle. . . . Ouch! Don't touch it!" The boy's contorted expression flipped from ecstasy to agony.

"Okay. Let's get you inside and have a look—no, not all you kids. You're going to have to stay outside. Roger, could you help me here?"

Roger Montgomery was Finca Fe's maintenance man. At sixty-three, with rounded shoulders and a spreading girth, he lived with his wife—who ran the kitchen—in the only independent housing at the academy, a tiny cottage set apart from the old manor house that had been divided into offices and staff apartments. Also on the grounds were a boys' and a girls' dormitory, a gymnasium (which doubled as the dining hall), a classroom building, and Nick's hanger. Nick lived in a back room in one corner of the hanger. On the other side of the hanger was a bunkroom for three guards stationed at Finca Fe to protect children of high-profile business executives from rebel kidnappers. One of those guards was assigned to David Tarkington and had been hired by his father's company.

The school did not like having armed guards on its premises, but what could they do? Private guards had become commonplace in a country as violent as Colombia. Terri didn't like them, either.

She found them uncouth and unsociable, men she could imagine selling out their charges to the highest bidder.

After working with David for an hour and making a few phone calls on his behalf, she headed to the dining hall looking for Nick. Their earlier interaction left her feeling a little embarrassed to face him again, but this time there was nothing personal. The sun was less than a finger above the horizon when she entered the cinder-block structure, and Arlene Van Loon, the towering gray-haired principal of Finca Fe, was standing ramrod straight at the end of the gymnasium reading announcements for the next day. In spite of the racket from stainless-steel trays and sixty noisy kids, Miss Van Loon made herself heard above it all. She could always be heard *clearly* anywhere on campus, as though she was born with a built-in bullhorn. She concluded by booming, "Don't forget, B-team is on cleanup tonight!" and marched out the door.

Terri spotted Nick and headed his way. "Oh, there you are." She tried to sound casual as though the afternoon's interchange had never happened. She studied his face to see if he seemed upset.

But Nick was his usual warm self. "What?" He pointed at his ear. "Hearing loss!" They both laughed. "By the way, you almost missed the Friday night special." He waved his hand over his tray like a magician revealing a rabbit. "Sloppy joes, mac and cheese, and Ho-Hos. I'll need an extra Precose with this load of carbs."

"*Precose?* You take Precose? How come? You got diabetes? You never told me about that, and I'm the nurse around here, you know." Oops, she didn't mean to scold, and she wasn't usually this touchy. But Nick just seemed to trigger something in her.

"Ah, ain't nothin'. I forget my pills half the time, anyway. Never seems to bother me. I work it out. Lots of exercise, you know. Doctor in the States said exercise is the best thing, anyway."

"Uhh, yeah. It can help some, but I want to check your blood sugar—maybe tomorrow, okay?" She took a deep breath. That would mean seeing him again, but what could she do? Everyone's health was her responsibility. "The reason I came over here—" She tapped a finger to the side of her head, recalling her mission and getting herself back on track. "—is to ask if your plane is ready to fly this evening?"

"Well, kind of. I finished the patches, but I'd have to put the wingtip back on. I could do that in about ten, fifteen minutes. Why? What's up?"

"It's David Tarkington." She noted Nick's blank look. "Didn't you hear? He broke his leg playing soccer. I've X-rayed it, and it's just a simple fracture. I could set it here, but I've talked to his father on the phone, and he wants him moved to a hospital in Neiva. And he wants it done this evening."

"This evening? But I wouldn't be able to get back before dark, and tomorrow . . . well, I promised to spend all day Saturday helping Hector and Isabella put a new roof on their place."

Terri felt relieved. She didn't like it that the people with big money could so easily dictate what happened at the academy. "Maybe I should call Tarkington back and tell him to send the company plane for him."

Nick leaned back and laughed easily, his dimples creasing his cheeks. "You don't land corporate jets on our little grass strip. No, I'll take him and just come back early tomorrow morning." He got up and wiped his mouth. Terri noticed the twinkle of a smile grow in his eyes as he said, "But hey, why don't you go with me tomorrow?"

"With you?" What? Was he asking for a date? "You mean . . ." No, he couldn't be asking for a date. "You mean to help you put on that roof? Like a service project?"

"Yeah, guess you could call it that. But it's really a cute little house. Isabella's got it fixed up real nice. It just needs a new roof, and it's only a mile up the river, shorter by the road. But I'm not going to carry those rolls of roofing on my shoulders, and I doubt Roger can get by without his tractor all day. So, we can take the outboard and be back by dark. Whaddaya say?"

She was almost tempted, and then she remembered. "Sorry, but I've got to plan tomorrow night's campfire." Her mind raced to think of someone to do the campfire for her. Wait! What was she doing? "You know . . . Saturday night sing for the older kids, remember? If we don't get rained out again."

"Oh, yeah. Sure." He sounded disappointed. Then his face brightened. "Then why don't you fly to Neiva with us this evening?

We can come back early in the morning, and you'd have plenty of time to prepare for the campfire."

"Uh . . ." It was so tempting, just to get away for a few hours. "But where would I stay? Where do you stay when you go up there?"

"Oh, I just crash on Armando's cot in a little room off his office. He's the service manager at the airport. We're good friends." Nick's face got red. "Course, you can't stay there. But . . ."

Nick kept talking, but those clothes-dryer feelings kept tumbling in Terri's stomach. Tarkington expected the guard to accompany David for security, but as his nurse, he'd probably be happy if she accompanied David, as well—oh the perks of the powerful and wealthy. "Nick, hey, Nick." She interrupted his strategizing. "Don't worry about it. I'll get Tarkington to put me up in a hotel."

Nick's mouth dropped open, and he stared at her for a moment. "Great, great! Then you just get David and his guard over to the plane in about fifteen minutes. By then I should have the repairs on my wing all buttoned up, and we'll be on our way before dark."

Terri watched him head toward the door with a doo-wop swing to his step until he turned back and said, "Be sure to call Tarkington and have someone meet us at the airport. I don't want to be responsible for getting that boy all the way to the hospital, and I wouldn't trust that guard of his to find his way out of a paper bag, let alone out of the airport."

Thirty minutes later, Terri was belted into the left rear passenger seat of Nick's plane. He'd removed the other rear seat so David could stretch out on a pad on the floor to keep his leg straight. The Cessna 185 had a tail wheel rather than the "tricycle-gear" favored by many pilots flying in and out of regular airports. Planes with front wheels sat up, nearly level so pilots could see better while taxiing. But many bush pilots preferred the old "taildraggers" because they could land on rougher fields.

After a warm-up, the engine roared, and the sturdy plane jostled down the strip and quickly rose into a painted sky. Terri had almost forgotten how peaceful it was up there. But not peaceful for everyone, she chuckled to herself a few moments later when she noticed the burly guard put a death grip on the side of his seat with one hand while clinging to the overhead strap with the other as Nick put the plane into a gentle bank, heading toward Neiva.

Chapter 2

High clouds had again taken their place over the Magdalena valley when they headed back toward Finca Fe early the next morning. Nick looked over at Terri in the front passenger seat, who was leaning back with a smile on her face. "Havin' fun yet?"

"You bet. I love flying."

Nick grinned and shook his head. *All that and a bag of chips, too.* It really did mean something to him that she liked to fly. After all, it was his life. "You do much of it before?"

"Some, a few years ago. Almost soloed."

"You took lessons?"

"Sure thing. Logged eighteen hours."

"No kiddin'? Then why am I doing all the work up here? You want to take the stick?"

"Sure," she said hesitantly, giving him an inquisitive look, to see if he was serious. Then she slid her seat forward a little and took the controls. "You know, the plane I trained in was a Piper Cub, and it really did have a stick."

"Really. So you know how to handle a taildragger on the ground."

"I wouldn't go so far as to claim that. Actually, on my last flight . . ." Her voice trailed off.

After a few moments, seeing that she seemed at ease, Nick ventured, "So what happened that you didn't get your license?"

"Life, mostly. Nursing school wasn't cheap, but that seemed to be the direction God was leading me, so . . . I had to make some choices, and flying got put on hold. But here I am—" She turned to grin at him. "—doing it again!"

A few minutes later, he said, "You see that bend in the river way up there? That's Finca Fe."

"It looks so much smaller from up here."

"Always does. You want to try and take it in?"

"Oh, I don't know. I'm sure I'm rusty." Her voice sounded hesitant.

"That's okay. I'm right here." Nick pulled back the throttle, gave the plane 10 degrees flaps, and reset the trim. "Now I usually come around from the west where there's less turbulence from the hills on the other side of the river—unless, of course, there's a crosswind." He kept encouraging her, giving little tips until they were on their final approach when he said, "We're a little high." He increased the flaps. "Gonna have to slip it in. You want to give it a try?"

"Uh . . . maybe I better go around again."

"Ah, you can do it."

"No, I can't! I really can't. Here, you take it." She released the wheel as if it had shocked her.

Nick glanced her way as he took the wheel. The color had drained from her face, and her eyes and mouth were as wide as a first-time flyer's. He refocused on the strip below and kicked the rudder, putting the plane into a steep slip. At the last moment, he straightened the plane out and set it down with plenty of runway for an easy rollout.

When he'd turned around and was taxiing back toward the hanger, he looked at Terri again. Her head was down and she was biting her lower lip. He decided not to say anything for the moment, but when they were finally stopped, and the engine had chugged its last, he couldn't help himself. "So, what happened up there? You were doing so well."

She shook her head and opened her door without answering. She grabbed her bag from the back and began to walk away, when she stopped and turned back. She stood under the wing, out of the light drizzle that had begun. "That last flight I started to tell you about? I was practicing slipping it in, but I no sooner set it down than I ground looped it."

"Really?" Nick stared at her in awe. "Did it go all the way around?"

"Yeah, and the wingtip scraped the runway. I thought I was gonna flip all the way over. And the expense of those repairs was the part of 'life' that happened that forced me to choose between flying and nursing school."

"Yeah, I can imagine. Must've been scary. That is one of the challenges with a taildragger. They can ground loop pretty easily, especially if there's a crosswind. Almost happened to me once. But you shouldn't let that keep you from flying."

"I didn't think it would until you wanted me to slip it in. Just froze up."

"Hmm." But he was sure he could help her get over that fear if he had time.

He looked at the buildings of Finca Fe. It seemed like the only other people who were up were the Montgomerys. The lights were on in the kitchen, meaning Betty had started fixing breakfast, and Roger, festooned in an orange poncho, was making his rounds of chores on his little tractor.

Terri cleared her throat as though she'd choked up. "I gotta get to my room and get to work on planning that cookout. You need any more help here?"

"Nah," he said as he chocked the big bush tires that allowed him to land on rough strips. "You go ahead. I'll tie it down and top off the fuel."

Nick watched her trudge across the campus, head down in a way that appeared to be more than an effort to keep the light mist out of her eyes. He wouldn't push it, but it was a shame for someone like her to be haunted by such a frightening memory, especially when it was obvious she really did enjoy flying.

As Nick climbed down from the ladder after filling his wing tanks with a twenty-liter gas can, he saw Roger coming his way with his little tractor and trailer. "Hey," he called above the noise of the tractor, "think you could give me a hand? I got three rolls of roofing and a box of nails in the hanger that I need to take down to the boat, and your little trailer would sure make light work of it."

Roger just nodded from under his wet and crumpled fedora and turned his tractor to follow Nick into the hanger. Nick pointed to the roofing materials and headed toward his little one-room apartment at the back of the hanger to change into some old work clothes and grab a rain jacket, his baseball cap, and some energy bars and an apple—not as good as Betty's breakfast, but it would hold him until later.

On his door was taped a small yellow note with his name on it. He ripped it off and opened it as he went in. "If it's not raining tomorrow morning, meet me at The Rock! —Me."

Whoa! She must have put that up before we even talked about going to Neiva yesterday. Nick grinned and used a pushpin to tack it to the bare stud at the foot of his bed. "The Rock" was a large bolder on the bank of the Magdalena where Terri had her morning devotions whenever weather permitted. Nick had come across her sitting there once and asked if he could join her. She said sure, and he sat down before he realized what she was doing. She continued her reading, and it was kind of awkward, him just staring out over the rippling water with nothing to do. Finally, he'd said, "It's sure beautiful, but I gotta get back. See ya." She had smiled and waved. Since then, he'd seen her there on other occasions when he took an early walk, but he just waved and steered off in another direction. But now, here was an invitation to her "personal place" and she'd signed it "Me" . . . as though he should know.

Nick felt like a shirker when he came out of his room and Roger had finished loading the wagon by himself. But Roger's thick PhotoBrown eyeglasses didn't clear indoors nearly as fast as the ads promised, so it was hard to see his eyes and guess what he was thinking, and his long, grey walrus mustache completely hid his mouth. But that was Roger; you took the whole and liked him—everybody at Finca Fe did.

"Where you headed in this rain?" he asked as Nick climbed onto the load, and they headed out of the hanger, rattling down the muddy road to the river.

"Goin' up to Hector and Isabella's. Promised to help them put on a new roof. They said the old one only leaks when it rains, so I guess today's the day."

"Ha, if that's the key, almost any day the last two months would've done just fine. I been thinking Noah might have been a little ahead of his time. Whaddaya think?" The churning waters of the rain-swollen Magdalena were the color of creamed coffee with islands of cappuccino foam swirling in the eddies. "Hey, you hear anything while you were in Neiva about when they're gonna to build us a new bridge? We can't rely on you usin' that tail-dragger of yours to fly in our supplies forever."

"Not a thing. All I know is that the army said the next time they come this way, they'd let us know, and they'd bring whatever. They say their big trucks can get across at the rapids if the water's not too high. But with this rain, who knows when that will be?"

"It's not right, you know." Roger turned his head back so he could be heard above the steady roar of the lawn tractor. "Government shouldn't leave a bridge out this long. I mean, it ain't just us. What about El Tabor and Betania on up the road? Don't those little villages count for something? It's just neglect. That's what it is."

They arrived at the river and unloaded the roofing supplies into the small aluminum boat. "Hey, Roger, if you need supplies, maybe you oughta take this tub down to Puerto Seco to get what we need. It's only about twenty kilometers."

"Twenty kilometers? What's that, thirteen, fourteen miles? I never can get used to the metric. Gigante's closer, but I'd have to hitch a ride from the river to town and back. Besides, don't know if that little outboard could make it back up against the current with a loaded boat, not with the river so high. You know, there's some fast water down that way." The older man stood up after untying the little boat and gave Nick a mock salute. "You take care, now."

Once Nick got the outboard going and had pulled back from the small pontoon dock, he gunned the engine and turned his face into the ever-present mist. With a glance back, he waved to Roger who still stood on the dock, and then smiled to himself. Wasn't that just like Roger, waiting to see that he was safely underway before going back to his own tasks. Always thinking of the other guy first.

The drizzle stopped by mid afternoon, and Terri recruited three high school guys to help her carry the plastic bins of hotdog buns, wieners, and all the fixings, plus marshmallows, chocolate, and graham crackers for s'mores. Then she sent them for dry wood from the shed and laid a fire.

She hoped the evening wouldn't be so muggy that a fire would be miserable. But she didn't need to worry. The dozen older kids eligible to come to the campfire and Saturday night sing were hungry enough by the time the evening's dark closed in that they were glad to suffer a little heat in exchange for food. And mercifully, the smoke seemed to keep the bugs down. By the time their stomachs were satisfied and they were ready to sit on the logs around the fire, they even sang a little.

Of course, there was the added incentive that certain guys were sweet on certain girls and jockeyed for certain seats, all with as many casual, I-don't-really-care airs as possible. But it made for a nice evening that caused Terri more than once to recall her own church youth group.

She had been a little late to mature, but there *were* dates in high school and a couple guys in college who might have wanted to get serious if she hadn't been so focused on her nurse's training. Not that her mother hadn't tried. Terri came from a very tolerant, secular Jewish family that hadn't objected when she became a Christian as a teenager. "To each his own," her father had always said. "*Her* own," her mother always corrected. "But can't you at least give me some grandchildren? That's not against your new religion, is it?" Terri had always laughed it off with, "Of course, Mama. At the right time." Her older brother, David, had married between college and grad school and now had three children.

But what might've happened to her had she taken another path? Terri wondered. What if she'd pursued a pilot's license, like Nick Archer? She knew the expense was only a drop in the bucket compared to renting—let alone owning—a plane. Would she have ever made it to the mission field? Might she have become a missionary pilot, too? *"I know the plans I have for you,"* declared the Lord in Jeremiah 29:11, *"plans to prosper you and not to harm you, plans to give you hope and a future."* She'd clung to that verse as she studied. And now she *was* on the mission field, getting to know a handsome pilot. Maybe God's plans for her were working out in ways she could never have foreseen. Maybe marriage and a family weren't out of the question . . . with a little flight time thrown in occasionally. What about that? *"O the depth of the riches both of the wisdom and knowledge of God! How unsearchable* are *his judgments, and his ways past finding out!"*

When the last strains of "Amazing Grace" died away—for the third time, being one of the few songs Lucy Mendoza could play on the guitar—and the teens had returned to their dorms in time to make their extended curfew, Terri began picking up the chocolate wrappers and stacking the plastic food bins inside one another. Like the return of a pleasant dream, Nick strolled into the dim glow of the dying coals.

"Looks as if I missed it."

She shot him a wry grin. "Got a couple of hotdogs and buns here. Probably been dropped on the ground a time or two, but hey, there's still plenty of mustard to cover up the dirt."

He plopped down on a log and looked around. "Got anything left to drink? I'm parched. Been thirsty all day. Been peein' all day, too. Oops! Sorry. You'd think a person wouldn't get so thirsty when it's so humid. But putting on that roof was hard work."

She looked at him sharply and handed him a can of root beer. "All that's left, but you better come see me tomorrow. I want to check out that diabetes."

"How come?" He popped the top and took a swig.

"You have diabetes, and you just told me you've been peeing all day. I want to check you out. Now, will you help me carry all this stuff back to the kitchen?"

"Hey, I thought you offered me some hotdogs."

"Sure. Come an' get 'em."

"Don't we have to cook them first? Where are some sticks? Let's enjoy what's left of the fire."

She hesitated and then grinned. "Sure, why not."

In a few minutes they were sitting on the damp ground, leaning against a log, mesmerized by the fire. "Hey, I found that note you pinned to my door."

"Ah, that was nothin'. Just thought we might pray together occasionally."

"Yeah, I'd like that . . . at The Rock. You go down there almost every morning, don't you?"

"When it's not raining, which we've had a lot of lately." She paused for a few moments. "I also was thinking that I might have been a little hard on you yesterday, about flying on the other side of the mountains, and—"

"No problem."

"And . . ." She took a deep breath. "And I was wondering . . ." She took another deep breath, inhaling enough courage to get personal. "Well, I was wondering why a guy like you isn't married."

He stared into the fire so long she feared she'd asked a forbidden question. Then he said quietly, "I was married once."

Terri didn't know what to say. She knew marriages broke up for all kinds of reasons that couldn't be blamed on one partner or the other. But it did raise the question: Could he have held it together?

It took him a while before he continued. "Not sure where to start . . . Guess I always wanted to fly, but a few months after high school, 9/11 happened, and I joined the army, thinking that was the quickest way to help stop Islamic extremists like Al-Qaeda." While fighting in the Second Gulf War, he said his unit accidentally shelled an orphanage near Tikrit. When he couldn't shake the nightmares that followed, he sought help from a chaplain as a way to find forgiveness. That's how he became a Christian and later felt the call to missions. Combining that with his love of flying, he looked into missionary aviation, but when there were no options to train on fixed-wing aircraft in the army, he welcomed his discharge in 2006 and enrolled in a Bible school with a missionary aviation training program. While acquiring an A&P mechanics license, a commercial pilots license, and logging enough flying hours to be accepted by MAST, he met and married Megan Williams. Upon graduation, they were assigned to the Philippines.

"At first Megan was excited about being a missionary, but Tubigan, the town where we were assigned, freaked her out. There wasn't anybody she could connect with, and I was off flying most days. On top of that, the Abu Sayyaf, an Al-Qaeda revolutionary group, were constantly terrorizing the Christians and all foreigners . . . ." Nick's voice trailed off. He grabbed a stick and stirred the fire, as if kicking up sparks from his private hell until Terri began to wonder whether he couldn't say any more.

Finally, he turned to her with a grimace. "God knows, none of us are designed to face such stress long term. I was afraid she was going to have a mental breakdown. But that was our first assignment, and I didn't want to wimp out."

Again he fell silent. Terri hesitated but finally said, "And then . . .?"

Nick shrugged. "I was off on a two-day support flight up in the hills when the Abu Sayyaf launched a major attack in the night—grenade launchers, automatic weapons, IEDs. When the resistance was suppressed and everyone was hiding, the terrorists went around torching houses." His voice caught. "Megan was one of twelve who died . . . seventeen others were injured, including four children—more died later. . . . Some of the neighbors tried to get her to come out, but she had huddled in the corner unable to move. . . . I never even got her body back or anything. Local officials just sent it back to her family in the States."

He crossed his arms on his knees and leaned forward, burying his face from Terri's view. Slowly his shoulders began to shake with deep, silent sobs. Not knowing what else to do, and feeling badly that she had dredged up such painful memories, Terri put her hand on his back and began to rub back and forth across his shoulders. Slowly the sobs quieted their surging, and finally Nick raised his head to wipe his nose on the backside of his hand. "Sorry," he muttered. "I've got a handkerchief here somewhere."

"Here. Take this napkin. I'm—I'm really sorry, Nick. Sorry about what happened, and sorry for bringing it up. I didn't mean to make you go through all that again. I—I just didn't know."

Nick blew his nose into the paper napkin. "That's okay. They told me in counseling that it's good to go over it, helps desensitize me."

Terri leaned back and shook her head. "Gee, I don't know. I'm not sure that's the kind of thing you'd ever want to become used to."

"No, not become insensitive—*desensitized,* so I don't bury the memories." He turned and managed a wet-faced grin. "It's been . . ." He looked up as though reading the last of the sparks that rose from the coals. "It's been almost four years now. Guess I haven't repressed my feelings too much." He sucked in his breath. "But hey, life goes on, and I'm . . . I'm hangin' in there." He took a sip of his root beer. "Ahh, So let's talk about something else. How about you? How has a beautiful woman like you avoided marriage? Surely your story isn't so grim."

"Not hardly. Pretty dull, by comparison." *Had he just called her beautiful?* "But we don't have to talk about me, now. Besides, it's getting kind of late, don't you think?"

"Not at all. Tomorrow's Sunday. We can sleep in." He straightened up and poked the fire with his stick again. "Look here, still some flames. Wouldn't be safe to go away leaving live coals, would it? Gotta be good Smokey Bears."

"Ha! This place is so soaked even Elijah couldn't call down enough fire to light it up."

"Probably not, but c'mon. Talk to me. You ever have a boyfriend?"

"Of course!" Oh, gosh. This could get embarrassing.

Suddenly, the voice of Arlene Van Loon bellowed from the direction of the academy. "Terri, are you still out there? Little Carla's sick again. Quite sick this time. Could you come?"

Terri groaned. "Oh no. Not again. Poor kid. Guess I better go." She stood up, brushing off her pants. "Coming," she yelled. "Just give me a minute to gather up this stuff."

Beside her, Nick muttered something under his breath.

"Saved by the bell!" she teased, making light of the interruption. But she hoped there'd be another evening like this, even if she did have to talk about herself.

"You go ahead," Nick said. "I can pick up around here. I'll drop the stuff by the kitchen, so Betty can clean it up. Or . . ." He looked a little sheepish. "I'll go over and help her do it in the morning."

"Thanks, but you better put everything in a sink of water or there'll be ants all over them by morning."

Terri hustled down the dark path unconcerned about tripping over roots or rocks. As far as she was concerned, she felt as though she could float back to the infirmary.

Terri rose early the next morning, mopping up after Carla's illness through the night. Poor kid had lost it from both ends, nonstop for three hours. Once her stomach finally settled down, Terri had put the child on a cot in a side room rather than take her back to the dormitory. There was no telling whether she might have another round of vomiting and diarrhea, and besides, by then Terri was too tired. She cleaned up the worst of the mess and went to bed, but with morning's light, the exam room definitely needed a good scrubbing.

It was another gray, drizzly day, so typical of Colombia's November rainy season. Most people at Finca Fe slept in because Sunday chapel didn't begin until 11 A.M., and it was too wet to play or work outside. However, tiredness, a gloomy day, and the nasty job had not dampened Terri's mood. *"This is the day* You *have made, O Lord, and I will rejoice and be glad in it."* Besides, there was still last evening around the campfire with Nick to savor. The memory made her spirit soar. And, painful though it had been for Nick to review what had happened to his marriage, there was nothing to suggest he hadn't been a good husband, in fact, nothing at all to call his character into question. He was sensitive and caring and good-looking, and he'd even said he'd always wanted to be married. What happened in the Philippines was a tragedy that left him single and alone and thousands of miles from home four years later.

She smiled as she finished mopping the floor and picked up the bucket.

A movement through the high bathroom window caught her eye. She finished dumping the dirty water down the toilet and looked more closely. Coming up the muddy lane to the academy were soldiers, a dozen, maybe more. Not marching in the open, but spaced out, sneaking along in the ditch, moving from bush to tree, weapons at the ready. They looked as if they were assaulting the academy! Curiosity flicked to fear. Why would they be doing that?

Then Terri noticed their armbands and knew they weren't government soldiers. They were guerillas, FARC guerillas, and they *were* assaulting the academy. She didn't panic but quickly dialed 1-1-1 on her local phone. She knew it would ring the emergency warning on phones throughout the school—the dorms, the gymnasium, the kitchen, the classrooms, the offices, and in all the staff apartments—sixteen phones, she remembered Roger Montgomery once saying.

It was a good warning system. Everyone knew what the signal meant and would know what was happening. Unfortunately, there wasn't a thing anyone could do to stop it.

Chapter 3

Pop! Pop! Ratta-tat-tat-tat!

"O Lord, they're shooting! Help us!" she whispered hoarsely.

Silence on the phone.

Terri glanced out the window. Still coming! She had only a minute, maybe two. Punch 0-9 for outside. It might take the army several hours to arrive, but they were the only help. Come on, come on! But no tone came. She hung up and tried again . . . and waited . . . and waited. Sensing Terri's anxiety, Carla got up and shuffled to Terri's side, a small dingy blanket hanging from one shoulder, her tired eyes full of questions Terri did not want to answer.

Still no dial tone!

The red phone light glowed, so the power was up. Maybe the software needed resetting. Terri looked out the window. Where were they? No time to run to the office. She clicked off, then on, and hit the 0-9 again . . . waiting, waiting . . . until loud banging commenced on the infirmary door.

"Espera." She bounced nervously as though she could force the line open. The banging increased . . . until a squat, solid man with a broad, angry face smashed open the door and stood there, surveying the room with the muzzle of his AK-47.

Terri froze.

The soldier stepped in. A half-smoked cigarette bobbed in his mouth as he asked, "You the only one here?" He checked Terri's room, the bathroom, and the side room with the cot, not yet clear of the sour tang from little Carla's heaves. Then he opened the supply closet. *"¡Nada!"* He hadn't seemed to notice the little girl plastered to Terri's right leg like a living cast. "Where's the doctor?"

Terri found her voice. "Uh, no doctor."

"¿Esto ės un hospital, verdad?"

"No. Just an infirmary."

He extinguished his cigarette on the door jam and then waved her outside with his rifle. When she was slow to move, Carla now hanging from her arm, he prodded them like cattle, and the image of his weapon exploding in her back hastened Terri's steps. He wouldn't shoot, would he? Why had the rebels come? She didn't know, but she didn't want to do anything to antagonize him. He didn't seem crazy, but—

Terri froze. There by the tree was the mangled, bloody body of one of the private guards. She clasped Carla's face to her breast so the girl couldn't see and was punished by a stabbing pain in her back from the muzzle of the AK-47.

"The other che-e-eken, he ran for the fields," the man growled.

Giving the tree and its sightless sentry a final look, Terri silently prayed from Psalm 9, *"O Lord, have mercy and lift us up from the gates of death,"* as she continued across the damp grass toward the gym. Other Finca Fe residents were streaming there like water down a drain, children wailing, adults buffering them from the guerrillas.

Inside the gym, the soldiers seemed more organized than most school administrators. The children who had already arrived were all on one side, sitting on the floor. Adults sat on the other side with their hands on top of their heads, fingers interlaced. Seeing the plan, Terri urged Carla to leave her side and join the other children. When Terri headed for the adults, her captor grabbed her shoulder and pointed toward the far end of the gym where the evident commander was already seated behind a long table, flanked by a male and female guerrilla fighter standing stoically, surveying the room with eyes of stone, weapons at the ready.

They were fast. Had already made this their headquarters!

Terri's captor spoke briefly to the commander in a voice too low for her to hear what he said above all the noise. Then he stepped back and pushed Terri forward, this time with his hand, his weapon pointed toward the ceiling.

"So, you are the doctor?" the commander asked in only slightly accented English. Unlike some of the other rebels who had mud splattered on their boots and damp stains on their fatigues from the morning's fog, he looked as if he'd somehow just stepped out of the shower—clean shaven, sharp mustache, and fresh fatigues.

"Like I told him"—Terri gestured behind her with her head—"we don't have a doctor here." When one of the commander's eyebrows went up, she added, "Day before yesterday we had to fly a boy to Neiva for a . . . for a simple broken leg. There's no doctor here."

"But he says you have a lot of equipment. Do you know how to use it?"

"Well, I—" Terri was noticing a thin scar that ran across the commander's right cheek and ended at a missing earlobe when the piercing voice of Arlene Van Loon echoed through the hubbub of the crowded gym. "What's going on here? Who do you think you are, barging in here uninvited? You people didn't even stop at the office to get a pass!" A pass? Terri couldn't remember the last time *any* visitor had been required to get a pass, but across the gym floor strode Finca Fe's principal, standing tall in housecoat and slippers with a sleeping net over her steely hair as she challenged a unit of mud-splattered, combat-hardened rebel soldiers.

Terri turned back toward the commander in time to see him flick one finger toward the kitchen. Miss Van Loon's captors quickly deflected her march and hustled her through the closed door where only her grumbling murmurs could be heard from the gym. He looked up at Terri. "As I was saying, Doctor, you know how to use that fancy equipment, right?"

"I'm not a doctor."

He stared at her. "So you say." Then he picked up a small radio, clicked the key, and said, "We're still looking for the doctor. Find that pilot yet?"

"No, señor," crackled the radio.

"Well, hurry up. I want to get out of here!"

Good, thought Terri. *The sooner FARC leaves, the less likely anyone else will get hurt. But why are they looking for Nick?*

Seemingly forgotten by the soldiers, Terri wandered over to the seated adults and noticed Lucy Mendoza was among them, head down on her raised knees, weeping. Perhaps because of her size they had taken her for an adult, though even the bigger boys were on the other side of the gym. "Lucy, you okay?"

When the girl looked up and saw Terri, she rose to her feet and lunged to embrace Terri.

"¡Siéntese! ¡Manos a la cabeza!" shouted a guard. "Sit down! I said. Hands on your head! Hands on your head! Sit down, right NOW!"

Moving with defiant slowness, Terri untangled the girl's arms from around her neck. "She's just a child. She belongs on the other side with the kids." Who were these people, anyway, terrorizing children? They certainly had no care for the common people. They were just bullies. But she sat down and put her hands on her head, nonetheless.

A half hour passed, during which the guards yelled at anyone not complying with their instructions. Terri counted fourteen different guerrillas posted in the gym or who came and went to confer with the commander—about the same number she had seen coming up the road. They brought in a hushed Arlene Van Loon, and she sat on the floor with the rest of them, legs crossed, all fifty-seven years of her ramrod straight with her hands on her head like some kind of a yoga pose. She avoided eye contact with anyone from Finca Fe as though she was embarrassed about what was happening.

Finally, after another delegation of soldiers reported, the commander stood up and announced, "All right, everybody, listen up." His English sounded more like an American coach rallying his team than a communist rebel. "I'm Lieutenant Fabián Ramírez, and I want the doctor and the pilot. So as soon as you tell us where they are hiding, we'll be out of here, and no one will get hurt. So let's have it!"

For some reason, Lucy Mendoza began wailing uncontrollably at the top of her voice. Her hands had slipped from the top of her head down by her contorted face as though she were holding an invisible basketball.

"¡Cállase la boca!" barked the commander, and a tall pimple-faced female soldier stepped forward. She grinned, revealing gaps in her teeth as wide as a jack-o'-lantern's, and backhanded Lucy

across the mouth so hard that her head snapped back. Her wailing crescendoed into a scream.

Terri hardly saw what came next, it happened so fast. The soldier who had brought her and Carla from the infirmary lunged forward. His AK-47 was slung over his back, but he grabbed the pistol from the female soldier's holster. He jerked back the slide with a loud clack and held the weapon stiff-armed against Lucy's head.

The FARC woman jumped back, hands out, as everyone in the gym watched in silence. The man with the pistol turned toward her slowly. *"¡Silencio!"* he said in a loud whisper with a triumphant sneer on his face as though showing her how it was done. Then he whipped the pistol toward the ceiling and pulled the trigger.

The explosion in the confines of the gym deafened and froze everyone until Roger Montgomery stood stiffly to his feet . . . to the loud clatter of three rifles cocking. "Now hold on a minute!" He held up both hands, palms out, as he slowly straightened up.

Out of the corner of her eye, Terri saw Lieutenant Ramírez raised a hand. "Sargento Rodriquez."

The terrorist compressed his mouth into a hard slit and returned the pistol to the woman.

Roger took a breath. "Now you listen to me, Commander Whoever-you-are, you ain't got no cause to be terrorizin' these children. You come in here pushin' us around, shootin' up the place, what else do you expect but some are going to fall apart? There's nothin' here you need, so why don't you just be on about your business, and leave us in peace."

"Don't tell me what I need or don't need!" the lieutenant snapped. "What I *need* is to find the doctor and the pilot." He pointed his finger at Roger. "Are you going to tell me where they are, or are these people going to see more trouble than your worst nightmare?"

Roger looked around him at his friends sitting on the floor, his big mustache working like a palm-leaf roof in a storm. Finally, he dropped his hands to his sides. "First of all, we ain't got no doctor here, and that's a fact! As for our pilot. Yeah, we got one. His name's Nick, but he ain't here right now."

"What do you mean, *ain't here*? His plane's sitting right out there in plain sight."

Roger cleared his throat as though preparing for a speech. "Well, sir, you can go see for yourself. I sent him off yesterday mornin'. He took the outboard and went up-river with some rolls of roofing paper. Went to help one of our neighbors put on a new roof. That's how *we* take care of the poor . . . 'stead of recruiting 'em into a ragtag revolution where they're bound to get killed." He looked around at the rebels, then offered in a more conciliatory tone, "Ain't no wonder he isn't back yet, what with the rain and all."

Terri bit her lip. Was she the only one who knew Nick had returned? Where *was* he? Had Miss Van Loon seen him when she called to her the night before about Carla? It was late and dark. Nick probably went straight to bed after his long day and their talk around the campfire. But where could he be this morning? And why were these soldiers so determined to find him and . . . and some imaginary doctor?

"You can sit down now," the lieutenant said, not taking the bait of Roger's cheeky speech. He looked at his watch. "But listen to me carefully, people. In thirty minutes, if I don't have the doctor and the pilot standing right here in front of me—"

"I will begin executing the students!" interrupted Sergeant Rodriquez. "Beginning with . . ." He took out a pack of Marlboros, studied it a moment, then tapped out a fresh smoke, putting it in his mouth as though he had forgotten what he was going to say. "*¡La bebé grande!*" he finally concluded, looking with a wry grin directly at Lucy.

No, no! Terri looked at the commander, but he was talking quietly into his radio. No! He wouldn't let that happen . . . would he? Terri felt as if she was going to black out as muffled crying spread through the gym. What should she do? Where was Nick? Had he gone for help? How? Should she tell the lieutenant she knew he wasn't up river? Perhaps he knew that already. Maybe one of his men had already reported a boat tied up at the dock. Otherwise, why would he allow such a ruthless threat? Several of the staff had begun praying and were urging others to do the same. Miss Van Loon emerged from her subdued state. "There's power in prayer," she said, loudly enough for those around her to hear. "More power than in all their guns. They cannot defy the name of Jesus. Everyone pray. Everyone pray! We must pray!"

The principal's efforts to take charge of the situation had some effect. The crying turned to praying, increasingly insistent until two guards brought a chair, picked up the principal and sat her in it. They tied her with ropes and gagged her. A hush again descended on the gym. Some people continued to pray softly; others—especially the children—cried quietly, but Miss Van Loon's brief suggestion of a supernatural deliverance slowly faded.

Terri tried to keep praying, tried to pray the Word as she had so often done, but somehow all those verses she had immersed herself in over the years wouldn't come to mind. Instead, she felt nudged in her spirit to *do* something. But what? Would it save the children if she confessed that Nick *had* returned last night? She still didn't know where he was this morning. Why wasn't he here? Anger bubbled up in her. He was the one who had been in the army. He was the one—the only one at Finca Fe—who really knew about military matters. He must have a reason for staying out of sight, but what? Would she betray him if she told FARC? And as for a doctor . . . suddenly it struck her: The reason they wanted a doctor was obvious: They needed medical help!

She got to her feet with her hands still clasped on top of her head, carefully watching the guards lest they think she were trying to do something rash, and made her way to the commander's table.

"Lieutenant . . . uh . . . Ramírez, we have no doctor here, but I am a nurse, a highly trained nurse. I . . . I can do anything a doctor can do outside a hospital. I mean, I can do just about anything except major surgery."

His eyes narrowed. "How about gunshots, shrapnel?"

"I worked in Cook County Hospital's ER for five years—that's Chicago. I've tended many people who have been shot. Never saw a shrapnel wound, but I've closed plenty of knife cuts and injuries from auto accidents."

"Chicago, uh? So there's really no doctor here? Who uses all that equipment? My sergeant said you had X-ray and everything."

"I do all that."

"Okay." He ran his fingers through his short, dark hair. "But what about the pilot?"

Terri froze her face, fearing any change in her expression would betray the frustration popping within her. Why wasn't Nick here when she needed him most? What was he doing? What could she say?

"I . . . I honestly don't know where he is."

The lieutenant looked at his watch, both eyebrows rising as he breathed in deeply and then blew out a silent whistle. "All right. Go sit down."

Chapter 4

The sharp leg of the pilot's seat cut into Nick's back. He looked at his watch. For over two hours he'd been cramped in this awkward position on the plane's floor and didn't know how much longer he could stand it, twisted like a pretzel and poked worse than on a hide-a-bed. Yet he knew he might be the only person in the academy able to call for help.

When the alarm rang earlier that morning, Nick had vaulted from his bed and looked out the window in the back of his hanger apartment. He swiped at the smeared windowpane—should have cleaned 'em long ago—to see someone coming up the road. No, two, three, four . . . at least a squad of camouflaged guerrillas, maybe more.

He punched 0-9 on his phone . . . No outside dial tone. He slammed it down. They must've cut the lines. That was the first thing he'd done back in Iraq when taking any installation. There had to be another way to call for help.

He ran through the hanger and was about to sprint to the administration building when gunfire stopped him. Across the campus he saw one of the bodyguards go down by an old tree. The shooting stopped as soon as it had started, and Nick considered his alternatives. His plane, parked on the grassy runway . . . if he could get to it unnoticed, he might have time to radio Neiva. The hanger shielded his view for the moment from the approaching rebels, but it was a slim chance. Surely he couldn't stay hidden within it for long before someone would find him.

Backpedaling so he could be sure the hanger remained between himself and the approaching soldiers, he made it the fifteen meters to the plane without anyone seeing him . . . he hoped. *Whack!* His head hit the wing strut, and he scurried around to the other side of the Cessna, opened the door, and tumbled in. Lifting his head just above one of the seats, he had looked through a window on the left-hand side of the plane.

There they were, a hundred meters away as they emerged from the shield of the hanger, and advanced up the driveway. No one seemed to be looking his way. They were scanning the administration building, the bushes, the trees. What? Did they think this place was defended like a fort? Good grief, it was just a school for kids, run by missionaries. But on they came, sneaking along, weapons at port, giving signals to one another to direct their approach.

Nick tossed one of the removable seats into the baggage bin in back, and lay down on the floor low enough so no one could see him unless they walked right up to the plane and looked through a window. Even then, they might miss him in the dim interior. MAST had complained about the expense of the tinted windows when he'd installed them. But now—Ha!—they just might save his life. He flipped on the master switch, then the radio, and pulled the mic down where he could speak into it.

"Neiva tower, this is Cessna five-three-four-niner-tango, over."

No response. He tried again . . . and again.

Nick knew it was often hard to reach Neiva from the ground at Finca Fe unless the weather conditions were just right. But he kept trying, switching to a general call for help, hoping someone—possibly a plane already in the air—would hear him and respond.

"Mayday, mayday, anyone monitoring this frequency, this is Cessna five-three-four-niner-tango. I am not airborne but am making an emergency call from the ground at Finca Fe, a boarding school situated seventy-five kilometers southwest of Neiva on the west bank of the Magdalena. We have been attacked by a FARC unit and are in need of immediate assistance. For more information on our location contact Armando Trujillo, the private plane service manager at Aeropuerto Benito Salas."

"Mayday, mayday, anyone . . ." He kept it up, minutes stretching into hours, feeling trapped, not knowing what was happening to

Terri and the children but not coming up with any better plan, either.

Then he heard voices: "Rodrigo! Go check out that plane. See if it's open."

It came from near the hanger. Must be FARC. His nerves tightened. They were going to find him. If he could only lock the door. He rolled over, hoping his movement didn't shake the plane. If he could just get his pocketknife out and wedge it in the door latch, he might foil a casual attempt to open the door. But he couldn't get it out without sitting up.

Ah, there it was. He flipped it open and jammed the blade between the door and the frame into the latch mechanism just as "Rodrigo" began wiggling the latch from the outside.

Suddenly from the radio came a faint, static-ridden voice. "Cessna five-three-four-niner-tango, say again. You're breaking up." *Static, static!* "Did you . . ." *Static, static!* ". . . Mayday . . . Sorry . . ." *Static, static!*

Nick stretched for the mic while keeping his knife jammed in the latch. But he couldn't reach it. Stretch farther! It was just another couple of inches . . .

"Cessna five-three-four . . ." *Static, static!*

"Hey Sarge," boomed a voice just outside the plane. "It's locked. *¡Aquí no hay nada!*"

The wiggling of the door latch stopped. A few moments later, Nick heard the voices drift away, presumably around the side of the hanger.

Franticly, Nick resumed his call: "Mayday, mayday, anyone . . ." But there was no further response.

A half hour later, Nick knew his contact was long gone, and he was about to sit up and relieve his painful back when he heard a woman's voice. *"Señor Nick, Señor Nick."* He tensed. Maybe FARC had left, after all. But who would call him Señor Nick? Maybe one of the students, but he didn't recognize the voice, and they usually called him Mr. Archer or Señor Archer. Staff members just called him Nick.

He started to rise enough to peek out when the voice called again. *"Señor Nick. ¿Dónde está? ¿Dónde está, Señor Nick? Venga aquí."* That was strange. And then he heard a man's voice speaking Spanish, saying something about getting a ladder to look in the hanger's rafters above his room.

Where was Terri—and the kids? He hadn't heard any sounds from them since the beginning when he'd heard some children crying as they crossed the campus. What was happening to them? Were they being threatened, robbed? And why attack Finca Fe in the first place? The school wasn't political, at least no more than the fact that most staff members were gringos.

His thoughts drifted back to Megan and the violence in the Philippines and how it had terrorized her. And now Terri was in danger! He couldn't go through that again. "Please God, no more of this. I've been through it once. I did my turn. It's time to be my Protector, my Rock, my High Tower, my Shield, my Defender"—he ran through all the names of God he'd heard on the sermon tapes and CDs friends from the States had sent him. What did it mean to call upon the name of the Lord in the time of trouble? Now when he needed it, he hardly knew. His prayer dwindled down to a hopeless murmur. "O God, no, no, no."

But where was God? His thoughts hardened, like drying mud. If he was going to get out of this, he'd have to do it the old way—by himself, like when he was in Iraq!

His mind swirled, seeking options. If there were just two soldiers in his hanger, and one was climbing up into the rafters . . . certainly they'd be distracted, compromised. He might be able to take out the one on the ground, grab her weapon, and shoot the climber. He imagined the sequence. A garrote . . . there had to be some wire lying around. But even best case, once he shot the other guerrilla, others would come running at the sound of gunfire. There was the old pump house made of concrete blocks, if he could get to it . . . he *might* hold 'em off—but for how long?

He exhaled the adrenaline wind-up. Dumb! Holding them off wouldn't buy much, and Terri and the others would still be captives. Nick shuddered. Once the shooting started, who could know how bloody it might get and who would die? These were experienced fighters, not likely to give up easily even if he could pull a Rambo.

Maybe he just ought to come out and say, "Hi, you guys lookin' for me?" as though he'd been relaxing like a martyr on the rack rather than hiding cramped on the floor of his Cessna for the past three hours.

But what *did* they want with him, anyway?

"¿Y el piloto?" Lieutenant Ramírez glared at the five soldiers who stood casually in a huddle around him. They shook their heads, some looking at the floor. "Stand at attention and answer me properly when I speak to you!" he snapped.

"Sí señor!" They straightened, but still couldn't give him the news he wanted.

Terri kept her head turned away as she strained to listen.

"You gave them a warning, *teniente.*" Sergeant Rodriquez surveyed the gym. "But no one has cooperated. Maybe they would talk if you—" He hefted his rifle.

Ramírez flicked his hand impatiently then frowned. "You sure you've searched *every* building?"

Heads nodded. He slammed his fist on the table and swore. "How about that boat? Is it gone, like the old man said?"

"No. There's a boat tied up down there."

"Then he's gotta be here somewhere!"

"Maybe he escaped, went for help."

Terri sucked in her breath. *"Yes, Lord. Let the wicked fall into their own snares, but let* Nick *escape!"* Maybe he'd be back soon with the army or . . . or—

"And just where would he go on foot?" snapped Ramírez. "No. I think he's around here somewhere." He turned away and paced back and forth, mumbling quietly to himself. Finally, he stopped. "We can't wait any longer. No pilot, no plane! Let's get out of here!"

"Señor . . ." It was Rodriquez again, squinting as smoke curled up from his cigarette into his eyes. "At least we could take a couple hostages. Get some *dinero* for all our trouble." He shrugged. "Aren't all gringos *ricos*?"

"Not as rich as you might think," Ramírez glared. "And kidnapping is never as easy as it sounds. *Pero, es posible.*"

"*¿Y la doctora?* What about her?"

Ramírez spat on the floor and shook his head. "Might have an alternative there. Not sure yet."

Terri shuddered as the soldiers continued to discuss plans in lowered voices. She'd been right. They needed a doctor, but she'd imagined a wounded man they wanted to bring here to her infirmary. She would've done what she could and worried about answering to the government later. She had as much as volunteered her services. But now, it seemed obvious they'd come to Finca Fe to commandeer a doctor and a pilot—with a plane—to serve their revolution. Commandeer! More like enslave. Hadn't the lieutenant used the word kidnap? No, no! She wasn't about to go along with that. Unless . . . her mind swirled. Unless they *did* take Nick, too. Maybe they could get through this if they were together.

No, no! That was crazy, absolutely crazy! This was a nightmare, not Disney's version of "Pirates of the Caribbean." She belonged here. God had called *here*, to serve these children. She couldn't leave them, no matter what. Her offer was off the table! Let the rebels bring a wounded comrade here if they wanted, but she wasn't leaving.

Terri watched as Ramírez broke away from his huddle. "*Señorita Doctora.*" He beckoned to her with his finger. She felt the blood drain from her face and worried she might faint as she got slowly to her feet. Could she be firm enough in refusing to go? As she approached the table, he gestured to his soldiers.

In a few moments, Arlene Van Loon and Roger Montgomery were pushed up to the table beside her.

"Tell me what you do here?" the lieutenant asked Van Loon.

She straightened even more, if that were possible. "I am the principal of Finca Fe, and I resent your—"

"Shut up. And you, *señor*?"

Roger cleared his throat. "I—I do the maintenance."

Ramírez raised one hand. "Good. We're about to leave. The three of you are coming with us. You have ten minutes to gather a few things. I suggest you put on your best hiking shoes, bring a rain poncho, a blanket"—he ticked items off on his fingers—"jacket, canteen and something to eat with, and any medications you might need. Pack everything in some kind of a backpack. Do not, I repeat, *do not* pack more than you can carry if you have to walk all day. You will be living rough for an indefinite time, so prepare for it. One of my men will accompany each of you to make sure you do not pack any weapons or . . . wander off. You have ten minutes."

It had been quiet for a long time when Nick suddenly heard automatic weapons firing. He opened the door of his plane and tumbled to the ground. In the distance he could barely hear children yelling, screaming.

O Lord, help us! Not a massacre. They're killing everybody! Just like the Philippines. A groan escaped from deep in his gut. He'd been a fool. He should've done something, made some kind of a stand, drawn their attention away from the children toward himself. Maybe he should've tried to take off in his plane. That might've given some of the children an opportunity to escape. But now . . .

He ran, stumbling on cramped legs that had been asleep for hours. Where were they? Somewhere . . . the gym? He rounded the corner of the hanger before he got ahold of himself. *Calm down, Archer. Panic won't help.* He, at least, was still free. Maybe he could still do something, but what? He proceeded more cautiously, darting from the hanger to some empty fuel barrels, then the pump house, and over behind Roger and Betty's cottage.

The gym—his stomach lurched. *Oh, no! O God, please no!* The windows around the top of the gray building were shattered; bullets had pocked the wall below. Were the guerillas still inside? How many kids had been shot? And why? *Why?*

And then he saw them: a small team of FARC soldiers, covering one another as they took turns backing down the lane in a classic retrograde maneuver as though they expected a blaze of gunfire to chase them off academy land.

Chapter 5

The chatter of automatic weapons fire ripped down the valley just as the FARC soldiers herded their captives out of the lane from Finca Fe and across the road that led to the Magdalena River.

"What was that?" Arlene Van Loon balked and swiveled her head, looking for the source of the sound. "That was shooting! Why is there shooting? Is the army coming?"

"Shut up and keep moving," growled Sergeant Rodriquez, giving her a shove.

"No! It's the army. They've come to rescue us!"

Lieutenant Ramírez, who had been near the rear of the ragged column, caught up to the captives. "*Señora,* it is not the army. There is no army within fifty kilometers of here. Believe me, if there were, we would know. *Mejor vamanos.*" And he held out his hand as though he were ushering her down the steps into a regal ballroom rather than into a muddy ditch and a field of briars.

"I am *not* a *señora*! But if that's not the army, why all the shooting?"

Terri wondered the same thing, a cold dread oozing down the back of her neck as she thought about the helpless children back at Finca Fe. She brought her hand slowly to her mouth, and Miss Van Loon caught the expression on her face, causing her own eyes to widen. She shouted at the commander even though she continued to stare at Terri. "You . . . you're shooting our children! You barbarians! You might as well shoot me too if you are going to shoot my innocent babies. I will not cooperate with any criminal thugs who kill children!"

"We don't shoot children—"

"Coulda fooled me," Roger Montgomery muttered. "Scared the wits outta that poor girl."

Ramírez waved his hand. "Ah, that was just my sergeant here— "

"But you're in charge, aren't you!" said Arlene. "You threatened to shoot us if we didn't tell you where Nick was, so—"

"You're not a child, *Se-ñor-i-TA*! But we have been known to shoot *viejas perras* who refuse to cooperate. Now get moving!"

"Wait a minute!" Terri stepped between Arlene and the scowling commander. "You still didn't answer our question. Why all the shooting?"

"¡Y perras jóvenes, también!" Then, apparently thinking an explanation might work better than threats and insults, he said, "I left a few men back there to cover our departure. They probably fired a few shots in the air to make sure everyone stayed in the gym."

"But you don't really know for sure, do ya?" Roger pushed his crumpled fedora back on his head, daring the lieutenant with a half-opened mouth, his thick PhotoBrown lenses hiding his eyes.

"I know my men!"

"Well, I'm going back to see!" Arlene's first stride was blocked by the side of Sergeant Rodriquez's rifle butt. He shoved, and Arlene tumbled into the ditch, mud spattering the baby blue of her Nike jacket. In a single stride that stretched Rodriquez's thick legs, he leaped across the ditch, tossing his cigarette down to hiss out in the brown water near Arlene's elbow.

When she didn't rise quickly, Ramírez kicked the bottom of her shoe. "Get up." He turned his head toward a movement across the road and back up the lane. "There come my men now. They did not shoot anyone. Keeping your friends in that gym was for their own good. If anybody *had* tried to follow us, that could've created a real crisis. We don't shoot unless we have to—but don't mess with us, either. It's best for everyone if you take orders and cooperate!"

Roger's face muscles tightened; then he turned and fell into line. Terri sucked in her breath. "Okay, Lord," she whispered, "your Word says, '*The wise in heart accept commands, but a chattering fool comes to ruin.'"* Perhaps Roger was right. She helped Arlene get up and followed the older man as they headed across the field and into the scrub trees lining the bank of the river.

As Terri snaked around bushes and down into and out of ravines, plodding along with an armed female soldier behind her, it began to sink in that she was a prisoner, a POW, a captive. With all the violence in Colombia between the government and the revolutionaries and their propensity to kidnap hostages, First Peoples Mission had conducted a training session nearly a year earlier with the staff at Finca Fe concerning what to do if anyone were captured. Nick had arrived by then and offered suggestions based on his army training. What was it he said? The best time to escape was immediately after being captured. That was when the enemy was least organized, you were closest to "friendlies," and still in familiar geography. And, unless injured, you might be in the best physical condition of your captivity.

Terri started looking for opportunities. Should she run? Would they shoot? Could she sneak behind a bush? Set up a distraction? At some point, they'd have to let her relieve herself, what if she just kept going? And what about the others—Roger and Miss Van Loon? Would it be wrong to go without them? On the other hand, what good could she do by remaining captive? She would look for her chance!

If only Nick were here. What would he do? Blast him, anyway! If he hadn't run off, she wouldn't be alone now! She was angry with him for doing that and being free. Except . . . now she was looking for an opportunity to do the same thing, perhaps leaving Roger and Arlene behind. Did that make her a hypocrite?

Nick approached the gym cautiously. Were some rebels still inside? The ones he'd seen disappear down the lane and the pockmarks on the walls below the windows suggested the shooting had come from outside the gym, but there was no assurance what he might find within. He listened but heard nothing. But if they weren't still being guarded, why hadn't anyone come out?

Cautious of rebels who might still be stalking the academy grounds, Nick worked his way around toward the kitchen door. If he could get in that way, FARC might not notice him even if they were still in the main room.

He rounded the corner and stopped. A fifty-five-gallon drum—one of Roger's trash barrels—had been wedged under the handle of the kitchen door, blocking anyone inside from opening it. His shoulders sagged in relief. The rebels wouldn't have locked themselves in. Maybe they were gone . . . or maybe they just wanted to make sure people didn't get out. Locking a door would mean fewer guards were needed inside.

He dislodged the barrel and rolled it under the kitchen window, the only low window in the building, and climbed up. No one was in the kitchen, but when he went back to try the door, it was locked. Around the corner, Nick found the two sets of double doors blocked from the outside by picnic tables. Certain now that the rebels were gone, he dragged one away. The first sigh of relief when he opened the door was swallowed by cheering and a rush to embrace him.

"Are they gone?" some of the teachers asked anxiously.

"I think so. Is everyone all right?"

Three people had been cut by glass blasted from the upper windows, but none seriously, though a boy of about ten looked as though he could use a few stitches.

"Where's Terri? She should get these kids over to the infirmary."

"Terri's gone." Mr. Barns, the school's math, science, and PE teacher was visibly shaken. "Terri and Miss Van Loon and Roger—the rebels took 'em all." To Nick's blank stare he added, "They gave them ten minutes to pack. Said they might walk all day—"

Terri gone? The cacophony around Nick faded like the soundtrack of a movie as he stared around the gym. Gone, kidnapped? And he'd just let it happen! How could he have failed her like that?

Slowly, Betty Montgomery's crying recaptured his attention. ". . . Roger, he can't do that. I mean, he works all day around here, but he's sixty-three, and no one minds if he takes a break now and then." She lurched with deep sobs. "But he's got a little heart condition. Remember?" She nodded at Nick. "Remember when you flew him to Neiva for that check up? He shouldn't be hiking all day. You gotta bring him back, Nick. You gotta—"

"Yes, Betty." He put his arm around her shaking shoulders. "We'll try, but . . ." Nick ran his hand through his short hair as he turned to Dick Barns. "Did they say anything about where they were headed or what they wanted?"

"They wanted *you*, Señor Archer!" Lucy injected. "And I was afraid they were going to find you, too. They kept lookin'."

"What do you mean, they wanted me?"

"They kept sending soldiers out for you—"

"What she means," said Barns, "is they kept asking where the pilot was. They wanted the pilot and the doctor. Of course, Terri's not a doctor, but they took her anyway. We told 'em you weren't here, but they didn't believe us."

"Yeah," added Lucy, "Mr. Montgomery said you'd taken the boat up to Hector and Isabella's to put on a new roof, but they didn't believe him, so they took him, too."

Nick's gut twisted. It *was* his fault. If the rebels had found him, maybe they wouldn't have taken— He shook his head, trying to piece together the information. "Okay, they took Terri, Miss Van Loon, and Roger." He forced himself to think. "Surely their ultimate destination is El Despeje, but they can't get across the river here, so where are they headed? Unless they're goin' all the way to Puerto Seco . . ." He had to act. He couldn't just stand there. How far could they have gotten by now?

"Barns, you take a couple of the older boys and walk the phone line until you find where they cut it. Repair it if you can and call for help. I'm going to take the plane, see if I can spot the rebels while we've still got daylight. Soon as I get high enough, I'll also radio Neiva for help and try to keep the army informed of their whereabouts."

"Wait a minute," said Barns. "I'm not sure it's a good idea for you to fly over them. If they see you flying around, they might come back here just to get you when you land. They wanted you awful bad. But we don't need 'em terrorizing us again." When Nick did not agree immediately, he added, "You gotta think of the kids, Nick. So far we got away with a few glass cuts, but no telling what might happen if they come back."

Nick clinched his jaw. "Yeah. Guess you got a point, but . . ." Everything inside him rebelled. "But they've also gotta know if I'm up there and flying, I can radio the army. Might even call in a helicopter strike if I have a positive sighting and can keep 'em under surveillance."

"But you wouldn't do that, would you? Not with Terri and Roger and Miss Van Loon as their hostages?"

Nick hesitated. "No, probably not. But I've gotta do something. You go repair that line; I'm goin' up."

As soon as he was airborne, Nick began searching for the rebels and their captives, following the winding road west into the rugged foothills, which seemed to be the only way they could've gone since the bridge over the river was out. When he was high enough, he radioed Neiva and reported the situation. The tower couldn't patch him through directly but assured him they would inform the army. Nick sure hoped so, and he hoped Barns had repaired the phone lines and made a direct call by then.

But where were the kidnappers? He was now over the village of El Tabor, some seven kilometers from the academy, and hadn't seen a sign of them. It had been less than an hour; surely they couldn't have walked much farther. He circled back to check the bridge area. Did they swim the river? None of them had been that wet when they arrived at Finca Fe. What about inflatable rafts? How could he know? He wished he'd gone down to the end of the lane to look for tracks before he took off. Perhaps they had vehicles waiting there. The road supposedly went west on into the hills past El Tabor and Betania and came out somewhere, but he'd never known anyone to drive it. It was always easier to use the bridge to cross over and go north by way of Gigante . . . until the fall rains this year had washed out the bridge.

Nick circled and again headed west along the narrow, winding track through El Tabor to see if he could follow it from the air. He flew for half an hour until he lost sight of it in the mountains. It was getting late and still no sign of vehicles or troops. Reluctantly, he turned back east and flew until he intersected the natural gas pipeline that ran from the south, north to Neiva and finally all the way to the coast. He turned south, and when the pipeline crossed the river, he cut off and followed it back to Finca Fe, essentially having flown a large fruitless loop. Shadows had spread across the landscape below, and he could see very little. He'd have to wait until tomorrow and track the rebels on the ground with the help of the army . . . he hoped.

As Nick started his decent, he realized he was shaking, probably from lack of food all day or maybe because he'd neglected to take his diabetes pills again. Or was it just the tension? He didn't know. Terri had wanted to check his blood, but now she was gone. Ha, he'd gladly let her stick him as often as she wanted if only she were still here. Night was coming, and she was out there, a captive of rebels. He couldn't keep his mind from imagining the dangers. Supposedly, more than thirty percent of FARC soldiers were women, but with a prisoner as attractive as Terri, there would be plenty of men who might take advantage of her. And after all, they were by definition outlaws. Would anything restrain them?

O God! Help me! Nick felt he had to do something! But what? He could hardly stand waiting until morning. Still, accompanying the army would be best. He couldn't do much if he found them by himself, anyway. He had to face it: There was nothing he could do tonight. Nothing, nothing at all, and that drove him nuts.

Something in the back of his mind prodded, *"You could pray."* Yeah, yeah, I should pray: *"God, God, please protect 'em. Don't let any harm come to them."* He stopped, his mind spinning as he set his Cessna down, again going over all the horrible things that might happen to Terri and the others. His prayer had been as feeble as a newly-hatched bird. Why would God listen? For the first time he wished he could pray like Terri, using Bible verses to conform his thoughts to God's thoughts, but he just didn't know his Bible that well. Was God even concerned about this situation? If so, why had God let it happen in the first place?

Nick wasn't getting anywhere. His mind was running berserk. He shut off the master switch as the Cessna rolled up to the hanger—if only he could shut down his run-away thoughts as easily. He sat for a few moments, trying to get his emotions under control. He could hardly stand quitting the search. Wasn't there something he could do even though it was getting dark? By morning, they would be farther away, harder to find. If someone had tracking dogs . . . but he didn't know anyone in Colombia who did that.

Finally, he got out of the plane, set the chocks, and headed dejectedly toward the gym. He needed something to eat. And had Barns repaired the phone line?

Terri, Roger, and Arlene had been walking an hour and a half, weaving around brush, climbing into and out of the steep rain gullies along the west bank of the Magdalena River. It was exhausting at the pace their captors drove them, and Terri was panting for breath after the first ten minutes. How long could she keep it up? And Roger, red-faced, stumbled with every step. Maybe she should have told FARC that Nick *had* returned and was somewhere around the academy. Maybe that would have caused them to go back, and she could have traded Roger and Arlene for Nick. Nick could deal with this far better than they, and he would be with her.

But no, she couldn't betray him. This was FARC's doing; that would've been her doing. She had to leave it in God's hands.

Ramírez had drifted back to walk near the captives. "How much longer?" she gasped. "Can't we quit for the day?"

"Not long. All we have to do is cross the river and meet our trucks." He stepped ahead, not interested in answering more questions.

Cross the river? How could they do that, certainly not swim. The bridge was out, and besides, they had passed it several kilometers back.

Terri thought she heard a small plane in the distance as they came out of a patch of woods, but Roger arrested her attention. "So that's how they propose we cross the river." He pointed to a large natural gas pipeline. Several rebels had already climbed up on it and were walking along, maintaining their balance by holding on to the suspension cables that supported it across the river. "There's no way I'm doing that!" he wheezed. "Not across the Magdalena! Not anywhere!"

The sun had gone down and the valley was smoky lavender dissected by cobalt shadows when Terri stepped to the ground on the other side of the river, her legs shaking. Somehow Arlene and Roger had made it across right behind her in spite of his declarations.

One of the soldiers skidded down the bank to where the group stood catching their breath. *"Nuestros camiones, ¡no están aquí!"*

"What?" demanded Ramírez.

"Our trucks, they are gone!"

The lieutenant swore under his breath. "Spread out," he hissed. "Could be an ambush."

Chapter 6

"Nick, thank God you are back." A tear-stained Betty Montgomery came running up to him as soon as he entered the gym. "Did you find Roger? Is he okay? What's happening?" She was wringing her hands in her apron more out of nervousness than any need to clean them.

Other staff members and several kids clustered around him.

"Did you see any sign of them from the air?"

"Where'd they go?"

"Hey, Señor Nick, why'd they take Miss Van Loon?"

Nick shook his head. "I'm sorry." He was feeling as shaky as a leaf in a stiff breeze. Moving the huddle toward one of the dining room tables, he swung his leg over the bench and sat down. "I really didn't see a thing." He raised both hands. "And I have no idea where they're going, though you'd think they would head across the river . . . somewhere."

His stomach growled. "Hey, Betty. You got any leftovers? I'm starving. And where's Mr. Barns? Has anybody seen him?"

Someone said Barns wasn't back yet from repairing the phone line. Betty delivered a bowl of chili and a basket of crackers so quickly it was as if she'd been expecting him. "What do you want to drink?" But before Nick could respond, she sank onto the bench beside him and broke into tears. "Oh, Nick, I don't know what I'm going to do. I can't . . . without Roger. We've been married forty-three years, and . . ." The sobs took over.

He patted her arm. "Now, Betty, we're going to find 'em." Trying to think of something practical for her to do, he added, "Can you get me a cola? I'd like a cola if there is one."

Mopping her face with her apron, she said, "Sure, Nick." She had no sooner disappeared into the kitchen than the kitchen phone began ringing.

Ah! The phones were up.

A moment later she called to him through the pass-through window. "You better come get it, Nick. It's the mission . . . from the States. They've heard about the attack."

Nick shooed everyone out of the kitchen and closed the door. For the next half hour, he explained what had happened, cradling the phone between his ear and his shoulder while leaning against the wall and grabbing bites of chili from the bowl in his hand.

Government officials had notified the mission but didn't provide details—probably didn't know any. Nevertheless, as soon as First Peoples Mission heard there had been a kidnapping, they convened a Crisis Team to coordinate responses.

"Great," said Nick. "And the army?"

"Should be there in the morning."

"Right." Morning. That meant another twelve hours. Where would Terri and the others be by then? "Okay, I'll help them track the rebels. Gotta get our people back ASAP."

"Yes, but . . . let the army handle that, Nick."

"Wait. No—"

"Nick," the mission representative cut in, "our first priority is the safety of the children and the remaining staff. What we need you to do is to begin flying everyone to Neiva."

"What? No, no! I don't think that's . . ." Nick's stomach felt like Betty's chili was doing flip-flops. An evacuation was the opposite of what he wanted to do. Terri—and Roger and Arlene—were the ones in immediate danger. He wanted to go after *them*!

"Nick, listen. You gotta understand, now that FARC has proven itself active in the area, we can't take a chance on anything happening to the children. Look, Mr. Tarkington, you know him—" The mission man rattled on while Nick struggled to pay attention. "—his son, David, attended the school. He's boiling mad that FARC attacked the school. Apparently, his oil company has a vacant building that's actually located on the airport that he's agreed to let us use temporarily. We'll bring in some bunks, and the kids can stay there. We'll have classes up and running again in no time—"

"Wait! Wait a minute." Nick had a hard time keeping his voice steady. "It'll take days to ferry everyone out of here in my 185. I can only carry a few at a time. Can't the army evacuate the school? Their trucks should be big enough to cross the river at the rapids."

Silence. Then: "All we could get them to promise was a few defenders for the school while they go after the rebels. Frankly, Nick, in a situation like this, we're lucky they're willing to do that much. Successfully retrieving hostages hasn't been their long suit, but they're the only game in town."

Oh, yeah, thought Nick. Very reassuring!

"But that's their first priority," continued the mission rep. "It's up to us to get the kids out of there. We're trying to arrange for a second plane, but . . . right now, the task is yours. Keep us posted, okay?"

Nick hung up the phone and slid down the wall until he was sitting on the bare kitchen floor. He knew the Crisis Team was right. But every nerve within him screamed to go after Terri.

Morning. The mission rep said the army would be here by now, didn't he? But it was nearly eleven before they arrived in two duce-and-a-halfs—old U.S. Army trucks, according to the faint star on the doors—specially outfitted with machine guns on top. They'd had trouble crossing the river and had to winch out one of the trucks after they nearly lost it to the current.

Nick had delayed evacuating the kids with the excuse that he was organizing them to pack only what he could carry. There was no way he was going to leave before he knew the army was on the trail of the kidnappers.

The army captain—business-like enough, but so young—dismissed the idea of FARC going west after a raid. "One of our patrols already picked up a couple vehicles, probably theirs, old pickups abandoned by the road on the other side of the river. So, we're in good shape."

"River? How'd they cross the river?"

"*¿Quién sabe?* Does it matter? They'll be headed back into El Despeje on the other side of the Cordillera Oriental Range as soon as they can. You can be sure of that. We'll get 'em."

Resigned to ferry duty, Nick made four runs to Neiva before dark, evacuating seventeen kids and three adults. Each time he landed, David Tarkington's father was there with a van to take the kids to their new "school." Rather amazing, Nick thought, for such a high-level executive of a multi-national company. He must really be committed to the school. But in his brief conversations with Tarkington, Nick learned it was the kidnappings that provoked him the most. SurPetro had gone through it a couple years before when rebels kidnapped over twenty of their oil workers. They ended up paying a huge ransom to get them back, so now Tarkington was willing to do almost anything to help. The building he'd offered, however, was nothing more than an empty warehouse with some offices at one end. Still, Tarkington said, it was dry and spacious, and there were even men's and women's bathrooms, though no showers . . . and no kitchen. But all that was promised even though the cots hadn't even arrived yet.

On each trip, Nick studied the banks of the river, sometimes diverting slightly over the surrounding countryside, hoping for some sign of the kidnapers and their captives. Droning along at three thousand feet, watching the landscape below, Nick couldn't keep from thinking about Terri. Why was he so gripped by her? It wasn't like they were engaged or married or anything. In fact, only recently had he even been able to imagine marriage again, and though he and Terri had been good friends for nearly two years now, it had only been the other night after the cookout that his feelings toward her had exploded. There were two other hostages out there, for heaven sakes. But his imagination was consumed with her. How was she doing? Had anyone harmed her? Did she feel threatened? Had she been able to stay dry? Did she have enough food? How could he rescue her?

The crisis itself seemed to have catapulted their relationship to a new level. In spite of the tension, he laughed at himself as he banked his plane to the right and started his descent to the academy. Relationship? You had to have two people interacting for there to be a relationship. This was all in his head! But that didn't make it any less powerful. He was obsessed with this woman, and he liked it . . . well, not the kidnapped part, but the fact that someone other than himself and his own plans filled his thoughts.

As exhausted as he was after his last trip, he phoned the Crisis Team at mission headquarters as soon as he landed, ostensibly to make a report, but really to find out whether there had been any news from the army. The four soldiers left at Finca Fe as "defenders" didn't even have a field radio that reached their captain.

But there was nothing to report from the search. Not a word! "Just get the rest of those kids out of there, Nick. We'll let you know as soon as we hear anything about the hostages."

Discouraged, he dragged himself to his quarters realizing he, too, would leave Finca Fe in a few days. This had been home for the last two years—home and where he had gotten to know Terri Kaplan. His room seemed dreary, as though the voltage in the lights was low, his hopes for a new life crushed by the events of the past couple of days. What if the army didn't get her back? He didn't want to think about that. But . . . he'd probably resign from MAST. He wouldn't be able to stay in Colombia. Yeah, that's probably what he'd do. He'd come here to serve God, but God had to do His part. He'd been making it okay without a woman in his life, and then he'd met Terri. Nick didn't like a God who teased him with good things only to snatch them away. *Huh. Didn't the Bible say something about God satisfying us with "good things"?* "You're not playing fair, God!" he yelled into the silence. Yeah, he could pray Scripture, too. Quote it back to God, make Him to do what He promised.

His outburst startled him. He ought to be praying . . . *"Yes, and with faith!"* He knew that. But he was tired, too tired. Without even taking off his clothes, Nick fell into his bunk.

Terri forced her legs to climb—around a bush, over those rocks. It seemed as if they were wandering without direction, forever climbing higher in the foothills of the Cordillera Oriental, but never following a path or road for more than a half hour before ducking off into dense brush or scrambling up a steep bank. Though she occasionally saw a small village or farm, the FARC seemed careful to keep its distance.

For a while, she tried snapping off twigs, tearing leaves, and bending down the tops of the coarse grass to leave a trail someone might be able to follow. After all, how could nearly twenty people go through the wilderness without leaving tracks that anyone could see? But by the end of the second day, it was all she could do to pick up one foot and put it in front of the other before her guard prodded her in the back with the hard muzzle of a weapon. Even if it never went off, Terri figured her back was covered with bruises.

And what was the use of trying to leave a trail? The mountains were covered with game trails and cattle trails weaving in and out in such a random fashion that no one could possibly distinguish one from another.

The first night had been a nightmare, sleeping on rocks, trying to stay warm, and forever worrying about scorpions and ants and other crawling things. But by the second night, she hardly finished the chunk of bread and piece of chocolate the soldiers gave her before she fell asleep, exhaustion overriding comfort.

Roger didn't look well the next morning. Sleep had done little to refresh him. It was a sign of dangerous exhaustion in a man of his age. That day, Terri noticed their travel changed. The terrain was too steep to wander over the hills on a seemingly indiscriminate path. Now they were following valleys and canyons, looking for the easiest pass to get over the next ridge. The altitude required her to reach deep in a second effort just to get a normal breath. What was it doing to Roger and Miss Van Loon?

"I'm not packed yet, Nick. Take someone else this time." Betty waved both hands as though Nick was asking just too much from an old lady. But he knew it was her reluctance to move away from where she had last seen her Roger. He felt the same way about doing anything that would take him farther from Terri, too. But this *was* the third day, and hopefully he could finish transporting everyone to Neiva by this evening and then concentrate on searching for Terri . . . though he wasn't sure how. Maybe fly as a spotter plane for the army. He didn't know.

Every kid had wanted to take more stuff than his plane could carry, and he was losing patience. They had to leave everything behind except for essentials. The mission would retrieve their personal possessions later when it could rent a truck big enough to get across the Magdalena. Some students were scared and wanted to go straight home—not to Neiva. Others refused to pack up at all and had become totally passive. Most adults seemed more concerned about their own needs. Families wanted their kids to go first, which was understandable because most of them were so young, but then the parents wanted to go with them, too. No one—except Betty—wanted to be left until last. Why did Nick have to be the one to comfort, guide, and organize everyone?

MAST, Nick's own mission agency, had asked him to use up the fuel reserves stored at Finca Fe to lessen the temptation for anyone to steal gasoline once the academy was abandoned. So, two or three times a day he had to refuel his plane by filling a twenty-liter gas can, climbing a ladder, and holding it head-high while he carefully filled his wing tanks. Each refueling required him to repeat the maneuver four or five times until with the last can he had to hold his breath and strain so hard his arms trembled, and he spilled the gas.

Breathing the fumes with his face so close to the gurgling gasoline, some of it inevitably splashing out, gave him a pulsing headache and left his brain as scrambled as a street kid sniffing glue.

No support plane arrived to help him, and in the last sixty hours, he'd had less than six hours of sleep. He felt numb with exhaustion, rubbing his eyes to clear his blurred vision.

Shortly after noon of the third day—Terri calculated it as Thursday, November 17—FARC started pushing them faster, for what reason, Terri couldn't tell. And by that time, she and the other captives were so exhausted they made few attempts to talk to their captors or even to one another. Walking and getting the next breath were all they could manage. Finally, Roger stopped on the edge of a deep, overgrown ravine and leaned over, hands on his knees. His guard poked him, and he slowly turned his head toward the young soldier, a mere boy. "I . . . can't go any faster. Give me a rest. I can't go any farther."

"You've got to. The army's coming. We can't let them catch us."

"The army?" Arlene Van Loon straightened up. "Did you say the army is coming?"

"*Sí.* And they're getting closer. *¡Vámonos!*"

Like hitting the afterburners, Arlene cut loose at the top of her lungs. "Help us! We're up here! *¡Ayúdenos!* FARC has kidnapped us! *¡Ayúdenos!*" She stopped for a moment as her voice literally echoed down the valley.

"*¡Basta!*" snapped Sergeant Rodriquez as he brought up his rifle.

But Arlene paid no attention and opened her mouth for an encore.

"Arlene, NO!" Terri shouted and lunged toward her as Arlene took up the call again, this time even louder.

"*¡Basta!*" Rodriquez yelled again and Terri stopped.

Up the trail she saw Lieutenant Ramírez wheel around at the angry yelling, raise his hand, and shout, "No—!" But Rodriquez pulled the trigger, shooting Arlene right through the head.

Terri stared in horror as Finca Fe's lofty principal crumpled to the ground, blood pulsing from the blown-off back of her head.

Suddenly, Roger came to life and charged the sergeant. Smoothly the man switched aim and fired at Roger, stopping the older man in mid-stride.

"No-ooo! No!" Terri wailed.

A blank stare descended over Roger's face like the blood that began streaming from under his fedora and down the side of his head. He staggered one step to the right and then tumbled over the side of the ravine, rolling down and down, crashing through trees and brush. Then all Terri heard was the skitter of pebbles following his limp body.

Chapter 7

Nick was so tired, he couldn't see straight. Only one trip to go evacuating the academy. It had already been a long day, but if he didn't take off soon, he'd be making a night landing in Neiva. Nick did one last check of the hanger. All his tools were locked up. The power was turned off, and he was ready to go.

MAST had told him they would retrieve his tools and equipment later. That might be awhile, given the difficulty the army trucks had crossing the river. Maybe they'd have to wait until the water subsided. Thankfully, there had been no rain for the last three days. Maybe the rainy season was coming to an end. Or maybe he would fly back in a few days and pick up as much as he could haul.

But right now, he needed to give his eyes a rest. Just fifteen minutes.

Nick wandered into his apartment at the back of the hanger and flopped down on his bare mattress, gazing around his digs. If he and Terri had gotten married, they wouldn't have been able to live here. They would've had to apply for an apartment . . . crazy thoughts! Terri was out in the mountains, kidnapped by FARC! And he was thinking about *apartments*?

He shut his eyes for a few moments but was too wound up to sleep. He stared blankly at the walls. *Wait* . . . Something was wrong with his eyes. He couldn't see the numbers on the calendar he'd left hanging on the opposite wall. He sat up, blinked, and rubbed them again. The right one was blurry, but his left one . . . there were some kind of smoky patches obscuring his vision. He rubbed again but to no advantage. He got up and stumbled to the mirror over his sink. The only light was coming in through the window, but there didn't seem to be anything floating on his eye, no dirt or anything.

Still, irregular patches obscured much of his vision like shadowy islands in a sea. Nick fought down a flicker of panic. This was not good. As a pilot, he needed vision correctable to 20/20. But right now, he wouldn't be able to pass a physical if he had to renew his license.

Calm down, Nick, he told himself. Probably just extreme exhaustion, both physical and emotional. He'd snap back when he got some rest.

But going back to his bed, he tried again to focus on the calendar across the room, first with his right eye—a little blurry, but not too bad—then his left eye. The dark areas were still there.

"Hey, Nick, we're ready to go."

So much for a rest. He stood up and nearly fainted. Ohhh . . . this was not good, not good at all. "Yeah, I'm comin'." As he walked out of the hanger, he bumped into the edge of the hanger door with his left shoulder—just tired? Or had he not seen it? He wasn't sure. He headed toward his plane muttering, "Oh God, don't let this be happening to me. Whatever it is, You gotta stop it. Please God, please!"

Climbing into the Cessna, he faced forward without saying a word to Dick Barns or Betty—who had managed to wait until last—and the three older boys from the academy who had stayed behind to help close the school. When they finally shut the Cessna's door, Nick opened his window and called, "Clear!" then started the engine. The sun was just setting, but he could still see well enough to fly even with the dark amoebas in his left eye. He did a quick pre-flight, turning his head all the way to the left to check the aileron movement with his right eye. Then pushed the throttle to the firewall.

Just one more flight—this would be his twenty-third trip in three days—then he could get some rest. Maybe that was all he needed, a little rest.

But once he reached altitude, anxiety about his eyes crowded his mind. What could cause dark patches in a person's vision? His panicky thoughts searched what he knew about eye problems: glaucoma—something about pressure in the eye. Macular degeneration—that happened to older people, didn't it? Brain tumors . . . brain tumors? Yeah, could happen to anyone. No, couldn't be a brain tumor . . . could it? He didn't have any headaches or anything. Must be something else. He had to quit thinking about it. But within a moment, he was closing one eye and then the other. Had the dark shapes changed? Were they smaller? Larger? *Arrrgh!* There was no putting this out of his mind. What he saw—or didn't see—was unavoidable, *all the time*! No getting away from it as long as he was conscious!

Twenty minutes later, he touched down at Neiva's Aeropuerto Benito Salas. Though an orange glow still lit the western sky, the runway lights were on, and he saw well enough to land, but in the shadows—whether on the ground or in his eye—he missed the turnoff ramp to the private service area and had to go all the way to the end of the tarmac and taxi back.

"You been kinda quiet, Nick."

"Yeah. Guess I'm bushed." Had Barns noticed his mistake? He hoped not. The others had been talking—nearly yelling to be heard over the engine noise—during the whole trip, but he hadn't paid attention to a word. He *was* tired!

"Well, thanks for all the work you've done, Nick. I don't know what we'd have done without your plane. You coming with us in the van to our 'new school'?"

"Thanks, but I need to tie down the plane, check a few things. I'm going to see if Armando will let me crash in his office." No way Nick wanted to be in a warehouse with sixty kids. He needed some rest, real rest. Tomorrow he'd ask the service manager to recommend a good optometrist in Neiva. Maybe a pair of glasses would help.

Roger Montgomery awoke shivering. The tropical sun just peeking over the Andean pass had not yet tickled the morning air. He pushed himself up out of the leaves and twigs, many of them glued to the side of his head like ruffled quills on a porcupine.

The pain of trying to brush them away was his first lesson of the day. The second had to do with the crumpled fedora with a hole through its side that lay in the dirt beside him. It meant something, but he couldn't quite identify what.

Automatically, he grasped the free earpiece of the wire-rimmed glasses that hung from his other ear, dangling about his chin like some crystalline necklace and hooked it in place—ouch, that hurt, too, but he could see better. He looked around. He was near the bottom of some kind of gulley, and it seemed obvious that he should crawl up out of it. But that was hard work. Every meter or so he slid back. Not fair! He didn't like things that weren't fair. After resting a minute, he again cautiously tried to touch the side of his head—tender, sticky with . . . what was this? Blood? His blood? He picked up the hat. It was *his* hat. He was sure of it, now. He turned it around in his hands until he got it just right and then tried to put it on. *Ouch!* . . . more punishment.

With greater care, he picked away the leaves and twigs and gingerly touched the sticky area. It was swollen, some kind of an injury. With stiff hands, he rotated his hat again. The hole was on the same side as his wound. It looked like a bullet hole. He'd been shot! *That* was his second lesson. No other explanation for it. He'd been shot. But who would've shot him and why? With as much tenderness as if he were dressing an infant, he put on his hat, delicately pulling it down over the wound. After a moment, the throbbing subsided, and he turned around to look up the steep bank again. He knew he had to get up there. In the back of his mind, there was a reason. Maybe another lesson. He'd always been a student in the school of hard knocks.

He crawled and slid and crawled and clung to bushes and finally, panting like a puppy, pulled himself onto an obvious trail. After resting a few moments, he stood up on wobbly legs and looked around. He was high in the mountains, but what mountains? A few steps away he noticed a large dark patch on the trail. With halting steps, he went over to it, stooped down—though the movement made his head pound—and dragged two fingers through the damp dirt. He rubbed his fingers with his thumb—brown, sticky. More blood? The dark patch was large, perhaps at least a meter across. That was a lot of blood! He tentatively touched the side of his head. He couldn't have lost that much blood, not and still be alive. How'd he know that? He shrugged. He just did, maybe because he was old. You don't get old without learning your lessons.

A wave of dizziness washed over him. What was he supposed to learn here?

When he got his bearings again, Roger gazed at the valley below. "FARC!" He spat out the word like a curse, then said it again: "FARC!" It was somehow connected to the evil in the dark patch beneath his feet. He needed to get off this mountain, away from FARC, whatever FARC was! Gingerly he touched the right side of his hat and staggered down the trail.

The optometrist Armando recommended peered into Nick's eyes with his little scope for a moment. He asked a few questions about how long Nick had been having trouble with his vision. Then he stepped back and scribbled a name on a notepad. He tore off the sheet. "Before we talk about glasses, Mr. Archer, I want you to go upstairs to the third floor of this building and see this ophthalmologist." He handed the sheet to Nick. "I only prescribe eyeglasses. You need to see someone who can examine the health of your eyes."

"Why? Is something wrong?" Stupid question. Nick already knew there was *something* wrong.

"I wouldn't be able to say, but he can."

Nick climbed the stairs, again rehearsing the possible eye problems he knew of: glaucoma, macular degeneration, brain tumors, cataracts . . . Cataracts, maybe he had a cataract. His mother had had cataracts. They were removed, and in a couple weeks, she could see just fine—no problem. "Oh, Lord, if I gotta have something wrong, don't let it be a brain tumor!" He checked one eye against the other as he approached the door with the frosted glass. He had to get much closer than usual before he could read the doctor's name with his right eye. And his left was still the same

. . . or maybe the dark islands were different shapes, obscuring new areas. He should've drawn a map of them.

Thirty minutes later, after the doctor had looked into his dilated eyes, Nick admitted that, yes, he knew he had diabetes, but it had never bothered his eyes in the past.

"Well," responded the doctor, "I'm sorry to tell you what's bothering you. You've had a hemorrhage in your left eye and a small leak of blood in your right eye. These have been caused by your diabetes."

He slid his stool back and folded his arms. "When not thoroughly controlled, new blood vessels can grow in the retina of a diabetic's eyes. These abnormal blood vessels are weak and tend to break, allowing blood to seep into the eye. If it is just a small leak, such as you've experienced in your right eye, you may perceive it as nothing more than minor cloudiness or spidery floaters. But if these vessels hemorrhage into your vitreous, it can block a substantial portion of your vision. That is what has happened in your left eye. It's called proliferative diabetic retinopathy."

The term meant nothing to Nick, but hemorrhage did. "What can you do about it?"

"We can cauterize the leaking vessels with laser in your right eye, but in your left eye, I can't see in any better than you can see out right now. We tend to wait. There's a chance the blood will clear with time, and then we can treat the retina with laser."

"How long until it clears?"

The doctor shrugged. "A few weeks, maybe months."

"Months? And . . . and what if it doesn't clear?"

"Then we'd have to do a vitrectomy . . . to remove the blood-soaked vitreous or jelly in your eye. We'd replace that with a saline solution, and proceed from there."

Nick left the doctor's office, miscalculating and bumping the left door jam, but he had an appointment to return the next day to begin laser treatment—hundreds of "spot welds" over the next few days to seal any abnormal vessels in his right eye. Clear vision should return to that eye within a week.

But as Nick hailed a taxi to take him back to the airport where Armando had graciously allowed him to bunk down in an unused office, his mind tumbled. Why had this happened now, right in the middle of a crisis? Had he missed the warning signs? What were the odds of getting full vision back in his left eye? Would he be able to fly again?

His mind replayed what the doctor had said. Wait a minute. If a vitrectomy—or whatever it was called—was the ultimate treatment for cleaning out a hemorrhage, why wait weeks or months to see if it cleared spontaneously? He didn't have time to sit around and wait. Terri and the other hostages were still missing. He had to get back to Finca Fe and find out what was happening. He had to get that vitrectomy . . . now!

Chapter 8

Nick knew MAST headquarters in Newton, Kansas, was waiting for his report. But should he tell them about his eyes at this point? They'd probably ground him. Nevertheless, he made the call and asked to speak to Michele Santos, bringing the Latin America field manager up to speed on the evacuation. "And, uh, there's another little matter I probably should tell you about."

"What's that, Nick? I know you've been awfully busy. Glad everyone's finally out."

"It's nothing, really, but I've been having some problems with my eyes. I guess it's related to my diabetes—"

"Diabetes? . . . Oh, that's right. Here, it's mentioned in your file. I'd forgotten."

File, she's looking at his file?

"Yes, well, guess I'd forgotten, too. Anyway, the first time I noticed it was yesterday afternoon on my last flight. My eyes started getting a little cloudy. Pretty scary at the time, I have to admit, but I couldn't do anything about it until today. Fortunately, the doctor says I should be okay. It's rather common with diabetes. He's scheduled me for laser treatment on my right eye beginning tomorrow." Nick stopped short of describing the more serious condition of his left eye.

There was silence on the other end, and then Michele said, "Could you hold on a minute, Nick?" When she came back on the line, she sounded as if she was speaking in a can. "We're not so sure getting treated *there* is a good idea, Nick. Maybe—"

"Who's 'we'?"

"I asked George to join me in here in the office. We're on the speakerphone. You know George Arthur, our controller?"

"Hello Nick."

"Yeah. Hi George." He'd fought with George often enough about the cost of equipment and other expenses.

"Anyway, as I was saying, we think you should come back to the States and get a second opinion—in Chicago, if you like. You don't want to take any chances with your eyes. Besides, we've been having some trouble with insurance coverage on nonemergency procedures overseas."

"But this *is* an emergency."

There was another silence on the other end, then, "But it can wait another twenty-four hours or so, can't it?"

The tension inside Nick had jacked up to twang-level, but he didn't know why. He'd rather get his eye "lasered" here and now, and have it over with, but . . . a second opinion was good, wasn't it? And by going home to Chicago, he'd be assured of the best treatment possible, and he could see his mom. Under ordinary circumstances, he wouldn't think twice. But now? Leaving Colombia meant moving days and thousands of miles farther from Terri, whose life was in jeopardy.

When he finally answered, he stumbled. "I . . . I don't know. Guess another day won't hurt. But I'm not the doctor."

"Then let's see what we can do."

"Yeah," George said. "I should have a ticket for you by morning. Okay?"

"Sure. Thanks."

"You take care, now," Michele added. "Goodbye."

The next morning, instead of going to the doctor's office in Neiva to begin his laser treatment, Nick was on a plane to Chicago with an eye appointment already set up for Monday morning with a Dr. Norman, "one of the best in the country," Michele had said. But Monday was three days after he would've received treatment in Colombia.

It was while he was staring down at the blue Caribbean, winking one eye and then the other to see if his dark patches had changed shape—and hopefully shrank—that a thought came to him, almost as though God were reminding him of his desperate prayer the day before: *"Oh, Lord, if I gotta have something wrong, don't let it be a brain tumor!"* Well, he didn't have a brain tumor! That was good news in itself. Was it also an answer to prayer? Or did the fact that apparently it had never been a tumor mean his prayer hadn't mattered one way or the other? Was God there and concerned about him or did he basically face life alone?

He didn't want to go there. It made him feel empty and adrift. Nick plugged in his earphones. But he couldn't seem to help himself stewing about where God was in this whole thing even with an old Buddy Holly song playing in his ears.

Nick's white-haired mother met him at the baggage carousel waving a large white handkerchief. "Nicky, Nicky!"

"Mom! Hey, I can see you just fine. Uh, Mom, you don't need to lead me by the hand through the airport. I won't bump into people. . . . No, I don't need to go to bed as soon as we get home." She was shorter than he remembered, and he didn't feel too secure when she exited Chicago's O'Hare Airport barely peering over the steering wheel as she pointed her big old Buick west toward her home in suburban Carol Stream. She had chosen to stay in the family home after Nick's father had died ten years before. But it was three times larger than she needed and a pain to maintain.

All the rest of that day and the next, Nick left messages for the Crisis Team at the First Peoples Mission headquarters in neighboring Wheaton. When he couldn't get through, he was tempted to go over there for a personal update, but if the team wasn't in the offices, that would be futile. Finally, on Saturday morning Thomas Hoover, the head of the Crisis Team, returned his call.

Nick missed the phone receiver on the first grab and had to reach for it again. With the vision in his left eye gone, and his right eye still a little fuzzy, he hadn't yet learned how to compensate for his diminished depth perception. "Thanks for getting back to me." He sat down by his mother's kitchen phone, nervously testing whether he could read her phonebook with his "good" right eye—he couldn't, not even the bold type. "Have you heard anything from the kidnappers, any ransom demands or anything?"

"Nothing from FARC. But . . . the army has called off the pursuit."

"What?"

"I'm sorry Nick. Seems there was a . . . a 'fatal confrontation,' I think is what they called it."

"A fatal . . . what do you mean?" Nick's insides flopped over.

"Apparently, they were closing in on the kidnappers when two shots rang out. They approached cautiously, because you can never tell whether they are drawing you into an ambush or what. But when they arrived at the site, they found the body of Miss Van Loon. She'd been shot once through the head and was lying dead on the trail."

Nick stopped breathing. Things were going from bad to worse. Terri and Roger, what about . . . "And the other shot? Was anyone else hurt?"

"Well, that's the thing. This is an old tactic FARC uses when they're cornered. They shoot a captive and then fire another shot simulating the execution of a second person. When the army gets there, they have to waste time looking for a possible second victim. It gives FARC time to escape."

"Did they . . . was there . . .?" Nick couldn't finish the question.

"They don't think so. Couldn't find a second victim. But after one execution, they called off the pursuit to avoid any more killings."

"*Called it off?* What about Terri and Roger?"

"Nick, listen. By executing one hostage, this FARC unit demonstrated they're willing to kill prisoners. Roger and Terri could have been next if the army kept up the pressure."

Nick blew out a long breath. Yeah, keeping Terri alive—Roger, too—that's what mattered. He could see that. . . . "So, what's next?"

"Well, we wait. Perhaps they'll radio with ransom demands. The army thinks we should negotiate."

"Negotiate *what*? I thought First Peoples Mission didn't pay ransom." That's what they'd said at the training session a year ago.

"We don't. But we're always willing to talk."

"Talk! Just talk? Has talk ever led to a release?"

There was a hesitation. "Yes. But it wasn't from organized insurgents, more like a gang of thugs, but we did get a couple back—the Fergusons. That was Indonesia, about three years ago. Besides, once contact is established, the army may be able to pinpoint the coordinates of the FARC base."

Nick sat there a moment. He couldn't believe it. The rebels had killed Miss Van Loon. Betty Montgomery was sick with worry for Roger—with good reason. And the search had been called off! Now they were supposed to . . . just wait? He took a breath to calm himself. "Please, keep me in the loop. Okay?" He ended the call feeling as if he ought to go over to the First Peoples Mission, but the executive hadn't even called from the office. He'd been at home. No one was in the office on Saturday. Besides, what could he do . . . or say? What could anyone do?

The Crisis Team was here, in their comfortable suburban homes. But who was down there in Colombia? Who was close enough to help Terri and Roger?

They'd been walking for three full days since the shootings, over high mountains where the wind cut like ice blades and then down into the steaming valley of the Amazon. *"Yea, though I walk through the valley of . . . death . . . Yea, though I walk through the valley . . . Yea, though I . . ."* Terri stumbled along, fending off the fear of evil—of Arlene and Roger having been shot, blood flying, bodies falling—by repeating words from Psalm 23. The soldiers grumbled about the lack of transportation and the blisters on their swollen feet, but Terri didn't care whether her feet fell off or if she dropped in a heap along the trail. Her friends had been shot, murdered by the great "People's Army" of Colombia. She walked in a trance, comforted only by the protective rod and staff of the Good Shepherd. But the trail—the many trails, the ever-branching trails—continued on into the thickening rain forest.

The jungle is its own defense, a fortress of entangling vines and towering trees, roaring cataracts, and barricades of fallen logs to which any intruder must bow, even crawl. Nevertheless, in the middle of all that arboreal security, the travelers came upon a campesino who had hacked his remote farm out of the very heart of the jungle. He stood by the trail, leaning on his hoe, nodding with a placid face to the passing guerillas.

Did this poor farmer know that she was a captive, kidnapped and brought here against her will? Did he have any idea that these murderers had slain her companions? Would this *campesino* be her *compañero* if she attempted to escape? Was he a victim like herself, or was he a committed insurgent? The questions swirled hopelessly in her mind. How could she know? How could she flee?

That evening they came finally into a camp, a virtual small town beneath the canopy of protective trees. Electric lights powered by some distant droning generator hung from wires and shone through tent doorways. Camouflaged soldiers welcomed the returning warriors and then went back to their tasks—breaking down the mess line, servicing a pickup truck, sweeping out a tent.

"Over here!" Lieutenant Ramírez waved Terri toward a small tent. "You'll bunk in there with Rosita. She will be your assistant." A sullen woman, younger than Terri, came out and looked her up and down. She wore fatigues and a pistol on her hip, and Terri immediately concluded "Rosita" was more of a guard than an assistant. "Drop your stuff in there and go over to the hospital. You can eat after you've seen to your patients." The commander strode off into the darkness.

"Need something to eat?" Rosita asked, but it wasn't a friendly invitation, and Terri had no interest in food. She'd thrown up every time she'd tried one of the stale tortillas her captors had urged on her. Somehow every attempt at eating brought up the images of Arlene and Roger getting shot in the head.

She turned to Rosita. "Can I at least use the restroom first?" When the woman stared blankly back at her, Terri added, "Restroom, *el baño?"*

"*Oh, sí.* Down this path." She grabbed a flashlight and headed off. "But you must hurry."

Ten minutes later Rosita led Terri into the makeshift hospital. It was one of the larger tents, with a wooden platform for a floor and a fan at one end to move the humid air. The lieutenant was coming out just as Rosita ushered Terri in. His face looked grim, and he made no eye contact with Terri.

Wounded men lay on two of the cots. Rosita pointed. "That one is Jesús; the other is Carlos Álvarez." Terri approached the patients tentatively. Her heart sank. They were just boys. Carlos seemed to be sleeping peacefully, but the younger of the two moaned softly, sweat glistening on his forehead. "You must save him!" hissed Rosita. "He's the son of Teniente Ramírez."

News that FARC had shot hostages and that the army had backed off put Nick over the edge. Somebody had to do something! *Why this problem with my eyes, God? Why now?* But if he couldn't do it, who could?

By the time Nick arrived at Dr. Norman's office Monday morning, he was again wrestling with his options: If a vitrectomy was the quickest way to remove blood from his left eye, why not do it first rather than wait? He needed to get his vision back. He needed to get back to Colombia by any means necessary! Do what he could to help Terri.

But he held his question while Dr. Norman examined him, confirmed the diagnosis he had received in Colombia, and gave him a firm lecture about the need to care for his diabetes.

Nick snorted. "Well, you better believe I've been a good boy the last few days. Scheduled all kinds of tests for my diabetes, too."

"Good." Dr. Norman folded his arms. "So, any questions?"

Nick almost asked about the vitrectomy but didn't want to appear too headstrong, so he led with another question. "You got any idea why this happened now, the hemorrhage, I mean? I know the condition has been developing for some time, but did I do something to cause the bleed now? Something I should avoid in the future?"

"Hard to say. Sometimes bleeds occur while a person sleeps with no apparent trigger. But there is the possibility that after working as hard as you say you did those three days, you were so exhausted you found it nearly impossible to lift those gas cans over your head. Maybe you resorted to a Valsalva maneuver. That's an attempt to increase lifting ability by holding your breath and creating a lot of pressure with your diaphragm and chest muscles. Unfortunately, holding one's breath can cause the blood pressure in your head to spike. That's why some people's face turns red when they try to lift something heavy. Perhaps this caused your hemorrhage, but . . ." He shrugged. "There's no way to know for sure. What is certain is that neglecting your diabetes was the real cause."

Nick nodded, feeling like a third grader without his homework.

"Okay, now for treatment—"

When Nick suggested going straight for the vitrectomy, the doctor balked. "I'm not sure I'd recommend that. It might be the quickest route to clear vision, but it is serious surgery with risks of further hemorrhage or infection. I prefer avoiding those risks whenever possible. Why don't we proceed with the laser work on your right eye for now, and see if the left clears on its own?"

Because, thought Nick, without my left eye, I have no depth perception. I can't fly—at least I shouldn't. I was lucky to make it from Finca Fe to Neiva safely. Without a plane, I'm just another helpless gringo. But with a plane . . .

An idea had been percolating in the back of his mind. If the FARC commander had wanted him and his plane so badly that he'd sent several people to search for him, then perhaps Nick could use the lieutenant's desire for a pilot to secure Terri's release. What if he went back to Colombia and offered to trade himself and his plane for Terri and Roger's release?

Whatever the prospects, he had to return to Colombia, and he had to be able to fly when he got there!

"Well, doctor, I hear your cautions, but I've made a decision. I want you to do a vitrectomy like . . . now! While it's recovering, we can do the laser work on my right eye. I know there are increased risks, but I need to pursue the shortest possible route to fully restored sight."

Dr. Norman frowned. "But you understand that I cannot guarantee that?"

"Yes. You've explained it clearly."

The doctor sighed. "All right. Tomorrow's my surgery day, and you're in luck. I just had a cancellation. If you can go right over to the hospital and do your pre-op this afternoon, I'll tell my assistant to schedule you for tomorrow."

Chapter 9

It was what Nick wanted—immediate surgery. Get it over with. Get back to Colombia. Help Terri. But emotionally he wasn't ready to go under the knife so quickly. Knife? Would it be a knife? How would they do it? He hadn't even asked. Dr. Norman had said they wouldn't need to put him out. Local anesthesia and relaxants would do the trick. Would he have to keep his eye perfectly still? What if he blinked or twitched at the wrong moment? A shiver shook him as he rode home on the Metra train.

His mother called her pastor as soon as Nick got back. The pastor and a couple elders came right over. They were actually from Nick's old home church of fifteen years before, and still supported him financially, though many members had moved on. They sat stiffly on his mother's doily-strewn couch and prayed that God would guide the hand of the surgeon and protect Nick from complications. Efficient, cover the bases, get it over with—like the surgery. "Amen."

"Now, let's see," the pastor said, getting out his Day-Timer, "since you'll be around for a while, can I schedule you . . ." He turned a few pages, then looked up. "First, why don't you tell me about some of the churches you've planted? We're a very missionary minded church, and I'm sure that would bless our people."

Schedule? Was he expecting Nick to speak? "Uh, I don't plant churches. I fly airplanes. I work for MAST. Support, you know?" Oops, *work for,* why did he say, *work for,* like his was just a job for a corporation?

The pastor had noticed, too. He raised his eyebrows and took a deep breath. "Well, then, tell me about some of your converts, some of the people you've led to the Lord." He turned and grinned at first one elder and then the other. "I find personal stories are sometimes the most powerful."

Nick's mind went blank . . . no, it wasn't blank. It was empty—nothing! In all his time on the mission field, he hadn't personally led anyone to the Lord.

"You mean all you do is fly planes?" the pastor asked as he slowly closed his Day-Timer.

Nick nodded. He could describe how essential his support ministry was, but these men obviously had their preconceptions, and he didn't feel like arguing with them.

"Well, we hope your surgery goes well." The pastor stood up, and the elders followed his lead. "Perhaps your mother can let us know how things turn out."

They all shook his hand and left.

Nick went to his mom's guestroom wondering what had just happened. Was this mechanical religion all there was any more? He knew his own prayer life had become rather perfunctory, but that's why he needed someone else to pray for him. He needed someone who really believed. Not just someone who believed *in* God, but someone who believed *God* and His Word. Uh, what was that old verse . . . oh, yeah: *"The effectual fervent prayer of a righteous man availeth much."* Sometimes speaking King James was like spitting out fish bones, but he knew what it meant, and right now he needed some *fervent* prayer by someone who was *righteous* and *effectual*—prayer that could affect the outcome!

He closed one eye and then the other. The dark patches were still there. What if the surgery didn't work? He needed help from someone who was more in touch with God than he was!

"Hey, man. What happened to you? Looks like you been fightin' *el diablo*!" They laughed, and one held up a dark bottle. "Like us! Eh?"

In the day's waning light, Roger staggered toward the two campesinos sitting on the tailgate of a rusted-out pickup. He waved his hand across his face as though he were wiping a mirror, his motion more intoxicated than the men in the truck. "Weren't no devil. . . . FARC!"

They stood up cautiously, suddenly sober, craning their necks to see up the shadowed path behind Roger. "Uh, *hasta luego,* man. We gotta be goin'." They staggered around to the cab.

"Wait!" Roger picked up his pace. "Don't leave! I need a ride. Come on, you guys, how 'bout a lift . . . anywhere?"

The driver was already in, but the other one hesitated. "Where you from, *anciano*?"

"I . . . I don't . . . uh, grew up in Hannibal . . . Hannibal, Missouri."

"Hey, we ain't goin' there, man. Sorry." And he got in the truck.

The old engine roared to life, ejecting a puff of blue smoke, and the truck began to roll down the hill.

"No! Don't leave me!" Roger was running, stumbling, waving his arms. "Wait! You can't. . ." Then he fell. Flat out, face in the dirt, crumpled hat rolling on ahead.

After a moment, he slowly looked up and saw a white light wink on in the broken lens of the truck's taillight.

The red glow from the digital clock winked at Nick as the numbers changed from 3:47 to 3:48. They were a little blurry, but he could see them fairly well with his right eye. But what if he had a hemorrhage in that eye, too? What if there were complications and he ended up virtually blind in both eyes? He was too old to learn Braille or some new job. What job? What could he do? Make brooms?

He flopped over. Had to get some sleep. Surgery in a few hours, and he was full of static. *Thump, thump, thump, thump.* He'd never noticed his heart beating before . . . not at rest, not in bed. His leg twitched, and he flopped over to lay on his other side. He sighed deeply, and looked again at the clock, this time with his left eye—dark patches glowing red around the edge. Right eye: 4:02.

Close eyes! Don't think!

But can you *not* think about something so incessant?

Terri. He would think about Terri. What was happening to her? Would he ever *see* her again? Oh, no! There it was again: *see* . . . his vision! Not just would he, but *could* he see?

His thoughts scrambled for he didn't know how long until he finally drifted off just before the same clock beeped him awake.

At the hospital, the proficiency and friendliness of the staff reassured Nick, and what nervousness remained washed away with the help of what the anesthesiologist called, "today's cocktail of choice." Dr. Norman came by the prep booth, and to Nick's relief, looked like he'd slept much better than Nick had the night before.

"Ready?" When Nick gave him a mellow nod, he patted his shoulder reassuringly. "This shouldn't take more than about ninety minutes. You'll be awake and can even communicate with us if you need to, but you shouldn't feel any pain. Okay? See you in there." Then the doctor grinned. "Actually, you won't see me, 'cause you'll be draped before I come in. Everything but the eye you can't see out of will be covered. But I'll say hello."

"Make sure it's the right eye . . . I mean, the correct eye, my *left* eye!"

"Oh, you'll know!"

Nick *humphed*! Cocktail must be working for him to joke about it.

As Dr. Norman had promised, nothing hurt except Nick's cramped back as he tried not to move while the instruments were stuck in his eye. The local anesthesia also froze the muscles in and around his eye, so there wasn't a danger of him blinking or twitching at the wrong moment.

As the surgery progressed and Dr. Norman asked for one instrument and then another, Nick began to recognize their names. One whirred like a miniature hedge trimmer. One sucked like a vacuum cleaner. Suddenly, he began to see more light with his left eye, and there inside his eyeball, he could actually make out the small tool sucking the darkness into the tip of a "soda straw." The light became brighter . . . and brighter.

"You're getting' it! You're sucking it out. It's clearing up." He'd spoken without realizing it.

"Yes," said Dr. Norman, his voice muffled behind his surgical mask. "We're replacing the contaminated vitreous with a clear solution now."

From the tip of a second instrument within his eyeball, Nick watched what looked like spreading heat waves as they irrigated his eye. Then there was more of the "hedge trimmer" and more suction. With each round another dark patch was cleared, and Nick's excitement rose until he thought he would weep for joy. Thank you, Jesus. Thank you! Thank you! It's working. Why did I ever doubt?

He could not see the doctors or anything in the operating room—the scope through which they watched what they were doing by looking through his dilated pupil blocked all outside view—but the world within was fearsome, illuminated by a fiber optic light that intruded into his internal universe through a third tiny incision. Nothing was in focus, but Nick could still make out the instruments, moving around, vacuuming up the consequences of his neglect. A fierce resolve rose in his spirit. Never again would he ignore his diabetes.

How long was this going to last? Terri had done all she could to make the wounded boy soldiers comfortable. After only forty-eight hours, the older one seemed to be responding, but the younger one . . . he needed a real hospital, not just this makeshift, mosquito-infested sickbay in the jungle. She would tell Ramírez, demand he take his son for intensive care if he wanted him to live.

But when she emerged from the tent, the unit was preparing for some kind of a trip—putting on backpacks, adjusting straps, shouldering weapons and belts of ammunition. They were a ragtag army: mismatched uniforms, interspersed with civilian clothes—Adidas running shoes or pull-on rubber farmer boots—it made little difference. But their weapons were another matter. Well armed, they stood around checking out one another to see that ammo pouches were full and plenty of grenades hung from their webbing.

Terri surged with excitement. Were they going to take her home? Was it over? "Rosita!" She hurried to her guard who was leaning over, filling her canteen from a hanging Lister bag. "Where are we going?"

"You? You're not goin' anywhere. You stay here and cook."

"What? But . . ." Terri couldn't miss this opportunity. Wherever they were going, it had to be closer to 'civilization' than she was now. "I don't know how to cook out here. What am I supposed to make? Why can't I go with you? Where are you going?"

Terri couldn't read Rosita's shrug. Didn't she know where they were going? Or wasn't she supposed to tell? Either way, it didn't look good. "You might need a medic along. What if someone got hurt?"

"Someone probably *will* get hurt! Just be glad it won't be you. Look," Rosita straightened up and faced Terri for the first time. "Beans and rice. Beans and rice! That's all they'll expect. Certainly you can do that."

Oh yeah. Terri turned away, deflated. She still had a hard time eating anything herself, and they wanted her to cook beans and rice? She had to think of something to tell Lieutenant Ramírez that would cause him to take her. But before she could come up with a convincing argument, the order was given, and the troops trekked off into the jungle.

Only half a dozen men remained. One was a man she had examined who had an ulcer on the top of his foot and couldn't wear his boots. A couple had just gotten over a nasty case of dysentery. But the others seemed fit. Why had they been left behind? Soon all six were playing volleyball on the court set up in the small clearing near the camp—even the guy with the sore foot.

Terri wandered down the trail to the latrine, shoulders sagging. On her way back, she sat down on a log beside the trail. Her thoughts drifted back to Finca Fe. What were they doing? Had classes resumed? Had more of the army finally arrived to protect them? She missed her cozy room and an infirmary with screened windows to keep out mosquitoes. She even missed Betty's cooking. Compared to this jungle, all else was luxury. Ever since arriving, she'd listened for a plane to fly overhead. Nick said he sometimes took a shortcut across El Despeje when he had mail or medicine to take to the Gustafsons. Would his route take him over this part of the jungle? Ha! The Amazon Basin was as big as some countries, and she with no idea where she was, let alone where the Gustafsons were stationed. It was a futile hope. Yet, she longed to glimpse Nick's white and red plane, flying freely overhead with him at the controls, possibly thinking of her . . . maybe even trying to spot where to direct an army rescue.

A squawking bird startled her, and she jumped up. Somebody would come searching for her if she didn't get back to camp soon. She headed up the trail wondering whether the army would come even if they knew where she was. But wasn't that their job, to make incursions into El Despeje, FARC's "safe zone" east of Cordillera Oriental mountain range, to rescue people? Or maybe at some higher command they would negotiate her release. On the other hand, why would Colombian officials care about her? Could the mission or the U.S. government bring enough pressure to force Colombia to do something on her behalf? The more she went through the possibilities, the more dismal each seemed.

She needn't have worried that the soldiers had noticed her absence. No one even glanced her way when she returned. The volleyball game was over and the men were playing poker.

Suddenly the thought struck her: She could have kept going and escaped! . . . Perhaps. She made her presence in the camp obvious, nursing her patients, asking the poker players where clean sheets were—all the time thinking about running for freedom. Where would she go? Could she make it without a map? The main thing was to get over the mountains to the west.

For lunch she returned to the card game and passed out tortillas and half-burnt, leftover chicken from the night before. Afterwards, a couple men took a siesta while others continued the poker game, gambling with enthusiasm.

While planning her escape, Terri wandered over to the men to remind them with her presence that she was still in camp. "Hey! When's the patrol coming back?"

"Who knows?"

"You should. Am I supposed to make food, or what?"

"Just get outta here, *¡Perra!* Leave us alone!"

Crude names and chasing her off had never sounded so sweet. They'd be glad if she disappeared, maybe for hours. . . . Enough time for a good start!

She hurried to her tent and stuffed a rain poncho, socks, a blanket, and her Bible into her tattered, brown backpack. A compass; she needed a compass! Rosita had one somewhere. Terri tossed Rosita's things without any luck. Many of the soldiers had them, but she couldn't find one even in any of the adjacent tents. Well, she couldn't waste more time. After all she was just heading over the mountains. Couldn't be that hard to figure direction. Going back to the mess tent, she wrapped up a dozen tortillas and the remaining chicken, filled her canteen, and opened the refrigerator. Cooled only during the evening hours when the generator ran, the door was supposed to be kept shut, but in the back she found three six-packs of beer. She had no idea who they belonged to, but to her they were a gift from God.

She put the beer in a battered foam cooler, grabbed a large bag of chips—in the middle of the jungle, no less—and a plastic container of cold, refried beans and carried it all out to the poker players. That should forestall any need for an early supper. The two men who had been napping were now up and looking over the shoulders of the other four. They all dug into the beer and chips without acknowledging Terri for her kindness, but that was okay with her. The poker stakes had risen sharply—someone would make out like a bandit—but her hopes were just as high. She was glad to become invisible as she returned to her tent.

A light rain began falling, and soon the drops worked their way through the leaves of the overhanging trees, driving the card game into a tent.

This was her chance!

Chapter 10

Backpack slung casually over her shoulder, Terri walked down the trail to the latrines like any other call of nature. The acrid smell gagged all stagnant air within twenty meters and sometimes, with the wrong breeze, invaded camp like a forest slug, overcoming even the smoke from cooking fires. She stopped, shooing flies from her face as she glanced around. Surely no one would think she came here for any reason other than bodily necessity, but she shivered in spite of the day's heat. *"When I am afraid, I will trust in you. . . . in God I trust; I will not be afraid."* She repeated the couplet from Psalm 56. So far, no one had followed. *"When I am afraid, I will trust in you. . . . in God I trust; I will not be afraid."* She continued beyond the latrines to where the trail narrowed to a rarely used crease in the undergrowth. She began to run, twisting and turning to weave between encroaching vines, ducking under bushes, sometimes stumbling over roots. She'd not been this far from camp since she'd come, but the path headed in the right direction . . . toward the mountains.

Before getting too winded, she stopped, breathing the words in and out: *"When I am afraid, I will trust in you. . . . in God I trust; I will not be afraid."* And listened. Birds, the buzz of ever-present mosquitoes, and . . . a whishing sound: water, fast-moving, off to her left. She continued along the trail, or what she thought was a trail, as it turned toward the water, and within a couple minutes came to a river as wide as a city street, rolling noisily over a rough bottom. She paused. Should have paid more attention when they brought her into the camp. At the time, she was still in shock from the shootings. But yes, she remembered a river. And she could wade these rapids and continue toward the mountains.

Terri crossed the sandbar to the water's edge, then glanced back. Tracks—her tracks—stitched the sand, distinct enough to be seen from fifty meters away. She froze as though one more step would trigger a landmine. What was most important, getting as far as possible away from FARC or covering her tracks? Distance or stealth? She'd probably left footprints all along the trail but certainly not as distinct as in this damp sand. What would Nick say?

Finally, she went back to the bank and grabbed a handful of driftwood brush snagged on roots along the bank and began sweeping away her tracks, backing toward the river. When she had stepped into the water, she surveyed her work. Pretty good, and it would look even better in a couple hours when the scrapes in the damp sand had dried. She turned and waded across the river, tossing her brush broom into the swirling current.

Fording the river had looked easy before she stepped into the water. But even though it was much clearer than the Magdalena, the slick, uneven bottom and the roiling waters were deceptive. She stepped in a hole, water up to mid-thigh. Her next step hit a sunken log, and she went down, rolling over as the torrent swept her twenty meters before she could regain her footing and rise like the monster from the black lagoon with water streaming from her soaked clothes and backpack. So much for dry socks and edible tortillas! "Next time, find a stick," she scolded herself. In fact, a hiking stick would be a good idea for the mountains, too. She'd get one on the bank.

The bank was steep and high, higher than Terri could reach. She moved along it until she stood below a towering mahogany with two blue-green macaws squabbling in its upper branches. The tree's roots hung exposed where the river had washed away the red clay, and Terri was able to use them—dirt falling in her face all the while—to climb up until she slung her leg over the edge and pulled herself up like a child mounting a too-tall horse. She lay there in the weeds, soaking wet and filthy until she caught her breath.

Twenty paces through thick brush that lined the river brought her to a single strand of barbed wire. What was a fence doing out here in the middle of the jungle? It was running up the center of a shallow ravine that probably drained heavy rains into the river she'd just crossed. Rather than cross the fence into thicker brush, she veered away from it and continued up a clearer but slicker incline. It was a mistake. Every few steps, she slid back, leaving skid marks in the mud, tracks that could be easily followed. She grabbed some dried brush and tried to sweep away the skid marks.

Soon she was out of the ravine, but the chance of being tracked mushroomed in her mind, and she tried to avoid breaking branches or stepping in mud where her footprints would be recorded. She tripped over a large arum lily, breaking off its beautiful flower. In a panic, Terri stooped, trying to reset the stem in the moss under the leaves to look like it was still intact. A foolish waste of time. The thing would wilt within an hour! *"When I am afraid, I will trust in you."* Forget leaving a trail. Leave hiding it to God. Just put more distance between yourself and FARC.

In minutes, she was panting from the faster pace, sucking heavy air, damp and smelling of rotting leaves and mold and fallen trees and moss-covered rocks by the rain pools dotting the bottom of every hollow. She panted, too, from the fact that the terrain had become corrugated—down and up, down and up. And then it dawned on her that she was no longer certain of traveling toward higher ground. She descended one small rise and hiked up the next, but by the time she reached its top, the thick forest hid whether it was higher or lower than the last hillock. Finally, the land smoothed out and the undergrowth of the forest opened up enough for her to occasionally see as much as a hundred meters ahead. She adjusted her direction so that she was proceeding gently but steadily toward higher ground.

The squall of capuchin monkeys overhead punctuated the twitter of birds and constant drone of insects until Terri began to slow down and surrender to the symphony of the rain forest. Perhaps she *would* escape. How could anyone find her this far from camp?

When she heard the gurgling of a stream, she made her way over to it, thinking there might be stretches of even easier travel along its banks. But when she arrived, something was wrong!

Her head spun! She reached out for a tree to keep her balance and realized she was in trouble: The water was moving the same direction she'd been traveling! Gentle as the slope had been, she'd been going downhill when she thought she was going uphill.

Terri stood still as her heart's pounding grew like an approaching stampede. How could she have been going in the wrong direction? And for how long? Maybe only minutes, but how could she know for sure? Should she turn around and follow the water upstream? It seemed totally backwards, and try as she might, she couldn't reorient herself, couldn't swing her mind around to "see" downhill when she'd been so certain she'd been traveling ever-so-slightly uphill. She peered past huge buttress-rooted trees and over shiny-leafed philodendrons. Was upstream really higher ground? She knew it had to be, but she couldn't make her gut feel it. It all seemed so backward.

She closed her eyes and forced herself to think. Upstream would certainly take her to higher ground, no matter how it appeared. Then another thought struck her: It might be toward higher ground, but would it be toward the mountains she needed to cross or merely up the opposite slope of an adjacent ridge? She looked up into the tree canopy. The rain that had driven the poker players inside a couple hours earlier had long since stopped, but the sky was still overcast. What patches of sky she could see were gray with clouds and gave no clue which way was west or east . . . but it was starting to get darker!

For the first time it struck her: She could die out here! She might never find her way over the mountains! She could fall and hurt herself! She could starve, and no one would know! Where were all those trails FARC had used bringing her to camp?

Calm down! Calm down and think! No, calm down and *pray*! Would God help her? Proverbs promised: *"In all your ways acknowledge Him, and He shall direct your paths."* Well, perhaps He would provide general direction for one's life by getting priorities straight, but expecting guidance out of the jungle, wasn't that too literalistic? Maybe she was taking this pray-the-Word thing a bit too far. But she'd made a habit of it, memorizing hundreds of promises. And to whom else could she turn out here?

Terri tried to tell herself darkness was not the issue. She'd always known she'd have to spend several nights in the wilderness before she reached safety. She'd imagined hiking until she came to a nice comfortable spot, maybe part way up the mountains, hunkered down between some boulders where she could safely build a small fire for her camp. (Ha! She hadn't even remembered to bring any matches!) But not this! Somehow being lost made the late afternoon gloom so much more threatening. No idea where she was going . . . no idea from which direction she had come.

"Lord, as Abraham's servant prayed as he stood by the well, '*Please guide me in a special way,*' 'cause nothing here looks right." Slowly Terri turned from the stream. She would not continue downhill, and she would not go directly upstream, either, even though she admitted to herself that would take her to higher ground. Instead, she would do her best to retrace her steps, which had for the last few minutes paralleled the stream, hoping she could ultimately discover where her sense of direction had gone wrong. Maybe then she could get reoriented.

But near the equator, night came quickly as if God pocketed the sun.

Though the ride home had brought Nick stabs of pain with every chuckhole in the Chicago streets, it was tolerable once he was sitting on his mother's couch in her overly decorated living room.

"Do you need something, Dear? How about some soup? You always liked my chicken soup. I could make some."

"Sure, Mom, but I don't want anything right now. Make it for later." That should keep her busy for a while. "And why don't you close the kitchen door. I want to turn the TV on."

"Oh, I don't think you ought to be using your eyes, Nicky. Not after what you've been through. You need to give them a rest."

"Mom, the bad one's patched, and the doctor said I could see whatever I could see. It doesn't hurt 'em, especially if I'm not looking from side to side a lot. Watching TV's okay. He specifically mentioned it." She was standing right beside him—on his bad-eye side—but he spoke like she was in the kitchen with the door already shut. "And could you bring me some Ibuprofen."

"Oh, you're hurting? You need some of that Tylenol 3 with Codeine we picked up from the Walgreens?"

"No, no. It's not that bad. I just want to keep ahead of any pain."

Nick laid his head back and closed his right eye. He couldn't tell whether his left eye was closed or open. A padded aluminum shield protected his eye so that nothing could bump it. That in turn was covered by a thick bandage that went from his hairline halfway down his cheek.

The phone rang. "Hello.... Yes, he's here, but I don't know. He just got back from the doctor, the hospital, actually. And he's not feeling—"

Nick's heart leaped! "Mom, bring me the phone! I can take it."

It was Thomas Hoover at First People's Mission in neighboring Wheaton. The Crisis Team had just received a call, patched through from the army in Colombia. On the line had been a man claiming to be Lieutenant Ramírez, a FARC commander holding Terri Kaplan.

Nick staggered to his feet and began pacing around his mother's small living room, one hand holding the phone to his ear, the other grabbing the chair backs, the doorframe, the TV. He didn't know whether it was the excitement of the news or his earlier operation that left him so unsteady. The guerilla commander had wanted to open negotiations for Terri's ransom. But he didn't have any proof of life. He described her accurately enough, but he refused to put her on the radio, and of course he didn't say anything about Roger Montgomery or Miss Van Loon.

For a few minutes Nick forgot about his eye. "Did you get a fix on their coordinates?"

"Actually, the army did. But that's the strange part. Ramírez didn't seem in any hurry to end the transmission. It was like he wanted them to locate him, or at least didn't care, but the army says these FARC guys are usually very careful about that. So we're not completely sure he's authentic. They're going over the recording now to see if he mentioned anything that could not be known from media reports."

"What's next?"

"We actually broke off the call, insisting we don't want to talk without proof that Terri's okay."

"*Broke off—!*" Nick swallowed like he was downing a cotton ball. "But why? Why not keep talking? Maybe Ramírez would have relented and put her on? I mean, it was our only contact! How could you hang up?"

"Now take it easy, Nick. This is the way it's done. We don't even know if this guy was legit. But in any case, he needs to know that we're in charge—"

"*In charge?* It doesn't seem to me like we're in charge of anything. I mean—"

"I understand how you feel, Nick. But just trust us on this one. Listen, I gotta go. I'll get back to you as soon as we hear something else."

It took all Nick's will power not to throw the phone against the wall.

Terri's river-soaked clothes had dried—as much as they could in a damp forest and while she continued to sweat in panic. She should stop trying to retrace her steps! It was just too dark. She couldn't be sure she'd even passed this way before. Soon she'd be doubly lost, if she wasn't already. She needed a place to spend the night. A hollow tree or perhaps a fallen log under which she could crawl in case it rained . . . anything. But suddenly she found herself on a trail, not one she recognized—she had paid no attention as FARC brought her through the jungle—but she hadn't been on any kind of a trail since crossing the river, and this one was at least going somewhere.

Suddenly, she broke into a clearing, with nothing but grass under her feet, not even the clumps of bushes you'd expect to find in the average meadow. Ahead, the closest silhouetted trees stood like a wall on the other side of the clearing. And when she looked from side to side, she realized the jungle she'd just emerged from, also created a wall, parallel to the far wall. It was as if someone had cleared a swath out of the jungle to build a road, and a fairly wide one at that. But it was probably a farmer's field.

As her eyes adjusted to the dim light, she realized that there was something across the meadow. Terri's heart hammered. It looked like . . . it couldn't be, but it was . . . some kind of a building. A little shack, maybe. God's answer to her need for shelter. Didn't the Bible say, "*He will cover you with his feathers, and under his wings you will find refuge*"? Well, there it was: Refuge! She stepped forward. Then stopped. What if someone were inside? There was no light, no fire, no noise. But they might have gone to sleep, might have heard her coming and were waiting in ambush.

She listened, trying to quiet her own breathing. No other sounds but the thousands of frogs and crickets and other insects. She took a step closer, then another, cautiously creeping across the field. She was almost to the little building, when she tripped over a root and thudded her foot as she lunged to regain her balance. Quiet! Listen! Still no response! Maybe it was empty.

In a few more steps, she reached the corner of the shack and stood for several minutes listening for movement or breathing or anything. Nothing. She worked her way around until she found a doorway, took a deep breath, and stepped through.

The place seemed empty, but she wasn't going to explore its recesses. It had a smell, a biting smell, like ammonia and something rotting. Terri cowered just inside the door. She wouldn't explore the whole place. She had a roof over her head, and that was enough. She pulled her blanket and poncho out of her backpack. The wet blanket was useless, but her poncho, while damp on the surface, might still protect her from some of the creepy-crawlies in the hut. She wrapped it around her like a cocoon and curled up on the dirt floor against the wall.

Ultimately, exhaustion overcame the fears that skittered through her mind like mice in the attic, and she fell asleep.

How long she slept or what woke her, she didn't know, but she was immediately aware of a presence. And then she heard it! The expulsion of air, a lot of air, from large lungs, followed by a deep guttural rumble. And then a movement at the door, just a few steps from where she huddled. Terri held still, not breathing, unable to see a thing. What was it? Jaguar? Puma? They were rare, but not unheard of in this jungle. Or perhaps an anaconda reclaiming its den. Did they sleep in dens? Did they have big lungs?

More breathing, and then the sound of something hard scraped against the doorway. Hard? The image of caiman's plated hide came to Terri. It might make such a grating sound, but surely a jungle alligator wouldn't venture this far from water. On the other hand, she had no idea how far she was from water. The last few steps before she arrived at the hut had been downhill, as though slightly down a bank. A swamp could be five meters further into the jungle on this side of the clearing. Maybe *that* was the source of the smell.

O Lord, if this is supposed to be a refuge under your wings, then help me now. You said I don't need to "fear the terror of night," but I'm scared!

There was a snort, and the creature backed away. Terri heard heavy feet receding—*thud, thud, thud.*

Was it gone? She held her breath, listening.

She could still hear an occasional heavy breath and—she couldn't really identify what—but a rhythmic grating, like someone dragging their knuckles over a washboard. It continued for a few minutes, then stopped. Was it a jaguar scratching the ground to bury its scat? Did big cats even do that? Or . . . or a caiman digging a hole for her eggs?

Terri was so tired she had almost fallen asleep again when the grinding sound returned: *Gr-r-rum, gr-r-rum, gr-r-rum.* How long the cycles continued, she had no idea, but every time they started up again, she startled awake. And then she awoke to a dim grayness filling the doorway and needling its way through cracks in the wall.

Was the creature still waiting for her? Could she sneak past it before dawn fully broke?

Chapter 11

Though Nick's night was relatively pain free, his sleep was as jerky as a car running out of gas. What little sleep he did get was tormented by half-dreams that the shield had come off his eye, and he'd rolled onto it causing a new hemorrhage. At one point, he thought he felt wetness—tears? blood?—running down his cheek. Or had his stitches popped allowing vitreous to leak out of the holes in his eye? He sat up and gingerly checked with his hand, but the shield was in place and everything was dry.

When he was not tossing from visions of no vision, Terri's plight haunted him. He wanted to listen to the tape of the army's contact with the rebel lieutenant—what was his name? Ramírez? He knew Terri better than the Colombian army, probably better than the Crisis Team. He could recognize details that might prove or disprove authenticity—like if she'd quoted a Bible verse or said something about one of the kids at Finca Fe. He needed to be involved in this. It might be the only key to her release, but here he was in the States with a patch on his eye! How could he help?

What was it Thomas Hoover had said about Ramírez wanting to open ransom negotiations? First Peoples didn't pay ransoms! That was their policy. So, what was going on?

His mind swirled without answers until he finally drifted back to sleep . . . dreaming about his days in Iraq, advancing with a team of his buddies from house to house in Tikrit until they finally found Terri, cowering on the floor in the corner of a bombed-out orphanage, tear-stained and sobbing. "I'm here, Terri! I'm here! Everything's okay!" But when he walked up to her, she morphed into the little orphan child he'd actually rescued that day in the Gulf War. . . .

He jerked awake in a cold sweat.

Terri! She was in trouble, more trouble than having been kidnapped. Somehow, he knew it in his spirit. She needed him right now, but what could he do? How could he help from such distance? "O God, go to her . . ."

That was it! Even in Carol Stream, Illinois, in bed with a patch on his eye, he could pray. He might not be able to pray like Terri, but he could still talk to God. He swung his legs out of bed and poured out his heart to his heavenly Father as the eastern sky began to define the black branches of the old elm tree outside the window.

It was getting even lighter when his mother called through the door. "Nicky? You okay? Sounds like you're crying, Nicky. Is your eye hurting? You need some pain medicine?"

He steadied his voice. "No, Mom. I'm okay. Just go back to bed. I'll see you later."

Terri stood deep in the doorway of the shack and strained her eyes toward the sounds she'd been hearing during the night until something focused into a shape. She blinked. It was still there, a light brown patch in contrast to the black-greens and grays of the surrounding foliage. Was that movement? *Gr-r-rum, gr-r-rum, gr-r-rum.* The grinding resumed, though she could barely hear it over the chirping birds, screams of distant monkeys, and other sounds of an awakening jungle. What was making that sound? Large animal, tan fur . . . Had to be a puma! Jaguars were spotted, weren't they? Or black? But puma or jaguar, what difference did it make?

A mosquito was biting her forehead, growing fat on her life's blood, perhaps infecting her with malaria, but she dared not slap it. Cats' eyes pierced darkness! Their ears caught every sound. She would never be able to sneak out of the shack.

The creature moved again . . . snorted . . . moaned long and low as it lumbered to its feet. It was getting up! Terri retreated deeper into the shadows of the shack. . . . But what was that? . . . A cow? *A cow*! Just a cow? . . . A cow that had snorted its disgust to find its foul-smelling "barn" occupied by a stranger! A cow with horns that had scraped the doorframe. Just a cow pastured in that farmer's field? Must have been chewing its cud most of the night, creating the grinding sound Terri had heard. And she'd imagined a lion pawing the sand or a caiman burying its eggs!

Terri expelled air like a breaching whale as she stared after the boney beast ambling up the slight incline and disappearing into the heavy mists that enshrouded the meadow. Stepping out of the shack, she leaned against its weathered boards.

The mosquito! She slapped her forehead and brought her hand away with such a large dark smear on it that she could see the red even in the dim light. She wanted at least another full night's rest before traveling farther. But that was impossible. She had to get going, find her way over the mountains.

With one last look toward the ghost cow, she went back into the shack, stuffed her poncho into her backpack, grabbed a handful of tortilla "mush," licking it off of her dirty fingers, and drank from her canteen. Then she left, plunging down the bank and into the jungle.

The shack had not been the neat camp with a fire tucked between mountain rocks that Terri had imagined, but it was shelter, and not too bad, either, if she'd only known it was just a cow she had usurped. "Thank you, Jesus. You did give me refuge and the 'terror by night' was only in my mind."

She had traveled only a short distance when she noticed rays of sun slicing through the jungle leaves overhead. Finally, the mist was boiling away, and for the first time in days, the air seemed free of the jungle's oppressive humidity. But while looking up and rejoicing at the sunbeams, she walked right into some thorns that painfully snagged her thighs.

But they weren't spines on a brier bush runner. They were spikes on a single strand of rusty barbed wire! A strange sense of déjà vu bubbled up within her. A second barbed wire fence running through the jungle . . . with only one strand? It kind of made sense if that cow was not a stray but belonged to a farmer trying to keep it in the pasture she'd crossed last night. But what about the earlier fence? Something wasn't right. And then she saw it—a wilted arum lily, the trumpet of it's once white blossom hanging down like a dirty skirt with a brown fringe. It wouldn't have fooled anyone. But worse, it was obviously the same broken flower she'd tried to camouflage less than twenty-four hours before.

Her heart sank. In her arduous day's excursion, had she accomplished nothing but to make a huge loop through the jungle? Where were the mountains she thought she'd been heading toward all day? With all her running and stumbling and fighting through tangled foliage, she wasn't more than a quarter of a mile closer than if she'd stayed in camp.

Terri dropped down to the ground and cried, her sobs rolling over her like breakers on a stormy beach. "I give up! I can't do it! *My God, my God, why have you forsaken me?* I can't do this by myself!"

At nine o'clock—as early as he thought the offices would be open—Nick phoned First Peoples Mission. Did they have a copy of the tape from the previous day's call? "No, I'm sorry," said Thomas Hoover's secretary. "But I'm glad you called. Mr. Hoover just got a call from Colombia—he's still on the line—and he seems very excited. I'll have him call you as soon as he gets off the phone."

"No, no, that's okay. I'll be right over."

Less than five minutes later, his mother was driving him to the mission offices under protest. "But Nicky, you can't miss your doctor's appointment this morning. He needs to check your eye."

"Mom, I'll see the doctor as soon as I can, but this is an emergency. Just trust me, and look out for those chuckholes. They still make my eye hurt . . . but only a little. I—I'm doing fine. Just get me to Wheaton."

Getting past the front desk took a little explaining, but finally Nick was directed to Mr. Hoover's office, and his secretary ushered him right in to where the chairman of the Crisis Team was speaking on the phone. Another man, whom Nick had never met, sat in a chair toward the right side of Hoover's desk. Hoover gave

Nick an enthusiastic thumb's up and continued: "So he's in Neiva now or he's on his way there? . . . And they'll take him right to the hospital?" Hoover put his hand over the receiver and whispered to Nick. "Roger Montgomery escaped. Gonna be okay."

He turned back to the phone. "Possible concussion? But he's coherent and seems stable at this point? . . . Good! Good! . . . Yes. Let us know as soon as you have any more information. . . . Okay. Good-bye to you, too."

"Well," said Hoover, leaning back in his chair with a smile as big as Thanksgiving dinner, "I suppose you were able to follow some of that. Oh, by the way, have you two met? Nick, this is Josh Kaplan, Terri's brother. Just got in from New Jersey. Josh, Nick Archer, the pilot at the school where Terri taught."

Nick shook hands with the slightly balding man who rose to greet him with his collar and tie loosened and a gray suit sufficiently crumpled to confirm a redeye flight.

As they sat down, Hoover continued. "It seems some Colombian farmers found Roger wandering down a road—"

"So, Roger's actually okay?"

"Apparently. Well, maybe not that great, but he's alive. He was up in the hills, and the farmers brought him into their village. He insisted on using a telephone even before they could wash him up and give him something to eat. They say he looked like he'd been dragged behind a bull at a rodeo. Anyway, there was only one phone in the village—at a little store—and he used it to call for help. He's on the way to the hospital, now."

Nick threw out his hands. "So, how'd he escape? From where?"

"Not sure. We haven't talked to him directly, but apparently he was shot at the same time Miss Van Loon was killed. The bullet only grazed Roger's head, but maybe they left him for dead. I'm not sure why the army didn't find him. Maybe he came to and walked away before they got there. I just don't know. At least he's alive."

"When are you going to talk to him? Did he say anything about Terri?" Nick realized the pitch of his voice had gone up, and he tried to calm down. "I just want to know if she's okay." He glanced at Kaplan who sat there expressionless.

"I know how you feel, Nick, but we don't know anything else. No one's had a chance to debrief him yet. I'm sure the army wants to ask all those questions, too." Hoover stood, indicating there was nothing more to tell.

Reluctantly, Nick started to rise, and then noticed Kaplan remained seated. Terri's brother cleared his throat. "So . . . what comes next? I presume you have some kind of a fund or insurance to cover such contingencies since you operate in these areas?"

"Not exactly." Hoover melted back into his chair and leaned forward on his elbow.

"Surely you don't expect the family to pay the ransom for getting her out of a situation that you put her in, do you?"

"We don't pay ransom, Mr. Kaplan. We believe that would only encourage the rebels to kidnap other missionaries all around the world."

"I don't care about other missionaries!" Kaplan snapped. "This is my sister, Mr. Hoover. We're secular Jews, so it wasn't a big deal to us when Terri found a faith that seemed to satisfy something for her. Religion's a comfort to a lot of people, but we do expect all modern religions to operate responsibly. If you want to send her off to the ends of the earth to help people, that's great. But what am I supposed to tell her mother? You don't seem to have any kind of a plan. Are you expecting us to raise the ransom ourselves? I'm just a university professor. We have other family and friends, but—"

"I'm sorry, Mr. Kaplan. But at this point, I can only promise you that we will keep you up to date on everything, and when the Crisis Team has enough information to formulate a plan for her release, you'll be among the first to know. We appreciate your concern."

Hoover turned to Nick to change the subject. "By the way, how's that eye coming?"

A few minutes later, as they were walking out, Nick said to Josh Kaplan, "How long are you going to be in town?"

"I have classes Monday morning. I told our mother I didn't think there was anything I could do in person that couldn't be done over the phone, but she insisted I come." The man looked back over his shoulder toward Hoover's office. "Does this kind of thing happen often?"

"More often than they'd like, I'm sure. Though in Colombia, oil company executives are far more vulnerable. They've got the money. Uh, where do you teach?"

"I'm dean of the economics department at Monmouth. Here's my card. Let's stay in touch." He blew out a troubled breath. "This could be a long ordeal, but I'm ready to do anything that might help."

Terri rose from the ground, her face stained from the long cry. No, she couldn't flee on her own. She'd been a fool to try. She looked up through the jungle canopy at white clouds drifting overhead. Had they come over the mountains or were they heading west toward them? Even if she had a compass, successfully escaping over them would take more than running toward them. On this side of the range they were so much higher and steeper than from the western side. Without directions, it might take several tries up rugged canyons just to find a pass.

Despair edged Terri's thoughts. Maybe she would never break free from the FARC. She headed down the ravine, and soon heard the river that separated her from the camp. Would she ever be able to sneak back into camp without being shot? Who cared anymore? But surely if Ramírez was so eager to have medical care for his son, he would allow her back. It was her only chance because she now knew she couldn't survive alone in this jungle.

Thirty minutes later, Terri smelled the camp latrines, her departure point for her failed escape. Could she sneak back into camp? What would she say if she were caught? What about Jesús? Would he be better or worse? She took a deep breath. There was nothing to do but try and see what happened. Just past the latrines, she tossed her backpack into the bushes and headed up the trail.

The camp looked the same as when she'd left the previous afternoon, except for the occasional beams of sunshine finding their way through the canopy instead of rain. The men had again emerged from the steamy confines of their tents to resume their marathon card game on a footlocker surrounded by mismatched chairs.

"Hey, *perra,* where's the coffee? We didn't get any coffee this morning. What's the matter with you? Make us a fresh pot!"

"Sí señores. Un momento, café caliente!" And she ran for the mess tent, panting with relief.

But when she came out ten minutes later with a pot of coffee in one hand and a stack of plastic cups in the other, the game had folded, and the men had scattered to various places around the camp. One was sweeping out the command tent. Another was pouring a bucket of water into the Lister bag. And then she realized why: In the distance, she heard returning soldiers. For a moment, panic seized her. Then Terri got a hold of herself and took the coffee and cups to the command tent, set them on the table—a "welcome home" for Commander Ramírez—and went to the infirmary tent where she began attending to Jesús and Carlos.

Carlos was definitely improving, but while Jesús wasn't in crisis, Terri's concern for him grew. The boy's body simply wasn't getting on top of the infection. She took his temperature and changed his bedding, occasionally raising the tent flap to watch the mud-splattered, exhausted soldiers straggle into camp and throw their dirty equipment into their tents, cursing at having had to march so far. Several stopped by the infirmary with scrapes and cuts they wanted Terri to clean and bandage. One man had been bitten by a snake. His leg was swollen twice its size, and he was unable to walk on it.

Outside the infirmary tent, Sergeant Rodriquez yelled to be heard throughout the whole camp. "*¡Escuchame gente!* . . . I said, listen up! This is no time to get caught with our pants down. Our position could be compromised, people. We need to be ready to move! There'll be a weapons and equipment inspection in one hour. I want everything clean and ready for use. One hour! *¿Comprendieron?* You can kick back later."

Groans and cursing skittered through the camp like heat lightening.

What was that all about? Compromised how? Move where? And what about the wounded boys? Not knowing what was at stake, Terri administered the anti-venom serum to the man with the snakebite, and then straightened up the infirmary.

An hour later, while Sergeant Rodriquez was conducting an inspection, Lieutenant Ramírez—washed, shaved, and in a clean shirt—entered the infirmary. Was she going to be inspected, also? But he went straight to his son's bed. "How's Jesús doing? Making any progress?"

Terri shrugged. "Still has a fever, and I don't think he's gaining any strength."

The commander sat down on the boy's bed. Terri busied herself on the other side of the small tent, checking on the man with the snakebite. After the lieutenant had talked to Jesús for several minutes in tones too soft for Terri to understand, he came over to her. With a jerk of his head toward Jesús, he said, "Give me a list of anything the boy needs—anything."

Terri nodded. "What he needs is rest. We're not going to have to move, are we?"

Ramírez shrugged. "I hope not, but he also needs good care." He looked Terri up and down with an expression she couldn't read, then grabbed her sleeve behind the elbow and pulled her away from the man with the snakebite. "Listen, I need to see you. Finish attending to the snakebite, then come to my tent."

Lord, have mercy, Terri breathed as the lieutenant left the infirmary. Jesús must have told him she'd been neglecting him during the last twenty-four hours. What if he'd figured out that she'd been out of camp, trying to flee? But he hadn't seemed angry. What did he want? Then a cold chill gripped her. Maybe he had other plans. The commander had never come on to her. In fact, she hadn't seen him take liberties with any of the women in camp, but he'd acted so . . . so clandestine, as though he didn't want anyone to overhear him. "O God," she moaned, clapping her hand to her mouth. *"Whom have I in heaven but you? . . . My flesh and my heart may fail . . . ."*

Chapter 12

Dr. Norman carefully peeled away the tape holding the padded shield over Nick's left eye. He extended his chin, tipped his head back so he could look through his bifocals, and leaned close as he moved his head from side to side examining Nick. "Looks like someone tagged you a good one." He chuckled at his own joke. "Can you see anything out of that eye?"

Nick was already experimenting by closing his right eye and looking around at the various gentle light sources in the examining room. "Yes. It's awful blurry, but . . ." Excitement grew as he turned his head different directions. "I don't see any of those dark patches like before."

"That's good. Here, hold this shield over your other eye. Now, can you see my hand?"

Nick saw an approximately flesh-colored blob wave somewhere before him. "Yeah."

"Good. How many fingers am I holding up?"

"Uh-h . . ." Nick strained to bring the blob into focus. "Um . . . two?"

"Three. But that's okay."

Huh. If the doctor had held his hand against a dark background instead of in front of what was probably his face, he might have been able to count all three.

"Here, rest your chin on this support and your forehead against the upper pad, and let me have a look inside with the slit-lamp." The exam continued with various instruments, looking inside, testing the pressure. . . .

Finally, Dr. Norman leaned back against a counter. "Everything looks good for one day out."

Relief flowed over Nick and washed fear away. For the first time he realized he'd been caught in a quagmire of raw fear. He'd never thought of himself as a fearful person. He'd faced death in the army in Iraq and in some tight spots while flying. But the possibility of losing his sight had swallowed him like quicksand, sucking him ever deeper the more he fought against it, without fully realizing it until now as its grip dissolved.

"I'll give you several kinds of drops to put in your eye," said Dr. Norman, "and I want you to continue wearing that shield at night—and no showers yet. You need to keep it dry. Check with the front desk and set up an appointment to see me again in three days. Okay?"

He had turned and was about to leave the room when Nick said, "Excuse me a minute, doctor. There's a serious kidnapping crisis going on in Colombia, and I need to get back down there. When, uh, when do you think I can go?"

The doctor frowned. "Hmm. I'm going to want to keep a close watch on your eye for a few weeks. And, of course, we've got that laser work to do in you right eye."

"Weeks! Uh . . . that's a problem. Someone's life may depend on me getting back down there." Nick's mind was swirling. He was grateful for Dr. Norman's care, but at this point he wished he'd never come to the States. He felt trapped, caught between two competing emergencies. He had just faced the fact that his vision felt more important to him than life itself, but on the other hand, there was Terri. . . . "I appreciate your concern, doctor, but what would my options be if I said I absolutely had to return to Colombia?"

"I don't like being . . ." The doctor looked away and sighed heavily. "Look,"—he unfolded his arms and gestured with both hands as though passing a basketball to Nick—"I can't tell you what to do, and I know this is a new day when patients are supposed to have a greater voice in their medical care. But that usually involves getting a second opinion or explaining options to patients in ways they can make informed decisions. It doesn't usually involve gross negligence, which is what I consider your notion of heading out of the country at this time."

The man stopped and looked down at the floor, chewing on his lower lip. "But . . . there's one man I know in Colombia. He's good. At least he was when we were in school together. I think we still exchange Christmas cards. You were in Neiva, right?"

Nick nodded, his hopes rising.

"Yes, well, I think that's where he is, too. I could call home and get the address from my wife if you want, but I want you to understand: I do not recommend this! My instructions to you—and I'm going to have my secretary put them in writing—is to use the drops and do the other things I mentioned and come back here to see me for an appointment on—what's today? Thursday?—then on Monday. You're to come in *here* and see me again on Monday. Is that understood?"

Nick smiled. He understood that the Dr. Norman was covering his butt while providing an alternative he figured Nick might take.

Ten minutes later, Nick left the office with his mother who'd been dozing in the waiting room. In his shirt pocket he carried two pieces of paper: an appointment for Monday with Dr. Norman and an address for Dr. Gerardo Gomez, an ophthalmologist in Neiva, Colombia. But Dr. Norman's strong words had sobered him. Should he stay? Eyes weren't something to mess with . . . and what could he do for Terri, anyway?

By the time Terri got to Lieutenant Ramírez's command tent, she was shaking as though she had a jungle fever. What was this all about? "*Teniente* Ramírez?" she ventured from the outside of the closed flap.

"*¡Entra!*"

With relief, Terri saw someone else was in the tent. Another man was seated at the communications table with earphones on, adjusting the radio. The lieutenant, who stood leaning over him, glanced back at Terri. "I'm going to put you on to verify that you are alive and well. But you are not to describe anything about where you are or any other details about this camp or the size of our force. Understood? We have a total of one minute and twenty-five seconds on the air. No more. You can have forty. Okay?"

"But—"

"Stand right here and keep silent until I hand you the mic . . . You ready yet?" he asked the radioman.

The man held up one finger for silence as he studied his digital watch. *"Sí, señor.* Starting . . . right . . . *now*!" In one swift motion he stripped off the earphones, handed them to the lieutenant, and added, "You're patched all the way through to *los evangélicos en los Estados Unidos."*

Ramírez sat in the chair vacated by his radio man and cleared his throat. *"Hola, soy Teniente Fabián Ramírez de la Fuerzas Armadas Revolucionarias de Colombia.* We want you to know that we have with us Terri Kaplan, a nurse who has been serving us in one of our field hospitals. She is in good health and wants to say hello—"

"Trenta secundos, señor," said the radioman as the lieutenant handed the earphones and mic to Terri.

She fumbled to get them on as quickly as possible. Not knowing what else to say, she ventured, "Hello? This is Terri Kaplan. Who's this? . . . Oh, yes, Mister Hoover. It's good to hear your voice, too. . . . Yes. I'm okay. Been helping in their infirmary. . . . No, nothing too bad. . . . What? Roger? . . . But I saw him get . . .! No. I don't think they know." She glanced at Ramírez. "Yes. All right. That sounds good. When—?"

The radioman hacked his finger through the air at Terri like a hatchet. *"No mas tiempo!"*

Ramírez grabbed the mic while ignoring the earphones still on Terri's head. "That's enough," he barked into it. "You've got your proof. I will call again in two days, 6 P.M." He made a slicing motion across his neck, and the radioman flipped a switch. "Did we get off in time?"

"Sí, señor. Un minuto y viente secundos." They exchanged thumbs up.

Ramírez turned to Terri, his face unreadable. "Now, *Señorita Doctora,* with a little encouragement from outside, are you ready to do your best for my . . . for comrade Jesús?"

"Yes sir." She turned, her dark eyes staring at nothing as she made her way out of the command tent and back toward the infirmary. Did he think she wasn't doing her best by his son? She was a nurse, after all, committed to providing medical care for anyone in need, regardless of affiliation. On the other hand, she had abandoned Jesús when she'd tried to flee. Could God have brought her back to the camp for the sake of the boy?

It was all so confusing, she couldn't think about it. "*Whatsoever things are of good report . . . think on these,*" she reminded herself. "Yes, thank you, Jesus. Roger is alive!" She shook her head. "What a great report. What a miracle! What a good God you are! Thank you Jesus!"

Nick spent all evening wrestling with Dr. Norman's counsel that he remain in the States to follow through on his eye treatment fighting with his sense of urgency to return to Colombia in case there was some way he could help Terri.

Before the surgery, he'd been able to make out various objects not hidden by the dark islands of blood in his left eye, but since Dr. Norman had taken off the shield, everything through that eye were indecipherable blobs. And yet, there were no dark patches. That's good news; that's progress, he kept telling himself. Yet he couldn't keep from testing his vision in that eye by looking toward first one light source and then another—as though it might improve any minute.

He tried watching TV with his right eye to get his mind off things—Dr. Norman had said it would do no harm. In fact, watching something that didn't require much eye movement was probably good—but vision with his right eye also remained somewhat blurry and afternoon TV programming was so insufferable, he gave up.

Late that afternoon he put in a call to Thomas Hoover at First Peoples Mission to see if there had been any more developments, but he didn't get a call back until 11 A.M. the next day, Friday.

"What? You got another call from the FARC commander yesterday? He even put Terri on the phone? Why didn't you tell me immediately?"

"I'm sorry Nick, but things have been so hectic, I just didn't get to it. But there's more good news." Nick could tell Hoover was trying to snow him with good news to compensate for not keep him up to date. "The guy promised to call back in two days at 6 in the evening. Uh, that'd be tomorrow. You're welcome to come over to the office and sit in. I think he wants to deal because he said it would be a very short call."

"Are you going to?"

"What? Deal? Nah. You know we don't pay ransom."

"Then what's the *point*?" Nick hit the table with his fist in frustration, but he knew what the point was even before Hoover answered.

"Every contact provides clues, information about where Terri is, what condition she's in, who's holding her, and what they are like. We're building a psychological profile that may provide the very key we need to get her back."

"Yeah. Hope so." But Nick thought he already had a fix on the lieutenant. Skilled military man: He knew the kind. "What about Terri's location? Did you confirm the coordinates?"

Silence on the other end of the line. Then Hoover sighed. "That's a bit of a puzzle. The army says it wasn't the same location, but at the same time they didn't get a new fix. Says he wasn't on long enough. I don't get it. How can they be so sure about one without knowing the other? On the other hand, it was short, rushed. They yanked her right off there."

"Hmm." Nick didn't know what to think, either. These people were the *Crisis Team*, the ones supposed to be finding Terri. But they seemed to be operating with the urgency and clear planning of a church potluck committee. "Well, keep me informed if anything else happens. I'd like to hear *right away* . . . if you don't mind."

Nick hung up the phone in the kitchen. Should he have added that last little jab? He felt as wound up inside as his mother's long phone cord. He was frustrated at being on the periphery of the case. He was frustrated because the Crisis Team was just flying by the seat of their pants. They had no plan. They were just reacting to whatever FARC did. And he was frustrated at being so far away from Terri.

There was only one solution. He would go back to Colombia in spite of Dr. Norman's recommendations. This was the second day since his surgery, and nothing had gone wrong yet. Besides he could see that doctor in Neiva. Normally, his own mission agency would pay for his return flight to Colombia, but Nick feared MAST might not approve if he notified them of his intentions ahead of time, so he decided to pay for the trip with his own money. He'd call MAST once he got there.

He sat down in the living room with the phonebook to look up the airline's number. It'd be so much easier if his mother had a computer.

"Uh, Mom, you got a magnifying glass I can borrow? This print is too small for me to see, even with my good eye."

"Sure Nicky. It's on the end table beside my rocker, can't miss it, about three inches in diameter and real glass, too. Doesn't scratch. I use it for looking up those cross references in my Bible. They print 'em so small anymore, I don't know how anyone can read them." Her voice was getting closer as she came from her bedroom.

"Mom, I can find it."

"Oh." She stopped in the living room doorway. "Well, sure. You can keep it if you want."

"Thanks, but I'm just trying to read a phonebook."

Chapter 13

Nick had wanted to leave Saturday, but the earliest flight he could book was for Sunday. His mother drove him to O'Hare airport, fretting all the way about his leaving before his eye had healed, though he hadn't told her about Dr. Norman's grave counsel.

She stood by the curb as he took his luggage out of the trunk. "You have that patch thing for your eye? Now don't forget to wear it at night like the doctor said. And how about my magnifying glass? You got it in your pocket?"

"Yeah, yeah. I got it." He could tell he'd been home too long. She was only trying to help, but . . . He glanced at her as he put his luggage down. She was wringing her hands like a lost refugee. "Aw, Mom, I'm sorry. It's just . . ." He gave her a kiss on the cheek.

"Nicky, when do you think you'll be coming home again?"

"I don't know, Mom. Probably when all this kidnapping stuff gets cleared up. I'll call you."

She had definitely grown thinner and more frail in the last few years. He wished his dad were still alive. It must be hard living alone when you're old. Heavens, it was hard enough being single when he was young and healthy. As he walked into the terminal and found the line for his airline, he thought about Terri. Getting to know her had been the beginning of hope to end his loneliness. Funny, he'd never really owned being lonely before, as though ignoring the condition lessened its bite. Besides, how could you be lonely on a mission station surrounded by a team of dedicated believers who cared about you and prayed for you if you asked, people you saw and worked with every day? And yet he *had* been lonely, existing for the most part in his private little world as though he were always flying at eight thousand feet, able to see everything, but out of touch.

Terri, however, had "touched" him. And it wasn't just her cute face and trim figure. Oh, yeah, he had to admit they were the first things to get his attention. But he remembered the day in staff meeting when she had first prayed for him. Everyone had gone around the circle naming details for which they could use prayer. He had joined in, saying something about waiting for a new seal for his variable-pitch prop or he wouldn't be able to fly. It was a small worry. If the part didn't arrive that day, it would come the next or the next. But Terri's prayer took him back a little when she prayed Scripture over him. He still remembered it because later he looked up the verses she'd used: *"Father, your Word says,* 'the greatest among us will be the servant of all. For whoever exalts himself will be humbled, and whoever humbles himself will be exalted.'" Then she went on to say something like: *"Our brother, Nick, has humbled himself to serve us and many others, but he needs the tools with which to serve. Exalt him by providing what he needs."*

Her earnest prayer had made him feel special, but a *servant?* MAST was a support mission. It was right there in the name: Missionary Aviation Support Team. But Nick had never personalized it to see himself as a servant. He had put more emphasis on the word, "team," as in: We're all in this together, equal partners, each doing a task! But Terri's prayer made him think about how Jesus had considered himself a servant, and the more he tried on the "towel of servanthood" for himself, the more it gave him joy. That woman was more than just the cute nurse who worked in the infirmary. Definitely an encourager!

Now he was definitely going back to serve her, to secure her freedom in whatever way he could. "O Lord, can I now ask You to exalt me to a place of effectiveness? To bring her out safely and soon?"

The check-in lines and security lines were long and slow, but he made his flight, and after a stop in Miami and changing planes in Bogotá for the hop to Neiva, he arrived late Saturday afternoon with no idea where he was going to stay. Well, there was always Armando Trujillo, his mechanic friend at Benito Airport who would undoubtedly let him stay a night or two in the office off his shop—after all, Nick was still paying for tie-down space for his Cessna out on the ramp.

Carrying his bags, he walked down the airport toward the parking for private planes. He could see his Cessna, still sitting there, just beyond a line of three crop dusters, ostensibly contracted for private agricultural use but rumored to fly herbicide missions for the government over the mountains where peasants grew cocaine for the FARC. Unfortunately, that herbicide often destroyed any legitimate crops they might be trying to cultivate, too.

Beyond his Cessna sat SurPetro's private Gulfstream 200, emblazoned with an elongated image of the oil company's blue logo. Nick's little plane looked like a toy beside the sleek monster. But something was wrong. The door of the cargo pod under the belly of Nick's plane looked open. He could see it from a distance, even with his bad eyes. He hastened his pace to investigate. Sure enough, someone had opened it. He dug his mom's magnifying glass out of his pocket to examine it more closely and make sure it would still close properly.

"Think we had some vandals out here the other night," a voice called. "Your plane wasn't the only one hit."

Nick turned to see Armando coming across the tarmac from his hanger, wiping his hand with a rag as Nick stood up. "Armando!" He reached out and gave his friend a firm handshake.

Armando frowned as he stared at Nick's eye. "It's good to see you. But can you see me? Your eye don't look so good."

Nick realized he'd been squinting with his left eye nearly shut in the midday sun. "Ha! You wouldn't want to look if I opened it wide. Had to have some surgery, but it's gonna be okay." He looked up as an airliner came in for a landing. "How 'bout yourself?"

Armando wobbled a hand. "Can't complain." He looked down at the open pod door. "Sorry, *amigo*. Hadn't gotten around to checking it yet. You going to be around awhile?"

"If I can find a place to stay."

"Hey. Still got the cot. It's yours except when the wife chases me out of the house. Then I gotta claim it. But what about that school of yours? Aren't they in that old SurPetro building over there?"

Yes, there was Finca Fe. Nick knew he could probably bunk in its temporary facilities, but he wasn't eager to spend his nights in a boys' dorm. Still, it was a place to start, and it might provide him with the best connection to First Peoples Mission and news of Terri. "Could I use your phone?"

"Of course. Just leave a little of that Yankee *dinero* on my desk."

After eleven rings, a woman's exasperated voice said, *"Hola,* Finca Fe."

"Betty, is that you?" Nick said.

"Yes, who is this?"

"Nick. I'm here in Neiva, at Benito Airport."

"Nick!" She sucked breath like a diver coming up for air and shouted, "It's Nick, everybody!" Then back to the phone. "When did you get in? Where are you? How's your eye?"

"Hold on. One at a time: I just landed. My eye is getting better, though you might not know it by looking at me, and I don't know how long I'll be staying. In fact, that's what I was calling about. I'm wondering whether there's any space in the new facilities — temporarily, of course?"

"Oh, you don't want to do that. Why, all these poor kids have are open dorm rooms. You want to be stuck in there with a bunch of hyperactive teenage boys? Come on, Nick, you wouldn't last the night. You're staying with Roger and me. We got a nice little apartment, even though I gotta climb the stairs. And there's room enough for you until you find something more permanent."

"Thanks, Betty. Maybe I'll take you up on that offer—if Roger approves. But what about him? How's he doin'? We thought he was dead. I can't believe it! I can't believe he walked out of there! Can I see him?"

"Sure, you wanna come? I'm leaving in a few minutes to go pick him up from the hospital. They're kickin' him out. Probably driving them crazy. You want to come? He'd love to see you."

"Sounds good. I'm at the hanger where they park private planes. Can you pick me up?"

Though he was still weak, Terri had "discharged" Carlos Álvarez from the infirmary. But the fever that boiled in Jesús' body on Sunday frightened her. Aspirin and sponge baths seemed to have no effect, and the antibiotics she had been administering were of no more use than injecting swamp water in his veins.

Ramírez saw it when he visited after lunch. "What's happening? He's delirious, unresponsive. What are you doing to him?"

Terri brushed a fly-away strand of limp hair from her face with the back of her hand. "It's the heat. It's exacerbating the infection. He'll never overcome it in this heat." She didn't know that for sure, but the heat was certainly miserable, and it was an answer to his question.

"We'll get an air conditioner." And he left.

The commander's commitment to his son was touching, but where would he put an air conditioner? She couldn't just blow cold air on the boy. They needed a sanitary, enclosed room.

Fifteen minutes later, Terri was folding sheets when Sergeant Rodriquez slapped open the tent flap and threw a soggy brown bag on the infirmary floor.

"*¿Que es esto?*" he snarled, his teeth gritted and his dark eyes boring through her.

In one glance, Terri knew what it was—her backpack with a blanket, poncho, socks, her Bible, and a bag with a few more globs of soggy tortilla. He obviously knew what it was and that it belonged to her, so how should she respond? She couldn't deny it outright. Should she feign gratitude and pretend she'd been looking for it? That would be risky. She shrugged. "It's my backpack," she said flatly, and went back to folding the sheets.

He grabbed her arm with an iron grip and whirled her around, his face only inches from hers, his rancid tobacco breath smelling of tin and sour grapes. "I know it's yours, but why was all your stuff in it? And what was it doing hidden out there under some bushes?"

"Ouch!" Terri pulled hard, but couldn't break his grip. "That hurts!"

"Then answer me!"

All she could think of was to shoot the moon. "Duh! I was planning an escape. But I got scared and gave it all up, so I just threw my stuff away." His eyes widened, and she used the opportunity wrench her arm free. "Let go! You're hurting me!"

"Don't play with me, *chica*!" His eyes narrowed to thin slits, and the skin of his face pulled tight. "You try to run, and I'll shoot you as quick as I did the others."

Terri watched him stomp out of the tent, his solid shoulders like fenders on a truck. She knew he'd do it, too. And there was no assurance Lieutenant Ramírez would intervene, even if he could.

When Nick and Betty arrived at the hospital, Roger wasn't ready to go. "It's just paper work," said the nurse. "Shouldn't take more than a half an hour. You can sit in the waiting room down the hall."

Betty headed in the direction indicated by the nurse, and Nick caught up to her. "You mind if I go across the street? I noticed when we came in that there's a cell phone store over there. I have no idea where my old one is. Probably doesn't even work anymore. But I'm going to need one here in Neiva. I'll be right back."

It took him a little longer than he expected, and Betty and Roger were waiting in their car when he returned. "So sorry to keep you waiting," he said as he climbed into the back seat. "That you, Roger? Could hardly tell with your shaved head and a white bandage wrapped round it."

Roger turned his head slightly in Nick's direction. "Well, it's good to see you, too. Hey, Betty, you bring my hat?"

"No, it's got a hole in it!"

"Well, so does my head. I just don't want this long drink of water trying to look inside."

"Oh, you don't have to worry about me seeing that it's empty in there." Nick tapped him on the shoulder. "I've known that for years."

"I heard you had some eye trouble. Is that all cleared up, now?"

"It's gettin' better, but I've got a ways to go."

Betty started the car and started to pull away but stalled the engine.

"You want me to drive, Betty?" Roger asked.

"You drive? You don't even know where we live."

"But I do know how to use a clutch, besides you told me it was on the way to the airport. How can I miss?"

Betty tried again and made it this time.

All the way back to the Montgomery's rented apartment Nick asked Roger about his ordeal with the kidnappers, quizzing him on every detail. "In the time you were with them, did you get a sense that they were in short supply of anything?"

"Ha, just their transportation. I guess the army picked up their trucks or something, and we ended up walking all over kingdom come. Why do you ask?"

"To get a full picture of what we're dealing with here. You've got to know your enemy before you can exploit his vulnerabilities."

"That's good. That's good, Nick. You oughta go to work for the Colombian army. They never asked me any of those questions."

"They what? Didn't they debrief you?"

"Oh, yeah. They wanted to know how we got across the river and how I found my way down out of the mountains, which was one thing I couldn't remember."

"That's all?"

"Pretty much. Oh yeah. They wanted to know everyone's name. Guess they keep files on these people, but I couldn't help much there."

By this time, they were sitting around the table after dinner, eating Betty's pie. Nick rested his elbow on the table and supported his bowed forehead with his hand. "They're never gonna find her. They're not committed or skilled enough to accomplish the mission." Now he was thinking in military terms. Someone had to go in and get Terri . . . or—and the bud of an idea began to form in his mind—entice them to bring her out!

Chapter 14

The plan growing in Nick's mind went back to something a year and a half earlier, just a few months after he had first come to Colombia.

He'd made one of his routine trips to Neiva to pick up some medical supplies for a missionary family in the bush when a light-skinned black man with a face so long and thin it looked as if it'd been squeezed in a vise approached him as he was tying down his plane and putting chocks under the tires.

"It's good to see another civilian from the States down here." His deep voice was a surprise coming from such a thin body. And with his accent he might have sung bass in a gospel quartet. "Most Americans hightailed it back home, given all the insurgent problems down here. Steven Lang"—he extended his hand—"with the Amazon Tribal Institute. We're mapping the migration of indigenous peoples . . . might have read about us in the newspaper lately. Colombian government now says they can't pay what they promised us." He shrugged. "But we're still trying to finish the job for the sake of the tribes."

"Good to meet you." Nick shook his hand. "I'm Nick Archer. I fly for MAST, Missionary Aviation Support Team."

"Yeah. I've been askin' around about you. Say, I was wondering if I might take you to lunch? We need some help, and you might be just the person."

"Ah, I don't know. This is the mission's plane, and I'm pretty booked up with—"

"I wouldn't be asking anything out of your way. Come on." He made a hooking gesture with his hand. "You gotta eat somewhere. How about La Restaurante Magdalena?"

Nick had grinned. "You talked me into it." The Magdalena was not far from the airport and definitely worth the time if only for their famous *Buñuelos,* the fried cheese puffs that could fatten up anyone. During lunch Lang had explained that all he wanted was for Nick to report when and where he noticed any human activity in the jungle. "You got a GPS, don't you? Good. All you gotta do is when you see some huts that aren't on the map, or a cultivated field, or any other human activity, you make a note of it, and the next time you see me, just give me those notes. You see, all this oil exploration and rebel activity is forcing the indigenous people to move, and that's going to negatively disrupt their life. We'd be hiring a plane and doing all this research ourselves, but . . ." he shrugged, "you know the Colombian government. Hot one minute, cold the next."

Nick had nodded. "Simple enough. See what I can do."

Over the next few weeks he had delivered three reports. They weren't extensive, but Lang seemed as appreciative as a kid at Christmas, and each time he took Nick out for a better meal than Nick could've ever afforded for himself.

The next time Nick saw him, the smile on Lang's face was as wide as a canyon. "Good news!" he said as they slid into a booth, once again at La Restaurante Magdalena. "Some funding came through. Not enough to hire our own pilot, but enough to get you this." He set a small leather case the size of a cigar box on the table and looked around as though checking that no one was watching. Then he unzipped and opened the lid, again shielding the contents from anyone else's view. Inside was what looked like a digital camera.

"This is a beauty, the ultimate point and shoot! Built-in GPS. In fact, it even calculates the angle of your shot so if you are in one location and take a picture of something five hundred meters to your right, it'll compensate to come up with the right coordinates of your subject. Then, through a satellite phone connection, it automatically transmits all the data straight to me. Now, ain't that something? You don't even have to take notes anymore. The only thing is, you gotta open your window a little, so you're not shooting the pictures through Plexiglas. That can throw it off."

Nick, a gadget geek like most pilots, was wowed. On his next flight, he took pictures of every hint of habitation he noticed in the jungle, even if it was only a column of smoke. The problem was, a week later, when he flew over the same areas, each little field that some campesino had previously hacked out of the jungle was withered and yellow. And on two of them, the shacks that had stood at the edge were burned to the ground.

Nick was immediately suspicious and did a little test the next day by skipping one very obvious field. When he came back three days later, it was green and healthy while the others he'd shot on that same trip were dead. Any dummy could see they'd been sprayed with herbicide. Off the end of one, the yellow and dying streak extended into the jungle where the pilot had failed to shut off his spray unit in time.

"You're using me!" snapped Nick the next time he saw Lang. "You don't have anything to do with charting indigenous peoples. You're all about drug interdiction!"

"Now calm down and get in my car."

"Why should I get in your car? Here's your camera." He tossed it to Lang, who caught it easily. "I don't want anything else to do with you."

"No?" Lang had shrugged. "But you're curious enough that if you don't find out what I'm really about, it'll bug you for weeks to come. Now get in the car. We may make better partners than you think."

Slumped against the passenger door of Lang's car, Nick had listened. Steven Lang was CIA, and he didn't care that much about the cocaine fields. That was just a side arrangement, passing on the information to the Colombian government, which sprayed the fields to keep the American government happy so it would keep its purse open—a symbiotic circle. What Lang was really interested in was confirming locations of rebel units in El Despeje. He had several contacts with high-level officers in FARC, both in Neiva and Bogotá, but he had to have a means of confirming the information they gave him. And some of that information had to do with the location and size of the rebel forces.

"Thought you did all that with satellites, right?"

"Most of it, yeah. But we like redundancy. You can never check too often."

"Well, I'm not your man." Nick opened the car door.

"Hold on! Listen, I can accept that, but The Company owes you. You were in the Gulf War—thanks for your service—and you've already been a big help to us here. As you probably know, we really aren't short of funds." He pulled a money clip out of the inside breast pocket of his smooth gray suit coat and began peeling off hundred-dollar bills.

"Keep your money. Iraq was a long time ago, and I don't know if you spooks are ultimately for good or for evil, but I'm in a different . . . a different army now and can't get entangled in your affairs."

Lang shook his head, pocketing the money. "Okay, pal. But if you ever need anything, just remember you have a little money in the bank where The Company's concerned. Here's my card. Things change all the time, but that number will always get a message through to me."

That had been about eighteen months ago. Now, if the "bank" hadn't folded, Nick needed to make a withdrawal.

There was nothing but an answering machine at the number Nick dialed, but two days later, while he was sitting in the plush waiting room of the ophthalmologist Dr. Norman had referred him to, waiting for his eyes to dilate from the drops the technician had put in, Lang called him on his cell phone.

"Took you long enough, but I can't talk right now. I'm in a doctor's office. Where can I call you back?"

"Same number, but it won't be direct. What if I call you?"

"No. I don't want to have to wait two more days—"

"No problem. Uh . . . meet me at the Magdalena in a couple hours. Good to hear from you, Archer."

"The restaurant?"

"Yeah, see you there."

Nick didn't know whether it was good to hear from Lang or not, but right now it was the only option he could come up with.

Five minutes later he was sitting in a dimly lit room while Dr. Gerardo Gomez examined the inside of his left eye with a slit-lamp, no different, as far as Nick could tell, from the one used by Dr. Norman back in the States. Not all of Colombia was primitive and poor.

"So, what can you see?"

"A lot more than I did a few days ago. I can see most of my surroundings, though I can't recognize people's faces across the room."

Gomez had him try to read an eye chart, and Nick felt embarrassed when he stumbled on the second line with letters the size of an egg.

"Don't worry about that. You're right on track. It'll come back to you."

Ah, what welcome words!

"But tell me, what's happening with your diabetes? Because there's no sense doing more with your eyes if we don't deal with the source."

"I'm being good. Check my blood twice a day—fingertips are even sore—and I take my pills regularly. So far, so good."

"Hmm. When do you want to schedule the first laser treatment in your right eye?"

First? Were there to be several? Nick put it off. He needed what vision he had in that eye—blurry though it still was—to get around and help Terri. Once she was safe or his left eye could take over, then he could afford some "down time" for his right eye.

Gomez wasn't too happy, but he agreed and scheduled Nick for another checkup in a week. He was free to shower and didn't have to wear the shield at night. "But just be careful. That eye has undergone a lot of internal trauma, and we don't want any complications. Call me right away if you notice any deterioration or pain."

As Nick rode the elevator down from the doctor's fourteenth floor office, he put on the flimsy, plastic wrap-around shades with cardboard earpieces that would protect his eyes from the bright equatorial sun on the street. Did he look like a cool gangster? No! He looked like a dork on his way to see Steven Lang, his secret CIA contact.

Nick leaned his forearms on the restaurant table. "Last time we talked, you said I had some money in the bank with 'The Company,' as you called it. Right?"

Lang nodded, his close-cut hair so short Nick could see the sheen of his scalp.

"Well, I don't want to get involved in doing any more of that 'research' for you, but I'd like to call in a favor." Nick watched the agent through his plastic lenses. The man's long face didn't flinch. "I need to make contact with a certain FARC commander. He's responsible for kidnapping three people from the academy where I was stationed."

"Yeah, I know all about that."

"Then you know that they killed one, thought they killed a second hostage, who actually escaped, but are still holding the third—"

Lang's eyelids closed as he nodded again with understanding. "Your girl?"

"She's not *my* girl, but she's in real danger, and we gotta get her out."

"I don't have any contacts east of the mountains."

"But I thought you said you needed my information to confirm your reports from inside FARC."

"Inside the *organization* . . . around here and in Bogotá, not out in the jungle. I don't know any rank and file soldiers."

Nick leaned back, peeled off his plastic glasses, and tossed them up in the air, unconcerned whether they might fall on someone else. He slapped both hands down on the table. "So what am I supposed to do? I've gotta contact these guys!"

"You want to hold it down a little?" Lang looked around. "This is a public restaurant, after all." He glared at Nick. "We don't control who comes in here."

"All right! All right. But what am I supposed to do?"

Lang pursed his lips. Then he leaned forward over the table and looked coldly into Nick's eyes. "I can put you in touch with someone here in town who might—again, I emphasize *might*—be able to reach your man in the field. But I can't guarantee it. And once you are in his hands, I can't help you at all. You'll be dealing with some nasty dudes who'd as soon cut your throat as make a deal. You tracking with me?"

"Sounds like someone I need to meet," said Nick.

But that night with an address in the pocket of his pants he'd dropped beside the bed, he couldn't sleep. He was closer to Terri than he'd been when he was back in Chicago, but was he any closer to helping her get free from her captors?

Chapter 15

The dappled sky over the Amazon Basin coalesced into a solid cloud cover by noon and then began to drift down and darken until they bellied like sagging blankets over the jungle where the FARC were camped. By three o'clock, Lieutenant Ramírez asked one of his men to start the generator. It usually ran only a couple of hours at night, but he needed to do some paperwork, and not enough light penetrated the leaves.

First one, then three, then a dozen soldiers found excuses to drift out to the volleyball court where they could look up at the slowly undulating sky. Intense storms were common over the rain forest, but they sensed this one was different. As the wind began to comb through the trees, dividing one from another, pulling apart the canopy, and whipping their tops from side to side, everyone felt their breath being sucked from their lungs by the plummeting barometer.

How different this was for Terri Kaplan than December as an ER nurse back at Cook County Hospital in Chicago. By this time of the year they would be dealing with homeless people suffering from exposure and sometimes pneumonia or families and elderly folks evicted from their apartments who ended up in the emergency room because they had no place else to turn . . . along with the regular stream of kids caught in gang violence—shootings, stabbings, and overdoses. But there was also the other Chicago—the snow and the ice skating in Grant Park, slurping scalding hot chocolate while viewing the animated Christmas windows at Marshall Field's, Salvation Army bell ringers and bustling shoppers, the squeal of the 'L' on overhead tracks, and always the hope that if the Cubs, Sox, and Bears weren't winning, the Bulls might make a comeback. Both bad and good, it was the City with Big Shoulders, the Windy City, the city that worked, and that brought a sense of order and comfort that was absent in the middle of the jungle, especially under a brewing storm.

In spite of the humidity, dust sandblasted her eyes and caked inside of her nose. Heat lightening chattered overhead like a worn-out neon sign, filling the air with the green metallic tang of ozone.

The rain did not start with what would commonly be recognized as drops but as sheets of water stripped off the leaves of the swaying trees to splat on the camp floor like miniature mortar shells. But their mission seemed merely to soften up the jungle's resistance. Soon the main assault descended, totally overwhelming the trees, and joining forces to battle the very air for the right to occupy the camp. Water splashed up as fast as it came down in a vertigo torrent while Terri tried to tie down the flaps on the infirmary tent.

The rope snapped out of her grip, and a wave of rain invaded her space, upending a bedside table and scattering cups and towels and a blood pressure cuff and all that was left of Jesús Ramírez's lunch.

"Help! Can I get some help over here? *¡AYUADAME!* Somebody HELP!" But no one heard her. No one could have heard her from more than an arm's distance. And then, as though taking a breath before another attack, the rain lightened enough for her to see a figure wading toward the command tent. She ran to intercept it, plunging through the four inches of water that threatened to float the wooden platform floors of the infirmary, the command tent, and the kitchen. Water rose across the entire camp like a tide on a flood plain, moving pots and boards and equipment as it came.

She grabbed the man's sleeve, pulling him to a splashing stop. "HELP! The infirmary!"

It was Sergeant Rodriquez. He flung her off. "Then get back in there and take care of it. You touch me again, *guapa,* and I'll drown you like a rat, and it won't be in this rain water!" He turned to go.

"But I can't tie it down. It's blowing away!"

"Not my problem!" And he was gone.

The storm resumed with even greater furry, making it difficult to locate, let alone get back to the infirmary. Terri tripped over someone's submerged rifle and went down. Except for the mud, it didn't much matter. There was no way she could've gotten any wetter.

Back at the infirmary, a tent rope had broken allowing the tent's roof to sag and fill with water so that from beneath, it mimicked the bloated clouds of minutes before. Terri dove into the tent, realizing the distended roof directly above Jesús looked like it could burst at any moment.

She stooped and sidled under the virtual cistern until she could get a grip on the cot, but it wouldn't slide. "Oh, Jesus, You calmed the storm on the sea, I need you to give me some relief right now. Please, Jesus!" She tugged again on the stubborn cot, her head pushing against the heavy bladder above her. "You said You are our *strength in the time of trouble.* Well, I need a little of that strength right now! Some raw, physical strength, Lord. Please!" She strained for all she was worth, her head pushing higher into the cool gut above her.

Suddenly, without warning, the canvas split from end to end, dumping its entire contents on her and Jesús. Weak as he was, he sat up, coughing and fighting for breath. Terri grabbed him around the shoulders and half lifted, half dragged him across the infirmary to an empty cot just as the whole front half of the tent collapsed.

Then, as fast as it had risen, the storm began to whip itself out, its violent gasps coming farther and farther apart. But Jesús was also gasping and shivering and convulsing into a semi-fetal curl from which he stared as though seeing nothing.

The floor of the yellow cab Nick caught that afternoon, hoping to find the address Lang had given him, was cluttered with gum wrappers, a folded newspaper, and a nearly empty McDonald's French fry container. The green plastic seats were cracked and smelled of too many unwashed passengers.

"¿Donde?" said the thick-necked driver, glancing at Nick through the mirror.

Nick looked at the slip of paper in his hand. *"Calle Cincuenta y Ocho, numero treinta y seis."*

Fifteen minutes later they pulled to a stop in a dirt street, surrounded by a patchwork of tile-roofed stucco houses. Each hovel was distinguished by its sherbet color and personalized security—bars on the windows and doors of some, literal "cages" of bars encompassing the entire concrete "lawn" of others, the rusted-out hulk of a wheelless car in the yard of another. Nick felt encouraged as he paid his fare and got out. Maybe it was the kids playing soccer in the narrow street or the sweet smell of hot *arepas de chocolo,* the fresh corn cakes that made Nick's stomach growl with hunger.

The woman who came to the door when he knocked shook her head and shrugged when he said, "Pablo?" as though he were speaking a foreign language. She started to shut the door, when a man inside with a two-pack-a-day voice said, *"¿Quién es"?*

"I'm Nick Archer. I need to speak to Pablo," Nick called over the woman's head.

A large man with drooping, hairy shoulders and a sweat-stained strap undershirt shuffled to the door and pushed the woman aside. His gut hung over his belt like a water balloon, and he had a week's beard on his puffy face. Straight, black hair stood askew on his head like iron filings that had come too close to a magnet. He stared at Nick from blood-shot eyes until Nick realized he was waiting for him to state his business.

"You Pablo?"

"What you want him for?"

"I need to contact Lieutenant Fabian Ramírez. He's east of the mountains in El Despeje." When the man returned nothing but a vacant stare, Nick added, "He's with FARC."

Instantly, the man's eyes sharpened as he glanced down the street at the yellow taxi that was just turning the corner. "Don't know him!" And he closed the door.

"Wait, wait, wait!" Nick rattled the bars of the security door. "I'm telling you. He definitely would want to talk to me. I've got something he needs."

The inside door opened a few inches. "What's that?"

Nick put on his most innocent smile and held out both hands as if he was offering the man a birthday cake. "I should probably just talk to Pablo."

"No conozco a ningun Pablo." And the door began to close again.

He had to know Pablo. *"Espere,"* he begged. "I got an airplane."

The door opened again. *"¿Un avión?"* The man scowled as though Nick had claimed to have the London Bridge in his pocket.

"Yeah—and I'm the pilot. Believe me, the lieutenant *will* want to hear about this."

The man sniffed deeply like a loud snore, hacked up some snot, and swallowed. *"Siéntese,"* he growled, gesturing with his thumb toward a weathered couch on the end of the veranda. Then the door closed.

Nick stepped over and tested the couch with his hand. Dust rose, and cotton stuffing protruded from a hole made by a broken spring, but it held him with nothing more than a pop and squeak when he sat down. Through the bars on the open window above his head, he heard the man making a phone call. From the brief snatches of one side of the conversation, he wasn't sure the guy was speaking to Pablo, but he did mention *"el gringo"* often enough to give Nick hope.

After a while, Nick picked up an old copy of *Cambio* magazine hidden halfway in the back of the couch and flipped through its pages with a different excitement. He was able to read the headlines and larger letters. He tried first his right eye and then his left. Even without his magnifying glass, he could make out the words of an article, though they were still quite blurry. His eyes were definitely improving. He could probably fly, and perhaps . . . perhaps with correction he would even pass his flight physical by the time he had to renew his license. For the next hour as he waited, he busied himself testing his vision with the magazine, looking down the street, and finally at the numbers on his watch.

The sun set behind scattered clouds and a streetlight came on at the end of the block, its orange glow distinct from the blue gloom of the neighborhood from which children had disappeared into the houses to get their *arepas* and rice and beans. The next time he heard the man speaking to the woman in the house, Nick called, *"¡Hey, hombres!* When can I speak to Pablo?"

"Whenever they come for you."

But it was night before a noisy Dodge panel van pulled up and two men got out and walked up to the house. The driver, small and thin with a light step, came up and banged on the barred door just as the secondary wooden door opened. "This him?" asked the driver.

"*Sí.* That's him."

Nick stood and extended his hand. "Yeah, I'm Nick Archer. You Pablo?"

He shook his head. "Turn around. Hands behind you." He stepped aside to make room for the bouncer to step up.

Nick complied and felt a nylon self-locking tie pull his wrists tight, the kind of tie intended for construction but often used in other "trades" when handcuffs were scarce. Then the bouncer quickly frisked him. *"Nada."* A dark hood came down over Nick's head, and the bouncer roughly guided him toward the van.

In moments he was pushed inside. "Stay on the floor." And the door slammed.

When the engine with an apparent hole in its muffler roared to life and he felt the vehicle pull away, he shuddered. *Am I on my way to rescuing Terri or will I end up dead in a ditch?*

Terri spent the afternoon fighting the chill that held Jesús in its grip like stones in an Andean glacier. The cool air brought by the storm had felt refreshing to Terri, but for Jesús' sake she welcomed the returning heat in spite of the rising humidity. Still, the boy remained rigid, his body temperature below 95° F, his pulse and blood pressure sluggish, and he still stared at nothing.

Terri dipped towels in hot water, wrung them out, and sealed them in plastic bags that she tucked under the blanket to warm the boy while she rubbed his limbs to improve circulation. Slowly his body temperature and blood pressure moved toward normal, and his body relaxed before he fell asleep.

Some of the men had temporarily repaired the infirmary tent, and as darkness settled over the camp, Terri sat alone beside Jesús with an oil lamp burning on the table an arm's length away. "O Lord, what happened today? Have You forgotten me? It was just as I was calling on You that all . . . all *hell* broke loose." She flinched at using a word some might consider swearing. It was not like her. She knew she hadn't been through literal hell, but this was a time for speaking frankly, and she trusted the Lord would forgive if her imagery were the best she could manage. After all, if the worst thing about hell was separation from God and His protection, she had never felt more forsaken than when she had called on Him only to have things immediately get worse.

In fact, the more she thought about it, her most urgent prayers seemed to have backfired every time since she'd been kidnapped. Was it possible that El Despeje, this "safe zone" for the FARC, was a region abandoned not only by the Colombian government but also by God Himself? There were those who believed that evil spirits had regional authority or that the absence of people of faith limited what God could do in a place. Perhaps with so much killing and all the drugs, this area east of the mountains had become a stronghold for the devil. Even Jesus, when He walked on earth, was unable to do many miracles in certain regions, namely His hometown of Nazareth. Why was that? Was she caught in such a zone?

Terri buried her head in her hands and sobbed. *"My God, my God, why have you forsaken me?"* Was this how Jesus felt on the cross? It was very dark.

Chapter 16

The old van bounced over rough streets, stopped at intersections, turned corners, labored up small hills, and then settled into the drone of highway travel, its loud muffler roaring in Nick's ears. He worked his head against the floor trying to loosen the hood. Even though it was dark outside, being unable to see held too much terror for him to take it calmly. But apparently some kind of a drawstring kept it secured below his chin. He coughed from the fumes of the leaky exhaust. "*Eh, hermanos,* where we goin'?"

No answer.

He tried to raise himself but couldn't get the leverage with his hands tied behind his back. "You guys think you could help me sit up?" He was sure they were far enough out of town that no one would see him, if that was their object. "I'm getting a cramp curled up here on the floor."

Still no answer.

"Can you at least remove this hood?"

He wasn't getting anywhere. Were both of the men riding in the van with him, or after throwing him in the back, had one of them stayed behind? He tried to replay the moment in his mind but couldn't recall whether he'd heard both front doors slam or not. The driver had spoken to the guy at the house before they left, saying, "Don't ever do this again. *¿Me entendés?* You understand?" But Nick had been too anxious over what was happening to him at the moment to note whether the bouncer had also gotten in. But why wouldn't he? On the other hand, why hadn't they been talking to each other during the trip?

Finally, the van slowed, turned off the highway, and traveled on a winding road until it came almost to a stop and turned onto a steep and bumpy road. Maybe a driveway? It stopped and *two* men got out—so they had both come—leaving Nick alone in the dark, listening to the ticking of the cooling engine.

The smells of animals and manure and rotting hay mixed with the odor of oil on the hot engine and brain-numbing exhaust. In a few minutes someone opened the van's side door and grabbed a handful of his shirt. Had to be the bouncer, given the strength with which he pulled Nick out. After such a long ride in a cramped position, Nick stumbled a little before gaining his balance. "Where are we?"

"Shut up and walk!"

The surface was rough and hard, like cobblestones. The hand on his shoulder pulled him to a stop as though his shirt was the reins of a horse. There was a clanging of heavy metal and then a protesting squawk as a steel door opened on some echoing chamber. "Get in there!"

Nick was given a tremendous shove and stumbled over a shin-high doorsill, sprawling into the cavern. For an instant as he was falling, he knew he was going to hit hard with no hands to break his fall. He tried to roll to one side and take the blow on his shoulder, but his head hit stone straight ahead. A flash, like a strobe at midnight, faded to black.

The pain in Nick's eye was what he'd expected from eye surgery, after people had poked around in his eyeball with strange instruments. But why did his forehead above that eye hurt so badly? And his shoulder? He remained very still. Was the operation over? He didn't hear anyone. Could he open his eyes? And why had they put him completely under? He thought it was just going to be a sedative, and that's how it had started out.

Wow, that anesthetic cocktail generated some wild dreams. Better not let it out on the streets or it would put the cocaine cartels out of business.

Wait a minute—details were coming back. It was no dream. His eye surgery had happened over ten days ago. He *had* come to

Colombia! He'd been trying to contact FARC. He'd . . . fallen, no, been thrown into a . . . a . . . what was this? A dungeon?

Ouch! Rainbows of light fired when he tried to move, and his hands were still bound behind his back.

He rolled over on the cold floor—a floor covered with something like pea gravel gouging into every unpadded bone. The bag over his head felt wet and sticky along the left side of his face. He tried to sit up, and knew as he did so that he was losing consciousness. Hang on! Hang on! Keep your head low. There, there. Now take a deep breath.

How long had he been out? Probably not long, but he had no way of knowing. And where was he? He pivoted—pebbles grinding into his butt—until his feet found the concrete wall that had stopped his head when the bouncer had thrown him like a battering ram through the door. He scooted himself across the floor until he came to another wall, then followed it along. It continued on and on, though he could tell by the close echo that the room was small. It was small and . . . and round, like a cistern or . . . or a silo. And the smell . . . coffee. Not the nutty smell of roasted coffee but raw beans. He was in a coffee bin, and the pebbles on the floor were old coffee beans. He remembered the animal smells upon arrival. This was a farm. Somehow a farm seemed less sinister than a dungeon, and yet he was just as confined.

Time passed. Light suddenly shown through the edges of his blindfold, and he heard the door creaking open and people step in, their footsteps echoing as they scraped beans on the floor.

"Take it off," came a new voice.

In a moment the hood was loosened and pulled off. It was such a relief to see anything that Nick hardly noticed the pain from peeling it off as though it were week-old adhesive tape. The glare of the light was so bright it took him several moments to see that the bouncer and the driver had been joined by a third man. Nick squinted at him. He was perhaps as tall as Nick, well built, with a square, weathered face, full mustache and thick eyebrows. He wore jeans with a heavy silver buckle, boots, a well-worn tailored maroon shirt, and a curled, white cowboy hat. He was an upscale version of any of Colombia's thousands of campesinos.

Bracing his hands against the wall, Nick tried to rise.

"¡Siéntese!"

Nick slid back to the floor as the new man leaned forward to stare at his head. Nick's vision wasn't so good again. Maybe it was just the glare.

"He give you trouble?"

"No, jefe," said the bouncer. "Don't know how that happened."

The chic campesino leaned against the wall and crossed his arms. *"Estoy Pablo.* What do you want?"

"Ah, Pablo! Good. Like I told the guy back in Neiva, I need to get in touch with Lieutenant Fabian Ramírez." He blinked hard, trying to clear his vision. "He's a FARC officer east of the mountains."

"How'd you get my name?"

"Steven Lang." Nick watched as Pablo shrugged. "Anyway," Nick added, "he gave me your name, told me you might be able to help."

"Why do you need Ramírez?"

Nick explained about the school nurse at Finca Fe getting kidnapped and that there'd been some radio contact, but he didn't think it was going anywhere, and he had something far more important to Ramírez that might be worth negotiating.

"And that would be . . .?" Pablo yawned and pushed his hat back on his head. In the glare, Nick couldn't tell whether his expression changed or not.

"I'm a pilot. When Lieutenant Ramírez hit—uh, I mean, visited our school down on the Magdalena, he made every effort to . . . to recruit me and my airplane. I wasn't . . . I wasn't available then. But now I thought perhaps I could volunteer my services for a short period in exchange for the nurse's release."

Suddenly terrified at what he was offering, Nick squirmed on the concrete floor as he looked up at the men. His hands, bound behind him for so long, were now completely numb. What if Ramírez took him up on his offer? What would be the consequences of assisting the rebels? He'd be deported and MAST might get banned from Colombia. He hadn't consulted anyone about those consequences, and the plane wasn't his to begin with. But surely, if he could accomplish Terri's release, all would be forgiven. And technically, neither mission would have paid a ransom.

"Of course," Nick said hastily, "I wouldn't be able to take part in any kind of hostilities. Just . . . maybe ferrying medicine or the wounded, that kind of thing."

The man snorted. "You think you could fly for FARC a coupla weeks and then go home like you'd been at summer camp?"

"Whatever we negotiate." But yes, there was that. Why would they let him go?

Pablo shrugged. "Then here's the deal . . ." With a little nod of his head, he pushed himself away from the wall and turned to the door. "No deal!"

"Wait a minute! Wait a minute! Don't you think—"

"Sit down," barked the bouncer, seeing Nick struggle to rise.

He slid back down. "Don't you think Lieutenant Ramírez should be the one to make that decision?" They were going out the door. "I mean, he's the one who initially approached us!"

The door slammed, and the light went out. "Ha! *Approached*!" Nick said into the darkness. "Attacked, was the word!"

He sat there arguing in silence with the departed Pablo. It was stupid of Pablo to pass up his offer. He ought to at least present it to Ramírez. Recalling how hard the lieutenant had looked for him at Finca Fe, surely Ramírez would go for it. So why wouldn't Pablo tell him? And why was he being kept in this prison? If they weren't going to make a deal, they should take him back to Neiva. What was going on? Another kidnapping?

Fatigue settled in the silence. After a while, Nick tipped over onto his side like a dead action figure and, in spite of the pounding in his head, fell asleep.

Terri spent the night on a cot next to Jesús so she could monitor how he was doing. He wasn't doing well. Since the first day Terri had seen the boy, she could tell the treatment she'd been giving him wasn't working. The infection had gotten too much of a beachhead in his body.

"So, what does he need?" Ramírez had asked when she'd explained that penicillin did not cover everything anymore, especially not some of the exotic tropical infections. Terri had named an array of new drugs, and surprisingly, Ramírez had delivered them within twenty-four hours, but they hadn't worked, either.

"The boy needs to be in a hospital," she'd said.

His eyes had narrowed. "If I take him to a hospital, the Colombian government will hear about it and hold him hostage."

"Like you're holding me hostage?"

He had rolled his head back, blowing up into the air like a smoker. "You're here because I need you to save lives—his life! I'm not using you to leverage anything else. But if the government gets its hands on him, it would be a true hostage situation: his life for mine."

"And my freedom? What price for it?"

"Just take care of Jesús!" And he'd walked away.

Now, a week later, Jesús was sinking lower, especially since the soaking that had shocked his body last night.

As Ramírez surveyed the tattered infirmary tent by morning's light, Terri said, "This didn't need to happen." When Ramírez frowned, Terri explained. "Before the tent collapsed, I ran out into that deluge and begged Sergeant Rodriquez to get some help because I feared this disaster. He just blew me off. Wouldn't do a thing."

The commander's eyes hardened as he surveyed the camp. "But Lieutenant," persisted Terri, "it's not just the tent. Jesús! Needs! Hospital care!" She emphasized each word with a stab of her index finger.

The lieutenant's attention returned from searching for Rodriquez, and he shook his head. "We've already been through this."

"Yes, but this is your *son*! Look, the antibiotics—even the ones you brought me—aren't tailored to fight his specific infection."

"Then order what you need!"

"I can't, and that's why he needs to be in a hospital. They would culture the infection, examine it in the lab, and come up with a more precise medication."

He stood there looking through her as if his mind was over the mountains in a bright, clean intensive care unit where his son needed to be. Maybe she was finally getting through to him. Would he sacrifice himself to save his son?

"You're right!" Ramírez said, returning to the present. "But he doesn't need to go to the hospital, only the culture does. You prepare it, then take it to be examined and get the medication, but you're not taking my son where the government might capture him and use him as leverage against me."

"But where?"

"Florencia. Rosita will go with you. You can tell them you're a nurse working with some of the interior tribes and need a quick diagnosis."

He looked around again at the storm damage and stepped off the tent platform into the mud as he started to leave. "I'll get someone over here right away to clean up this mess."

Terri returned to her work in a daze. Florencia? Could the rebel camp be that close to a city? A city under government control, a city with an airport and commercial flights? Ramírez had out flanked her efforts to "transfer" her patient, but he was also authorizing her to travel into a free territory.

Hardly knowing what to think, she prepared a cell culture medium in a jar and seeded it with the swabbings from Jesús' wound.

In less than an hour, Rodriquez showed up, repairing and cleaning up the infirmary, and not as the sergeant in charge, either. He sneered as he walked past her. "I'll get my stripes back, because he needs me. But you'll pay for this, *guapa*!"

Chapter 17

When the clank of steel awakened Nick, the dim gray of morning was already outlining the door and weaseling its way under the corrugated roof overhead. It was the bouncer who entered the coffee bin with a white, five-gallon plastic bucket that he sat on the floor. "Don't foul our five-star accommodations. Use that!"

"Hey, wait a minute! Let me out of here!"

But the door slammed, and the latch clattered home again.

Ten minutes later he was back with a two-liter plastic Coke bottle filled with water and a paper sack with a loaf of bread and a banana in it. Breakfast!

"What's goin' on? Why're you guys keeping me?" If they weren't going to buy his deal, why not take him back to Neiva? Nick was afraid he knew the answer: He'd just been kidnapped himself!

As the big man turned without answering, Nick said, "At least cut my hands free. They've been numb all night. I don't want to lose 'em."

The guy looked over his shoulder, eyeing Nick. "Roll over. Lemme see."

Nick detected his arms being manipulated from side to side but couldn't feel any touch to his hands.

"They ain't black yet."

"But wait! How am I supposed to eat? How am I supposed to do anything?"

"You'll figure a way." The bouncer's laugh sounded like rocks rattling in a can. "Give you somethin' to do."

The bread was easy. Just smash his face into it and start biting. That even worked for the banana as long as he didn't mind a little peel. Water? He had to manipulate the bottle to an upright position where he could hold it between his legs while he twisted the lid open with his teeth. Then he spilled most of it. But the white bucket . . . well, he never did get his pants pulled up on his own. But the two-hour effort restored enough circulation in his hands for some feeling to return.

Nick had to laugh at himself with his pants halfway down to his knees like those street kids back in the States. "Yeah, I'm bad! I'm bad!" This must be the best crime deterrent ever attributed to a fashion. Who could run away like this?

But laughing made his head throb, and he noticed that he didn't seem to be able to see as well as the day before—though in the dim light, it was hard to tell. One thing he noticed was that his eyebrow seemed to be so swollen that it cut off his upper-left peripheral vision. But when he gently leaned forward to touch that tender area to his knee, the abraded flesh didn't seem to be hanging down that far. Also, when he looked quickly from side to side, he saw an echo of the flash he'd seen just as he lost consciousness the night before. Maybe a little concussion, but at least he was conscious.

When the bouncer returned, Nick was on his side again, trying to find some relief from the coffee beans that seemed to forever grind into him.

"*Ay muchacho, sus pantalones.* Better pull 'em up. We're goin' for a walk."

"Uh, haven't been able to manage that, but—"

With one hand, the guy grabbed Nick's shirt and pulled him all the way to his feet in one motion, then turned and found the hood he'd thrown on the floor.

"No, no! Not the hood!" But Nick's protests didn't even slow the man from jamming it down over his head and leading him out.

He marched Nick like a hobbled horse across the cobblestones until they turned into what seemed to be the hacienda where the air was close and pungent with the aroma of real coffee.

"*¡Alto!*" said the bouncer, yanking back on Nick's shoulder.

"*Buenos dias, Señor Nick Archer,*" said Pablo. "Pull your pants up, will you! What were you doing out there?"

"It's these hand restraints, and if you don't take them off, I could end up losing my hands. I haven't had any feeling in them for hours."

After a moment, there was a tugging on his arms, and his hands were cut loose. He brought them around and tried to rub them together like empty gloves on the ends of two sticks, then worked to pull up his pants. "I think I need to relieve myself, again, too."

"You'll want to hold it for a few more minutes while you hear what I've got to tell you—"

"How 'bout the hood?"

"Stays on. You don't need to see the inside of this house."

Nick considered just pulling it off now that his hands were free, but decided he'd be inviting trouble.

"It's been a long morning, back and forth on the radio trying to make contact with this Lieutenant Ramirez you were telling me about. Finally reached him shortly after lunch. You enjoy lunch? Ha, ha, ha! . . . Uh, why don't you get our guest a candy bar or somethin'." Footsteps shuffled off.

"Anyway, apologies. You were right. He is interested in your offer."

Nick heard paper rattle as though Pablo were flipping the pages of a notebook.

"Uh, let's see . . . Here are his conditions: He has a wounded man he wants you to fly to the hospital in Calabozo—that's Venezula."

"Yeah, I know," said Nick, his voice muffled in the hood.

"Once you do that, the nurse can leave, but you stay with Ramírez. Understood?"

Nick tried to think quickly. What was he agreeing to? What was the hitch? How could he guarantee they would release Terri?

"Take it or leave it, man. This isn't the marketplace open to haggling."

"Yeah, yeah. How do I find him?"

"First, are you in?"

Nick knew his stalling was obvious. If they didn't release Terri, maybe he'd be able to look for his chance and just fly away, maybe take her with him . . . unless they always sent a guard in his plane to monitor what he did. He couldn't control that. There were a lot of things he couldn't control, but this was as close as anybody had come to freeing her. He had to take the chance.

"Okay, I'm in."

"Good! Then this is Thursday. Commander Ramírez has to get some things arranged. Next Tuesday, you're to fly to the little town called Otás, just this side of the mountains in the foothills. Know where?"

Nick nodded his head.

"All right. There's a road going east with a straight stretch about five kilometers from town. Land there at noon, *only* if there's no one around. One of his men will meet you and fly with you over the mountains. Any tricks, and you're dead."

Nick licked his lips inside the hood. "Understood. Won't be any tricks. I'll be there." His stomach quivered with the success.

"Okay, get him out of here."

"Jefe," said the bouncer, *"¿al baño?"*

"Nah, not in here. He'd make a mess with that hood on, and it's not to come off until you get him back to Neiva."

Rough hands pushed Nick outside and walked him out into some weeds. "Hurry up!"

Nick's hands still tingled with numbness, but he managed. After his triumph with Pablo, he could manage anything. *Yes, thank you Jesus!* as Terri would say.

Nick promised to stay on the floor of the van with the hood over his head if his captors didn't retie his wrists. The trip back seemed a lot shorter than when they took him out into the country, but maybe it was because his mind was buzzing with details. "What if there's bad weather, and I can't fly into Otás? What should I do then?"

No answer from "bouncer" or "driver."

"What's with you guys? Come on, *hombres.* You weren't afraid to talk to me back there with Pablo. Can't you just give me a phone number? You know, there could be a legitimate need to get in touch with you guys again. Anything could happen."

But their silence was as stubborn as an old tree root. Even when the van stopped and Nick heard the bouncer climb over the engine cover and come back to where he'd remained lying on the floor as instructed, it was all without a word.

The man undid the hood, pulled it off, opened the door, and jerked his head toward the exit.

Nick stepped out into the bright sunshine, and the moment his feet hit the street, the van roared off. He turned to watch it go, unable to focus his troubled eyes on the license number. It was just a dark green panel Dodge Caravan with a bad muffler.

He was standing in the street next to a building, the total side of which was an advertising mural for Aires Airlines with a beautiful blue and white turboprop De Havilland Dash 8-300 soaring off to other Colombian destinations. But the sign on the fence at the corner declared that the building was the Neiva airport headquarters for the *Policia Nacional*! What audacity! The FARC rebels were brazen enough to return their "victim" to the door of a police station and calmly drive off as though they'd merely given Nick a ride to work.

Well, in a way they had, he decided, as he walked around the corner and headed into the airport. He would check out his plane, run up the engine, top off the tanks, and be ready to go. It'd be good to check in with Armando Trujillo, pay his parking fee, and see how everything was. This was a great day. He was going to get Terri back, and if God was with him, the price would be small—just a little "service" to the rebels. No one needed to know.

"Hey, there you are!" Armando glanced up from his desk where he was doing some paperwork as Nick came in. "A Roger Montgomery phoned here this morning trying to find you, said you'd been missing, and they were worried about you."

"Uh-oh. Didn't mean to worry them. Didn't expect to be gone overnight, either. Mind if I borrow your phone to let 'em know where I am?"

"Help yourself. I'll just put it on your tab."

"Speaking of which, could you top off my fuel tanks while I make that call, and then could you figure up my bill through . . . let's see, figure it through Tuesday. I'm expecting to make a little trip and am not sure when I'll be back."

"Sure thing."

"Check the oil, too, would you?"

"Always do." Armando waved as he went out the door to gas the Cessna. Nick called Roger and Betty to apologize for worrying them, but he didn't offer an explanation of where he had been. Then, as an afterthought before hanging up, he said, "I'm here at the airport right now checkin' out the plane. I think I'm going to take it up for a little flight. Might go down to Finca Fe and see how things are. Anything you want me to pick up?"

Betty had a whole list of things from the kitchen. Nick wrote them down and said he'd get what he could. Then he looked out the window. "You know, it's getting a little late. There's probably a lot of things need doing down there. I might stay over and come back in the morning, so don't worry about me."

"You gonna stay down there all by yourself?" asked Betty.

"Don't see why not. My cot's still there, if the rats haven't made a nest of the mattress. Just have to knock the dust off."

"But food, what will you eat?"

"Ah, I'll find something. See you tomorrow, Betty."

Nick was starving—especially after the poor cuisine at "hotel FARC"—but the fast food he grabbed at the airline terminal was a long way from healthy for a diabetic. Still, this is a unique situation, he told himself. He'd get back on his diet soon enough. And he'd better get an extra supply of his medication before "volunteering" on the other side of the mountains. There was no telling how long he'd be there. And he'd have to tell Roger and Betty about that, too.

When he returned to Armando's office, he handed his credit card over to pay his bill. Armando looked at him and frowned. "That eye of yours still don't look too good. Did you have another operation? It's all red. There's a bunch of scratches around it, too. What happened?"

"Looks kind of bad, huh? Well, you know, the proverbial doorknob and all that. You got a first aid kit I can borrow? I'll go in the bathroom and clean it up."

In the bathroom, Nick soaked off what blood still remained around his eyebrow and the top of his cheek. He had slammed into that wall almost eye first, but there wasn't as much blood as he'd expected. And though a real shiner was developing, the swelling wasn't what he imagined it might be. In fact, what little swelling remained in his eyelid seemed hardly enough to bother his peripheral vision the way it seemed to.

He'd been so wound up and excited by the prospects of gaining Terri's release, that he hadn't been giving much attention to his vision. But he had to admit, that dive into the wall had caused a setback. Something was happening. His vision certainly wasn't as good as it'd been just twenty-four hours before when he could read a magazine. In fact, it was as though a shade was starting to be pulled down on that side of his vision in his left eye. Not good. He'd have to get it checked out with Dr. Gomez before Tuesday.

Now, however, he was going flying, and it was a beautiful evening for it, too—clear, light breeze, sun low to the horizon. He said goodbye to Armando and walked out onto the ramp just as the tires of an Aires flight squawked—*yip, yip*—as it touched down. A few moments later a whiff of kerosene exhaust blew his way. Yeah, he knew air pollution was a terrible thing, especially in bigger cities, but there were some smells that spelled adventure to Nick, and jet exhaust was one of them. Sure would be nice if he had a turboprop someday. They flew so smoothly.

Chapter 18

The village of Otás was less than ten kilometers off a direct route from Neiva to Finca Fe. Nick circled the town once, high enough to not draw undue attention, then followed the gravel road east. And there, about five kilometers east, was a straight stretch. He dropped down to inspect the surface and make sure there were no trees or power lines to obstruct a landing. Everything looked clear.

He smiled to himself as he regained altitude and headed southwest toward Finca Fe. Everything was lining up. "Hang on, Terri. It'll just be a few more days!" he said out loud into the drone of the engine and the whoosh of air over the cabin.

In the west a golden sun was setting, casting a lavender hue back on the jagged mountains of the central range as Nick buzzed the strip at Finca Fe to chase off a dozen sheep some local *compesino* had allowed to graze the lush grass. He touched down on the next round and rolled right up to his hanger. Then, with one last goose of the throttle to clear the engine with his right brake set, he swung the plane around and shut down the engine.

The blades chugged to a stop, leaving an eerie silence when he opened the door and stepped out, throwing back his shoulders and stretching the muscles still stiff from his previous night's rough sleep. Birds and insects had retired—except for an occasional bat—and all he could hear was the slow ticking of his Cessna's cooling exhaust. No children playing ball, no rattle of kitchen pots being cleaned, no purr of Roger's tractor as he mowed one last patch of grass before it got too dark.

He entered the hanger and lit a lantern. His little "apartment" looked the same as when he'd left, but somehow all the rustic warmth of home was gone. He unfolded the mattress and laid it out, then pulled a thin blanket from a plastic bag. The bed would be ready for him when he returned from surveying the campus.

With keys in hand, he went from building to building. A window had been broken in the old manor house. Hard to tell whether it'd been some local kids—no one lived very close—but it didn't look like any further damage had followed. He'd find some plywood to screw over it before he left.

With the power off, there was barely enough pressure in the water system for him to fill a plastic jug for his own use. He propped open the refrigerator and freezer doors. They were empty, but someone had left them closed to grow musty. A can of tuna, one of peaches, and a box of crackers from the nearly bare pantry would be supper.

Dropping in on the school to check around had seemed like a good idea earlier, but Nick almost wished he hadn't come when he entered the gymnasium/cafeteria. He hadn't been inside during the FARC raid, but to him it still seemed haunted by the terrified stories of the students and staff. The tannic smell of their fear had mixed with old sweat, stale food, and dust until the atmosphere of the cavernous room seemed like a tomb. He wanted out. The mission needed to send some trucks and empty this place—the whole school—of all its equipment and supplies and close it securely, or sooner or later it would invite theft and vandalism.

So far, however, most everything looked untouched. That's what he thought, at least, until he came to Terri's infirmary. The door had been forced, and the place had been stripped of all medical supplies and equipment—even the X-ray machine. That thing was heavy; Nick had helped set it up, and it would've taken at least a pickup truck to haul it away.

So, who got a trophy worth thousands of dollars? Had FARC returned? Were they watching the school even now, perhaps from the hill across the river? Had they seen him land? Were they likely to "recruit" him before he had a chance to complete his deal with Lieutenant Ramírez?

He turned off the lantern before returning to the hanger. As quietly as possible, he opened the doors wide and dragged the

Cessna inside, tail first. Then, in the failing twilight he closed the doors and went to his room. A candle was enough to eat by, and for once, he felt justified in not having cleaned his windows.

It was only 7:45 when he let himself flop back on his cot. He was exhausted, and his last thoughts as he pulled the blanket over him were: This place doesn't even smell like home anymore.

But Nick's thoughts in the morning light were quite different. No one had bothered him during the night, and the first thing he saw when he woke up was the little yellow note stick-pinned to the wall stud at the end of his bed: *"If it's not raining, meet me at The Rock! —me"*

He pulled it lose and read it again. Something *had* been percolating between him and Terri. He hadn't imagined it. They'd never managed a rendezvous at The Rock since the attack happened the next day, but the night before around the fire had been just as intimate, asking personal questions of each other that only special friends dared ask. He wished he could sit with her now in the early morning and share her devotional time. Using the stick-pin, he stuck the note back on the wall stud. Maybe some other time.

Since the FARC raid, Terri's kidnapping, and Nick's eye problem, all semblance of a devotional life had gone by the wayside for him. On the other hand, he'd reached out to God more intensely than he had since his wife, Megan, had died—maybe more desperately than ever. Whether that was better or worse, he had no idea, but it struck him as time now to renew his daily quiet time, if only to thank God for helping his eye recover and providing a plan to rescue Terri. And he needed to keep praying about those things, too, because they certainly weren't yet "in the bag."

He didn't have his Bible with him, so he rummaged in a box of his personal belongings until he came up with a little Gideon New Testament and Psalms that he'd had since his time in the army and went out to muscle back the hanger door wide enough to step outside. A glittering sun was lapping up the last wisps of a thin fog that undulated over the narrow runway. He headed off down the landing strip toward the river, picking up sticks and stones and tossing them to the side so his prop wouldn't catch them on take off.

When he got to The Rock, he sat on the edge of the huge, flat-topped boulder, facing upstream, like he had that first time, his feet dangling almost to the water. Terri had sat on the downstream side so they could only see the other by turning and looking over their shoulders. It was easy to imagine her there now. He got out his magnifying glass so he could read the small print and flipped through the pages of his New Testament until he stopped at Psalm 139 in the back. Its first words were comfortingly familiar: *"O Lord, thou hast searched me, and known me. Thou knowest my downsitting and mine uprising, thou understandest my thought afar off. . . ."* But it was verse seven and eight that stopped him. *"Whither shall I go from thy spirit? or whither shall I flee from thy presence? If I ascend up into heaven, thou art there: if I make my bed in hell, behold, thou art there. . . ."*

He wondered whether Terri was finding that to be true? *Even if I feel like I'm in hell, will You be with me?* Could she really sense God's presence even though she was a captive in that green hell on the other side of the mountains? She prayed the Scriptures all the time. She seemed to know them inside and out, so well that she probably didn't even need a Bible to have devotions. In addition to praying for God to help his plans succeed, he ought to pray about that. "God, I don't know how Terri's doing right now, but be close to her like you promised in this psalm. Help her to realize *you will never leave her or forsake her.*" Wasn't that another Bible promise? "And, God, help this plan to exchange me for her to work out so she can come home. Amen."

Yes, it seemed right to pray that. Nick continued reading Psalm 139 as the writer rehearsed all the far-flung places and circumstances in which God would never leave us. The psalm ended with, *"Search me, O God, and know my heart: try me, and know my thoughts: And see if there be any wicked way in me, and lead me in the way everlasting."* He'd heard it many times and had certainly read it himself, but this time it seemed as though God was nudging him to pray it, to make the psalmist's prayer his own prayer. Did he dare invite God to search him, to know his heart and thoughts and see if there was anything wicked in him? Didn't God know all that already? Of course, but maybe there was something to inviting God to reveal them to him. Maybe that was what God wanted to do. He said the words over again, and then said them again as tears choked his eyes. Yes, he would trust God with his life at this new level. He needed something new.

When he stood up and Terri was not there behind him on The Rock to talk and laugh about a few details of the upcoming day, it didn't seem to matter so much. He had touched God, and God had responded, assuring him that God *was* present with Terri. And then God had nudged him to trust more deeply. It was a connection.

Lieutenant Ramírez, looking as fresh and crisp as ever, stuck his head in the infirmary tent. "Hey Doc, you still working on that culture for Jesús?"

He *knew* she wasn't a doctor. Why did he keep calling her that? But it didn't do any good to correct him. "Yes, I already checked it this morning. I think it's taking. Be a couple more days."

"Good. We might not need it, but just in case."

"What do you mean, we might not need it? Jesús needs—"

"I'm workin' on an alternative. But keep it going. By the way, if you can take a few minutes right now, head on over to the command tent. I've told Hernandez to try and patch you through to your people again. Same rules as before: one minute and twenty-five seconds, no details about the camp, me, or our location. Understood?"

"Yes sir. *¡Gracias! ¡Gracias!*"

She watched him walk away. What was going on? Why all the optimism and magnanimity toward her? You'd think the war was over . . . after nearly fifty years? Could it be so? "Thank you Jesus if that's true. And even if it's not, You told us to give you thanks in all circumstances."

She quickly changed the I-V for Jesús and hurried over to the command tent. Hernandez was ready to make the connection as soon as she got there. He went over the rules again, and then made the call. Moments later he said, "Okay," handed her the earphones, and looked at his watch. "Beginning now!"

Fumbling to get the earphones on, she grabbed the mic. "Hello? Who's this?"

"Welcome to First Peoples Mission. Our regular office hours are eight-thirty to five, Monday through Friday. If you know your party's extension, please dial it now. Otherwise, enter the first three letters of his or her last name, and—"

Terri searched the table in a panic. "The dial? Where are the numbers?"

Hernandez shrugged.

"¡Los números! ¿Dónde están los números del teléfono?"

Suddenly, the buzz and the repeating instructions in Terri's ear went dead. "Hello, hello. Anybody there?" She pulled the earphone away from her head and turned to Hernandez. "It went dead."

Then from outside the tent she heard Sergeant Rodriquez's voice. "Ahh! What happened, soldier? How clumsy! You cut the line. Well, no problem. Head over to maintenance and tell someone to come fix it." A moment later he poked his head in the tent. "Sorry about that, Lieutenant. One of the men had a little accident out . . . Oh." There was a crooked grin on his face. "The lieutenant's not here? Tell him we'll have it fixed by noon." Then he left.

Terri fought down her anger. "Can you try again?"

Hernandez shook his head. "Not a good idea so soon. Too easy for the army to figure out where we are."

Frustrated, Terri returned to the infirmary. She was beginning to believe that perhaps the Prince of the Power of the Air was indeed sovereign over El Despeje!

Chapter 19

The items Betty wanted Nick to retrieve from the school's kitchen clattered, didn't pack easily, and took up so much space in the back of the plane that there was little room for Nick's personal items and some of the tools he wanted to fly out of Finca Fe before they were stolen. But by noon he had boarded up the broken window in the manor house and was ready to go.

He surveyed the grounds one more time, vaguely aware that the "shade" on the peripheral vision in his left eye had dropped a little lower. It left him with the uneasy feeling that the "other boot" was about to fall, but he had no idea what that meant. He just knew that he had to have the doctor check his eye soon. At the same time, he didn't want to acknowledge there was a problem. Probably just part of the normal healing process after his operation, or maybe a slight set back, but his body was strong He'd overcome it. Right?

The sheep were again on the runway and didn't seem at all spooked by the slow approach of his taxing aircraft. In fact, Nick had to stop the plane, set the brakes, and get out to chase them away before he could take off.

Back at Neiva, Roger arrived at the airport with an academy van shortly after Nick called, and together they hauled Betty's kitchen utensils to the temporary school where the older man also showed Nick a closet that had plenty of room to store his tools and anything else.

"I'm not really back to work, yet," Roger said, clinging to the steering wheel with both hands as they drove back to the Montgomery's apartment. "Still get little dizzy spells, but you know me: can't sit around all the time."

"Yeah. I'm kinda the same way."

"I know you are." Roger squinted at Nick through his thick PhotoBrown lenses. "So, what exactly you up to, partner?"

Nick took a deep breath and blew it out, letting his lips flap like air through a balloon nozzle. Should he tell Roger his plan? He ought to let somebody know, and there was probably no one better than Roger. "You're a nosey cuss, ain't ya?"

"Always have been."

"How 'bout we talk over lunch?"

"Cheese and onion sandwich work for you?"

"Whatever you got. I'm just grateful for a place to hang my hat for a few days."

Half an hour later, Roger set food on the kitchen table and waved Nick into a chair. "So?"

Nick took a big bite of the sandwich of hard bread, sharp cheese, and thick onion slice, making his eyes water. "Well," he said around his mouthful, "I'm not sure your mission's makin' any headway on getting' Terri out. Have you heard anything hopeful in the last couple days?"

Roger looked down and shook his head. "Haven't heard a thing."

"That's what I thought. And from the rebel's point of view, I can't see why they would let her go. I mean, what's in it for them? First Peoples aren't going to pay any ransom, are they?"

Again, Roger shook his head, his mustache working under his bulbous nose.

"Anyway, I began thinking. What do they want? What do they want that we have? If it's not money, what else? And then it came to me: They were looking for a pilot, for me. So I offered them a trade."

"What?" Roger looked startled. "You for Terri?"

"Yep."

"How'd you get in touch with them?"

"You don't wanna know."

Roger stared at him. "So, just like that, they get you and release Terri?"

"That was my offer." After watching the skepticism grow in Roger's face, Nick added. "Well, they bought it. I fly in on Tuesday."

"Oh." Roger's round mouth revealed his rarely seen lips, usually hidden beneath his bushy moustache. "So it's not just you, it's also the Cessna—or rather *MAST's Cessna* you're throwin' into the pot? Guess that'd sweeten the deal."

"Well, sure. But it'd just be temporary." Nick took another bite of the sandwich.

Roger belched from his first swig of Pepsi. "Let me get this straight. You're offering your services and the plane, and you're hoping . . . you're just *hoping* they'll let Terri go. And then you think that after a little while, they'll let you and the plane go? Is that the deal?"

Nick nodded. He was getting tired of Roger playing with him.

"Know what I think?" said the older man.

"No, but I'm sure you're gonna tell me."

"I think you're a bad businessman. You always gotta make it worthwhile to the other guy to do what he says he's going to do. Never make him a loser for keepin' his promise. What I see here is Ramírez has every reason to keep you both and virtually no reason to let you go once you're under his control. That's not good business."

Nick thought about that a few moments. He didn't like the way this conversation was going. "Okay. You probably know this guy better than any of the rest of us. Is he the kind of guy who'd be inclined to go back on his word?"

"Hmm. Don't think it'd be his nature, but you're temptin' him. I don't know what he's dealing with out there. We never got that far, but there's some other men with him I wouldn't trust to wake me in a fire."

Nick leaned back and sighed. "Well, the deal's set up, so I can't back out now."

"No, that's true. It could put Terri at greater risk."

They ate in silence for a couple minutes. Then Nick said, "You know, I'm not gonna help them in any military efforts or anything. I wouldn't do that. I made that very clear."

"I wouldn't expect you to . . . knowingly."

"What's that supposed to mean?"

Roger stared at him for a few moments, then said, "You served in the military, so you know even noncombatants are just as essential to a war effort as those who pull the triggers."

Nick clamped his mouth closed. Roger was making him mad. Finally, he blurted, "I ain't claiming to be a saint, I'm just trying to get Terri outta there! The first thing Ramírez wants me to do is to fly some guy to the hospital, so maybe what I'll be doing is not that different than what they're forcing Terri to do. As I see it, once I'm there, I'll at least have more leverage to free Terri than I do now. After all, my plane won't fly by itself. If he won't keep his word, I won't fly."

"Hey, Nick. I admire you for what you're trying to do, but there are ways to make you fly! And threats to Terri's well-being could end up being one of those ways."

Nick hadn't thought of that.

Somewhat shaken by Roger's blunt talk, Nick excused himself to call Dr. Gomez and try to set up an appointment before Tuesday, but the doctor had gone to Bogotá for a weekend ophthalmology conference and wouldn't be in until Monday morning. Trying to keep busy, Nick spent the rest of the day preparing for his "trip into captivity," as he thought of it. He got more Precose pills for his diabetes. Bought a new pair of sneakers, a new poncho, a couple cans of bug spray, a canteen, a backpack to replace his ripped one, a new hat with a brim and a mosquito net—*Guess I look like bwana, now*—all things he thought he might need in the jungle. What about a pistol? If Ramírez caught him with a gun, it could be bad, but the chance he might need one in a tight spot seemed persuasive, especially if he were trying to make his escape. In Colombia, it was no harder to find a pistol than some unrefined cocaine. He picked up a 9 mm Baby Glock, and a box of ammunition for $215, U.S. It would fit nicely in the map pocket next to his seat in the Cessna.

He waited until evening when he expected everyone to have gone home for the weekend from the MAST offices, and then called the States, leaving a message on MAST's answering machine. He didn't say anything about his plans, just wanted to let them know he was back in Colombia but wasn't immediately able to take up his support duties for the missionaries in the field.

That night, the flashes in Nick's left eye were like distant sheet lightening, going off silently whenever he looked from side to side, and it seemed to him as if the curtain in his left eye had come down slightly more.

On Saturday, Lieutenant Ramírez asked Terri if she thought she could leave Jesús for most of the day. He wanted her to make a trip into Dos Ríos with Rosita. Terri knew the town was controlled by FARC, and it was where the unit got most of its supplies, but she couldn't figure why Ramírez wanted her to go there. Nevertheless, she said she thought Jesús would be okay for the day.

A half hour later, she wished she'd said no. A couple of the men climbed into the cab of the '54 Chevy pickup while she and Rosita sat in the back, wedged against each corner of the tailgate, Rosita cradling her ever-present AK-47. The driver ground the starter until the old engine roared to life, spewing a billow of blue smoke, but then they waited while it idled like an old woman trying to do the samba. In a few minutes Rodriquez, who was again *"Sargento Rodriquez,"* climbed aboard with an M-60 and belts of ammunition across his chest. "A little trip to town, eh, *guapa*?" he smirked at Terri. Then he rested the machine gun on the caved-in roof of the cab, blew out what seemed as much smoke as the engine had, and slapped the cab twice. *"Vamonos."*

Terri had to brace herself as they bounced along the rutted road and took a fast run at muddy sections in hopes of not getting stuck. But Rodriquez traveled standing up like a surfer, barely hanging on. Flecks of the red mud flipped through the rusted-out floor of the truck bed and splattered Terri's pant legs. After about an hour of rough travel, they bounced up onto a gravel road that Terri had no idea was anywhere near the camp.

"Where did this come from?"

"This road?" said Rosita.

"Yeah. How'd the government ever build a road way out here in the jungle?"

Before Rosita could answer, Rodriquez turned and gave her a sneer. "They didn't. FARC built it."

"Well, we didn't build it ourselves," Rosita corrected. "But when someone in the villages is convicted of a crime, the sentence usually is public service, often road construction, or maybe something for the community like a new well for clean water."

Not a bad idea, Terri thought.

In another thirty minutes, they came to the village of Dos Ríos, located at the confluence of Guayas River and Caguán River. The town actually sat on a peninsula formed by an oxbow in the Caguán River just before it joined the Guayas River.

"My home town," said Rosita as the pickup stopped in front of a *mercado* plastered with tin signs—Coca-Cola, Marlboro cigarettes, Coors Beer. (*Could this little store really carry all those products from the States?*) "C'mon. I'll show you around while those guys load up our supplies."

Just down from the store they passed a large shed, it's wide doors open, with several people working inside. One was wading around in a huge tray of green leaves, running a gas-powered Weedwacker through them, chopping them into tiny bits. Another was shoveling the "slaw" into 55-gallon steel drums. Others were raking a grainy white substance back and forth on blue plastic canvases out in the sun. Terri stared. "Are they making cocaine, right here in plain sight?"

"Yeah. That's their only source of income."

"And FARC doesn't try to stop it?"

"We tax 'em. How else do we get money for the Revolution? You didn't think the U.S. Government funds us, did you?" She giggled briefly. "But U.S. citizens do pay for all of this." She waved her hand indicating the whole town. "You should've seen this place when I was a *niña*. This town was as rough as—how you say it?—as your wild west? Shootings every night, prostitutes, everyone drunk. All the men gambled every peso they got trying to win a little more, 'cause there was no work. My own father was stabbed to death in a poker game. And my mother . . ." Her voice trailed off.

"I'm so sorry, Rosita," said Terri. Her heart went out to the young soldier. "But . . . you're just exporting all that evil"—she gestured toward the cocaine production—"to *my* home. It ends up Stateside in little baggies of white powder—white death!"

Rosita shrugged, but at the same time her face cringed as though she'd bitten a piece of gravel. "Well, I'm sorry, too, I really am. But we don't make anyone buy the stuff. Most campesinos would be glad to grow other crop—corn, beans, tomatoes—but even when they try, their fields get sprayed, so they have to raise the crop that makes the most money even if they lose half of it. But as you can see"—she gestured around her—"things are better now in our village. All the kids are in school. The streets are clean. There are no drunks sitting around. And the last bar fight was a couple months ago. No one got hurt, but those guys are right over there." She pointed between two whitewashed adobe houses to an open field beyond. "They're now cutting the grass on our new soccer field."

"So that's FARC justice, huh? That's a lot of grass to cut."

"Yeah. We don't throw people in jail anymore, not unless they're totally uncontrollable and a danger to others."

Terri had to admit the town appeared to be one of the neatest, most pleasant villages she'd seen in Colombia. Is that why Ramírez sent her along on this supply run, to indoctrinate her in the "virtues" of FARC? Still, she knew what was on the other end of the drug trade—from rich yuppies frying their brains in the suburbs to gang wars on the streets of Chicago where a kid could easily make a thousand dollars a night supplying those yuppies . . . if he didn't get shot or go to jail or both.

Terri brought her thoughts back to the present. "How 'bout the army? If this is a FARC town, doesn't the army attack it?"

"Who would they shoot? The storeowner? The teachers? All the campesinos from the surrounding farms? How can they tell who is FARC? We come and go. All the people support us, but the town's not a military unit. And the army can't afford to police every little village. Now, eight kilometers downriver there's Catagena Del Chairá with a population of 7,500. They do have government police there and the army comes and goes as it pleases, sometimes making raids out into the jungle. But there are also plenty of trustworthy people even in that town who support us."

The two women had arrived at the end of the main street where it emptied onto an enormous beach, a sandbar the length of three soccer fields across the end of the peninsula like a flat fingernail on the end of the land's thumb. Kids were playing everywhere. Various boats were beached on the upstream side, some aluminum, some canoes with outboard motors. From one of the larger canoes, an old man struggled to transfer a huge blue-tarp bundle of what Terri assumed was newly cut coca leaves onto a wooden-wheeled cart.

She watched for a moment, thinking the man was going to lose control and dump the whole load into the water, but then she turned and gazed downriver. *Just a few kilometers away were government police officers, perhaps the army, and the prospect of freedom.*

Chapter 20

In spite of the recent deluge—perhaps the last one for this rainy season—dust boiled over the back of the speeding pickup and settled on the occupants like rust-colored pollen. It was a good thing Terri had learned to spit while living rough, because there was no room to maneuver and pull out a handkerchief while sitting among the sacks of flour and cornmeal, bags of beans and tins of oil and other supplies as they headed back to camp.

Her excursion to Dos Ríos had been a refreshing break from FARC camp life, but the contradictions she'd observed troubled her. Seemingly, the only way for these poor people to survive came from an addictive pharmaceutical industry defended by violent revolutionaries. She had faced a similar dilemma in Chicago where it took an unusually strong moral resolve for kids to resist dealing drugs when it seemed as if the only alternative was a minimum wage job at McDonald's. Some of the brightest, most polite, and capable young entrepreneurs she'd ever met were kids from the streets who had ended up in her ER at Cook County Hospital. They weren't junkies. "Blow" was for the fools from the suburbs. They were just young "businessmen" who had encountered a "lead" setback.

Sometimes the world seemed so upside down. *Maranatha, come quickly Lord Jesus!*

As the truck came around a bend in the road, the driver slammed on the brakes and the pickup skidded sideways. A tree lay across their path. Terri began to rise up on her knees to see what was going on when Rodriquez turned around and knocked her to the floor. "Stay down!" He put one foot on her shoulder and pushed. "Make sure she stays down, all the way down behind those bags."

Everything was quiet as the last of the dust floated like microscopic confetti twinkling in the blistering sun. Suddenly, there was a pop from the tree line, then Rodriquez, Rosita, and the two men in the front opened up with their automatic weapons, spraying both sides of the road in a steady roar, interrupted by momentary breaks as one weapon or another seemed to gasp for breath. In those pauses, Terri heard the cacophonous firing from the assailants in the trees, some of it pinging off the pickup. And then came explosions, first on one side and then on the other, so loud that all that followed was swallowed by the ringing in her ears.

The battle couldn't have lasted more than a minute and a half before silence returned. Air that had been stirred to the speed of lead, now hung heavy with the scent of cordite, ripped metal, and vaporized gun oil. Terri heard Rodriquez speaking as though he were at the other end of a long cotton tunnel, "Pull Talavera over. Rosita, get up there and drive. You can make it around the end of that tree. Just go for it."

In a moment, Rosita started the engine and roared down into the ditch, around the top end of the tree, and back up onto the road. Slowly, Terri sat up. Rodriquez was still standing, but blood was spreading from his shoulder down the back of his camouflaged shirt like an advancing plague. "You're hit!"

"Yeah, but not like Talavera. They got him good."

It was then that Terri noticed the driver's head, lolling over the back of the seat, the top blown off, blood smearing the back window of the cab. *O God, have mercy.*

She tried to control the shaking in her voice. "You need to sit down so I can attend to your shoulder."

"No way!" He locked a new belt of ammunition into his M-60 and pulled back the bolt to cock it. "Could be more paramilitaries. Do what you can, but I'm staying up here."

Terri pulled open the first aid pack on Rodriquez's belt and noticed it was U.S. Army.

"No morphine!" he shouted back at her.

She stood up behind him, jockeying to keep from falling, and ripped open his shirt. The wound, which looked to have come from shrapnel, was bleeding freely, but there was no pink foam, no gurgling bubbles to suggest the lungs had been punctured. Terri slapped on the field dressing and pulled the ribbons so tight Rodriquez cried out, "Hey! Take it easy!" But if she didn't get enough pressure to stop that bleeding, he might pass out soon.

She finished just as Rosita turned off the gravel road onto the trail that led to camp. Only then did Rodriquez feel safe enough—or so weak—that he sat down on the bags of flour. He kept his machine gun across his lap as he leaned forward, resting his elbows on his knees and his head in his hands. "*Gracias.*"

Terri didn't know what to say, so she remained silent as they bounced through the jungle. Rodriquez probably saved her life back there by pushing her down onto the bed of the truck. And then another thought struck her: What if that attack was an attempt to rescue *her*, and the sergeant had only pinned her to the floor to prevent her from bolting over the side and running for freedom? Even if it wasn't a rescue attempt, could she have gotten away in the middle of the chaos, run into the trees, and hooked up with the paramilitaries as soon as the shooting stopped? What if they weren't paramilitaries at all, but army soldiers? She hadn't actually seen any of the attackers, and she wasn't sure she would've been able to tell who they were even if she had seen them.

But she couldn't get the thought out of her mind: She hadn't made it over the mountains. Now, had she blown a second chance at freedom?

By Sunday morning, Nick was scared! A quarter of the peripheral vision in his left eye had gone dark, and he didn't know what was happening. This was different than the dark islands that had spread when his eye had hemorrhaged. It was like a curtain falling on the stage of his sight. When would the curtain stop falling? If this kept up, his left eye would again be useless. He sat at the breakfast table with his right eye tightly closed, trying to map just how far the darkness in his left eye had invaded his sight.

"You okay?" asked Roger as he shuffled to the table with coffee in his hand.

"Uh, having more trouble with my eye. Hoping to see Dr. Gomez tomorrow." He took a deep breath and reached for the milk to pour on his cereal. Then he picked up the Cheerios box. "Cheerios," he read the larger print, "distributed by General Mills, Minneapolis, Minnesota. You think they ship this stuff all the way from the States, or does General Mills have a plant down here?"

"Wouldn't know." Roger sat down. "Want to talk about it?"

"What, the Cheerios?" Nick shook his head. "Just makin' conversation."

"Of course not the Cheerios. Who gives a rip? I meant your eye."

Nick shrugged. "What's to talk about? I simply don't know what's happening."

"But you know how you're feelin'. You can talk about that."

"What are you now? Some kind of a shrink?"

"No. Just a friend . . . sometimes a guy needs a friend."

Nick hesitated. Then . . . "Don't know how I feel. I got a lot on my mind, and I just gotta make it through. Know what I mean?"

"Sure. Oh, by the way, I don't mean to put more on your plate, but somebody from your mission, MAST, called last night. They want you to get in touch with them."

"Yeah, I bet, but I just can't deal with them right now."

They ate in silence—Nick and his Cheerios and Roger and his coffee and toast. In a few minutes, Betty bustled in. "Well, aren't we a chipper bunch this morning? Hey Nick, want to come to church with us? I found this little local congregation on this side of town, *La Iglesia Christiana*, some of the dearest people you could ever meet. Why don't you come?"

"I didn't say for sure *I* was goin'," injected Roger.

"Of course you are. You're plenty well enough."

"Yeah, 'spose I can say this bandage around my head is a halo, and no one will ask any questions. Think that'll work?"

"Poof. If that's a halo, somebody needs to tell you it's been slipping a little bit lately, and church'll do you some good! How about it, Nick? You wanna come with us, too?"

The small storefront, converted into a church, was packed. Lots of grinning kids racing around while the praise team set up the keyboard and drums on the makeshift stage and the guitar and base player tuned their instruments.

"All right, everybody, let's find our seats and get started." Seats were plastic red, yellow, green, and blue stackables for the kids up front and benches for everyone else.

Nick urged Roger and Betty to sit down while he hung back to see if there were enough places for everyone. But a leather-faced usher with glossy black hair wouldn't allow him to stand and tapped one of the members on the shoulder to surrender his seat. Nick tried to wave him off, but there was no deterring the man. At least he was close enough to the back to not attract too much attention as a gringo. He didn't want anyone asking him to come forward and "say a few words." *Just let me be and get used to this!* He actually hadn't been in church since he'd left Finca Fe.

They sang several songs and then seemed to get stuck on "Santo Es Tu Nombre." Some of the women and children were dancing in the front, twirling in their brightly colored dresses, smacking tambourines while they repeated the words: "Holy is your name. Holy is your name." Nick realized that their shrill voices did not grate on him as they might have in any other setting. Perhaps it had something to do with their authenticity, and a wave of longing rolled over him. Praising the Lord with abandon, that's what Terri would do, but why couldn't he?

A couple of the men joined in the dancing, awkwardly swaying around, not smiling down to humor the children or impress the women, but with hands held high, looking up as if the only thing that mattered was praising the Lord. You could laugh at them like Michal had laughed at King David, but Nick knew they wouldn't care. They would probably say what David said: *"I will celebrate before the Lord. I will become even more undignified than this."*

But when they began singing, "Lávame," Nick wiped a tear from his eyes when he realized what the words meant: "Wash me in the waters of your pardon. Purify me, cleanse my life and my heart. Time and time again, like this time, I need to be washed by you." Could he really say that? Did he really mean it? He knew he needed it. But did he dare? He couldn't stop wiping his eyes during the message, delivered by the wiry, young pastor who urged the people to *"Seek the Lord while he may be found; call on him while he is near,"* from Isaiah 55:6.

Was this his chance to reach out and touch the Lord again? But could he . . . after so many prayers about his vision seemed to have gone unanswered?

Roger Montgomery insisted on driving Nick to the doctor's office the next morning. "What makes you think I can't drive?" he shot back when Nick protested. "I'm not dizzy and I can see better than you can. Besides, I'm off work this whole week. What else am I supposed to do with my days?"

"Well, thanks for the early start, 'cause I sure hope this doesn't take all day. You may have the day off, but I've got stuff to do," said Nick.

But Dr. Gomez hadn't yet arrived when they entered the waiting room.

"Do you have an appointment for today, señor?" asked the twenty-something assistant as she eyed her computer screen.

"No, not exactly. But I think this is an emergency, and the doctor told me to get in touch with him if I was having any problems."

"Okay. We'll let him know as soon as he arrives."

Nick and Roger flipped through magazines for a half hour without saying much to each other until a nurse finally invited Nick into a dimly lit exam room, asked a few questions, and put some drops in his eyes to dilate them. Another half hour passed while Nick hoped Roger wasn't regretting his decision to accompany him. Finally, Dr. Gomez came in and asked what seemed to be the problem. Nick explained about the darkening curtain, and the doctor examined him with the slit lamp Nick had become familiar with, as well as a hand-held lens and other instruments.

"You said this began after you fell and hit your head?"

"Actually, I hit right there by my eye, on my cheek bone and eyebrow."

"Was there a lot of pain?"

"Not as I recall."

"But you were having flashes?"

"Yeah. Like a strobe light off to the side every time I looked quickly in that direction."

Dr. Gomez wrote on Nick's chart for a few minutes, then he tucked it under his arm and cleared his throat as though something unpleasant were stuck there. "Any surgery is traumatic to the body. That's why you wore that shield over your eye for the first few nights. The whole eye was weakened. But it was healing nicely until this blow to your eye. That was more than it could take in its delicate condition. A retinal tear seems to have resulted."

Nick flinched. This didn't sound good.

"Fluid has been leaking through that tear, getting between the retina and what we call the sclera or the wall of the eyeball. The more fluid, the more the retina pulls away, something like when wet wallpaper peels away from the wall of your house before it dries. You described it perfectly when you said it was like a blind or a curtain coming down. So far, the tear is not too big, but unless we stop it, the retina will continue to detach resulting in total blindness. Time is of the essence. You're fortunate that it hasn't progressed faster. This is an emergency. Hours count. We need to schedule corrective surgery for today. I'll cancel some other appointments and make the arrangements with the hospital."

Nick took a deep breath. "Today?" He let out air. "Well, okay. I guess today's better than tomorrow. Tomorrow I've got an important appointment I don't dare miss."

Dr. Gomez chuckled. "You won't be doing anything tomorrow or for the next several days. Let me explain what we have to do."

Chapter 21

A crawling feeling traveled up Nick's shoulders and neck as his next breath eluded him. "I—I can't miss my appointment tomorrow. In . . . in fact, I'm going to be tied up for several days. Is there anything we can do to kinda postpone this?"

Dr. Gomez frowned. "Mr. Archer, I'm not sure you're getting the picture. If the detachment were to progress over the macula—that's the 'bull's-eye' center of the retina, the place where you focus—the chance of visual recovery is greatly reduced, and the longer it is detached, the worse. You're likely to end up totally blind in that eye. Given the risk of hemorrhage in your right eye because of the diabetes, I would not recommend gambling against those odds."

"Well . . ." Nick looked around the dimly lit examining room as though searching for an escape. "Uh, is this the kind of thing I ought to get a second opinion on?"

"By all means. Second opinions are always wise, especially when the stakes are so high. There aren't any other retinal ophthalmologists in Neiva, but in Bogotá . . ."

"How about calling Dr. Norman back in the States?"

"That would be good. You can call from here and talk to him alone if you want, or . . . I'd be glad to get on the line for part of the call and explain what my exam reveals, then you could talk to him."

Nick agreed and soon the assistant at the front desk put the call through. After Dr. Gomez explained what he had observed, Dr. Norman asked several technical questions while Nick listened in. Then Dr. Gomez excused himself, and Nick's Stateside doctor spoke to him. "I'm sorry to hear of this setback, Mr. Archer. It sounds like your recovery was going well until you had this . . . this accident."

Nick didn't think it was necessary to explain that the "accident" involved being thrown handcuffed into a concrete wall by revolutionary guerrillas. How he'd received a blow to his eye was not as important as discussing what had to be done now. Dr. Norman, however, was as adamant as Dr. Gomez that prompt surgery was essential.

The call ended. Nick sat alone in the small examining room trying to decide what he should do. He had a deal with FARC, a deal that promised to free Terri. As Roger had said, it might not succeed, but it was the most promising option to date. Now, however, it looked as if the price had risen for him to keep his side of the bargain. Nick might have to sacrifice the sight in his eye. Could he do it? What would his life be like if he could never fly again? What would he do?

Nick sat still a few more moments, breathing heavily. On the other hand, how could he ever live with himself if he didn't do everything possible to rescue Terri?

He had no choice. Nick went out to tell Dr. Gomez his decision, but the doctor was busy with another patient.

"So, what's up?" asked Roger. He was the only one in the waiting room.

Nick explained, pacing as he talked. Finally, he concluded: "Is it hot in here?"

With his head tilted, Roger eyed him for a moment. "Not particularly. Leastwise, don't seem that way to me."

"Well, I'm drippin'." Nick walked to the window and looked down on the city. "You don't agree with my decision, do ya?"

"It's not for me to agree or disagree. You want to trade the sight in one eye for a chance to get Terri out of there? Only you can make that choice."

"But . . .?"

"I didn't say 'but.'" Roger raised both hands.

"But you're thinkin' it."

"What if I am?"

"Well?" Nick walked back and sat down opposite Roger.

"You really want to know what I think?" Roger waited for Nick to nod. "I was with those guys for a while. They murdered Miss Van Loon. Shot me, thinkin' they'd killed me, too. They're terrorists, Nick. After fifty years of fightin', they've forgotten the ideals for which they took up arms. Now they're no different than the drug cartels. I don't think you can trust 'em. But that's my view on it. Take it for what it's worth."

Nick leaned forward, elbows on his knees, head in his hands as he stared at the floor. Roger's insights ought to be worth a lot. He ought to heed his advice, but . . . In a matter of moments he found himself searching from left to right across the floor with his bad eye, flashes firing whenever he jerked his sight around. Had the "curtain" fallen even more? A shiver gripped him.

"Tell you what I am willin' to do," said Roger, his voice barely penetrating Nick's fears. Nick looked up to see the glint in the older man's squinted eyes. "If you choose to get this surgery, I'll drive up to Otás tomorrow and tell those buzzards what has happened. I'll tell 'em you'll be out of commission for a few days, but then you'll arrange a new rendezvous as soon as you can fly again. At least that way you'd have a shot at saving your sight."

"What makes you think they won't shoot you the moment they lay eyes on you, finish what they started?"

"They never planned on killing me. It was just the heat of the moment—though I doubt I could convince Betty of that."

"See, we're both the same," said Nick with a wave of his hand. "You're worried about me takin' a risk, but you're ready to do the same for me."

"No! It ain't the same. They knew kidnapping me was a mistake. I'm too old, more of a liability than I'm worth. I doubt they'd have any interest in me again."

"You ain't that old. They could get ransom for you."

"We don't pay ransom. Remember?"

Nick shook his head. "That still leaves Terri at their mercy for who knows how long. And she doesn't even know we're trying to help."

"Oh, she knows. She knew while we were hiking up that mountain. But she puts her trust in Jesus. He'll make a way."

"Yeah, but what if *I* am that way?"

"Nick, you ain't."

"Whadda you mean? Aren't we supposed to be God's hands and feet on this earth?"

"It's a fine point, Nick, a fine point. But trust me, you ain't *the way* like you're thinkin' of it!"

Nick blew out a frustrated breath. "Well, I still gotta do what I can."

"Hmph. Figured you would. I'll go get the car and meet you down front."

When Dr. Gomez came out, Nick thanked him and assured him that he accepted his analysis of how dangerous waiting was. "But someone's life may depend on my keeping my appointment tomorrow. I'll be back for the procedure as soon as I can."

With thick high clouds over the jungle and a fog drifting among the trees, Tuesday morning felt claustrophobic to Terri. Until Lieutenant Ramírez bounded up onto the infirmary platform more out of breath than he should have been after only running from the command tent. "Get Jesús ready to travel. I'll have an ambulance here for him in twenty minutes."

"Where are we going? Florencia? I have the culture ready!"

"Not Florencia. I already told you that. We're taking him to Dos Ríos. Now hurry, and be careful." Then he was gone.

What was in Dos Ríos? Certainly Rosita would've proudly pointed out a hospital or even a doctor's office had the "model" town had one.

When the "ambulance" pulled up at the infirmary ten minutes later, it was just one of the old pickups FARC used, this one equipped with a battered camper shell mounted on the back. A couple men brought a stretcher in and loaded Jesús on it. "Where am I going?" The boy looked around like an old man with Alzheimer's. "Where am I going?"

But the stretcher-bearers only shrugged. Finally one of them said, "Your dad . . . I mean, the lieutenant's taking you somewhere."

That seemed to satisfy the boy. He laid his head back and closed his eyes again.

When Terri climbed in the back with Jesús, one of the men challenged her. "Where you think you are going? We were only told to pick up Jesús."

"He's my patient, and anywhere he goes, I go."

The soldier shrugged and turned away.

As they left camp, the old Chevy pickup with a machine gunner standing behind the cab, weapon at the ready, went first. Several other soldiers sat in the back. Lieutenant Ramírez rode in the front of the "ambulance," and hadn't acknowledged Terri except to look momentarily in the doorless back of the camper to see that Jesús was okay.

They traveled more slowly along the rutted jungle road, perhaps out of deference to the wounded man in back, but once they got to the gravel road, their speed increased until it seemed recklessly fast, fast enough to foil another ambush, Terri hoped.

When they slowed, Terri began to recognize the occasional roadside houses, a narrow bridge, then the dusty streets of Dos Ríos, the store, and the cocaine shed. The vehicle turned and went down a slight hill and onto the large beach. Ramírez opened his door even before they stopped and jumped out, slamming it behind him. "Cover that man!" Terri heard him yell.

Terri heard more loud voices as she began to climb out of the back of the camper—men yelling, Ramírez ordering, "Search him! Search the plane! Keep him on the ground!" She hopped down onto the sand herself and turned toward all the action.

A red and white plane—Nick's plane?—sat on the long beach. And Nick! It *was* Nick, spread-eagle on the ground, three men around him, weapons pointed at his head.

"No!" she screamed as she ran toward him. "What are you doing?"

"Stay back!" Ramírez grabbed her arm.

"But what are you doing? Let him up!" She wrenched herself free and ran the remaining steps, shouldering one of the guards aside as she crashed into the circle and fell on Nick.

"*Ooph!* Is that you, Terri? What's happening?"

"That's what I want to know." She raised herself up, glaring at Lieutenant Ramírez. "What's going on here? Nick hasn't done anything! Put your guns down!" Her words were so commanding, the men let the muzzles of their weapons sag toward the ground.

"I know this plane," Ramírez snapped. "High wing, belly as fat as a pregnant guppy, and those numbers." He pointed toward the plane. "4-9-T, 4-9-T, those were the numbers on the white and red plane spotting for the paramilitaries when we got hit!"

Terri and Nick were getting to their feet, but Terri held him behind her with her hands. "No! This is Nick Archer, the pilot you were looking for. Of course, you saw his plane before, it was sitting right there on the field at Finca Fe when you kidnapped me."

"No. Keep him covered!" The men raised their weapons again. "I never saw the plane at your school. I was inside the building with all your people. But I have seen this airplane before, when it flew low over us, spotting for the paramilitaries. That's when Jesús got wounded. I remember the numbers on the side of his plane: 4-9-T."

"But that's just the last three numbers. There could be a lot of planes with those numbers in its license," Terri protested.

"Hold on." Nick moved around in front of Terri. "Maybe he has seen my Cessna. I fly for MAST, the Missionary Aviation Support Team, so I fly over these jungles all the time. And I was stationed out of the school you attacked. So maybe you saw my plane there and didn't realize it. But I'm no spotter for anyone. I'm here to follow through on our deal. You gonna keep your end of the bargain or not?"

Terri touched his shoulder. "What bargain? Nick, what deal did you make?"

Everyone was silent while Nick and Ramírez stared at one another. Finally, the lieutenant spat. "How'd you make contact with us? Who gave you Pablo's name?"

"Steven Lang. He had an address for this fat guy who phoned Pablo."

"Who's Steven Lang?"

"He's . . . he's just a guy I met a long time ago. Look, I got nothing to hide. Let's just say he owed me—"

"So Steven Lang owed you, huh? As a matter of fact, I *do* know who he is. But why would a CIA agent owe you?"

"Nick? What's he talking about? Who's CIA—"

"Teniente Ramírez." It was the man who'd been searching Nick's plane. He was approaching the small group clustered on the beach, holding up a pistol in his left hand.

The lieutenant took the gun and weighted it in his hand to feel the balance. "A Glock. Very nice, but not a Bible, not what most missionaries carry, is it?" He ejected the clip. "My, my, and loaded, too." He slammed the clip back in, cocked it, and raised the weapon, sighting over the barrel at Nick as though he admired the view. "So tell me, Señor Archer, why *exactly* did the CIA owe you? What were you doing for them? Spotting, maybe? Don't stand there winking at me like we have some joke between us. This is no joke!"

Chapter 22

Nick tried to stop his left eye from blinking, only half aware that the curtain Dr. Gomez had warned about might keep falling. At that moment, his vision didn't much matter if his whole plan unraveled, if Ramírez shot him right there on the Dos Ríos beach. But he couldn't seem to control the involuntary reaction in his eye. And how much did he need to tell Ramírez? How much did the man already know? Too much, Nick feared. Truth was the only hope.

"Look, you're right. Steven Lang tried to get me to report on what he called the 'migration of indigenous peoples.' At first, I believed him when he said he worked for some preservation organization, the Amazon Tribal Institute, I think he called it. But when farmers' fields turned yellow a few days after I reported them, I figured I was being used—"

"Nick, how could you?" Terri's voice rose in alarm. "You know it's against mission policy to assist any government agency."

He glanced at Terri and raised both palms. "But I quit! As soon as I realized who Lang was. That was eighteen months ago." He looked back at Ramírez, down the wrong end of the gun's sights. "Like I said, I quit immediately. I—I even refused to take any money. That's when Lang told me he was CIA and said if I ever needed a favor . . . Anyway, when I was desperate to contact you, I remembered that he said he knew some FARC people. So I gave him a call. He's the one who told me how to get in touch with Pablo."

Nick raised his hands. "The pistol—could you please put it down? With all these men around, I'm not gonna try anything." But Ramírez kept it pointed right at Nick's head. "All right, all right," Nick said. He looked down at the ground for a moment, trying to control the twitch that had taken over his eye. When he looked up again, he said, "And I'm not winkin' at you. I can't help it. One of your guys did this to me when I was at Pablo's. He slammed me into a concrete wall. I'm liable to loose my sight over it."

Terri grabbed his arm. "Oh Nick, let me see!"

"Get back, Doc." Ramírez reached out and gently pushed Terri away as he slowly lowered the pistol and stared at Nick. "A year and a half ago, huh? Then how come I saw your plane a month ago when we were being attacked?"

"I have no idea what you're talking about . . . unless—" Memory of the pink tracers that had stitched their way across his wing came back to mind. "Unless you were the guys who shot up my plane. But I wasn't spotting for anyone. I was just flying home from delivering some medicine. You can ask Terri. I got back with holes in my wings. Take a look at the patches yourself." He pointed toward the plane.

Ramírez's eyes hardened. "Señor Archer, they say the best lie is *almost* the whole truth, and I think that's what you've just told me. But when I add everything up, I don't like what I hear. You're a pilot. You've worked for the CIA. You were in the vicinity when we were attacked, and Jesús was almost killed. Now you tell me you've been back in touch with the CIA, and you want me to let you take my son in your airplane—"

"Your son?" Nick's face grimaced in unbelief. What was the lieutenant saying? The wounded man Nick was supposed to transport to Venezuela was this officer's son? Is that what this was all about?

"Yes, *my* son! Of course, you anticipated I would send along a guard, so you hid a loaded gun under your seat. I don't like those odds, Mr. Archer. You're not taking my son anywhere. The deal's off."

He turned away, and then glanced at one of his men. "Shoot him and get rid of the body. We'll dismantle the plane and hide it later."

"NO!" Terri ran after him. "You can't do that! You can't shoot him!" She grabbed his arm. "If you shoot him, I . . . I . . . I won't care for your son!"

That turned Ramírez around. In a voice Nick could barely hear, he growled, "You wouldn't dare!"

"I could, and I would. You could beat me, you could even shoot me, but if you kill Nick, I will not treat your son under any circumstances."

Ramírez glanced back at the "ambulance" that held his son, and then over Terri's head he glared at Nick. He jerked his chin toward the Cessna. "All right. Get out of here!" he yelled at Nick. Then he pointed at Terri. "But you're going to take care of Jesús!"

She backed away from him. "Yes. I will." Then she walked back to Nick and hugged him.

"Why did you say that?" Nick hissed. "The man's not playing!"

"They would have shot you," she whispered.

"Yeah, but I'm still scared for you!" He pulled her head to his chest. "Are you okay? Are you getting enough to eat? Is anyone bothering you?"

"No, no. I'm okay. It's better than you think. Believe me, I'm safe. But you're not. You've gotta go!"

"Can you get away and come back to this beach?" he whispered, still holding her close. "I could pick you up . . . later."

"Enough talking," Ramírez shouted from a distance. "Get outta here before I change my mind."

Terri untangled himself from Nick. "You gotta go. We're hours from here." She backed away and spoke in a normal voice. "Call my family. Tell them I'm okay," she called after him as he headed for the plane.

As Nick climbed into his plane, he hesitated, then called to Ramírez who was standing by the pickup. "What would it cost to buy her freedom?"

"More than you've got!"

"But how much?"

"Forget it!" The commander waved his hand dismissively as he started to walk away. Then he turned back and gave Nick a dead-eye stare. *"¡Un millón de dólares, Americanos!"*

Terri watched as the red and white Cessna taxied to the upstream end of the sandbar and turned around. It remained stationary as Nick ran the engine up to full throttle, blowing sand back over the river. Then the brakes released, and the plane jostled past them like a lumbering bird, slowly gaining enough speed to leap into the air before it reached the water and skimmed down the river. She'd watched Nick take off so many times, but this time it was over the Amazon Basin instead of their comfortable home at Finca Fe.

Unfortunately, Nick would not be returning before dark or with the next day's dawn. She closed her eyes for a moment. The memory of his arm around her felt as fresh as if he was still standing there, but she knew she might never feel that security again. "O God," she breathed, "from the beginning You said it was not good for man to be alone. And I know that applies equally to women. So can't You provide a helper suitable for me? Your Word says nothing is too hard for You. Work a miracle, Lord; let it be Nick."

Lieutenant Ramírez's voice startled her out of her reverie. "Move it. Let's get out of here."

Terri climbed into the back of the "ambulance" and checked on Jesús. She turned up the drip on his I-V, and then sat on the floor facing the open back of the camper shell, watching the dirt streets and houses of Dos Ríos recede from view. Why was she praying about Nick becoming her "helpmate" as if they had the option of moving into a house with a picket-fence in the suburbs, when in reality she was the captive of a bunch of guerrillas in the jungles of South America? Shouldn't she be dealing with first things, first? And yet, it seemed as if being with Nick was the most important thing right now.

In spite of the sickening feeling in the pit of his stomach, Nick adjusted the fuel mixture and the prop's pitch as the Cessna settled into the climb that would take it high enough to clear the mountains.

What had gone wrong with the plan to secure Terri's release? Had Ramírez never intended to make the trade? No, he'd wanted to get his son to a hospital. So what was it? Nick reviewed the events of the day.

He'd flown to Otás just as he'd been instructed by Pablo. The landing on the gravel road east of town had occurred without incident. He had stood outside his plane for several minutes. At first he had a sense someone was watching him, maybe from the rocks in the hill above, but when no one stood up to wave or give him a signal, he began to worry that the plan would fall through. Then suddenly, he heard the roar of an engine, and a jeep bounced up out of a ravine he hadn't seen just a sort distance up the road. Two men stood in back aiming automatic weapons at him as the jeep approached. He'd put his hands on top of his head as he'd been instructed to do and waited until they stopped, and one man jumped out to search him.

No problem. There was a brief argument as the men vied for who would drive back in the jeep and who would fly with Nick. It was pretty clear that none of them had been up in a plane before and weren't eager for the adventure. Finally, the youngest soldier was pushed forward.

Nick's FARC passenger kept a pistol on his lap when they took off, but Nick had grinned to himself: If he'd wanted to take control, one quick stall and the kid's heart would be in his throat as he begged for mercy. Nick wouldn't need to touch the Glock in the door pocket. But he couldn't go that route. His plan required cooperation, so he flew as smoothly as possible.

They had landed without incident on the sandbar at Dos Ríos and waited until Ramírez and Terri arrived. All had gone according to plan . . . until Ramírez recognized his plane.

Nick shook his head. There was nothing he could've done about that, but maybe he should've refused to leave when Ramírez had "let him go." After all, they had a deal, and he'd kept his end of the bargain. Surely he could've thought of something to reassure Ramírez. Why had he left so quickly? Okay, he knew why! Because the guy had already ordered him shot, and Nick believed his men would've gladly followed through.

Admit it, he told himself. *You were scared.* That's why he'd gotten out of there. Or maybe—what was it Shakespeare had said? "The better part of valor is discretion." But as Nick recalled, that was Falstaff's rationale for cowardice. Not much comfort there. And yet, "He who lives to fight another day, rules!" Nick shook his head. This was foolishness. There were proverbs to justify anything. He'd better stick to the Bible like Terri did.

He glanced out his side window and thought he saw something familiar. Why not? He'd flown over this area a dozen times. And yet . . . He grabbed his chart out of the side pocket and his mother's magnifying glass from his shirt pocket so he could read the fine print. Where was it when he'd been shot at several weeks ago? Yeah, this was it—right down there. He remembered the coordinates he'd planned to report to the army, but when he'd failed to raise anyone in the Florencia tower, he'd forgotten about it. But there it was, a thousand feet below, the field—probably cocaine—beside the narrow road that led into San Lucas. That's where he'd taken fire. But San Lucas wasn't a FARC base. Word would've gotten out, and besides, the army sometimes paid visits to the villages. Though since declaring the area "El Despeje," they'd pretty much ignored the region.

Nick put the plane into a steep bank and circled over the small village, tracing the road in and out of it before it disappeared under the jungle cover. Nick felt certain this area was Ramírez's theater of operations. Had the army ever pinpointed the coordinates of the radio transmission? Yes, they'd done that once, but the position they had calculated had been twelve kilometers west of here, and for the next call, as Nick recalled, they said the broadcast came from some other place, though the transmission didn't last long enough to pinpoint the location.

But twelve kilometers west of here would have been back toward Dos Ríos. Nick leveled his plane and cut the throttle to half to allow the plane to descend more quietly. He didn't want to get too low and attract more ground fire, but he wanted to be close enough to spot anything out of the ordinary to the right or the left.

He closed his eyes and rubbed his forehead. Perhaps what he *couldn't* see had as much to do with the condition of his eyes as with the hypnotic monotony of the sculpted carpet of forest below him. He blinked, trying to focus. Was the curtain continuing to fall in his left eye as Dr. Gomez had said it might? *"If the detachment progresses over the macula . . . the chance of visual recovery is greatly reduced, and the longer it is detached, the worse. You're likely to end up blind in that eye."*

He blinked again, straining to focus on what was below him. And there . . . right *there*, carved out of the forest, was a landing strip! Or were his eyes playing tricks on him? No, it didn't go away when he blinked. It *was* a strip, not unusual for this side of the mountains. Small villages often had an adjacent landing strip—that's how he delivered supplies to several missionaries. Oil and mining companies built strips wherever they were developing the resources. Sometimes the government put one in near a meteorological or other environmental testing station. They were all over the Amazon basin.

But this one—he quickly checked his location by GPS and compared it to his chart—this one was not on the map. There was a small river just beyond the strip, and he found the river on the chart, but no indication of an airstrip. And rising from the jungle canopy a hundred meters beyond was a haze of blue smoke. Or was that his eyes again? It could be a blur in his vision, but Nick didn't think so.

"That's gotta be Ramírez's FARC camp. I'm sure of it!" Nick muttered as he banked the Cessna away, still in a semi-glide, hoping to remain as quiet as possible until he got as far away as possible.

The more Nick thought about that airstrip, the more sense everything made. When Ramírez had raided Finca Fe, he'd been looking for two things: A doctor—obviously to care for his wounded son—and a pilot and plane, probably to help with the insurgency. But a plane would be of no use unless you had an airstrip for its base, one that was close enough for easy access as well as the ability to defend it.

But the reason Ramírez had not directed him to land at his "private" strip to pick up the boy was also obvious: To do so would have revealed the exact location of his base. So he had Nick land at Dos Ríos—close, but not too close.

That had to be it! A flicker of hope ate away at his sense of failure. Pushing the throttle in, Nick began climbing over the mountain range. But he'd be back!

Chapter 23

"Well, Mr. Archer, glad to see you back so soon." Dr. Gomez swung the headrest for the slit lamp around in front of Nick and pulled his stool close enough to begin the exam. "How's the eye?"

"Not sure." Nick rested his chin on the support. "It doesn't seem too much worse."

"I hope not. But even waiting one more day was a dangerous gamble." He leaned forward. "Let's have a look."

The slit lamp that Nick had previously experienced as brighter than staring into the headlight of an oncoming train, didn't even penetrate the "curtain" as it had the hemorrhage. He was afraid he knew why: The blood from the hemorrhage had indeed been something through which a bright enough light could shine. But the detached retina was not actually a curtain blocking his vision. He was unable to see anything in its area because the photoreceptors in the eye that recorded light—the actual cones and rods—were virtually "unplugged" after being pulled loose from the wall of the eye.

"Well, you're a lucky man," said Dr. Gomez after a few minutes. "It's progressed only slightly. Wish we could have caught it on Monday, though. You prepared to let me operate today?" The tone in his voice was almost a threat, as though he might wash his hands of the case if Nick continued to delay treatment.

Nick nodded. "Yes. I did all I could . . . in terms of my business, at least for now. We can go ahead." But had he really done all he could? What kind of a man was he to leave the "love of his life"—as he was starting to think of Terri—with a band of kidnappers? His mind transported to that sandbar in the middle of the jungle.

What if he had . . . But that didn't matter. He'd located the FARC camp, and as soon as he got his eye fixed, he'd fly back out there and get Terri. Perhaps he could drop in at dusk, make a dead-stick landing, and then—

"Mr. Archer? You with me here, man?" The doctor's voice pulled him back to the darkened room. "You need to go over to the hospital and check in. My assistant out front will call ahead and make the arrangements. I'll be there as soon as possible, but you need to understand that even though this is an emergency, I can't neglect my other patients. Some of them also need attention today."

Nick recalled how he'd been in and out of the hospital in a few hours in Chicago. "Is this going to take all day?"

"Hopefully not. But I should explain a little more of what you can anticipate." He leaned back against an exam table and crossed his arms. "You had a vitrectomy before, right, to remove the hemorrhage? Well, we'll need to do the same thing again, but this time it will be for the purpose of creating room in your eye for us to insert an air bubble. The bubble will float up to where the retina has detached and gently lift it back into place. We'll give it a few days to reattach and begin healing, then we'll give you some laser treatment to—shall we say—rivet the retina more securely to the wall of your eye. Your body will slowly absorb the bubble and replace it with clear liquid. Hopefully, if there hasn't been too much damage, you'll be able to regain sight again in the affected area. But there are no guarantees." Dr. Gomez stroked his chin as though he had a goatee. "I understand you work for a mission. Is that right?"

Nick nodded.

"Then, if you're a praying man, this would be a good time to pray. I'll do my best, but success or failure is really in God's hands."

Nick bit his lip and nodded slowly, comforted that the doctor seemed to believe in God. "All right. Let's do it."

"Oh, before you leave, there's one other thing I should mention. While that bubble is holding your retina in place, you'll need to keep your head down and turned about forty-five degrees to the right for a few days. That should 'keep the bubble on the trouble,' as we say."

"What do you mean?"

Gomez held up his hand, cupping it with the palm down. "The bubble will, of course, float to the top, like this." He brought his fist up inside the cup. "You need to make sure the top is always on the area of the detachment. It does no good for it to lift some other portion of your retina. Get what I'm saying?"

Nick tried to digest the explanation. Very ingenious. Being a pilot who regularly worked on planes, such mechanical explanations made perfect sense to him. Except, how was he going to keep his head down and turned to one side for a few days? That seemed impossible. And if by *a few days*, the doctor meant three, that was too long. He couldn't just sit around town. He had to get back out there and find Terri! But how could he do that if he had to keep his head in such an unnatural position? In fact, how would he eat or sleep with such contortions?

Terri tensed as Lieutenant Ramírez sat down beside her on the bench where she was eating her lunch. "Do you think Jesús has recovered from the trip to Dos Ríos?" he said.

Avoiding his eyes, Terri took a bite of her beans and rice. "Yes. Pretty much."

"Does that mean he's getting better?"

After he'd threatened to have Nick shot, Terri didn't really want to talk to this man. But what could she do? All he wanted was to know how his son was doing. "No, it doesn't mean he's getting better. It means he doesn't seem to be worse after yesterday's trip." She took a sip of lukewarm coffee, tasting as metallic and bitter as the aluminum canteen cup that held it, and then turned to look at the commander. "Why didn't you tell me you were planning to have Nick fly him to Venezuela? Jesús would've been safe with him. I could've guaranteed it."

"You saying he'd have been safe and it being so aren't necessarily the same thing."

"Look, Nick keeps his word. If Nick said he'd take him to Venezuela, he would've done it. He'd've honored your 'deal'."

Terri said it, but the whole idea of Nick taking her place as a FARC captive troubled her. "How long would you have kept him?"

"What do you mean?"

"Well, you were going to make him your slave like me, weren't you?"

Ramírez rolled his eyes. "You don't understand! Nobody's a slave. Didn't your country have a military draft in the past?"

"Yes. I guess."

"Well, this is no different. I'm sure some of those young boys your government rounded up didn't want to serve any more than you or your pilot friend does. But it's a duty, something we do whether we like it or not. All this talk about making slaves of you is—how do you say it—hyperbole."

Rather than the Spanish—*hipérbole*— Ramírez pronounced it as perfect English. Terri frowned. He often used English when speaking to her and sometimes surprised her with how well he knew it. But more troubling was his twisted logic. "You aren't the legitimate government of Colombia, and we aren't your citizens. You have no authority to conscript us into your service."

"Who legitimately represents the people of Colombia is still a matter of political debate," said Ramírez.

More a matter of military dispute, thought Terri.

"But I can assure you that if it weren't for the U.S. meddling in our affairs, those people in Bogotá wouldn't be in power. As for you being foreigners, that doesn't exempt you from service. It doesn't exempt foreigners in your country. You conscript aliens when you want to."

Was that true? The idea rattled Terri. "Yeah, but . . . but why'd you say you'd release me for a million dollars? That's a ransom demand. You're really nothing but a kidnapper, a common criminal."

Ramírez waved his hand as if shooing away a mosquito, just as he had on the sandbar the day before. "Huh. I said that just to get rid of him. But even if I had been serious, it's not an unheard-of idea. Wealthy people have bought their way out of military service for centuries in countries all over the world. Our government needs two things: service and money. Sometimes they are interchangeable." He stood up and gave Terri a cold stare. "Maybe

I ought to get rid of you and find a real doctor. A million *bucks*"—he used English slang—"could go a long way toward finding one."

"Then why don't you?" she called after him as he started to walk away.

"You just get that culture ready. You can take it in tomorrow."

"Mr. Archer, can you hear me?"

"Yes. I'm here." Nick's response from the operating table was as muffled as Dr. Gomez's question had been.

The Neiva hospital had not been as modern as the stainless steel and glass structure in Chicago, but it was clean and bright, and the staff seemed just as competent—as though Nick could tell—and friendly. The operation had gone much the same way as his earlier one, except he may have received a little more of the "cocktail." In fact, now that he thought of it, he must've dozed off several times. He could remember snatches of what happened, the whirring "hedge trimmer," the suction thing. Or was that from the Chicago surgery?

"Yeah . . . what was that?" Whoa, he could tell that his speech was a little slurred. He'd better pull himself together. "I hear you."

"Okay, Mr. Archer. We've removed nearly as much of the vitreous as we planned, but we've run into a little problem."

Problem? Nick came alert. "Huh? What do you mean?"

"I said we have a little problem here. You need to make a decision. Can you do that?"

"What problem?"

"This is very unusual, but do you know what a cataract is?"

"Yeah, my mom had cataracts."

"All right, then. You know it's the clouding of the eye's natural lens, not the cornea, but the lens within the eye. It usually happens gradually to older people, but cataracts can also develop after an injury or trauma. In rare instances, they develop almost instantaneously. That seems to have happened in your eye. In fact, it's so cloudy, we can't see through it well enough to continue the procedure."

"Really? So what can you do?"

"The only thing we can do is remove the lens. But I need your permission for that. We could do it right now, or we could close everything up, and come back to it later when you've had a chance to consider it."

Nick felt as if he'd ridden too long on a tilt-a-whirl at an amusement park. There were questions he should be asking that would help him make this decision. But his mind felt foggy. "What . . . could happen later?"

"Same thing as we'd do today. We'd remove the lens and then complete the procedure to insert the bubble. The only thing is, as I told you before, the longer we wait before getting that retina back in place, the greater the risk for visual degradation."

Visual degradation. That meant worse sight. Whoa! That "cocktail" left his thinking a little fuzzy. "What . . . if we did it now, would you put the new lens right in?"

"Uh . . . no. We'd have to wait until substantial healing had occurred before we could determine the correct prescription."

Lying there on the table, unable to move, Nick let out his breath. That would mean he'd have to fly with only one eye for a while. Not easy, but he'd known a pilot back in the States with a "monocular waver" on his license because he could only see with one eye. In an emergency, Nick felt he could probably do the same—and this *was* an emergency. He had to get Terri. So there didn't seem to be any other options. It was either now or later, with increased risks for waiting. "If it were your eye, what would you say, doctor?"

There was a long silence. Finally, Nick said, "Doctor?"

"Yes, I'm here. . . . If it were me, I'd go ahead and remove it now so the retina could be put back in place as soon as possible. You're already pushing the envelope."

Nick's rational side kicked in, the "pilot" who had to make split-second decisions, react instantly to avoid disaster. "Okay. Do it," he said, but he had to admit, he was terrified.

Everything possible seemed to be going wrong. Why? Where was God? He thought he'd already been through this test—his trial, learned his lessons, whatever they were. But how could he trust a God when he reached out to touch Him and there was nothing there, no mighty Protector, no solid Rock, no everlasting Arms? Nick was falling into a darker and darker place.

Wait . . . what was that? Some kind of a little instrument was moving around in his eye, a little probe. There, over on the side where the curtain had not yet descended, something was falling, falling like he was falling. No . . . it was actually floating around in his eyeball like an opaque Frisbee.

"Is that . . . is that my lens? I can see it floating around in there."

"Yes, that's your lens."

Fascinated in spite of the horror that threatened to flood over him, Nick watched as the whirring "hedge trimmer," or some similar tool, cut up his cloudy lens and the little vacuum tube sucked out the pieces.

"Oh, oh you missed a piece. Just to the right, to the right. There . . . you got it!"

Somewhere in the back of his mind, he realized that getting involved in the mechanics of what was happening was the only way he could avoid completely freaking out.

Chapter 24

Nick's first eye surgery had lasted ninety minutes. This one took three and a half hours. When he was released from the hospital, Roger was waiting for him downstairs to drive him home. With his hands, Nick tried to support his head while he rode in the car. He leaned forward and tipped his head to the right as Dr. Gomez had instructed. But it wasn't easy. With a patch over one eye, his balance wavered . . . or maybe it was the remnants of the anesthesia that made him feel slightly dizzy and nauseated by the smell of "hospital" that seemed to exude from every pore of his body.

Once Nick got back to the Montgomery's apartment Wednesday night, he felt as if he'd left one hovering mother in the States only to land in the home of another one in Colombia: "Do you need a pain pill?" "We've got *arroz con pollo* for supper. How's that sound?" "How are you going to keep your head down when you sleep?"

Fortunately, several pillows made that possible, at least for the first few hours of the night. Then Nick woke up, alone, uncomfortable—though not really in pain—and feeling far removed from the rest of the world. He got up and shuffled to the bathroom, staring at his feet to keep his head down. But when he returned to bed, he couldn't get back to sleep. The hours dragged on, and he began to think of all he'd gone through: the death of his wife years before, Terri's kidnapping, his eye hemorrhage and subsequent surgery, and now retinal detachment and more surgery. Worse still was the prospect that his eye problems might not be over yet, and there was no assurance his vision would fully recover. What did that mean for a pilot? Even if he ended up with a monocular waver, would MAST keep him on?

And why was all this happening to him? He knew the Bible said trials produced patience, endurance, and strength—like learning how to climb a cliff or learning to shoot whitewater rapids. But this was no Outward Bound adventure. Adventures increased *self*-confidence and developed innate skills, and that was all well and good. But Nick was way beyond his own strength and didn't feel like he had any skills to sharpen. He was going down for the third time, out for the count, with no one to hear his cry. "O God, I'm not up to this. I don't know what's happening! It feels as if You're punishing me. Are You?"

That must be it. What was the proverb his father used to quote? *"Correction is grievous unto him that forsaketh the way: and he that hateth reproof shall die."* Well, if God was trying to correct him, then he would submit. He'd had enough. He was throwing in the towel, accepting his correction . . . whatever it was.

He did not go back to sleep, but the idea of God punishing him gave direction to his worrying for the remaining hours of the night. What had he done? How had he gone astray? Why was God punishing him?

The hours crept by slowly. In the dark of his bedroom—a darkness that now seemed more prevalent than all the light in his life—he prayed, he cried quietly and repented in spirit if not in fact. But no answers for why God might be punishing him rose in his conscience. Not that he thought he was perfect. He knew better. There were innumerable times and ways he could've done better. But that was different than any clear conviction of sin for which he needed to repent. He couldn't see any purpose in what he was going through—nothing to learn, nothing for which he was being corrected, no brave witness like a martyr, no sacrifice to benefit others. What was the purpose?

Even though he finally drifted off, he awoke when it was still dark wishing the Holy Spirit would convict him of some sin rather than leave him in this purposeless abandonment, this spinning out of control through a desolate wasteland, forgotten by God and useless to His kingdom. Nick had once heard a preacher hold forth on the many times in the Bible where God promised, *"I will never leave you nor forsake you."* But those promises must've been specific to His favorite people. It certainly couldn't be a universal promise. Either the promise didn't apply to him, or—Nick began to teeter on the edge of the abyss—maybe there was no God to be either close to or far away from!

He tried to push that thought aside. It terrified him! If there was no God, there was no meaning to life! Not for him, not in all of history, not even for people like Terri, whose faith seemed monumental! Perhaps everyone who imagined that life had meaning was self-delusional. But there was one theological concept he knew was true, and that was the reality of hell! If hell was separation from God, then he was on the edge looking in. Separation from God, or the possibility that there was no God there in the first place, it was all the same thing.

That was hell!

"O Jesus, if You're there, You've got to help me. The Bible says You healed so many sightless people, so why not me? WHY NOT ME? Do You hear me, Jesus? Are You there?" Nick exhaled like an old tire going flat. "Oh, I'm sorry. I'm sorry, Jesus. I really do believe. But *'help me overcome my unbelief!'*" Where had that come from? He knew it was a Bible verse, but Terri was the one who prayed Scripture. Nevertheless, it somehow brought him a scrap of peace to recall that someone else had struggled to believe, and Jesus hadn't rejected that man. In fact, wasn't that the story where Jesus had healed the man's son? Somehow, even in the middle of his doubts, Nick knew he had no place else to turn but to Jesus.

"Hey! Wake up!"

Someone was shaking Terri's arm. She opened her eyes to the gloom of early morning. Her sleep in the infirmary had been interrupted several times during the night when Jesús had moaned in distress. He was not doing well. But this was someone else calling her.

"Come on. We gotta go!"

Terri turned over and forced her eyes to focus on Rosita. "Go? Where? What for?"

"Teniente Ramírez. He wants us to go to Florencia. Get that special medicine you told him about."

Terri sat up. "Right now? How come so early?"

"Truck's going to . . . you don't need to know where it's going. But it'll drop us off at the river, and we can take the ferry over to Catagena Del Chairá. From there we can catch a bus to Florencia. He wants us back as soon as possible, so we gotta go now."

Terri stood up, running her hands through her hair. She looked at Jesús. "I can't go without getting someone to look after him."

"I'll get Joel, then."

"No, not Joel." Joel had resented the times he'd been assigned to infirmary duty as though it were a punishment for irresponsibility, and maybe it had been. "Get Maria. She's a better nurse."

"All right. All right. You just get ready. We're leaving in fifteen minutes."

Like armies everywhere, standard operating procedure for FARC was hurry up and wait. Fifteen minutes became two hours before the pickup pulled away with Terri and Rosita riding in the back. Terri was dressed in the usual cast-off clothes she had picked up, but instead of fatigues, Rosita was dressed in civilian clothes—so she would not attract attention when they arrived in Florencia, Terri presumed. Instead of army ponchos to keep off the morning mist, they both sweated inside large, black plastic garbage bags. Rosita had a narrow-brimmed, felt fedora like what many Andean Indians wore. Terri had a crumpled cowboy hat and carried the precious jar of Jesús' cultured infection in a brightly colored wool carpetbag along with a change of clothes.

They'd been riding in the back of the pickup at least two hours when they broke out of the jungle and fields first appeared on one side of the road and then on both sides. Some were even fenced off with cattle in them. The next tree line proved to be the bank of the Caguán River, where the road ended at a ferry landing. They got out, and the pickup headed back the way they had come.

"Who's gonna pick us up when we get back?"

"Don't worry. They'll be here, but this isn't a good place for them to park. Who knows who'll be on the ferry when it comes across?"

"How often does it run?"

"Whenever it's worth their while." Rosita sat down on a log by the river's edge, and Terri joined her. "The ferrymen see us sitting here, but two passengers aren't enough, usually they want a vehicle or two from this side or that side."

Terri gazed at the bustling town of Catagena Del Chairá on the opposite bank. It was the most civilization she'd seen since she'd been taken from Finca Fe—numerous boats going and coming up and down the river, cars on the streets, the spires of multiple churches, light poles and power lines, and even a Terpel gas station right along the river bank. "It's a small city," she murmured.

"*Sí,* and we have many *amigos* there. But there is also the *la policía y el ejército*—the army. We must be careful."

They only had to wait about twenty minutes before the ferry departed from the opposite shore with a truck and a SUV and several motorbikes. When it arrived and discharged its passengers, Terri followed Rosita up the little ramp for the return journey. The pilot nodded at Rosita, but didn't collect a fare. Was he one of the "friends" Rosita had mentioned?

In Catagena Del Chairá they walked about eight blocks to Hotel Los Corceles, where they waited for the bus while enjoying coffee at a sidewalk café. The 12:45 bus was thirty minutes late, but when it arrived, it was modern and air-conditioned. And other than jostling over some muddy ruts, the four-hour ride to Florencia was as comfortable as Terri had been in weeks.

For a city under government control, Terri was surprised at the number of FARC operatives she met in Florencia: the man who picked them up in his Honda from the huge Florencia bus terminal; the apartment building he took them to where they had a scrumptious meal with several families—all of whom seemed to be FARC—and spent the night; and the two men in a car from somewhere else who drove them to *La Hospital María Inmaculada.* But then, Florencia was a city of almost a 130 thousand people on the edge of El Despeje. So why wouldn't there be a number of FARC operatives?

"I have a specimen for the lab," Terri said when she and Rosita arrived at the desk.

With unease, she watched the receptionist who hadn't looked up yet. What if they asked too many questions? Ramírez had said to tell them she was a nurse working with some of the interior tribes and needed a quick diagnosis. But wouldn't there be forms to fill out, documentation about an incident of a "strange new infection"? What should she say? How much should she lie?

On the other hand, what if she told the truth and said she'd been kidnapped by FARC and needed help. What could Rosita do in the lobby of a busy hospital with lots of other people around? Terri knew she had a pistol hidden in the back of her pants, but surely she wouldn't shoot her right there.

"Rosita, ¿eres tu?" The woman behind the desk stood up and reached across the counter to grasp Rosita's hands.

"Camila! I didn't know you worked here. When did you get this job?"

Soon a happy reunion was in full sway. Then with one quick phone call Camila assured Terri the people in the lab would see her. "Just go down that hall to the end, turn right and continue until you come to red double doors on your right. That's the lab. Can't miss it."

Thinking Rosita would come with her, Terri hesitated for a moment until Camila said, "Go ahead. Raul is waiting for you."

She walked down the hall with the carpetbag under her arm, afraid to look back. What if she kept on walking, right out the back door of the hospital? There were probably several doors in the building. When they'd arrived at the four-story hospital, she'd seen parking lots and delivery ramps and emergency room signs, just like any institution. But there was also a tall fence around most of the building. Her mind was buzzing as she went to the end of the hall and turned right as instructed. A few steps further and she came to the red double doors on her right. Should she enter or flee? Without deciding, her hand reached out and pushed them open. What could she do but ask for Raul?

As though programmed like a robot, she explained to him that she needed an analysis of the culture in the jar she handed him and a recommendation for the most effective antibiotic to fight it. Raul filled out a couple items on a form and asked her to sign it.

"Should have it in a couple hours. You want to come back later? Or do you want to just sit out front in the waiting room?"

"I'll . . . wait." Terri went back through the double doors and looked right. The hall kept going. She could have followed it to an exit, but she turned left and returned to the front desk where Rosita and Camila chattered on about old times, current boyfriends, and family gossip. She caught Rosita's eye and smiled as she went over and sat on one of the chrome and green vinyl couches in the waiting area along with a dozen family members and sick people.

What had happened? She'd had a perfect chance to escape, but she hadn't taken it.

Chapter 25

When Nick awakened Thursday morning, he was no closer to an answer about where God was than he'd been when the question first arose, but with the morning came practical challenges to fill his day. Betty left early to cook for the school children, leaving Roger with instructions to fix Nick a good breakfast. Dr. Gomez wanted to check his eye to make sure no problems had arisen overnight.

At first, Nick's one-day checkup seemed routine—been there, done that—remove the bandage, check for hemorrhage or early signs of infection. Check internal pressure. No, he wasn't experiencing any undue pain. Yes, he'd put the drops in this morning, he was watching his diabetes, and maintaining his head in the correct position—keeping "the bubble on the trouble."

Did he have any questions? Yeah, why was God putting him through all this again? Why didn't God answer his prayers? But those weren't the questions Dr. Gomez could answer. Dr. Gomez couldn't even tell him if God was there.

"Looks pretty good for one day out," his doctor finally declared. "But I want you to remain face down, apply these drops twice a day"—he handed Nick two bottles—"and keep using that eye shield at night. And don't get any water in your eye. In other words, no showers yet. I want to see you in three days. That'll be Saturday, but I'll come in anyway. Okay?"

Three days! "If everything looks good, will I be able to fly then—I mean, even if I still can't see too well?"

"Fly? No way, Mr. Archer. Imagine what would happen to that air bubble in the thinner air of higher altitudes. It would expand like a party balloon."

And burst my eyeball you mean. Nick struggled to keep his voice even. "So . . . how long are we talking about before I can fly?"

Dr. Gomez shrugged. "Even though the detachment obscured quite a bit of your vision, you were fortunate that it wasn't really that large. So I injected an air bubble rather than a slower dissolving gas bubble. And I'm going to want to pin it down with a laser treatment as soon as we can shoot past the bubble. Perhaps we can do that on Saturday. But it will still be day five or even seven before it would be safe for you to go up in a plane."

"That's clear into next week!" Nick grimaced. He *had* to make a try to get Terri, but at the moment he felt too discouraged to say anything more than, "Okay. I'll make an appointment for Saturday with the girl out front."

When they got home, Nick went into the bathroom and removed the shield and bandage to inspect his eye with Betty's hand mirror. If *"looks pretty good for one day out"* was the doctor's assessment, Nick was stunned! His eye looked like a ball of hamburger. Gomez was right: Recovery would take a long time. He had to come up with some other way to rescue Terri.

That afternoon, Roger built Nick a double mirror contraption that allowed him to see ahead while looking down. He could talk to people, watch TV, and see something more than the floor.

"Aren't you afraid they'll fire you if you don't put in your time with the school?" he asked Roger. "You've been tending to me all week."

"Ha! They don't want me back at work until they're sure my head injury's okay. But don't worry about me or Finca Fe. At the warehouse all they've got is concrete. They don't have ten acres of grass for me to mow like we did down at the academy. And it was you who wanted me to keep that runway as trimmed as a golf course."

"Golf course?" Nick laughed even though it sent pricks of pain into his eye. "I never said a golf course lawn was required. With my bush wheels, you have no idea of some of the rough fields I've flown in and out of, sometimes nothing but a pasture that even a cow would stumble trying to cross."

Rosita finally turned from talking to Camila over the counter in the Florencia hospital and joined Terri. "How long do we have before they'll have that report for you? You think it'll be enough time for us"—she indicated herself and Camila—"to go get something to eat, and not from those cheap vendors out front, either?"

Terri shrugged. "He said a couple of hours, but . . ." When Camila didn't invite her to go with them, she added, "That's okay. If you want to go eat, I'll wait here."

Just then a young man in hospital scrubs arrived, and Camila rose to give her replacement her seat. "Two hours is plenty of time," she said, retrieving her purse out of a tall cabinet against the back wall.

"Want us to bring you something, Terri?" Rosita said.

"Sure. Whatever you get will be fine." Terri didn't have any money. Rosita had paid the bus fare to Florencia with money Ramírez had given her and presumably had additional expense money.

In minutes they were out the door, still chattering like a couple of schoolgirls. Terri couldn't avoid thinking that was the life Rosita should be living instead of the hardened existence of a revolutionary in the jungle. And yet she was coming to see that it was the same poverty and hopelessness she saw in the eyes of the mother sitting in the waiting room with her two sick children that drove people to grow cocaine or join a revolutionary group like FARC. Somehow the complications of life in Columbia were confusing her, making her think the FARC revolution was at least understandable if not downright legitimate. They didn't call themselves terrorists, and it'd been many days since she'd thought of them in those terms.

What was happening to her? Like right now. Here was another chance to run. Rosita was gone—a foolish blunder for a revolutionary guard watching over a captive, but hey . . . the hospital wasn't locked. No one knew she was supposed to remain in the waiting room. She could walk out the *front* door now and find a government office, perhaps a police officer, someone to help her, and be on a plane to safety before dinner. But should she? What about Jesús? Who would nurse him?

She got up and wandered down the hall toward the lab, passed the red doors and continued on. Why did she feel so personally responsible for Jesús? Rosita could pick up the special antibiotics and take them back. Maybe Ramírez could get someone else to nurse his son. Certainly he was influential enough to call for the assistance of some other FARC medic.

Or could he? He'd seemed desperate enough to find a doctor for his wounded son that he'd marched into Finca Fe with an armed band of guerrillas and captured three hostages—one of whom was now dead. What if she was the closest thing to help for his son he could find? What would happen to Jesús if she didn't return?

Before her was a door with a window in it that led to the outside. It didn't appear to be locked or alarmed. She could see the busy street only a short distance away. Why not just disappear into the crowd? But what if she were caught? What if one of the FARC operatives in the city recognized her? She could scream and yell for help, and if no one came to her rescue, the most they could do to her would be to throw her in the back of a van and race away. Would she be any worse off than she'd been so far?

Terri stood staring out the door. Where was her courage? This was her chance. And yet . . . for some reason, Lieutenant Ramírez had trusted her to come into the city on behalf of his son. What was most important—her own safety and freedom? Or the life of this young boy?

Slowly, she turned back and returned to the waiting room. She wasn't even certain she knew why.

That evening some of the Finca Fe staff came by to visit Nick and wish him well, but in spite of their efforts to encourage him, he felt as if he was in a separate room from everyone else and the door between them was slowly closing, shutting him off from the rest of the world. Even the mirrors Roger had devised to help him see his surroundings didn't bridge the void between himself and others. People tried to talk to him but ended up talking to one another about him. The old adage that the eyes are the windows of the soul had never seemed truer. They were how he looked out and apparently how others looked in, but now the distance seemed to be increasing. He longed for someone's touch to restore his sense of personhood. If only Terri were here. Would she touch him? Would she give him a warm hug like she had on the beach at Dos Ríos? Or even rest her hand on his arm or shoulder or maybe even touch his face. Yes, his face, would she touch his face? He just wanted the human contact. His spirit was waning thinner. Like a ghost drifting away, he felt as though he was fading from this world and needed a hand to pull him back.

In the night Nick again found himself wrestling with God . . . like Jacob? Or was he just wrestling with a phantom, with a "nothing"? What a sorry missionary he was, to come so far from home to help spread the Gospel and end up with such doubts! Others might worry whether their donors would pay their pledges on time, but he was struggling with the very existence of God.

"You seem awful quiet," Roger observed Friday morning over breakfast. "What gives? Here, let me butter that toast while you keep your head down like you're s'posed to." After a moment, he added, "Your eye hurtin' you?"

"No. It's not hurting. It's just that Dr. Gomez wants to see me again tomorrow."

"No problem. Like I said, I'll give you a lift."

"Yeah, thanks. But it's not that; it's that I can't keep wasting days." Nick hesitated. "I guess I didn't tell you before, but I'm pretty sure I found where they're holding Terri."

"You what?" Roger leaned down to stare at Nick through the mirrors. "How'd you find that out?"

Nick described how he'd discovered an airstrip that wasn't on the maps and how it coincided with the coordinates the government had triangulated for the first radio broadcast. "And just east of there, less than a quarter of a mile, I saw smoke rising out of the trees. My guess is, that's their camp."

"Mmmm. Sounds rather speculative to me."

"No, no. That's only half the reason I think it's their base. The main thing is, from the very first, Ramírez wanted a pilot and a plane, right?"

"Yeah . . . and a doctor."

"But a plane wouldn't be much use without a place to land it. Right? And yet, when he wanted me to fly his son to Venezuela, he had me land at Dos Ríos, and I'm positive they'd been traveling in that old pickup quite a while before they met me on the beach. Don't you see, it all fits."

"Yeah, but—"

"No *yeah-buts* about it. He couldn't have me land close to his camp, or he'd give away his location."

"Hmm. Okay, say you're right. What you gonna do?"

"That's the problem. I can't fly because of this bubble in my eye. But each day that passes is another day Terri's in captivity. Who knows what might happen to her . . . or whether Ramírez might even move his base? I can't wait! But Gomez said I have to wait five to seven days after surgery before I can fly and maybe even longer if there are any more complications or procedures."

"Now hold on there a minute, son. You were thinkin' of flying out there to rescue her like Rambo? That's crazy. You could get yourself *and* her killed! Why not just call the army?"

"First of all, because I doubt they'd pay any attention to what I say, but even if they did, they'd be the ones going in there blazin' like Rambo. I was thinkin' more of a stealth extraction—fly in just at dusk and make a dead-stick landing with my engine off so there'd be no noise. Then when it was really dark, I'd recon the camp until I found her and could whisk her out of there before they knew it."

"Oh, man, you're just plain loco! You know that, don't you?"

Chapter 26

Roger's less than enthusiastic response to Nick's plan to fly in and rescue Terri didn't do anything to cheer him up Friday, but it did cause him to review everything that had happened in connection with the FARC attack, looking for any other alternatives for how to free Terri. Maybe he ought to be working on more than one front at a time. The offer to exchange himself for Terri had failed, but he had found the FARC base, or at least he thought he had, but now he couldn't fly. However, Ramírez had mentioned a ransom—"*¡Un millón de dólares, Americanos!*" he'd said. Had he been serious?

Obviously, First Peoples Mission would never pay a ransom. That was their policy, and they'd not wavered from it in the past. Besides, they wouldn't have that kind of money anywhere in their budget. But Nick's mind was churning: What if he could arrange payment from other sources? Certainly Terri's family and friends were frantic for her release. A million dollars was a lot of money, but friends and relatives and perhaps people in her church might be able to loan that much from their savings accounts, insurance policies, home equity lines of credit, or maybe even organize a crowdfunding effort. People ought to respond to a plea to free a kidnapped nurse, wouldn't they? There had to be away to raise the money. But how could he ever get that much money out of the U.S. and into Colombia, especially on such short notice?

Wait . . . hadn't David Tarkington, the father of the boy who'd broken his leg at Finca Fe the day before the FARC raid, said the rebels had kidnapped twenty of his SurPetro employees? And his company had paid a huge ransom for their release! Maybe Tarkington could tell him how to do it. He certainly had been concerned and helpful when Nick was evacuating the students after the raid.

After Roger left for work that morning, Nick got on the phone and doggedly insisted on getting through secretaries and assistants until he made contact. "Mr. Tarkington, you may remember me. I'm the pilot who brought your son David up to Neiva after he broke his leg at Finca Fe. And you helped us over the following days with each load of students and staff as we evacuated the academy."

"Of course. Nick Archer, right?"

"That's right. And you might recall that our nurse, Terri Kaplan, who accompanied your son when we brought him up, was kidnapped during that FARC raid."

"Oh yes. David seemed very fond of her. How is she doing?"

"Well, we hope she's okay, but we haven't succeeded in securing her release. The government hasn't been much help, and the only attempt to arrange a trade for her release has fallen through. However, at one point the commander of the unit said a million-dollar ransom would do the trick."

"What? Look, can you fill me in a little more?"

Nick didn't want to explain the debacle of his failed attempt to trade himself for Terri, but Tarkington insisted on all the details so he could "assess the validity of the offer," as he put it. So Nick told him.

Tarkington sighed deeply over the phone. "First of all, you realize that the U.S. government considers it illegal for private citizens to negotiate and pay ransom in hostage situations. It undercuts their policy of refusing to pay ransom."

"I know, but this isn't a political hostage situation between terrorists and the U.S. government. They're not asking any concessions from the United States."

"That may be true, but that's not the way the U.S. Justice Department sees it."

"So, how'd you get past that?"

Tarkington laughed. "As they say in spy movies, I'd have to shoot you if I told you. But essentially it had to do with how SurPetro is legally organized. It's not an American company, so even though we have offices in the U.S., we're not subject to all the U.S. regulations."

Nick frowned. Corporate loopholes? Still, he needed this man's help. "Okay, but can you give me some tips for how to deliver that much cash—presuming we could raise it?"

"Do you think you can contact this Lieutenant Ramírez again?"

Nick thought about what he'd gone through trying to go through Pablo. Was he ready to get beat up again? Nevertheless, it had worked. He'd made contact with FARC, a contact that brought him face-to-face, not only with Terri, but with Ramírez himself. "Yeah. I think I can get to him. I did it before, and I'm willing to try again if I can just get the money out of the States."

"Okay. But you have to realize there's no way an average citizen can go into a U.S. bank and walk out with a satchel full of a million dollars in cash without making some extended arrangements and answering a lot of questions. Even if you succeeded, your attempt to leave the country with a satchel of cash might be discovered when you go through security before boarding the plane in the U.S. or as you deplaned and tried to enter Colombia." Tarkington paused.

"So what do I do? Ship it overnight like a box of books?"

Tarkington laughed. "You're worried about getting it into Colombia when you haven't even figured out how you'd get that much money out of a bank in the U.S. The average noncommercial bank has no more than twenty to fifty thousand dollars in cash on hand at any one time unless special arrangements have been made—and those arrangements involve a lot of documentation. Business is done electronically these days. Very rarely does a legitimate transaction need or even want to take the risk of handling large quantities of cash. So that's the way you'll have to go to get the money out of the U.S. But tell you what I can do. If you can raise the money, I can give you an account number in the States you can transfer it to. It's a SurPetro account, so the money can then be wired to our bank here in Colombia. Then I can withdraw it for you in cash."

Nick sucked in his breath. "In U.S. dollars?"

"Probably. I'd have to give them a couple days notice that we're going to need that much. But we often have to pay cash down here for various projects, and people do like the U.S. dollar."

Nick couldn't believe it. He'd just gotten his answer—if he could raise the money that is. He spent the rest of the day calling Terri's family and friends in the States.

By Saturday, the air bubble in Nick's eye had diminished in size from large enough to block his whole field of vision to something he could look around, the size of a soccer ball held at arm's length—though the bubble appeared black. When he visited Dr. Gomez for his checkup and was allowed to look straight ahead, the bubble appeared to float *down* at the bottom of his eye. "It's just like a camera," explained Gomez. "Your eye inverts all images, so the bubble is actually in the top of your eyeball."

Yeah, and Nick could look right "over" it. "But everything else is a complete blur. Can't recognize a thing!"

"That's because you have no lens in your eye," Dr. Gomez handed Nick a shield to hold over his good eye. "But let's see how much you can see."

"Not much." It was as bad as the day after the vitrectomy for his hemorrhage. "I thought I'd see better by now."

"Well, without a lens, there's no way for your eye to focus. But how about the dark area? Is it gone? Can you see this light?"

The doctor was holding a penlight in front of Nick. Its bulb a bright glare.

When Nick confirmed that he could see it, Gomez said, "Okay. Keep looking straight ahead but tell me when it disappears."

He moved it from side to side and up and down, and Nick realized that except when it disappeared behind the bubble, he had what seemed like a normal field of vision, no more "dark curtain."

"That's pretty good," said Gomez." You're a very lucky man. Can you see that eye chart on the wall?"

"What wall?" Nick said with a laugh, nervous humor being better than none at all.

"Okay, okay. Here, give this a try." He handed Nick a different shield—one side to cover his right eye and the other side perforated with a cluster of pinholes. "Try looking through those little holes."

Nick felt like the leper Naaman being told to dip seven times in the muddy Jordan River to cure his disease. What good would it do to try and look through pinholes when he could barely see large blobs of dark and light? But he did as he'd been told. And to his astonishment, when he looked through the holes, he could actually make out the doctor, the room, and several things in the room. "Wow!" Everything was dimmer than normal—undoubtedly because the light coming through the pinholes was only a fraction of what normally entered one's eye—but things were recognizably clear. "How do those holes make a difference?"

"You ever make a pinhole camera when you were a kid? The pinholes act like a crude lens. How about the eye chart on the far wall? Can you see the top letter?"

"Yeah, I can see it . . . uh, the fourth, maybe the fifth line. Not quite the fifth, but I think the fourth one is L-P-E-D."

"Not bad. Try the fifth."

"Umm. Z-B . . . no, maybe that's an E. I'm just not sure—"

"That's okay. Line four is six over fifteen . . . uh, that would be, let's see . . . about twenty over fifty for you Americans who don't use metric. That means you have to be within twenty feet of something to see what people with normal vision can see at fifty feet. And that's a lot better than not even being able to see the chart at all."

Nick snorted. "But I can't go around looking through pinholes."

"Of course not. But that simple device gives us an indication of your visual potential, and it seems pretty good in spite of the detachment. When your eye has fully healed, you might even do better than that with a lens implant." He took the pinhole shield from Nick. "If you have a magnifying glass, you can duplicate the same thing at home by holding it a couple of inches in front of your eye. You should be able to find a focus."

"Does that mean I don't have to keep my head down anymore?"

"Mmm, not yet. I want to give your retina some support for a little longer. But I think you're far enough along to do the laser treatment today, if you're up for it. Then we'll check again on Monday. If everything looks good, you won't have to keep your head down anymore. Okay?"

"Uh . . ." Nick wanted to follow the doctor's orders, but the urgency in getting Terri made it so hard to promise to keep his head down for two more days.

"Look," Gomez said, "I can see you're struggling with that. I can't force you to do anything you don't want to do, but you push the envelope at every edge. Let me just say this, if you raise your head, at least make it for only short periods of time. Keep it down *most* of the time, and for heaven's sakes, no flying until that bubble is as small as a BB. Agreed?"

"Agreed!" Nick grinned and instinctively put his head down.

Nothing could have made Nick happier . . . until Dr. Gomez began firing the 162 shots of laser into his eye, creating tiny burns in his retina that when healed were supposed to create minute scar tissues between the retina and the outer wall of the eyeball. He'd explained that if targeted away from the macula or central focus of the eye, these "rivets" would not interfere with normal vision but would prevent any future detachment.

But the pain was excruciating, each burn getting more and more intense until the green laser stopped firing. Perhaps they were more powerful than the shots he'd earlier received to simply cauterize the rogue blood vessels in his right eye, but by the time the procedure was over, Nick was exhausted trying to hold perfectly still while absorbing all that pain.

"Just hang in there," Dr. Gomez encouraged. "The pain should subside within a couple of hours."

The laser treatment had been so draining, Nick collapsed on the couch in the Montgomerys' apartment when Roger dropped him off. He listened to Betty's praise music and tried to pray. The verse, *"With thanksgiving, present your requests to God,"* replayed again and again in Nick's mind until he found it in Philippians 4:6. The verse began with, "Do not be anxious about anything . . . " Easier to do now that he had some hope regarding his vision. So he tried thanking God. That was good!

He thought again of the sightless people Jesus had healed and decided to read some of their stories in the Bible with his good eye, or rather his "pretty good eye," the right one. When blind Bartimaeus, who begged by the roadside, heard Jesus was passing by, he began shouting, "Jesus, Son of David, have mercy on me!" And no one could stop him. So Jesus asked, "What do you want me to do for you?" And Bartimaeus simply replied, "I want to see."

Nick understood that. That poor beggar could have asked for many things—riches, fame, justice, revenge, longevity, power, wisdom—but he had only one request: "I want to see." Bartimaeus hadn't asked for eternal life or even forgiveness. That's how important sight is. "I want to see."

Nick knew he would've said the same thing. No theological vision. No godly insight. No eternal perspective. No fear of darkness. No walking in the light. No aspirations of glory. All those spiritual concerns are first understood by humans in metaphors for sight—not feelings, not memories, not hearsay. No wise person bases their life on such shifting sands. But sight, that is more tangible! Even though we must rise above sight to live and be saved by faith, we all still cry: "I want to see!"

Apparently, Jesus understood this human need because he healed Bartimaeus. "Are you healing me, too?" murmured Nick. It seemed as if He was, and so Nick thanked God again and again and again.

It may have been the right thing to do, but it didn't lift Nick out of his funk Saturday afternoon. Time was passing, and Terri was still in captivity. He called her brother in New Jersey to see how the fundraising for the ransom was going.

"Pretty well," Josh said. "We've tagged over $480,000. So, I think we could send half the requested amount to you Monday morning. But we've pretty much tapped out family and friends, if you know what I mean."

"How about the crowdfunding?"

"That piece is more complicated. I'm sure there'd be a lot of sympathy out there even among strangers. I have to say you Christians are pretty generous people when it comes to something like this. But it's going to take several days to get it off the ground. You know, it's got to be approved and everything. And who knows how fast the actual money will come in?"

That was discouraging, but when Nick called Tarkington, the oil magnate encouraged him to go ahead and try to set up the transfer. "These things are always negotiable," he said. "You never pay what the kidnappers ask, but if you have real money, that can be pretty attractive to them. You know, *bird in the hand*."

"How about cash? Would the bank have that much by Monday afternoon?"

"I'll make sure of it."

Chapter 27

The special antibiotic Terri had brought back from the hospital in Florencia seemed to be working on Jesús. After three days, his fever was down. He was more alert and drinking sips of water on his own, and the wound looked less angry.

"Father, I thank you that you have heard me," she murmured, quoting Jesus when he had raised Lazarus from the dead. *"I know that you always hear me."* She lit the propane stove to heat water. "Carlos, you want some oatmeal?" Carlos Álvarez was the only other patient in the infirmary—back again after breaking a bone in his foot the day before.

"Sí, señorita. Muchas gracias."

Terri pulled down the large box of individual servings of Quaker Apples and Cinnamon Instant Oatmeal from the shelf and emptied packets into two bowls. Perhaps she could get Jesús to eat a little. She read the information on the side of the box: made in Cedar Rapids, Iowa. How had FARC managed to acquire a big box of oatmeal made in the USA? She shook her head. Ramírez had said they were reserved just for patients, but surely he wouldn't mind if she had one in celebration of Jesús' improvement. She prepared a third bowl.

Sergeant Rodriquez, on the other hand . . .

After two bites, Jesús refused to eat anymore. She shrugged as she put down his bowl and took her first comforting bite just as Rodriquez swatted open the screen door of the little canvas hospital. He frowned as he watched Terri set her bowl aside and try again to tease one more bite between Jesús' lips.

Rodriquez eyed Álvarez. "You ready for duty?"

"*Light* duty!" Terri said hastily. "He can't put any weight on that foot just yet. But he could probably get around camp on crutches."

Rodriquez shook his head in disgust. "You want to see the hole in my shoulder? Yet I'm not on sick call. But with you, Álvarez, it's always something with you, isn't it?" He turned to Terri. "And *guapa,* you're the camp medic, not his *mamacita*!" he snapped. "Right now, you need to get ready to move out. Bring a fully equipped first-aid bag and whatever personal items you need for a week—but it has to fit into this." He tossed a small backpack onto one of the empty cots. "And wear camo, not that stupid red shirt!"

"What? Why me? Where're we going?"

"You don't need to know. Just be ready in ten minutes."

Terri's mind was buzzing as she watched him look around the tent and then lean over to stare more intently at Jesús. She extended her hand as though to stop him. "You're not taking him anywhere. He's getting better, but he's not ready to move."

"I can see that," he sneered. "But for this mission we need everyone who's fit, including a medic, so get going." He wheeled and headed for the door.

"Wait a minute. Did you say *mission*? I'm not going on any mission! No way!"

He shrugged, "All I know is, Teniente Ramírez said to bring you, so you're coming. Tell Álvarez how to take care of Jesús while you're gone."

"What? There's no way I'm leaving Jesús in the care of someone who doesn't know the first thing about nursing and can barely walk. You tell Ramírez I'm not going anywhere, and that's final."

Rodriquez didn't even acknowledge her defiance before leaving the tent.

Terri pushed her bowl of oatmeal aside, suddenly feeling queasy. What had she gotten herself into? Rodriquez's order was certainly a wake-up call. The whole process of trying to save Jesús' life—and now seeing him finally making progress—had so consumed her these last few weeks that she'd deeply identified with her patient. It wasn't easy camping out in the jungle for so long, and there'd been the hide-and-seek avoidance of the army and police when they'd traveled to Catagena Del Chairá and Florencia. But that had been more like a challenge, a game. She'd even bypassed opportunities to escape, emotionally denying the fact that she was supporting a military unit at war with the government of Colombia.

But being ordered to accompany FARC on a combat mission hit her with reality. Missions meant raids and attacks that killed people. She couldn't be part of that!

Stepping out onto the wooden platform that formed a porch for the hospital, her eyes searched the camp for Ramírez. He was almost out of sight behind some trees, checking items off on a clipboard while two of his men loaded them into the back of a pickup. This did look serious. She ran up to him. "I'm not going!"

He glanced at her. "Yes, you are. I need you." He checked something off on his clipboard. "Go get that other box of ammunition," he said to one of the men.

"I'm telling you, I'm not going with you!" Should she threaten to stop caring for Jesús? That had worked to save Nick's life. But Jesús was getting better, and Ramírez knew it or he wouldn't have ordered her to leave camp, leaving his son behind for the next few days. "The only reason you want me is that you're going to kill people—and get some of your own fighters shot up in the process. I won't be a part of that, and there's nothing you can do to make me."

He finally turned to her, sighed heavily, and dropped his arms to his side. "I could make you come, you know."

"How, tie me up? I wouldn't be any good to you then."

He glared at her. "I could take Jesús with us. Then you'd come."

She stared at him, horrified. "You wouldn't do that! He could relapse. He's just starting to respond, and that could set him back. You don't understand infections! Every time it prevails, it gets stronger, and Jesús might not be able to fight it off another time. He needs a full recovery. And you can't leave him with Carlos Álvarez, either. That boy wouldn't know the first thing to do if Jesús took a turn for the worse."

That stopped him. He stared at her, eyes narrowed, jaw tight. "All right. You stay—but have that hospital ready when we get back. We might need it."

Terri turned away before he could change his mind. But as she ran back to the medical tent, she realized she needed to consider the implications of staffing an infirmary that was obviously essential to an ongoing war effort. And yet, wasn't that what she'd been doing since the day they'd brought her here?

O God, what am I doing here? Her thoughts and emotions felt as if they were running amuck. She had always been committed to nursing *anyone* who was sick or injured, regardless of affiliation or behavior, saint or sinner. And yet . . . medical support for a military unit was as essential as food and ammunition. Without it, they couldn't operate for long, could they?

Nick was still on his phone when Roger returned home Saturday evening. "No!" he said, turning his back to Roger as though keeping the conversation private. "This is important! Don't try to send it to me. Just deposit it into the account Josh gave you, and he'll let you know when we've reached our goal. We're gonna do this! All right? . . . Great! Goodbye."

But Roger hadn't been blocked out. He put his bag of groceries down on the counter and eyed Nick. "So, you're gonna do what?"

Nick stood up, keeping his head bowed. He hadn't really been trying to keep his plans secret. There just hadn't been a good time to explain them to Roger yet. "Uh, I think we have another way to get Terri back."

"Oh, you mean without goin' in there with guns a blazin'?"

"Come on Roger, I never said anything about guns." Nick sighed in exasperation. "But I've been talking to David Tarkington—though he might not want me throwing his name around, so keep it under your hat. Okay?"

"Done took my hat off while you wasn't lookin'."

"Ha, ha! Very funny. I'm just tryin' to keep my head down like the doc said, so I didn't see your shiny dome. Anyway, you know Tarkington, the CFO of SurPetro. He's given me a way to pay the ransom for Terri."

"He's gonna pay?"

"Of course not—not a million bucks. But Terri's got friends and family back home. If everyone puts up what they can—you know, savings, home equity, insurance, plus we're hoping to do a crowdfunding campaign—it shouldn't be impossible to come up with the money. In fact, we're almost halfway there. I've already got people from her family and church working on it. And Tarkington thinks he can help get the funds we collect into Colombia."

"Oh yeah? Like the drug cartels do all the time? You better be careful, brother."

"No, no. Tarkington's on the up and up. But the challenge I've got to work on now is making contact with Commander Ramírez."

"Ramírez? Now that sounds like another knock in the head. Hey. Sit down over there and use that mirror so I can look you in the eye."

Nick sat down and focused the mirror contraption so he could see Roger.

"Humph! Not much better." Roger shook his head as he took a seat across from Nick. "You know you're gonna die, don't you?"

What? Nick almost jerked his head up to see if Roger was joking. "Well, I suppose that's a possibility, but—"

"No. It's a certainty! We're *all* gonna die . . . unless Jesus returns first—at least that's what they tell me. But the odds for dyin' are pretty high."

"Oh. Well, sure, if you put it that way. But what's that got to do with getting Terri back?"

"Perhaps nothin' directly. But it has a lot to do with how we navigate the difficult things in this life. There are things we can't change, death being one of them—"

"Look here, I'm no fatalist, Roger, so if you think I'm just gonna roll over and sing, '*Que será, será*. Whatever will be, will be,' when Terri's life's on the line, well that's just not me, man!"

"Of course not. I get it. But you've also probably heard of the Serenity Prayer that Alcoholics Anonymous uses: 'God, grant me the serenity to accept the things I cannot change, courage to change the things I can, and wisdom to know the difference.' It's that last phrase that's the stickler, especially these days when we have preachers and advertisers who constantly pump the notion that we're entitled to everything our minds can conceive. You know, 'Believe and receive!' 'Name it and claim it!'? They try to tell you that's what faith is all about."

"Maybe, but I can tell you, I'm not about to give up on Terri. Besides, I don't think that little prayer for drunks comes from the Bible, does it?"

"Not sayin' it does, not directly, anyway. But this is one alcoholic who can tell you it's full of Bible truth."

"You? . . . You used to have a drinking problem?"

"Let's just say, 'My name is Roger, and I'm an alcoholic.' 'Nough said? Lost my job. Lost our house. Nearly ruined my marriage and my whole family. Always thought I could handle it. Didn't have the sense to know the difference between what I could handle and what I couldn't."

"Sorry. I never knew. Didn't mean to make light of your . . . your experience. But you're right. Of course, we gotta have God's help. And I've been praying from dawn to dark."

"You've been prayin' that God would do what?"

"That he'd help me rescue Terri, but . . ."

"But what?"

"Guess I have to admit . . ." He sighed deeply, shoulders dropping. "Does seem like everything has gone wrong, and now I can't even fly."

"And that's why I mentioned that we're all gonna die. Jesus died, even though he prayed that he wouldn't have to. All the apostles died. Every human died—except, some say Elijah and Moses—and for most people it wasn't a very pleasant experience, often accompanied by a lot of pain and suffering."

"So . . . what's your point with regards to trying to help Terri? Are you saying that because we're all going to die anyway, I shouldn't try to help her?"

"It's not that you shouldn't try to rescue her. May God grant us all the courage to change the things we can. But it's our attitude. Jesus prayed that he wouldn't have to drink that cup of death. He prayed for that very *specific* outcome with such urgency, the Word says, he sweat drops like blood. Don't know that I've ever prayed that hard. But Jesus also added: 'Nevertheless, not my will but thine be done.' That's the revolutionary perspective these prosperity preachers leave out when they tell people to just believe and receive. God's not a vending machine! You can't just put in your faith coin and out comes whatever you want. No one had more faith than Jesus. But what God has promised is that He'll be with us, even when we go through these dark valleys. We need to remember that we neither get everything we want, nor are we responsible for everything that happens in this world. But God is with us. That's all I'm saying."

Nick's bowed head slowly nodded. "Yeah. I guess He's been trying to teach me about that. But I still don't get what you're trying to say about Terri. Are you saying we shouldn't try to ransom Terri either?"

"Not at all. If Betty and I had any money, I'm sure we'd contribute. But what I am askin' is, what's your attitude about it? What are you going to do if it doesn't work out?"

"I don't know. But isn't that faith, believing what you can't see?"

"Depends on what you're believin'. If you're believin' you can raise a million bucks and ransom Terri, that might not happen. You already made one attempt to rescue her that didn't work out."

Nick shrugged and inadvertently raised his head to look right at Roger. "But isn't that life? You just gotta keep on, keeping on?"

"You mean, keep on hitting your head against the wall? That's how the prosperity preachers want you to think. Just keep sendin' in your money to make *them* rich and ignore the reality or even the possibility that you might never get what you want. God doesn't expect us to ignore reality. He just wants us to become aware of a greater reality. You know, the Apostle Paul was a man of great faith, and he prayed three times that God would heal him of something he called his 'thorn in the flesh.' Didn't happen! But that didn't really shake Paul's faith, because his faith wasn't in being healed, it was in God Himself. God said, 'My grace is sufficient.' And *that's* what carried Paul through—that greater reality."

Nick lowered his head again to "the position." Roger was trying to tell him something he intuitively knew was important, but he couldn't quite grasp it. And in the moment, it felt like Roger was simply throwing cold water on a great idea. But somewhere at the edge of his understanding twinkled the freedom of doing what was right—what he felt God was leading him to do—without fear that it might fail. The possibility of an obedience that left the outcome to God relaxed him . . . just a little.

Chapter 28

Paying attention during the Sunday worship service at *La Iglesia Christiana* was more than Nick could manage. He sang along with "Santo Es Tu Nombre," apparently a favorite of the little congregation, but when the Puerto Rican guest speaker began to preach, the man spoke so fast, Nick had to strain to keep up and finally let his mind drift.

Last night Josh Kaplan had said they'd already raised almost a half-million dollars and could have it transferred to Neiva on Monday. And Tarkington had promised the bank would have the cash available. He needed to make the deal with Ramírez today. Everything had moved so fast—while he was so busy with his eye problem—he hadn't done that yet, but he would do it today . . . as soon as this church service was over.

He set his mind to planning while the preacher droned on.

The only way he knew how to contact Ramírez was to go back to that house on 58th Street and ask for Pablo again. He dreaded the abuse he was likely to receive, but he couldn't think of any other way. At his appointment tomorrow morning, Dr. Gomez would hopefully commute his face-down "sentence." But he couldn't wait until then! He had to try and contact Pablo this afternoon.

Should he tell Roger what he was going to do? He could sure use a partner in an endeavor like this. On the other hand, the people who could contact Pablo were pretty wary. They'd probably slam their door and not open it again if two people came knocking, even though one was old and wore a hat with a bullet hole in it and the other couldn't raise his head to look them in the eye. No, he'd have to go by himself. But he would leave an envelope behind with the address, *Calle Cincuenta y Ocho, numero treinta y seis,* with instructions to not follow him for twenty-four hours. By then, if he hadn't succeeded, there wasn't much hope . . . and probably not much of a chance of the police finding him, either. But what else could he do?

The taxi ride to 58th street that afternoon went faster than Nick had remembered, and he was soon banging on the bars of the security door of the dilapidated pink bungalow. He held his small double-mirror box in hand so he could keep his head down.

"¿Qué deseas?" The man who answered looked as if he was wearing the same sweat-stained strap undershirt as before. "And what's that box? You tryin' to sell something? . . . Hey, I know you!"

"I'm not trying to sell anything," Nick said hastily. "It's just got mirrors in it. Your hombres beat me up so bad last time, I almost lost my eyesight. So I have to keep my head down so my eye will heal."

"¡Madre de Dios!" said the woman who'd opened the door the first time and now came up behind the man.

"You should've learned a lesson and not come back here." The man started to push the door closed.

"Por favor, no cierres la puerta." Nick reached through the bars to hold it open. "I have to reach Teniente Ramírez. I have money for him."

"¿Dinero? ¿Cuánto dinero?"

"You don't need to know how much. Just call Pablo!"

"Oh, you don't need to speak to Pablo." The man's voice was suddenly all friendly. "Look what he did to you last time. I can arrange it for you."

"No, no, no! Pablo. *Solo Pablo*. I will only speak to Pablo!"

The man shrugged his hairy, sagging shoulders and retreated into the dark house. A few moments later, he returned to the door and handed a cell phone through the bars to Nick. Hesitantly, Nick held it up to his ear. "Is this Pablo?"

"Yeah. What d'ya want? Ramírez told me you tried to double-cross him."

"I didn't double-cross anyone. I was prepared to fly his son to Venezuela like he wanted, but he got scared." Nick quickly added, "And he said the only way he'd let the nurse go was for a ransom."

"How much?"

Nick turned his back on the eavesdropping man in the doorway and took a few steps away. *¿Habla Inglés?*

"Of course."

Nick spoke as quietly as possible, "I got half a million bucks."

"A half mil? And you can deliver that when?"

"I think by tomorrow afternoon."

"You *think*? That means you don't have it yet, right?"

"But I will have it—in U.S. dollars. Look, I'll give you my phone number, and you can call me by noon tomorrow to confirm. Okay?"

"Hold on." Nick could hear muted conversations going on. Finally, Pablo came back on the line. "All right. If Lieutenant Ramírez approves, we'll call you at noon tomorrow. If you have the money in hand, we'll set up the exchange."

As soon as Nick gave him his cell number, the phone went dead.

Nick folded the phone and handed it through the bars to the man in the house. "Gracias." Then he walked away, trembling as he tried to keep his head down. After a couple of blocks, he used his own cell to call a cab.

The first night after the FARC unit left camp, there'd been no one to start the generator, so Terri had to make do with a propane lantern and flashlights in the infirmary. Figuring out how to start the generator was just one of the chores they'd have to pick up over the next few days. The soldiers had nearly emptied the Lister bag when filling their canteens. Carlos Álvarez might not be able to haul water on crutches, but hopefully he could start the generator, and maybe he could do some cooking.

By Sunday morning, Jesús had improved enough that Terri spent time interacting with him, knowing the young man needed all the encouragement she could give him as he clawed his way back to health.

An hour later, she heard the generator start up, and the light bulb in the infirmary lit up. Carlos had succeeded! Terri expected the engine to go quiet after a few minutes since they needed to ration gasoline for the week, but it kept running. Did she have to tell the boy every little thing? She stepped out on the porch to yell at him when she noticed lights were on in the nearby communication tent.

What was he messing with now?

And then it struck her: Communication tent . . . Radio . . . Help! Perhaps she could radio to call for help. If she was able to contact the army and they came while no one was in camp, there wouldn't be a fight, and she could escape and take Jesús with her to a hospital where he could receive better care. She'd have to distract Carlos in some way, but then he didn't seem like the type to stand up against an army unit by himself. At the very least, she would encourage him to hide in the jungle and dream up some excuse to tell Ramírez, or . . . maybe he would choose to wander off by himself and melt back into the population. Not too easy for someone on crutches, but that was his problem.

She entered the com-tent, expecting to find Carlos in there playing with the radio. But no one was there. Apparently, the lights had been left on the last time the generator was shut down. Terri stared at the radio, sitting on the table just as it had when the lieutenant allowed her to speak to Mr. Hoover at First Peoples Mission to prove she was alive. She sat down in front of it as though approaching a bomb that might go off with the wrong touch. Tentatively, she reached for what she thought was the on/off switch when the sound of the generator died and the lights in the tent went out.

Terri had to restrain herself from running out and yelling for Carlos to restart the generator. But on what pretense during daylight? She couldn't think of one in the moment. She didn't dare let him know she intended to radio for help. He might be inept and clumsy, but he was smart enough to know that unapproved use of the radio could give away the camp's location, and he was loyal enough to FARC to do something about it. Instead, she turned the switches off on the already dark bulbs and left.

That evening after Carlos had started the generator and they'd eaten supper, Terri got up from the table, grabbed a flashlight, and said, "I cooked, so you're on cleanup. Also, see if you can get Jesús to eat a little more of this rice gruel. He found it too hot earlier, but he needs the nutrition."

"What d'ya mean, I'm on cleanup? I outrank you. You don't have any rank at all around here. Besides, why d'ya need to go out for a stroll?"

"It's a personal matter," she said, rolling her eyes and holding up the flashlight. "Besides, Rosita told me that in FARC, men and women are equal. Share and share alike is the revolutionary motto, isn't it? So what's your problem?"

He shrugged, and she went out the door.

Inside the com-tent, she only used the flashlight. If Carlos looked out, she didn't want him to get curious about why bright lights were on in another tent. The radio was a jury-rigged device with two components that didn't even look military, perhaps leftovers from some amateur operator. She hit what she thought was the power button, and two dials lit up. Excitement coursed through her as though she'd grasped a couple of live wires from the generator. But how would she know what frequency to select? Their current settings were undoubtedly the last used by the radioman, probably to contact another FARC unit—not the best people to notify that she was on the air. So how would she call for help?

She spent the next ten minutes searching the tent for some kind of a manual or notebook with a list of previously used stations. If the operator kept records, they might even include the frequency she spoke on when they called Thomas Hoover. But time was running out, and Carlos was likely to become suspicious about her long absence.

She decided to take a chance on dialing some other frequency at random in the hope that by broadcasting to the heavens, she would reach someone who could help. In the back of her mind echoed Psalm 73: *"Whom have I in heaven but thee?"* as she sat down and reached out . . . only to realize that the earphones and mic were not plugged into the front of the radio. Where—? She quickly searched all around the radio, the floor, even among the other equipment. They simply weren't there. In her excitement over finding the radio, she hadn't noticed their absence earlier, and she hadn't seen them while searching for a manual or notebook.

Plopping down on the one cot that was in the tent, she buried her head in her hands. Of course! Ramírez and his radioman weren't so careless as to leave a functioning radio in camp, just inviting her to call for help. And all they had to do was take one essential part in order to totally disable the radio.

"Whom have I in heaven but thee? and there is none upon earth that I desire beside thee." She sighed deeply. "Okay Lord, I'm turning to You, and I thank You that I can speak to You without either a mic or earphones."

As Nick returned wearily to the Montgomery's house Sunday evening, Roger greeted him with, "You got in touch with them, didn't you?" It sounded like a challenge.

"Well, yeah. I'm not trying to keep any secrets from you. I know you didn't think it was a good idea, but I have to make every effort. I can't just leave her there."

"Wait a minute. I didn't say your plan was a bad idea. Don't forget, I said Betty and I would contribute if we had the money. So I don't blame you for trying. Just tell me how it went."

"Oh, yeah, you did say that. Sorry." Nick realized his emotions were on edge. "Well, I made contact without being thrown into a coffee bean silo and getting my head cracked open again. That's progress, huh?" Nick allowed a wry grin. "And I was able to talk to Pablo by phone. He's going to call me back tomorrow. If Ramírez approves and I've got the money, they'll give me instructions for making the exchange."

"But you don't have the million bucks. What're you going to do?"

"Pray, I guess. I told Pablo I had half that—or will be tomorrow morning. And Tarkington said there's nothing wrong with negotiating. 'Bird in the hand,' and 'Money talks.' That sort of thing. So . . ." Nick shrugged.

"Well I'm gonna pray God blesses this. We just need to keep our focus on Him. But if there's anything I can do, let me know."

"Thanks, Roger. I appreciate it." Maybe everything would work out. But the knots in his stomach . . . were they normal stress over such a big deal, or was it something more? Terri had so often quoted Scripture for every situation—sometimes a prayer, sometimes a word of reassurance—that Nick had sometimes considered it trite. But right now, a verse from the Bible might resonate as a personal word from the Lord for him, and he needed that.

Chapter 29

The next morning, Roger drove Nick to see Dr. Gomez.

"The retina looks good," the doctor said. "We'll keep a watch on it, but I think we've got it pinned down. However, your cornea has taken a beating. It's quite swollen. It's going to be a while before we can consider a lens implant."

"What do you mean by 'a while'?"

"Hmm, weeks, maybe a couple of months. It's hard to tell. We don't want to risk losing your cornea. Cornea transplants are . . . well, they're major events even when you can find one. Maybe we'll have to resort to giving you a contact lens, putting the optics on the outside of the eye rather than inside."

That was discouraging. "But I don't have to keep my head down anymore, do I?"

"No, I think you're good to go there. But don't forget about your diabetes. You're still vulnerable to bleeds if you don't keep it under control."

On the way home, Nick called David Tarkington. "Is your bank ready to release the money?"

"Let me check, and I'll call you right back."

As Roger was parking the car, Tarkington called back. "They've received the five hundred thousand, and they do have the cash in U.S. bills."

"Just five hundred K, huh?" Nick realized he'd been hoping somehow for the whole amount. "You think I've got a chance?"

"It's worth a try. Even if they say they need more, you've opened the negotiations, and that's more than we've had so far."

"Okay. I'm expecting a call about noon. Do you think you could withdraw the money? Then as soon as I get word, I'll drop by your office."

"I'll have it for you in thirty minutes."

At the Montgomerys' apartment, Nick couldn't stop pacing, and he didn't even think about how good it was to not have to keep his head down.

"Sit down at the table, will ya? You at least gotta have a bite to eat," Roger said, slapping down a toasted cheese sandwich and a glass of iced tea on the table.

Nick kept pacing. "I've gotta think of a good place to make the trade, a place they'd accept, and a place where they would release Terri."

"Ha. You think you're gonna set the terms? Look, they know a lot more about this business than any of us. It'll be a place and a time of their choosing, I guarantee it. In fact, I doubt they'll even bring Terri to the rendezvous. For most of the political kidnappings I can recall, once FARC got the money, they just released the hostages on some desolate road and let them walk to the nearest town."

Nick nodded absently and finally sat down. But after his first bite, he was up and pacing again. "How can I be sure Ramírez will keep his word and release her?"

"Huh, you can't. But like I said, FARC's been doing this for years. If they didn't usually keep their word, they couldn't keep makin' more ransom deals, and that's been a rather profitable scheme for them. So, I think the odds are in your favor. But who's to say? Just keep alert."

The call came before Nick finished his sandwich.

"You got the money?" The voice did not sound like Ramírez or Pablo, but it had to be someone calling on their behalf. Who else would have his number and know of the plan?

"Yes, I got it, five hundred thousand in U.S. dollars." He certainly hoped Tarkington hadn't run into any hitches.

"Good. Remember that road going east of Otás where you landed before?"

"Yeah." It was only fifteen minutes away by air, but he couldn't fly.

"Meet us there by two o'clock."

"Uh. You gotta give me more time." He'd have to borrow a car and drive. It was only about fifty kilometers, but it might take two hours by the time he went by Tarkington's office. "There's no way I can get there that soon. Give me 'til four."

"Four? *¿Estás loco?* . . . Or are you thinking you need enough time to set up an army ambush?"

"No, no, no. No tricks. I just can't get there that soon."

There was a long silence. "I'll give you until three, but you better come alone. If we see anybody, even dust on the road, the deal's off!"

"Don't worry. No tricks. I'll be there by three." But could he get there by then? "And I'll be alone. You don't have to worry." But he was only bringing half the money Ramírez had demanded. He'd better make that clear, but he wouldn't say *half*. "I'll be there by three with five hundred thousand U.S. dollars . . . in cash!"

"You'd better!" The line went dead.

Nick just stood there for a few moments, breathing hard. It was happening! He was making a deal to free Terri.

"So, is it on?" asked Roger.

"Yeah, I think so. Can I borrow your car?"

"I guess, but you only got one good eye. Maybe I oughta drive you."

"No! I gotta go alone. They said if they saw anyone else, even in the vicinity, the deal would be off. As it is, they're expecting me to fly in, but of course I can't, so I have to drive."

"They . . . what? Why didn't you just tell them you gotta drive? If they see a car instead of a plane . . ." Roger shook his head and threw up his hands.

"I . . . I don't know. Guess I was tryin' to keep it simple, not make a lot of changes besides the time."

"Lord, have mercy." Rather reluctantly, the older man held out his keys to Nick. "Where is this meeting, anyway?"

Nick headed for the door. "Otás, that little road going east of town, same place I met them before. Thanks for the car."

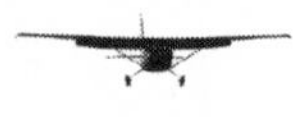

With an attaché case on the seat beside him, Nick pushed Roger's old car to its limits, hoping to make the rendezvous on time before he ran out of gas—he'd failed to check and wouldn't have had time to stop and fill up anyway. If Otás had been large enough to have a cop, he'd certainly have gotten a speeding ticket for racing through town. As it was, the chickens and goats were lucky to get out of his way.

It was five minutes to three when he came up over the little rise and saw the long, straight stretch of the dirt road where he'd landed before. He let his foot off the gas and allowed the car to slow down, realizing he was making his own cloud of dust the kidnappers had warned him about.

Finally, the car rolled to a stop in the middle of the road, at the exact spot where he'd stopped the Cessna on his earlier visit. He sat for a moment, watching the ravine the jeep had come up out of the last time, but nothing moved. Slowly, he opened his door, grabbed the attaché case, and got out, holding the case high with one hand, and his other hand equally high. He walked slowly forward, still studying the ravine.

"Walk a hundred meters straight ahead," came a shouted command from some boulders on the hillside to the left.

Nick obeyed, studying the rocky high ground for the speaker as he went.

He'd almost reached the designated distance when he saw a man stand up. With horror Nick realized the tube on his shoulder was an RPG-7 rocket launcher. Nick fell to the ground, flattening himself in the gravel just as the rocket fired and he saw it streak overhead back down the road. The enormous concussion as the rocket found its target knocked the breath out of him, only to be followed by a second explosion as the nearly-empty gas tank in Roger's car blew up, turning the whole wreck into a plume of orange and black flame.

Why had they done that? His heart was pounding. This was not a good start.

Slowly, he got to his knees and finally to his feet—hands high with the money case still dangling from his right hand. The guy who'd launched the rocket had disappeared, but Nick continued to study the boulders for other threats, not that he could've done anything about them. In fact, there wasn't even a place nearby where he could take cover.

The only sound was the roaring and popping from Roger's burning car, a hundred meters behind him. There didn't even seem to be any birds about or the whoosh of a breeze.

"Hello!" he ventured. "We got a deal here or what?" He waited a few more moments. "I got the money! Five hundred thousand American dollars." The thought crossed Nick's mind that it was strange Ramírez hadn't pressed for the whole million. In fact, that glitch had been nagging at the back of his mind since the call at noon, but he'd been too excited about making the deal to think much about it. And he didn't have any more money, so he'd figured, go with what you've got! Besides, if the rest of the one million came in at all, it would be days before he could deliver it.

"Hello, I know you're there! I want to see Terri!" It was time to be more assertive in this exchange . . . take control! He glanced over at the ravine on the right side of the road just as three men emerged, widely spaced, advancing along the road toward him.

All pointed Kalashnikovs toward him.

Chapter 30

Where's Terri? I want to see Terri Kaplan!"

"Put down the case, and back off." It was Pablo's voice. So this was Pablo—short and wide, though not fat. He wore Levis, a camo shirt, and a New York Yankee's baseball cap. A week's growth of salt-and-pepper beard shadowed his face.

"First, I want to see Terri." Nick tried to sound decisive, unrelenting.

"Señor Nick, you are not in a very good position to make demands. Either you put down the case and back off so we can check the money or we shoot you, and *then* we check the money. Which will it be?"

Nick's mind was spinning. Would Pablo actually shoot him? This was the second time he'd met the man, but it was the first time Pablo had allowed him to see his face—not a good sign. If Pablo had been so concerned about hiding his identity before, was he already planning to eliminate Nick as a witness this time? Having seen him, Nick could identify him, connect him to the kidnapping, the ransom demands, and . . . even the destruction of Roger's car. Nick wanted to say, "But I have no idea where you live. No one would be able to find you." He relented. Pablo was right. He wasn't in a very good position to argue.

"Look, I'm putting down the money." When it was on the ground, he began backing away, still keeping his hands high.

A nod from Pablo directed one of his men to pick up the case and take it to him. Pablo opened it and fingered through the stacks of bills. After a few moments, he looked up at Nick. "Okay, today you live. You can go now."

Nick breathed again. "Not without Terri. And how about a few of those 'Benjamins' to pay for my friend's car? Why'd you blow it up, anyway?"

"Why'd you drive instead of fly?"

"'Cause I can't fly my plane right now. It was the only way I could get here."

Pablo shrugged. "We had to make sure there wasn't someone else hidin' in it. No tricks, as you said."

That made Nick mad, but he bit his tongue. The car didn't really matter in comparison to Terri. "Yeah, we agreed, no tricks. So where's Terri Kaplan? It's time for you to deliver. I want her back, and I want her now!" He tried to make his voice commanding again, but he was afraid it sounded like a whine.

"Oh yeah, that nurse you're so worried about. Next time I hear from Lieutenant Ramírez, I'll ask about her. Who knows, maybe he doesn't need her anymore."

"What?" Nick cocked his fist and took a step toward Pablo before the man fired off a short burst into the air above Nick's head.

"I think you better leave, *amigo*," the man leered. "It's only a short walk back to town, no more than two or three kilometers. Maybe you can find someone going into Neiva who'll give you a ride, get you out of this sun. I think it's affecting your good judgment." He lowered his weapon and pointed it right at Nick's middle. "Now! *¡Sal de aquí!* Unless you are tired of living."

Nick slowly lowered his fist. He knew he was on the edge. A flick of the man's finger would end his life, and by now he had no doubt Pablo would do it, too. Rage seethed in his gut as he realized the truth. He'd been double-crossed. Pablo was here on his own. He'd never told Ramírez about Nick's ransom offer.

Just as suddenly, the rage was swallowed by an overwhelming sense of despair. He'd failed once more to rescue Terri. What did his life matter now? And yet, his feet turned his body around and began walking him toward Otás.

As he plodded past Roger's still burning car, he looked back toward the scene of the showdown. There was no sign of anyone on the road or in the boulders on the left or the ravine to the right. He was alone.

Nick's mind was as numb as if a concussion grenade had gone off beside him. And when coherent thoughts finally began to assemble themselves, they were from far away—somewhere over the mountains where he imagined Terri was being forced to nurse dozens of wounded rebels just as uncouth and dangerous as Pablo.

He'd failed her . . . again! He should have known something was wrong on the phone when Pablo didn't demand or even hint at the full million that Ramírez had set as the ransom fee. He'd just been too excited, too eager to be the one to rescue Terri.

He shuffled along the road to Otás. Now that the rainy season was over, his feet kicked up little swirls of dust with every step. A groan escaped from his dry mouth. *O God! O God!* He'd failed Terri! And he'd lost *a lot* of other people's money! "OPM" they called it when unscrupulous investors risked it. Was that who he was? And Roger's car . . . destroyed, too. How would he ever replace it? He glanced back one more time. The column of black smoke continued to rise over the last small hill, probably from the still-burning tires. Maybe it would attract the attention of an army unit. But what good would that do? They'd never catch Pablo, and even if they did, that wouldn't help Terri.

"O God, where are You when I need You?"

Feelings of abandonment thundered in on him like a monsoon rain that could turn dust in the road to mud in minutes. One minute he'd been so confident God was helping him rescue Terri, and the next minute all hopes were drowned. It had happened again and again. How could God be so fickle? Where was He? Did He even exist?

Almost an hour after his confrontation with Pablo, Nick finally got to Otás. A farmer on the edge of the village was loading crates of tomatoes onto his small truck. "You taking those in to Neiva?"

"Sí, para el mercado de mañana."

Nick glanced at the adjoining field where more crates sat at the ends of the rows. "I'll load the rest of 'em for you to take to market if you give me a ride."

The man straightened up, holding his back with one hand and pushing his hat up on his head with the other. He shook his head with regret. "No room *en mi camioneta—mi esposa y niños."*

"No problema. You take the wife and kids in the cab, and I'll ride in the back."

"Bueno." The man smiled broadly and waved his hand toward the field.

As Nick went for the boxes of tomatoes, the man headed across the road into the small orange house with a red tile roof, calling for his wife and children. Nick finished loading all the boxes in twenty minutes, reserving a space on the back corner of the flatbed for himself. But the sun was nearly setting before the family was loaded and they were rumbling through Otás on their way to Neiva. There seemed to be a lot of haze in the air, perhaps from Roger's car, but the column of black smoke no longer rose over the foothill to the east.

How would he ever explain this day to his old friend?

Chapter 31

Nick couldn't believe Roger's reaction. The older man seemed to dismiss his apologies with a wave of his hand. "Hmph. Don't worry about that old junker. It was about done for anyway. I'm just glad you're okay." Roger pulled on his mustache. "You look dead on your feet. I'll pour you some coffee. Had anything to eat?"

"You kidding? Had to walk halfway across Neiva from where that farmer let me off."

"Then sit down. Sit down. Here's your coffee. It'll only take me a few minutes to heat up Betty's leftover stew."

Nick collapsed into a wooden chair with its chipped white paint showing it had once been red. His hand was shaking as he accepted the mug of the bitter mud Roger called coffee. "What am I gonna do, Roger? Terri's still a captive, and no telling what indignities and hardships they're puttin' on her. And . . . and I've lost our only chance to buy her freedom."

Roger shrugged and sat down across the table from him. "Heck if I know what to do." He absently brushed a hand over his bald head. Roger's beat-up fedora was so much a part of him, that without it he seemed like an older and smaller version of his blustery self.

"I thought you'd at least tell me to pray about it."

"Why? Have you quit prayin'?"

"No."

"Well then, I don't need to you tell you to keep on. But otherwise, I don't know what to do. But if you must know, right now . . ." He got up and dished up a bowl of stew and put it before Nick. "Here, eat this, and then go to bed. I'm headin' that way myself. Betty's still at that quinceañera for Lucy Mendoza over at the academy. Said the poor girl needed something really special for her fifteenth birthday, so I don't expect her back till late. But you—you need some rest."

Nick fell asleep within minutes of hitting the pillow but woke up about four in the morning with the heavy feeling that he hadn't slept nearly long enough. But the name *Bartimaeus* was ringing in his mind. *Bartimaeus, Bartimaeus.* He was one of the blind people Jesus had healed. Nick switched on the light on his bedside table and opened his Bible, flipping through the Gospels looking for the story. He finally found it at the end of Mark 10. Bartimaeus had been begging beside the road outside the city of Jericho when Jesus came by. Verse 47 said, "When he heard that it was Jesus of Nazareth, he began to shout, 'Jesus, Son of David, have mercy on me!'" Apparently, he kept yelling the same request until Jesus finally responded and called him to come over.

How long had he been blind?

How long had he been sitting by the road begging?

How many times did he call out to Jesus?

Nick shook the thoughts out of his head. Trivial curiosities. Nick kept reading.

When Jesus finally responded, Bartimaeus threw off his cloak, jumped up and came to him.

> "What do you want me to do for you?" Jesus asked him.
>
> The blind man said, "Rabbi, I want to see."
>
> "Go," said Jesus, "your faith has healed you." Immediately he received his sight and followed Jesus along the road. (vss. 51, 52).

Nick's questions were more personal: Surely Jesus heard Bartimaeus because the man made such a ruckus people tried to shut him up. So why didn't Jesus respond to Bartimaeus's first call? *Why hasn't He responded to my calls for help?* Nick lay back on his pillow and looked up at the ceiling. The bubble rolled up the center of his vision. It was smaller now, more like the size of a softball held at arms length. He rolled his eyes and the bubble swirled around with the motion like a BB in a child's handheld pinball game. He gave one half-hearted laugh at the comparison as he reached over and shut off the light. He didn't want to play games. He wanted to fly airplanes so he could go get Terri.

"Jesus, Son of David, have mercy on me! Jesus, Son of David, have mercy on me!" Nick made the cry his own, and like Bartimaeus, he didn't care whether he disturbed anyone else, not even Roger and Betty. "Jesus, Son of David, have mercy on me!"

He knew his eye *was* getting better, but that didn't really matter anymore. The oscillation between hope and terror had worn his faith so thin he wasn't even sure he believed in God anymore. And even if God existed, did he want to have anything to do with such a God, one who was so incomprehensible, so un- . . . un- . . . so unmanageable? He had tried praise. He had tried thanksgiving. He had tried submitting his requests. He had tried to trust, but he couldn't make it work! There was no way to manage God, no way to *make God work*! Maybe God just didn't exist!

A cold claw gripped Nick's soul—the chill of being totally alone, the abyss of "no God." Was that a taste of hell's separation? Was that what it meant to exist forever without God?

Nick sighed deeply and closed his eyes. "Jesus, Son of David, have mercy on me! Jesus, Son of David . . . just be with me," he whispered. "Just be with me! Just be with me! That's all that matters, Jesus. Just be with me! Let me know You are here!"

Slowly . . . somehow being able to know Jesus really was there in that dark room became more important to Nick than managing God or even getting his sight back. He wanted to be aware of Jesus' presence! He wanted to know that Jesus was with him. Yes, if Jesus had asked him what he wanted, he would have answered like Bartimaeus, "I want to see!" But that would have come *after* Jesus had confirmed his presence. Wait . . . how had Jesus put it elsewhere in the Gospels? That it was better to lose your sight and enter the kingdom of God than to have two eyes and be cast into hell? Nick now knew what that meant. Even if he never flew again, even if he couldn't rescue Terri, even if he became completely blind in both eyes, he needed to know Jesus was there. Here! Now! Nothing mattered more!

"Jesus, Son of David, just be with me!"

Somehow in that early morning hour, something changed. Like rumblings in the bowels of the earth beneath, something shifted. At first Nick couldn't grasp it, but he sensed it. He had learned something. By looking over the edge into the abyss, he had learned it was more important to know that Jesus was with him than to be able to see, even though at one point he'd counted sight more valuable than life itself. But now he knew . . . Jesus's presence was even more important than either. And that lesson had somehow changed everything!

It changed everything because he began to realize it was Jesus who had taught it to him. And *in the teaching,* He had shown himself present. Not only was He there, but He cared enough to teach Nick something—something Nick hadn't known before, something he couldn't have discovered on his own. It was a lesson, taught by a Teacher, a master Teacher who had proceeded with purpose and love through pain and anguish. Someone had taken the trouble to teach him the most important lesson of his life, and that someone was Jesus. And in so doing, He had shown Nick he hadn't been alone through the whole difficult journey. Jesus had never abandoned him.

"Jesus, Son of David, have mercy on me!"

Jesus, Son of David, had indeed had mercy on Nick Archer.

The engine whine of a vehicle bouncing over the ruts of the road into the camp woke Terri. She jumped out of bed, glanced at Jesús, who was still sleeping soundly in his bed on the other side of the infirmary, and pushed open the screen door.

"Carlos," she called, "who's coming?"

Out of convenience, Carlos had moved his stuff into a tent closer to the infirmary, but Terri figured he'd already be up. He'd gotten good at getting around on his crutches and was usually up at dawn fulfilling small chores around the camp. "Can't see it yet," Carlos responded, "but it sounds like the meat wagon."

Meat wagon. Terrible name for the makeshift ambulance. Terri stepped out onto the porch. Bad news if it was the ambulance coming in so fast! She would be busy.

A minute later it skidded to a stop in front of the infirmary and Sergeant Rodriquez jumped out. "Help me with the stretcher," he barked as he came around to the back and began to pull it out, still favoring his wounded shoulder.

Terri grabbed the other end. To her surprise, Jesús had gotten up, tottered to the doorway, and was holding the screen open. "You better get back to bed," she said, seeing his pale face as she passed him. "I don't need any more problems here."

They set the stretcher on the long table. "Carlos," she yelled as loudly as she could, hoping he could hear her, "get that generator going. I need more light." She pulled back the thin blanket covering the patient. Her breath caught.

Rosita!

Terri leaned her face close, hoping to detect a breath, and then grabbed the young woman's wrist for a pulse. When she finally found it, it was faint and very fast.

"Rosita, Rosita! Can you hear me?" She glanced at Rodriquez. "What happened?"

"We were ambushed by paramilitaries. She got hit in the thigh and the chest."

Terri had noticed the huge dark stain on her leg. She ripped open Rosita's shirt. Someone had tried to stop a sucking chest wound with plastic wrap and a field dressing, but there was still frothy blood seeping out around the edges. "Sergeant! Can you put on that blood pressure cuff? I need to know what's happening. I've got to pull this off and put on a vented chest seal."

Rodriquez stood there shaking his head.

"Right *there,* hanging on that pole. Wrap it around her arm. Pump it up and then release the pressure slowly. Use the stethoscope, and watch the dial. Tell me when you first hear a pulse, and then again when you don't. Come on, Rodriquez, surely you've seen this done dozens of times."

"Yeah, but I—"

"Just do it!" By this time, Terri had pulled off the initial dressing. The frothing blood had slowed to a slow oozing, but there was no evident chest movement. She checked for a pulse and couldn't find one. "Give me that stethoscope!"

She detected no heartbeat. Desperately she began compression, which produced more frothy blood, but still no heartbeat. She frantically worked on Rosita for another twenty minutes, but finally stood back, defeated. Tears clouded her eyes.

"She's gone."

Breathing hard from the extended exertion, she stared at the closest person to a friend she'd met in the FARC . . . and she'd been unable to save her life. The wretched war! Would it never end? She had to get out of here. She couldn't take it anymore.

"But I got her here in time!" Rodriquez said. "She was still alive."

"In time? The only *in time* would've been before the ambush, before you ever went out, before all of you began fighting this damned war!" Terri rarely swore, but if there ever was something deserving the term *damned,* this was it.

"You have no idea!" Rodriquez turned and strode toward the door.

"What a minute. What are we going to do with her body?"

The man paused. "We'll take her to Dos Rios so her family can bury her, but not today. I'm whipped. I've been up for thirty hours. I'm gonna sleep."

Terri stood there for a long moment and then began cleaning Rosita's body, washing off all the blood, putting bandages over the wounds so her family would not have to see them, and dressing her in clean clothes. She struggled with a body that weighed as much as she did as she moved Rosita onto her own cot and laid her out to look as peaceful as possible. Finally, she combed the girl's hair and applied a little makeup to try and hide the gray of her face. The job took most of the day.

"You okay with me leaving her in here with you while I go sleep in the com-tent tonight?" she asked Jesús. "I'll be close enough that if you need me, you can call."

The boy glanced at Rosita's body a moment, then looked away. "Uh, I guess so."

"I'll see if I can get Carlos to cook something for us. I think Sergeant Rodriquez is still sleeping."

The small votive candle had almost burned out when Terri's eyes popped open. A dark figure loomed near her.

"Hey *guapa,* why so jumpy? Why didn't you wake me up to eat?"

She sat up. "I ain't your *guapa,* Rodriquez. And I didn't call you 'cause I figured you needed the sleep and would wake up when you got hungry."

"Oh yeah, yeah. Come to think of it, I am kinda hungry, but not for any more beans and rice." He took a step closer. "However, you look mighty fine in this candlelight. So why don't you lay back down? There's room for both of us on that cot."

"Get out of here, Rodriquez." She tried to keep control of her voice. "If I told the lieutenant about this, you'd be in big trouble."

He moved toward her.

"Rodriquez! I'm warnin' you!" She yelled, and feared her voice communicated the panic she felt. "Don't come any closer!" She could see the sneer on his face in the dim candlelight.

"You owe me, *guapa,* for that day you got my stripes pulled. I told you you'd pay, and now's as good a time as any."

"No. NO! Don't touch me! Get off me!"

Click—schlock . . . Rodriquez whipped around at the unmistakable sound of a 45 automatic being cocked. He leaned back and raised both hands. "Hey there, Jesús. You still look a little pale there. Better get back to bed before you pass out. We're just havin' a little fun here. Nothin' that concerns you."

Jesús thrust the gun toward Rodriquez, his right hand steadied with his left. "Get out." The boy weaved slightly from side to side, but the 45 remained pointed toward the sergeant. "You get out right now—out of camp. I don't want to see you around here anymore."

Rodriquez stood up. "Now Jesús, let's not get carried away. This was no big deal, and you don't want to make trouble for yourself with your . . . with the lieutenant."

"Doc," Jesús said, ignoring Rodriquez, "why don't you fold up that mat and take it back to the infirmary while I make sure this idiot gets in his pickup and leaves camp. Put Rosita on it on the floor . . . or you can sleep on it yourself, whatever."

Terri didn't hesitate. As she ducked out of the com-tent with the mat she'd been sleeping on, she gave Jesús a grateful smile. He might just be a boy in terms of his age, but right now he was acting like a true man.

Chapter 32

By the time Roger returned home the next evening from work, Nate had been working feverishly for over three hours with his flight charts spread out on the kitchen table, punching numbers into his pocket calculator and taking notes on a small tablet.

"Okay, Roger," he said, tapping a pencil on his notepad, "I've been doing my homework, and I think I can go get Terri outta there. I've found a route over the Cordilleras where I wouldn't have to fly any higher than about seventy-five hundred feet. Now, Neiva's almost fifteen hundred, so my gain would be no more than six thousand feet. You with me so far?"

Roger rolled his eyes. "Not really, but I've got an idea where this is goin'."

"Great! Because a gain of only six thousand feet means a decrease in air pressure of only 18 percent. So, the bubble in my eye wouldn't increase very much when you consider how small it is now. I'm sure I can handle a little increase with no problem."

Roger shrugged "That much calculatin's a little above my pay grade, but don't you think it'd be a good idea to check all this out with your eye doctor first?"

"No."

"Why not?"

"'Cause he's got to cover his butt, so he's going to give me his most conservative opinion, and I don't want his most conservative opinion. He thinks I'm going to be soaring around up there at ten or fifteen thousand feet. But I'm not planning on doing that. I can weave my way through the mountain passes and not go very high at all. Besides, that bubble's almost gone, so it shouldn't be any problem."

"And it won't be . . . unless it is, and then your eye's gonna pop like a balloon. And you'll be wonderin' where was God, and why He didn't protect you. Are you forgetting you only got one eye you can see with?" He shook his head. "You baffle me, Nick Archer. You truly just baffle me. That's all I gotta say."

The glow of dawn was just painting the eastern sky with a hint of light when Nick took off from the Neiva airport Wednesday morning. Earlier he'd intended to go in at dusk, but even a few minutes miscalculation would leave him in too much darkness to land. Besides, he figured, most people were still awake at that time of the evening, awake and alert enough to recognize any unusual noise made by his Cessna touching down. So he'd chosen the early morning, hoping to arrive with just enough light to find and land on the overgrown strip at a time when most of the soldiers were still asleep or at the most groggily staggering to the latrine before getting their first cup of coffee. The only problem was, he wouldn't have the cover of complete darkness to find and extract Terri.

But as the lights of Neiva passed under him, he considered it a beautiful morning, a beautiful day to rescue her. He banked in a gentle turn toward the mountains.

That morning before he'd snuck out of the Montgomery's house he'd checked the size of the bubble at the bottom of his vision in his left eye. It wasn't as small as a BB, more like a golf ball at arm's length. But then Dr. Gomez had said he'd only need to wait five to seven days before flying, and this was day six, so it was all relative anyway . . . he hoped. Besides, he'd devised a way to minimize the altitude he needed. He checked his compass and adjusted his heading slightly for the first pass in the mountains, feeling like he was flying pretty well with only one usable eye.

It got a good deal dicier weaving through the mountain passes, though. It wasn't so much his lack of depth perception—that came more into play with things closer at hand, like how high the next step was when climbing stairs. But he was flying between mountains with barely enough light to see them on either side of him. A couple of times he was too uncertain, and chose to go higher, but only once did he go up to eight thousand feet.

"O God, don't let my eye—" He couldn't say *burst!* "Just keep it okay, God."

It took an hour before he approached the coordinates where he thought the FARC outpost was. He'd timed it right in terms of the light. The sun was ready to break over the eastern horizon, and the pink patches of mist scattered across the jungle below looked like shreds of cotton candy that had snagged on the treetops.

He throttled back, set his flaps to 10 degrees, and began his descent even though he hadn't yet spotted the scar among the trees he'd taken for a landing strip. It was highly risky to land on a strip he hadn't carefully scouted at least by a low fly-over, but there wasn't any alternative, and he had no plan B. If he had to add power and come around a second time, he'd lose his stealth advantage. If that happened, should he abort or land anyway and hope for the best?

And then he saw it—or thought he did, just before a wisp of mist moved over the spot. Yes, that was it! He cut the ignition and feathered the prop. Now . . . could he set the right glide path to hit the end of the runway? He increased his flaps and slipped the plane to the left for a better view. Yes, that was it. It looked good. It was a short strip, but it had to be enough. It was, after all, a landing strip and not just the start of a road . . . he hoped. The trees at the beginning were pretty high, however. No one had been taking care of it or they would have been cut down or at least topped.

At the last minute he straightened out and set it down. *Wham, baloom, baloom. baloom! Rattle, rattle, baloom!* The Cessna bounced and shook, making so much noise Nick was sure it could be heard a mile away. Finally, it rolled out. He'd never been more grateful that he'd installed oversized "bush tires" on his plane that could roll over such a rough field. It'd felt like a cow pasture with deep hoof dents everywhere.

He opened the door and listened. Everything was quiet except for a couple of parrots squawking in nearby treetops that the sun was just beginning to tip with gold. He got out and listened again. He could hear a stream or river to the east, in the direction he thought the camp lay, but no voices, no one yelling to rally the FARC defenses.

However, as he looked around, he saw a problem. His plane had stopped two-thirds of the way down the strip, probably slowed by the foot-high grass and rough ground. He looked back at the trees he'd come over at the beginning of the strip. There was no way he could just turn around and take off in that short of a distance and be sure of clearing those trees. He'd need the full length of the strip. That meant turning the Cessna around and dragging it by hand all the way to the other end of the strip so it'd be ready for a quick takeoff . . . or trusting that when he and Terri came running to make their escape, there'd be time to taxi to that end, turn around and take off before any pursuers arrived with weapons that could shoot them out of the air.

Nick gritted his teeth. He couldn't take that chance! He had to give himself a better start. Hurrying to the back of the plane, he pulled out the tail-pull handle—again, thankful he'd taken the time to add that modification years before—and turned the plane around. Then he began dragging it tail-first toward the end of the field. The high grass, bumps, and hoof-holes made the job nearly impossible. The small tail wheel, in particular, seemed to get caught in each depression. Nick had to stop every five meters to rest. Soon he became so fatigued he could only manage three meters at a time before catching his breath. Dragging a ton of aircraft the length of a football field was exhausting enough even on a smooth ramp. But across a rugged cow pasture it was nearly impossible and left him panting and drenched in sweat.

He felt as if he was going to black out, with darkness closing in from every side. In desperation he hung on. He was almost to the end of the field. Yes, yes . . . he was going to make it. Just one more push to make sure the main tires as well as the tail wheel weren't caught in holes that would make it hard for the plane to get going again.

There, he'd done it! He closed his eyes and let his body collapse over the rear of the fuselage just in front of the vertical fin, his arms hanging down on the other side like a rag doll until his heart rate finally slowed. Now all he had to do was find Terri and get her out of that camp without getting caught.

He rested for another five minutes and then opened his eyes and stood up . . . but something was terribly wrong with his vision. His left eye was as before—a total blur because of no lens, as though he were looking through a piece of frosted glass. The distinct bubble still rolled back and forth on the "bottom," maybe as small now as a BB. But his right eye, his *good* eye, was like someone had thrown mud into it!

Nick tried to fight a rising tide of panic. Without a doubt, those large islands of brown came from another bleed!

Terri awoke, momentarily disoriented by sleeping on the floor beside the surgery table. What was she doing down there? And then she remembered. She sat up. At least Rodriquez had stayed out if the infirmary for the night. Could Jesús' threat actually have convinced him to leave camp? She hadn't heard the old pickup start.

She scrambled up and checked on Jesús. He still slept peacefully, so she went to the door and looked out. The pickup was gone, and hopefully so was Rodriquez.

"Carlos, you awake?"

"Sí, Señorita Doctora," Carlos answered from inside his nearby tent.

"Where's the sergeant?"

"He went to meet the lieutenant. Said the whole unit's coming back later this afternoon, and they need the pickup to help transport stuff."

Terri sighed with relief. She was safe for the moment! But when Ramírez got back, should she tell him what happened last night? Or would that simply cause Rodriquez to schedule his retaliation for the next time he caught her alone? Deep down she knew abusers and sexual predators were opportunists. Lack of opportunity did not mean they had changed. It didn't mean she was safe. He would simply wait until he could attack with impunity.

She had to get away! How did David put it in 2 Samuel 22? *"I will call upon the Lord, who is worthy to be praised, So shall I be saved from my enemies."* She stepped back into the infirmary murmuring, "Yes, Yes! *So shall I be saved from my enemies. So shall I be saved from my enemies.* I need to call upon the Lord!"

Terri poured an inch of water into a basin and washed her face. Then she grabbed a roll of toilet paper and headed toward the latrines. As she walked down the trail, she began to call upon the Lord by singing the words of Scripture as made popular by the group Petra: *"So shall I be saved from my enemies!"* She sang them over and over until she got to the makeshift canvas booths surrounding the latrines.

When she came out, she started to sing again, and then she heard something.

"Terri, Terri . . ."

She stood still. Was someone calling her? Couldn't be. Carlos and Jesús were back in camp. And yet she was certain she'd heard her name. She started back toward camp and then heard it again. "Terri, is that you?"

She turned around and cautiously went back, past the latrines, this time along the much narrower path toward the river.

The voice came again, barely above a whisper. "Terri, over here!"

All her senses went on alert. "Who's there?"

"Me, Nick."

"Nick!" Her heart did a leap. "How'd you get here?" His voice had come from a pile of driftwood and heaped-up brush deposited by some recent floodwaters. She glanced back along the path to be sure no one was coming, and then waded through the high weeds toward the thicket. "Are you in there, Nick?"

"Yeah, but . . ."

"What are you *doing* here?" She pushed her way into the thicket, hardly believing her ears until she saw his face, with a trickle of blood rolling down his forehead. "You're bleeding!"

He wiped the back of his hand across his forehead. "It's nothing. I just took a header off a bank back there into the river." But he seemed to be squinting and blinking as though something was in his eye . . . or had he seen someone coming?

She quickly checked the path again. "It's okay. We're alone. There're only two people back in camp, and they're still in bed."

She wanted to touch him, to wipe that blood off his face. But they were still several yards apart. "How in the world did you get here?"

Nick steadied himself on some of the thick brush. "I flew in. Landed on the strip across the river."

"You came with your plane?"

"Yeah. To fly you out of here But now . . . now I can't do it!" He choked up as though holding back tears. "I'm so sorry, Terri! I'm afraid I've messed up everything!"

Chapter 33

Nick could see the vague image of Terri silhouetted against the morning sunshine, but he couldn't focus on her, couldn't actually see her. In attempting to climb out over the sticks and logs to get closer for a better look, he kept missing his handholds and almost fell face first into the tangle of brush.

"Nick, look out!" Her hand grabbed his arm and steadied him as he stepped over the last log. "What did you mean, you've messed up everything? What's the matter? Are you hurt? Did you crash? Are you injured?"

"No, no, didn't crash. I came to get you, but . . . O God, I no sooner landed than I had another eye hemorrhage, in my right eye this time. And now I can't see anything but vague shapes."

"*Another hemorrhage*? What're you talking about? What do you mean, you can't see?"

Nick suddenly realized Terri didn't know anything about his eye problems. They'd all happened after she'd been kidnapped. Did he have time to explain? "It's my diabetes . . ." He tried to give her a quick rundown—not watching his blood sugar, too much exertion, sixteen hours a day flying everyone out of Finca Fe. lifting so many gas cans up onto the wing. "They called it 'Valsalva' or something—when you hold your breath while straining too hard. And just now I had to push the Cessna all the way to the end of the runway. I guess it was just too much. It's just like the first bleed in my left eye, so I'm pretty sure that's what happened."

"*Valsalva* . . . never heard of it. But it'll go away, won't it? Can you see at all?"

"From what my eye doc told me, I doubt it'll go away on its own. As for seeing . . . can't see much. I can see the sun coming up, and that you're standing there, and that there's a tree line behind you. But I couldn't see well enough to notice I was stepping off a bank into the river. Must've fallen a meter or more before hitting my head." He reached up and wiped his forehead again.

"Don't do that. You're getting mud in the cut. Here, let me stop the bleeding with this."

He felt her grab the back of his head with one hand and press something soft against his forehead.

"It's a roll of toilet paper, but it's clean, at least a lot cleaner than your hand." She dabbed at his forehead a time or two. "I don't think it's too deep. You're going to be okay as soon as it stops bleeding."

He grimaced as she put pressure on his head wound. "I'm so sorry, Terri. So sorry! I was just trying to get you out of here, and now I've messed it all up. I don't know what to do."

She started to hum as she tended his forehead, and then softly sang, *"I will call upon the Lord, who is worthy to be praised, So shall I be saved from my enemies."*

He groaned. "Everything I've tried to do has gone wrong."

"*Shush*! I don't believe this was an accident, Nick." She pulled away her makeshift compress. "There, it stopped bleeding. You got a first-aid kit in the plane? We can put a bandage on it when we get there."

"What do you mean, 'when we get there'? You gotta go back to the camp before they come looking for you." He realized she didn't understand. He couldn't fly her out. It wasn't that he wanted her to go back, but he didn't want her to get caught trying to escape—caught and perhaps shot.

"I'm not going back. I told you—there're only two people in camp, my two patients. Look, the whole unit is away right now, and that kid you were going to fly to Venezuela—he's finally doing okay, so I can leave him. But he can't follow us, and neither can the other guy. He's got a broken foot. The rest of the unit won't be back until this afternoon. So we've got a few hours."

"But—"

She grabbed his arm and began guiding him back toward the river. He had no choice but to follow her lead. He could hear the water before he could see the glimmer of the river's surface, and he'd stepped into it before he knew they were at it's edge.

"O Lord, I'm calling upon You!" she said as she steadied Nick so he wouldn't slip on the rocks. "We need an idea here, Lord."

It took them a full ten minutes to scale the bank once they'd waded across the river. Nick kept missing his handholds even as Terri tried to guide him. But once they were up on flat ground, they both laid there catching their breath. "I tried hiking over the mountains once," she said quietly. "But I got myself lost and ended up going in a big circle right back to here. Hey—" Nick saw her image suddenly sit upright. "You've got a hand-held GPS in your plane, don't you? And some maps of this area? If we used them, we wouldn't get lost."

Nick sat up as well, and tried as hard as he could to make her image come into focus. "I guess it's worth a try, but . . ." He was thinking how much he would slow her down. If the soldiers chose to follow them, they'd have no problem catching up in short order.

"Of course it's worth a try." Her tone was resolute. She stood up and grabbed his hand to help him up. "Let's get as much of a head start as possible."

They pressed on and soon had to climb over a single strand of barbed wire fencing. Then Nick realized they'd come out of the trees and were on the rough runway.

"There's your plane down there." And she turned him to the left. But they walked a good way before Nick was able to pick out some blurred red and white that slowly took the vague shape of his Cessna when they were within six meters. "Yeah," Nick muttered in disgust, "I'm what Dr. Gomez described as 'legally blind.' I have to be within twenty feet of something the average person can see at two hundred. There's no way I can fly that thing!"

"Probably not," Terri said in a perky voice. "So that's why we're going to hike over those mountains."

"What mountains?" Nick mockingly gazed back and forth in a generally westward direction. "This isn't going to work, Terri! There's no way I can keep up a pace to stay ahead of anyone following us, and every time I stumble, I'd leave scars on the ground even a blind person could follow. Ha, ha." His forced laugh was sour.

"I will call upon the Lord," she quietly sang, *"who is worthy to be praised, So shall I be saved from my enemies."*

When they got to the plane, Nick said, "You're right about one thing, Terri. *You* can be saved. Take the GPS and the charts, and high-tail it over those mountains without me. That's our only chance."

"Not gonna happen, Nick Archer. I'm not leaving you under any circumstances."

"But why not? I can get on the radio and call for help." He'd never told her how difficult it was to make radio contact from this side of the mountains even when he was up at altitude. "But even if I don't get through, you could send help, because now you could identify exactly where this FARC unit is . . . where I am."

"Ha! You think the FARC would stay put? They'd move out of here before night—after they destroyed your plane. And they'd take you with 'em . . . if they let you live. No, I'm not leavin' you."

They walked around to the far side of the plane, and Nick brushed his hand along the side until his fingers slipped into the door handle. He pulled it open, grabbed the seat, and raised his foot to the step. But he missed, and his shin grated painfully down the step. "Ahh!" He bent over to grab his leg.

"You okay?" She moved him out of the way. "Here, let me do it." She hopped up into the pilot's seat. "Here's your GPS, on the passenger seat. Where are your charts?"

"In that side pocket down by your left foot."

"Got it! Let's go." She started to get out.

"Wait!" Nick put his hand up and touched her shoulder. "Stay in the pilot's seat."

"What for? We shouldn't waste any time."

Nick stood there a moment, one hand on the open door of the Cessna and the other on Terri's shoulder. He took a deep breath and slowly blew it out. "*You* can fly this thing, Terri. You flew all the way back from Neiva. And you said you almost soloed, right?"

"Yeah, but—"

"You can fly us out of here. This field's pretty rough, and I can't see, but I can talk you up and help you land when we get to Neiva."

"Oh, Nick! I don't know . . . like you said, it's pretty rough. I turned my ankle and almost fell down a few moments ago when I stepped in an animal hole of some kind."

"That's why I put these big bush tires on this old tail-dragger. It'll be rough, but you can do it."

"But Nick, there are trees sticking up at the other end."

"I know. I dropped in over them when I came in. But if you bank to the right a little bit, isn't there a corridor where nothing sticks up?"

"Yeah, I guess."

"Then that's our way out."

Terri was silent for several moments. Then . . . "But what about landing. I told you what happened that time."

Nick felt for her hand and gripped it tightly. "You can do it, Terri. I know you can. And you won't have to slip it in this time. The tower can talk you down even if you have to come around a second time. Piece of cake."

He could feel her hesitation. "Hey," he said gently. "You're the one who keeps singing that we're gonna be saved from our enemies, and if you're not willing to hike out of here by yourself, then this is our only way to escape."

Terri sighed. "O Lord, have mercy on us," she murmured, then let go of his hand. "Okay, let's go. Can you make it around to the other door by yourself?"

Nick managed to climb in, get the door closed, and belt himself into the passenger seat. "I'm pretty sure I landed uphill. Right? So going downhill will give us a little advantage on takeoff, but the high grass will hold us back—at least it's dry—but the bumps will also knock us from side to side. That'll be your biggest challenge, holding us straight until we lift off."

They waited in silence a moment, and then Terri said, "Will you pray?"

"You said there're only two guys in camp, and they're both incapacitated, right?"

"Yes."

"All right, but it's gonna be a very short prayer." He asked the Lord to keep them both calm, to give Terri courage and help her make the right decisions, and to bring them home safely. "Okay. Find your instruments." He talked her through the basic ones.

"Even though those guys in camp are supposed to be stuck there," he muttered, "we're not going to do a full run up. Once they hear the engine, I don't want to give them time to begin shooting at us. So we'll check a few things and then go."

He ran through the steps. "When it looks good, bring the power up to 2,850 RPM, but don't just shove the throttle in. Push it in slowly, over two or three seconds, and give it a lot of right rudder, because with 300 horsepower, sudden torque could . . ." He was going to compare it to her dreaded ground loop. "Let's just say, it could be worse than the chuckholes. Once we're rolling, keep the tail down because it'll tend to bounce, and then you can't use the tail wheel to steer us, and all you've got is the rudder.

"Don't worry about your airspeed indicator. Concentrate on keeping the plane straight. Let it fly off in that tail-low attitude. *Then* check your airspeed. You want to get us over those trees, of course, but it stalls at about 56 miles per hour. Once you're clear, drop it back to twenty-five hundred RPM and fly us out of here."

"Hear my cry, O God," Terri said softly. *"Give heed to my prayer. From the end of the earth I call to You when my heart is faint; Lead me to the rock that is higher than I."*

Nick gritted his teeth. How could she do that? We're fleeing for our lives, I'm trying to instruct her on how to fly this thing safely, and she prays a Bible verse.

But then without another question, Terri flipped the main switch and went through the sequence of starting the engine. After checking the essentials, she said, "I think we're ready."

"Okay, give it 20 degrees flap, and let's roll!"

She eased the throttle forward, and the Cessna leaped down the runway, bouncing and rattling, and jerking from side to side. Nick could hardly keep from asking what was happening, but he knew she needed to concentrate. Without sight, there wasn't much he could tell her that would help. But she wasn't screaming, and it felt as if they were maintaining a relatively straight course as their speed rapidly increased.

And then they were off the ground, and it was just the roar of the engine . . . until, *Yeeeeep.* "Stall warning! Stall warning!" he yelled. *Yeeeeeep!*

The plane immediately dipped forward like going over the hump on a rollercoaster, and then *WHAM!* It shuddered and jerked to the left worse than from any of the chuckholes back on the strip. Terri screamed, and Nick grabbed the doorpost to brace himself, thinking for sure they were crashing. The plane wallowed for a few moments and then seemed to stabilize, but Nick held his breath. He was flying blind and so couldn't coach her and certainly didn't want to distract her if she wasn't yet out of danger. But when nothing more occurred in the next few seconds, he finally said shakily, "Are we okay?"

"I think so," she blurted, "but we've got a bunch of leaves flapping from the left landing gear. I'm so sorry, but I think I clipped one of those trees."

Nick sighed and leaned back. "It wouldn't be the first time for this old bird." After a moment, he asked, "Can you see? Is it just leaves, or is there a big limb caught in the gear?"

"It's a stick about the size of my thumb, maybe eighteen inches long with a bunch of leaves on it. I'm so sorry, Nick. I was afraid of stalling even before I took off, and then the warner went off, I pushed the yoke forward."

"Well, if it's just a small branch, it shouldn't be any problem. Like I said, I've clipped the tops of trees a couple of times. But I have to say, with you having prayed, *Lead me to the rock that is higher than I,* I thought for a moment there you might have found it." He hoped his attempt at humor had broken the tension, but when he reached over and touched her leg, he realized she was trembling like the wings of a humming bird.

He almost wanted to laugh. "It's okay, Babe! It's really okay. We made it. You can throttle back now and slowly release the flaps. We made it!"

Forty-five minutes later, Nick was on the radio with the Neiva tower trying to explain their emergency. "I know the weather's clear and the visibility is good, but, uh, I can't see."

"What d'ya mean, you can't see? Are you the pilot?"

"Yes, but I had a medical crisis before we took off, and I can't see."

"So who's flying the plane?"

"Uh . . . an inexperienced . . . student, you might say."

"But you're the pilot?

"Yes. Listen, we were escaping the FARC, and I let her take off, but now we need some help landing. She's flown before, but you need you to talk her in."

There was some chatter in the background, and then a different controller who sounded older took over. He dispensed with the questions about how Nick could be the pilot while flying blind and focused on helping Terri land. Nick felt frustrated, not being able to see or help at this critical point, but he held his tongue while the tower gave instructions. Terri's replies to the tower were terse: "Got it" . . . "OK" . . . "Now?" He knew she was tense after what happened with her previous attempt to land the Cessna.

When he felt the wheels touch down with their comforting squawks and only a minor bounce, and knew the plane had slowed enough that a ground loop was unlikely, he huffed in relief, only then realizing he'd been holding his breath. "Beautiful, Terri," he breathed, grinning. "Flawless."

When they rolled up to the service hanger, no one asked them about the stick with its few leaves dragging from the left landing gear. Nick, however, found it by feeling around by hand and pulled it loose.

The word spread quickly, and within twenty minutes Roger and Betty and several other people from Finca Fe were running toward them, shouting their names and giving them both big hugs. Everyone was talking at once, wanting to know, "What happened?" asking Terri if she was all right, and slapping Nick on the back. "You did it, man! You did it!" Roger cried.

"But, actually, it was Terri who saved *me*!" Nick protested two or three times without anyone noticing until Roger grabbed his arm and pulled him aside.

"What're you talking about? You don't seem right. Are you okay?"

"No. That's what I'm trying to say! I had another bleed in my eye—my good eye this time. Couldn't see a thing. Terri's the one who flew us back here."

"She . . . what?" Roger chuckled. "Well, I'll be darned." Then his voice sobered. "But . . . your eyes. Nick, I warned you!—oh forget that. How bad is it?"

"Right now, can't see worth mud in your eye. The first eye is coming along. Don't think any harm came from flying. But," he admitted, "I still haven't been attending to my diabetes like I should, so while I was out there, I had to drag my plane the length of a football field over some pretty rough ground. Did me in, I'm tellin' ya. Guess it triggered another bleed."

"Hmm. Guess we better get you to the Doc this afternoon, then."

"I'd appreciate it, but . . . don't tell everyone about it right now. It'd throw cold water on celebrating Terri's return. But before we go, maybe you could ask Armando if he could park and tie down the Cessna for me."

"You got it." Roger threw an arm around Nick's shoulders. "Still, you did good, Nick. You did good! And just ten days until Christmas. What a heck of a Christmas present this'll be for her family—for all of us, really."

Chapter 34

It wasn't until the following July that the bridge over the Magdalena River was repaired, making the road to Finca Fe and beyond to the villages of El Tabor and Betania finally passable. And now, a month later, Finca Fe was finally reopening.

Roger Montgomery backed the pickup close to the hangar door and got out, then leaned back in to speak to Nick. "Hey, why don't you decide where you want to put these barrels while I go tell Betty we're here—I think she said they're cleaning up the dining hall today."

"Yeah, yeah," Nick smirked. "You just want to snitch a snack *before* you help me unload all this fuel."

"Who, me?" Roger winked and headed for the school's dining hall.

Nick remained sitting in the pickup. How quickly things had changed. The bridge was repaired. The army had established an outpost less than five kilometers up the road to ensure the safety of the local civilians—even though there had been no further FARC activity in the area—and the Colombian Government was confident lasting peace accords would be signed by next Christmas.

Peace efforts had frequently faltered in recent years, but Nick supported the decision of the Crisis Team for First People's Mission to reopen the school this September. Leaving the property abandoned too long invited vandalism, along with the natural deterioration to unused facilities. It was a use-it-or-lose-it situation, even though everyone realized some of the more wealthy parents might hesitate to reenroll their children for a while. All the staff had agreed to stay with the school—including Cynthia Beale, the woman who'd come from the States as acting principal while the school had been operating at the Neiva airport.

And for Nick, relocating his base of operations back to Finca Fe would cut twenty to thirty minutes off his support flights to the missionaries in the southern region. Better yet, he would again be close to Terri Kaplan.

And *she* was supposed to arrive today after almost eight months back in the States.

Eight months! Nick had no idea she'd be gone that long when Terri went home for Christmas after being rescued from FARC's jungle camp. She hadn't either. But both the mission and Terri's family had urged her to take a complete rest for the second half of the school year, as well as get some extended counseling to come to terms with her ordeal . . . which had left Nick in Columbia dealing with his own medical crisis and wrestling with his MAST mission executives over his "going rogue" in his unorthodox efforts to rescue Terri.

Because Terri was part of First Peoples Mission and not on staff with MAST, Nick hadn't technically violated their policies about not paying ransom for one of *their* staff members should they have been kidnapped when he delivered ransom money for Terri. But ransom payments were illegal, and he certainly had violated the spirit of the mission's policies, especially in frequently avoiding communication with their office. Nick readily acknowledged that he'd gone off script and hadn't kept them informed of his activities or the continuing eye problems, but it had been because he knew they would have grounded him.

"I know all that," Nick admitted, "and believe me, if I had ultimately failed or even lost the plane, I would have tendered my resignation. And I know my 'cowboy tactics,' as you call them, could have gotten the mission in trouble on several fronts. But First Peoples Mission had run out of options, and the Colombian government wasn't doing a thing to rescue Terri. She could have lost her life, as Miss Van Loon had. I was in the military where we had a motto: 'leave no soldier behind,' and I could do no less in this case."

They debated the matter for several days until MAST finally allowed Nick to continue on a provisional basis, provided neither the Colombian or the U.S. governments demanded his removal from the country and that he would promise to fully communicate with them over any future "difficult situations."

He tried not to burden Terri too much with these tense negotiations in the many emails they exchanged and the occasional Skype calls they enjoyed, but those long-distance communications were never enough. Now finally, he would see her again.

Suddenly restless, Nick got out of the pickup and pulled up on the handle to open the hangar door, eyeing the empty space for the best place to store the three barrels of aviation fuel he and Roger had hauled from Neiva. Once Roger cut the grass—it wasn't really necessary with his bush tires, but he wasn't going to tell Roger that—he'd relocate the Cessna and make this "home" again where he had a hanger and no ramp fees. Dr. Gomez had given him the okay to fly again a couple of months ago . . . "As long as you keep that diabetes completely under control," he'd warned solemnly, "you shouldn't have any problem, but we're going to keep a close watch on it."

Like wrestling those barrels today. Even though Nick had become religiously careful to attend to his diabetes, take his meds, and check his blood sugar regularly, with his body's tendency toward eye hemorrhages, he didn't want to overdo that Valsalva maneuver. Every day he thanked God for restoring his sight. After undergoing a vitrectomy in his right eye to extract the blood from his second bleed, and after his left eye had sufficiently healed, Dr. Gomez had successfully implanted a lens—the same procedure tens of thousands of people received in routine cataract surgery. So far, no complications—no detached retina, no need for a bubble, no face-down time.

"What?" said a voice, startling Nick out of his reverie. "Thought you'd have those barrels rolled in by now." Roger was stuffing his face with what was left of a submarine sandwich as he strolled into the empty hangar. "Guess I didn't stay away long enough."

"Ha. You didn't happen to bring me one of those subs, did you?"

Roger snorted but pulled something wrapped in a wax paper out of his pocket and handed it to Nick. "Huh. Sneaking food out of the kitchen before supper with that Mrs. Beale hanging around is like robbing gold from Fort Knox. That woman acts like a drill sergeant." The older man rolled his eyes and pressed his lips together.

Nick grinned but let the matter drop and devoured his sandwich. Once the two men had set up a ramp to roll the barrels out of the pickup and into the hanger, they both stood back to catch their breath. Roger removed his crumpled fedora and wiped the sweat off his head with the back of his hand and then studied the bullet hole in the side of his hat as if seeing it for the first time. "What time did you say Terri's comin' in?"

"Supposed to get here this afternoon. James is driving the van up from Neiva with some more supplies and a couple of short-term volunteers. Terri's supposed to come with them."

Roger put his hat back on and gave a tug on the front brim to pull it down over his forehead. "Does Betty know?"

"Yeah, she asked me last night before we went to Neiva for the fuel. I think she wants to cook up something special for dinner."

"So . . . you haven't seen Terri since she returned to the States last Christmas, right?"

"How could I? I'm here, and she's there. But we emailed and have Skyped occasionally."

"Skype? Oh, yeah, that internet video thing." Roger waved his hands back and forth. "I oughta try that with the grand kids . . . except now we're back out here where we can barely get internet." Roger turned and walked over to his riding mower, which was parked alongside the hangar. "Guess pretty soon, you won't be needin' no Skype, will ya?" He winked at Nick and turned the key to start the little tractor chugging. "See ya. I got a lot of mowin' to do around this place."

"Hey," yelled Nick above the noise. "When you gonna to take care of my landing strip? I need to bring the Cessna up here, sooner the better."

"Ha, you told me you didn't need it to be like no golf course." And he drove off.

Nick shook his head. *That guy's impossible . . . and the best friend I've ever had.*

Going through the empty hanger to the little room where his bunk was, he glanced at the yellow note pinned to the wall stud and grinned to himself. Nope, pretty soon he wouldn't need Skype. He un-pinned the note: *"If it's not raining tomorrow morning, meet me at The Rock! —Me."* Grabbing a pen, he put a comma after the word "Me" and signed it, "Nick," then folded it once and put it in his pocket.

The van with Terri and the two volunteers didn't arrive until dark, leaving Nick plenty of time to imagine all kinds of ominous things that could've gone wrong—from car trouble to Terri getting sick . . . or even changing her mind about returning to Colombia. But the culprit was only some bad weather over the Caribbean that had delayed her flight.

Nick had a hard time keeping his eyes off Terri as he helped carry her luggage into the infirmary. He'd given her a big hug when she climbed out of the van, but there was so much he wanted to say . . . if he could just make all the other staff disappear for a couple of hours! Not likely, he thought glumly. Betty had cooked up a feast for a "welcome home" party that night.

He'd have to go with Plan B.

When Terri went out to make sure she hadn't left anything in the van, Nick did a quick re-con of the room. There . . . her Bible was sticking out of her open backpack. Pulling the yellow note out of his pocket, he put it into her Bible with about an inch of it sticking out at the top. Even as tired as she obviously was, he figured she'd get her Bible out and put it on the small lampstand by her bed before going to sleep that night, and if she did, she'd be sure to notice the note.

At first, nobody seemed to have energy for much of a party, but they all dug into Betty's enchiladas and salad for dinner. Perked up by the good food, soon there were cheers and grateful toasts and so many stories about what had happened over the summer that Nick had no personal time to connect with Terri, even though he'd managed to sit by her. Be patient, he told himself. Maybe he could walk Terri to the infirmary after it was all over and give her a proper good night—a warm hug, perhaps even that kiss he'd been imagining for so long. But Mrs. Beale, the new principal, had so much to tell Terri that she insisted on accompanying her to the infirmary "to help her get settled for the night."

Frustrated, Nick just headed back to his dark hanger, hands in his pockets. Why couldn't that woman wait until the next day—a work day, during working hours? Not that anyone kept strict hours at Finca Fe. But with Mrs. Beale rummaging around, trying to help Terri get settled, would Terri even see his note? Would she read it? Would she be too tired in the morning to come?

Terri awoke up with a start and for a moment couldn't place where she was. Then as the dim gray light through the window brought her surroundings into focus, she recognized the comforting furnishings of her small room in the infirmary. It certainly wasn't the open-beamed ceiling, board walls, or the rough floor—all painted institutional foam green—that attracted her. And the lumpy cot still made her back ache. But Finca Fe was the place where God had planted her, and she was glad to be back home.

Besides, Nick Archer was here. She didn't know for how long, given the ordeal he'd been through, but for now he was here, and he'd asked for "a date" . . . well, kinda. She turned over, flipped on her bedside lamp, and pulled the little yellow note from her Bible. *"If it's not raining tomorrow morning, meet me at The Rock! — Me, Nick."* She couldn't help smiling. He'd saved the note she'd written so many months before—that had to mean something—and then he'd added his name.

She jumped out of bed and went to the window, pushing back the red-checked gingham curtain she'd made to give herself a little more privacy. Water still dripped from the trees outside, and the sky roiled with heavy clouds . . . but it wasn't raining at that moment. She checked the time on her digital clock: 6:03. It was a little earlier than when she usually went down to The Rock, but why not?

She could get her shower later. Pulling on her clothes, she went into the infirmary, brushed her teeth in the sink, and combed out her hair. Should she put on makeup? She seldom wore more than a touch, but no, not this morning. She'd be her plain self. Grabbing a windbreaker with a hood in case it began to rain, she headed for the river.

Would he come? It had been Nick's idea, but the note said, "If it's not raining . . ." And it wasn't at the moment, but it was certainly a rainy day. She needed to keep her expectations low. She'd wait at The Rock until seven. If he hadn't come by then, she wouldn't feel disappointed. She'd go on up to breakfast and see him there . . . and wouldn't say anything about his not showing.

But when she came around the bend in the little road down to the river, she saw a figure in a yellow slicker sitting on The Rock. The person was facing downstream, and Terri couldn't see the face. Drat! Had someone commandeered her special place, the place she and Nick were scheduled to meet? Seemed like everyone was scheming against them having any private time together! *"Why have you conspired against me?"* She knew King Saul's complaint to the priest Ahimelech didn't apply here, but that's the way she felt.

And then the figure on the rock moved . . . and the way the person straightened his shoulders took away her breath. Was it Nick? She'd never seen him wear a yellow slicker like that, but . . . She quickened her pace, and when she was twenty yards away, she couldn't help calling out, "Nick?"

He turned and jumped up. It *was* him!

"Ha, ha! You came! I didn't hear you approaching. Must've been the rush of the river, and I wasn't even sure you would, given the fact that it *was* raining and might start up again any minute. But here you are!" With a huge smile he scrambled off The Rock and opened his arms to her.

Terri couldn't help herself. She ran into his embrace and held him as though she would never let him go. "Oh, Nick, Nick, I've missed you so much! Those phone calls just didn't do it." What was she saying? She was talking as if she had some claim on him. Something had been happening between them that they'd never acknowledged with words. But it was real!

They stood on the riverbank for several minutes, clinging to each other and swaying back and forth like a slow dance to the music of the river. Finally, Nick untangled their arms and held her hand as they climbed back up on The Rock and sat down beside each other.

They sat silently for a few minutes, staring at the river until Nick finally spoke.

"I don't know how to say this, but it's kind of like that water. It keeps rushing by, and once it's past, you can't bring it back. And I'm old enough to realize that's my life, and I don't want any more of it to just go floating by when I *know* what I want to do with it. So . . ." He reached into the pocket of the yellow slicker and brought out a small square box. As he opened it, she saw a lustrous Colombian emerald ring flanked by two small diamonds, nestled on the velvet lining.

He held it out gently toward her. "Will you marry me, Terri Kaplan?"

Tearing her gaze away from the ring, she looked him in the eye, gulped and took a deep breath. "Yes! Oh, yes! I *will* marry you, Nick Archer." She flung her arms around his neck and kissed him, trying to sustain it long enough to make up for all those unspoken—even unacknowledged—longings over the months of separation.

Finally, they came up for air and Terri nestled under his arm, staring at the river until rain started peppering the water's surface. She stood up and held out her hand, grinning so hard she thought her face might crack. "Let's go back to the infirmary. We've got so much to talk about and plan. I don't know how we're going to do this. I mean . . . a wedding and everything."

"Well, I was thinkin'," Nick said as they headed up the road, "as soon as school starts, they're going to need you on site."

She nodded slowly. "Yeah. I guess we could wait until Christmas break. A lot of the kids are gone then, so I could probably take time off. But what about you?"

"You're right, that doesn't help me. But whenever we do it, I'm just gonna have to tell MAST I need the time off. So I was thinking . . ." He hesitated, and then spoke in a rush. "Why don't we do it right now? We've got a three-week window until school starts, so let's just squeeze in a wedding!"

Terri opened her mouth to say, *"Squeeze? Now?"* But Nick was already rushing on, as if trying to get the idea out before it evaporated. "There's no advantage to MAST for me to wait until Christmas. Either way, the missionaries will have to make do for a few days, but this is definitely the best time for you, don'tcha think?"

"Yeah, but . . ." Terri's mind was racing—now? Before school starts? They pushed open the squeaky door to the infirmary and went in, hanging the wet slicker and windbreaker on the nails along the wall. Stalling, she grinned at Nick. "We're gonna miss breakfast."

"Who cares?" he laughed and pulled her into his arms for another long kiss.

Finally, they broke it off and sat down on either side of the little table Terri used as a desk. She sighed. "Okay, I'll be honest. My family might kill me if I ran home for such a quick wedding. Mom's about given up, but her dream is a great big wedding with four bridesmaids, huge reception dinner, the whole works."

Nick shrugged. "Well, I don't want to add to any more family disappointments, but maybe we can explain. Hopefully they would understand."

"What do you mean, you don't want to *add* to family disappointments?"

"You know . . ." he grimaced, "after I lost everyone's money?"

"Don't worry about that. They understand, they really do, and they have a very high opinion of you. But . . . it's not just the wedding. We've also gotta figure out where we're gonna live. The apartments here are all taken, and we certainly can't live in this infirmary."

"Ah! I've thought about that, too—"

Terri raised a cautioning hand. "Don't you suggest we live in your little room in the back of the hanger!"

"Oh, Babe, why not? Anywhere with you would be heaven," he laughed. "No, no. But remember Hector and Isabella's place that I put the roof on the day before the attack? Well, Isabella's elderly mother took a real turn for the worse, so last week they moved to Bogotá to take care of her. They were asking all around for someone to rent their place."

Terri made a face. "And we'd go back and forth in that outboard?"

"No, no. The road. You can walk it in fifteen, twenty minutes."

"And in the rain?"

Nick grinned and shrugged. "Most people gotta go to work, rain or shine."

There was a loud banging on the door, and then it swung open as Roger Montgomery stuck his head in. "Oh, there you guys are. It's time for that planning meeting, and everyone's looking for you."

Nick and Terri grinned at one another, and Terri said, "Guess we were having our own little planning meeting."

Roger stepped all the way into the infirmary and took off his hat. "Hmm. You don't say." He stared back and forth between their grinning faces. "So you *do* say. . . . Well, how about them apples?" He squinted his eyes and started pulling at the edges of his mustache.

Terri reached out her left hand to him. "Yeah, and how 'bout *this* green apple?"

"Oh my. Oh my." Roger took Terri's hand and examined the ring closely and then broke into a hearty chuckle. "Now you've gone and done it, Nick. Now you've gone and done it. Well, good on you both!"

Epilogue

Three days later Nick was sitting on The Rock as the sun came up over the Cordillera Mountains. The cloudless sky was unsullied by haze or jets or anything but a solitary hawk circling high overhead. Below his feet, the Magdalena River flowed peacefully and clear—well, as clear as it ever got. And even though Terri was not sitting by his side at that moment, he felt at peace.

They'd announced their engagement to the staff at Finca Fe, and almost everyone—except Mrs. Beale, the new principal—agreed they were old enough and knew each other well enough to choose such a quick wedding . . . especially since it meant both of them would be back on duty to help out when school opened. And to that end, Terri had flown back to the States to meet with her board at First Peoples Mission and to make arrangements with her family and church. Nick would follow in a few short days. They'd decided to have a very small wedding, realizing there'd be relatives and friends who couldn't come on such short notice, but most would be there, and they both were confident most of the others would understand.

Nick shook his head and breathed thanks to God. Less than ten months earlier everything had seemed so dark. "Ha, and not just because I was blind," he mumbled. At some points, he'd not even been sure God existed. The true depth of the void he'd been in was beyond his active memory, but he certainly didn't want to recreate those feelings just to confirm their reality. It had been bad, bad, BAD!

But now everything was so good!

If he'd only known then what his life would be like today, he wouldn't have found it nearly so hard to get through those dark days. He laughed out loud. Now he felt as if he'd lived through a Hallmark movie where, within ninety minutes, everything works out just fine. Then it struck him . . . the only difference was *time.* He'd been stuck in time. God was not! Outside of time, Nick's darkest moments were illumined by the brilliance of today.

Ha. Terri would probably quote 2 Peter 3:8, *"Do not forget this one thing, dear friends: With the Lord a day is like a thousand years, and a thousand years are like a day."*

Was it ever possible to get outside of time? Was doing so the essence of faith? Could he remember that when future troubles came . . . as he knew they would? He'd been around the block a time or two, like with the death of his wife, Megan, in the Philippines. At that time, people had tossed biblical platitudes at him, like Romans 8:28: *"In God all things work for the good of those who love him."* Force-feeding that mystery to someone locked in the moment was a cruel affront. Even today, years later and in the glow of his love and future with Terri, Nick couldn't wring one shred of good out of that pain. But he would keep reaching out for it, because he now realized the only possible way to experience that peace was outside of time.

For now, however, everything was copacetic.

Until that afternoon, when he got an email from Terri.

Dear Nick,

I hope you're sitting down. I had my meeting with the board this morning, and they're saying our marriage flies in the face of their policy against romantic relationships on the field. Furthermore, they never assign newlyweds to an overseas position until they've been married at least a year. And they grumbled about the complication of one spouse working for one mission and the other working for another. They said the only other time they tried that, it didn't work out too well.

But the bottom line is, if we go ahead and get married, they'll let me return to Finca Fe only until they find a replacement. (Finca Fe can't operate without a nurse on site.) After that, I'll be suspended for at least a year. But if my replacement works out well, they may have to reassign me to some other location.

They say they're sorry, and say they understand our circumstances—that they know we weren't carrying on an active romance behind their backs—but they feel they must uphold their policy.

Oh, Nick, what are we going to do?

Nick reread the email two or three times, feeling the darkness threatening to wrap itself around his spirit. *No, no . . . not this. Not when everything was looking up and going so right!*

And yet . . .

What had God just been teaching him this whole past year? That God was real. That God was with him—and Terri too—through the toughest times. That it was God who'd brought him and Terri together. That his timing was not always God's timing.

Nick sat and stared at Terri's email a long time. Then he hit Reply and started typing.

Dear Terri . . .

Acknowledgments

This novel has been a long time in the making and probably began with my father, **Bev Jackson**, who, with my mom, pastored small churches in logging and ranching villages in the northwest. He'd also worked for Lockheed Aircraft Company during the war and had developed a love for aviation. As I entered adolescence, he left the pastorate to learn to fly and obtain his A&P (airframe and powerplant) license so he could become a missionary pilot. The transition didn't happen as quickly as he'd hoped, but during my high school years he owned and rebuilt two airplanes, the second of which was a Cessna. He let me help, got me jobs at the airport each summer, and took me flying for hours and hours. Unfortunately, by the time he was prepared to apply to his chosen mission agency, it had set a new age limit for incoming pilots, and he was one year over that limit.

Like me, my college roommate, **Dean Berto**, loved cars and somehow got permission to rebuild the engine of his Buick while it was parked near the dining hall. We lost track of each other after graduation. But when I discovered he'd become a pilot for Missionary Aviation Fellowship, serving many years in Africa and Central America, I asked him to review this story to make sure I hadn't "crashed" Nick's plane.

In recent years, I've admired **Jim Fitz**, a church friend who has taken many trips to Colombia to work for peace between the FARC, other revolutionary groups, the Colombian military, and some of the paramilitaries. His dangerous work yielded some remarkable testimonies of Christ's transforming love in the midst of violence.

The late **Lee Hough** was our agent when I first conceived of this book. He believed in it wholeheartedly but was unable to find a publisher for it at the time. I was tempted to give up, but **Robert Peterson**, a missionary in Colombia, encouraged me and arranged for **Hermano Santiago**, one of the members of his little church, to take some three hundred photographs for me along the Magdalena River where this story is set. In telling Hermano what I wanted pictures of, I never described Nick's plane, but among the photos Hermano sent back was a distant, somewhat fuzzy shot of a Cessna 185 sitting on the ramp of the Neiva airport, equipped and painted exactly like Nick's plane. I pinned a copy of that photo beside my desk as a reminder that someday I needed to finish the story.

Sephanie Boogaard's husband is a pilot for an aviation missionary team in South America that does much the same work Nick did in supporting other missionaries. His family was also part of a missionary base in Colombia that had to be closed due to FARC threats and kidnappings. And Sephanie is close friends with a missionary who had been captured by FARC, so her input was invaluable in bringing authenticity to this story.

I couldn't have written this book without the constant encouragement and help from **Neta Jackson**, my wonderful wife and most-excellent editor. I also need to thank **Fernando Mercado** for correcting my rusty high school Spanish and **Michelle Redding** for copy editing the manuscript.

And finally, I must thank **Dr. Norm Blair,** friend and retinal ophthalmologist God used to restore my vision after I lost the sight in my left eye. I do not have diabetes like Nick, but my vision problems were similar to those diabetes can create. To read more about my personal experience, go to . . .

www.daveneta.com/support-pages/dave-eye.html

Made in the USA
Columbia, SC
04 December 2017